ALSO BY ALLAN TOPOL

Spy Dance

DARK AMBITION

ALLAN TOPOL

AN ONYX BOOK

ONYX
Published by New American Library, a division of
Penguin Putnam Inc., 375 Hudson Street,
New York, New York 10014, U.S.A.
Penguin Books Ltd, 80 Strand,
London WC2R 0RL, England
Penguin Books Australia Ltd, 250 Camberwell Road,
Camberwell, Victoria 3124, Australia
Penguin Books Canada Ltd, 10 Alcorn Avenue,
Toronto, Ontario, Canada M4V 3B2
Penguin Books (N.Z.) Ltd, 182–190 Wairau Road,
Auckland 10, New Zealand

Penguin Books Ltd, Registered Offices:
Harmondsworth, Middlesex, England

First published by Onyx, an imprint of New American Library,
a division of Penguin Putnam Inc.

First Printing, January 2003
10 9 8 7 6 5 4 3 2

 REGISTERED TRADEMARK—MARCA REGISTRADA

Printed in the United States of America

PUBLISHER'S NOTE
This is a work of fiction. Names, characters, places, and incidents either
are the product of the author's imagination or are used fictitiously,
and any resemblance to actual persons, living or dead, business
establishments, events, or locales is entirely coincidental.

*This book is dedicated to my wife, Barbara . . .
my partner in this literary venture.*

Chapter 1

Jeb Hines saw a man in a trench coat walking from the bottom of the cul de sac. A typical Washington lawyer, Hines thought contemptuously. The city would be a helluva lot better if half of them—no, make that three-fourths—were buried at the bottom of the Potomac River. This one had a suit and tie under his dirty Burberry coat, black horn-rimmed glasses, and a briefcase. On his head he wore a flat round gray cap that made him look effeminate.

Hines had been an agent in the U.S. State Department's Office of Diplomatic Security one week, and already he hated it. Having spent four years as a part of the Secret Service detail that guarded the President, he had jumped at the State Department job, which promised higher pay and frequent travel around the world as part of Secretary of State Robert Winthrop's personal entourage. Too late, Hines realized he had been better off in his former job. At least when the President was at home, he could lounge in the warmth of the White House. Now he was sentenced to spending most of his time on Linean Court, in front of the Secretary's house, as he was on this Saturday in mid-November with a bitter west wind whipping through the trees.

A rustling noise behind him caused Hines to wheel around quickly. Yet it was only Clyde Gillis, the Winthrops' gardener, struggling with another huge pile of leaves hauled on a piece of burlap. His black forehead was dotted with perspiration that made the scar above his left eye glisten. Gillis unloaded the pile into the back of his truck. When the burlap was empty, Gillis tossed it over his shoulder and trudged wearily toward the backyard. Jesus, that fucker works hard, Hines thought. Gillis had been raking nonstop for almost three hours, dressed only in a blue denim shirt and jeans.

Hines tapped on the window of the navy Ford Crown Vic to get the attention of Chris MacDonald, his partner, sitting inside to warm up, while studying the sports page of the morning *Washington Post*. With a yellow legal pad in his hand, MacDonald stuck his head up out of the car.

"Hey, Mac, it must be the Secretary's two o'clock," Hines said.

Mac scanned the first page of the pad, which had the secretary's schedule for the day. The only visitor for this afternoon was at two o'clock. "George Nesbitt, State Department business."

"So what did you decide about tomorrow's game?" Hines asked.

"I'll take the Skins and ten and a half."

"Dallas is only a seven-point favorite."

"But you'll give me ten and a half 'cause you love them asshole Cowboys."

"Bullshit!"

The man in the tan coat approached the end of the driveway, where Hines and Mac maintained their vigil. Close up, he looked younger, in his thirties, Hines thought.

"Can I help you?" he asked.

Without saying a word, the man reached into his jacket pocket and extracted a black leather billfold. It was expensive shiny leather with the Gucci insignia embossed in gold. It figures, Hines thought. A bunch of goddamned parasites.

With a gloved hand, the man took a California driver's license from the wallet and held it out to Hines, who scanned it quickly. The photo ID was for George

Nesbitt. The picture matched the man standing in front of him—minus that stupid hat, of course.

Hines nodded to Mac, who picked up the cell phone resting on the hood of the Crown Vic and hit the one and five buttons, connecting him to the house. As he expected, the secretary, home alone, picked up. "Mr. Secretary, George Nesbitt is here."

"Send him right up," Winthrop said.

Hines nodded to Nesbitt. "He's expecting you."

Slowly the visitor put away the driver's license, then crossed to the flagstone steps that led to the front door.

"Talkative fellow, isn't he?" Hines said to Mac.

"I don't care if he says shit. I'm interested in what you're going to say. Will I get those ten and a half points or not?"

"Eight and a half."

"Nine and that's my last offer."

"You've got it for nine. Twenty bucks. And I win on a tie."

"Deal."

Hines glanced up the stairs. Nesbitt was approaching the front door. He even walks like a damn woman, Hines thought. Suddenly he felt tired. It was his turn to get into the car and out of the cold. He might even take a short nap.

Inside the house, Robert Winthrop was trembling with excitement, as he had been since the call came this morning from Alexandra in New York, telling him to expect a surprise at two o'clock today. It was an absolutely perfect Saturday afternoon. The maid had the weekend off, and Ann wouldn't be back for another couple of hours. Eagerly, he climbed the stairs from his lower level study to the front entrance hall. Dressed in charcoal gray slacks and a blue oxford button down shirt, he opened the door as soon as the bell rang.

"We're going downstairs," he said to his visitor. Then he proceeded to lead the way down the dark

blue–carpeted stairs to the two rooms below. The first
functioned as his study, with a green leather–topped
antique desk in the center that held a red phone running directly to the White House. He wasn't worried
that the phone would ring this afternoon. Philip Brewster, the President, was at Camp David for the weekend. Today, the agenda was domestic policy, and
Philip was working with Jim Slater, his chief of staff,
trying to reshape the administration's proposal for a
tax reduction in the face of congressional opposition.
With only twelve months until the voters decided on
his reelection bid, Philip desperately needed to find
some way to stimulate the economy, and he was pinning his hopes on a retroactive tax reduction, if he
could pull it off in Congress early next year. Tomorrow morning, the presidential helicopter would be taking Winthrop down to Camp David to meet alone with
the President for a broad-ranging review of pressing
foreign policy issues. It had been a struggle, but Winthrop had managed to exclude Marshall Cunningham,
the Secretary of Defense, from tomorrow's meeting.
Winthrop had known Brewster a lot longer than Cunningham, and he was getting damn tired of the SecDef
wanting to run everything in Washington the way he
had run Blue Point Industries in Dallas.

In one corner of the room, a television set was
broadcasting a Notre Dame football game. He decided
to leave it on to drown out any noise.

The room in the back was a library with three of
the walls overflowing with books that he had begun
collecting in his Exeter and Princeton student days.
Against the fourth wall was a brown leather sofa that
opened into a king-size bed. The spacious backyard,
dotted with trees, mostly hickory and oak, could be
seen through the window behind the sofa, but Winthrop had drawn the drapes. Through the window, he
heard Clyde Gillis's bamboo rake scraping the ground.

At the bottom of the stairs, Winthrop said to his
visitor, "We only have an hour. The bed's in the other

room. Why don't you go in there and get ready? I'll find some money for you."

The visitor's mouth opened. The sound that came out was a woman's voice, soft and enticing. "I understood that Alexandra was paid direct."

He laughed. "She always is, but you wouldn't refuse a little gratuity."

She removed the cap, then a man's black wig. After that, she shook her head until long blond tresses fell to her shoulders. "Tips are always welcome. Give me a minute to go into the other room and change clothes. I'll call you when I'm ready. I promise, you won't be disappointed."

Still carrying her briefcase, with Winthrop's eyes riveted on her rear end, she disappeared into the other room. When there was nothing left to leer at, he walked over to the credenza against the wall and opened the third drawer on the right side containing several red file folders, the first two of which were crammed with diplomatic papers. He untied the third one, then reached inside, groping around until he found what he was searching for: a roll of hundred-dollar bills and a box of three condoms.

For several minutes he paced, waiting for her to return. She would be well built, he knew that, with large round breasts that he could bury his head in and a firm, tight ass, because Alexandra knew that was what he liked. Ah, Alexandra, he thought. No matter what he paid her, it was never enough. In his current position, he needed someone like Alexandra to work for him, and she had contacts all around the world from her Upper East Side apartment in Manhattan. He had been delighted when the woman now in the other room, Laurie, had called him this morning an hour after he'd spoken to Alexandra, on his private number that Alexandra always used. "I'm the surprise," she had said. "I'm visiting from New York. I'll be there at two o'clock."

"It might be difficult," he had replied.

"I can dress as George Nesbitt, and I have a California ID to match," she had said in a soft, sensual voice.

God, what a voice. He had felt a stirring in his loins even then on the phone. Still he had hesitated. "I don't know."

"Alexandra tells me that you're special. If you have an hour, I'll make it worth your while. If you doubt me, call her. She'll tell you how good I'll be for you."

He had quickly yielded. Now he tried to visualize what she would look like when she stripped off that man's shirt, suit, and tie. He didn't have long to wait.

"Robert," she called to him from the other room, "you can come in now."

She was standing next to the couch, dressed in black leather gloves, a black leather G-string covering a sea of blond pubic hair, and nothing else. Her breasts were round and full, the nipples jutting out like little peaks. Her legs were long and sinewy, with powerful calf muscles as evidence of the long hours she spent jogging. She stood, legs spread, rubbing her tongue over her lips, while she stroked her right hand over the front of the G-string. She moaned softly, then slipped her hand inside and cupped it over her vagina.

"I told you that you wouldn't be disappointed," she said.

"Why the gloves?" he asked nervously.

"I'm into leather. Haven't you noticed?"

"Not S and M."

"Of course not. Only pleasure for you, Robert. No pain."

He could feel his penis stiffen in his pants. He reached into his pocket, took out the roll of bills, and peeled off ten hundreds. "A thousand altogether," he said.

She walked over to him. With her left hand she took the money, and with the fingers of her right, she touched him gently on the tip of his erection. His whole body trembled.

"That's a preview," she said. "I'm going to put the

money in my briefcase. You stand here with your eyes closed, and let me take care of everything else."

Winthrop meant to do exactly what she said, but he peeked slightly, when she was leaning over the briefcase resting on the couch, with her rear facing him. She was so beautiful from this view. He couldn't wait to take her from the back. He would put her up on the bed on all fours, and he would—

"Remember, eyes closed," she ordered. "I'm in charge of the fun."

He closed them tightly.

"You can look now," she said softly.

Quickly he opened his eyes—and gaped. She was gripping a .380 Walther PPK automatic pistol with a Sionics suppressor in her gloved hand. Rays of late-afternoon sunlight cut through a narrow opening in the curtains and glinted off the metal.

Stunned, Winthrop cried out, "Hey, what is this?"

In response, she squeezed once on the trigger. A bullet slammed into Winthrop's chest and drove him up off his feet. She squeezed again. This time Winthrop collapsed on his back on the Oriental carpet. Blood oozed from his chest, saturating his blue shirt, and spilled freely onto the carpet.

Still clutching the gun, she hurried across the room to Winthrop's body, then reached down to check his pulse. He gave one final shudder, and his hand clutched for her head, grabbing her hair for an instant, then dropping helplessly to the floor.

After returning the gun to her briefcase, she reached into his pants pockets and extracted the rest of the money, mostly hundreds. She also removed the package of condoms. The Mark Cross wallet came next. Inside, there were more hundreds. She took those, then tossed the black leather wallet into the pool of blood on the floor. Most of the money and all of the condoms went into her briefcase. Glancing at the antique grandfather clock in a corner of the room, she saw that she had been in the house for a half hour. No point rushing. Slowly and methodically, she put on her man's suit and tie, the wig, and the cap.

Fully dressed, she walked toward the staircase that led up to the first floor. Halfway up the stairs, she scattered half a dozen hundred-dollar bills, trying to make it appear as if they had fallen from her hand or her pocket. She wasn't worried about fingerprints. The gloves had never come off. Calmly she walked out. She didn't want to seem out of breath to those two bozo guards in front of Winthrop's house.

Clyde Gillis finished raking the last pile of leaves onto his large piece of burlap, slung it over his right shoulder, and carried it to the front of the house. Last one, he thought with relief. He tossed the leaves along with the burlap into his truck and then walked around back to gather up the rest of his equipment.

Raking on a windy day like this was a lot tougher than normal, and Clyde would have preferred to have skipped today. The difficulty was that he didn't like missing a Saturday because that was the one day of the week either Mr. or Mrs. Winthrop was usually at home. Then they handed him a check for the week's worth of gardening. If they weren't home, he had to leave a bill and wait for the check to arrive in the mail. Mrs. Winthrop was real good about paying promptly, but he needed to take that check to the bank every Monday morning.

Clyde's fourth child and first boy, Clyde Junior, now seven years old, had been diagnosed last year as having a rare kidney disease. That meant dialysis on a weekly basis, which was expensive, and insurance didn't pay all of it. The medical bills had already taken every cent he had saved in the twelve years since he had moved his family to Washington from southern Mississippi, and he had no other way to make more money. He worked every daylight hour, but he couldn't make enough. Once, when he was thinking about it, he began crying. Mrs. Winthrop had asked him what was wrong. He had worked at this house before the Winthrops bought it when they moved to Washington from New York three years ago, and he had always found Mrs. Winthrop to be a kind person. He told her about Clyde Junior. She wanted to lend him money, but he knew he could never pay her back. "Consider it a gift," she had said. He couldn't do that. It was a matter of pride. That night, at home, Lucinda had told him he was crazy to turn down Mrs. Winthrop's money, but he refused to change his mind. If a man didn't have pride, he didn't have anything at all. So he toiled, he squeezed his money, and he prayed.

Behind the house, Clyde picked up his rakes. Then he approached the back door, put everything down, and rang the bell. He waited. There was no answer. So he rang again. Still no answer.

Before leaving the house, Mrs. Winthrop had told him that the back door would be unlocked and that he should come right in if no one answered the bell. "You find Mr. Winthrop in the house," she had said. "He'll have your check."

Clyde heard the football game on the television set downstairs. At the top of the stairs, he called, "Mr. Winthrop, it's Clyde Gillis."

He waited. There was no answer.

Cautiously, he walked down the stairs. "Mr. Winthrop?" he called again.

That was when he saw the hundred-dollar bills scattered on the stairs. Alarmed, he drew back and stopped. Then he continued down. He needed that check. He had to get it to the bank Monday morning.

Still no answer, but he was detecting a powerful odor from the other room. With hesitation, he walked toward the doorway. Seeing Winthrop's body lying in a pool of blood, he stopped short and screamed. Instinctively, he knelt down and placed his hand against Winthrop's heart. He felt Winthrop's wrist for a pulse. The man was clearly dead.

Perspiring heavily, trembling, Gillis was enveloped by panic. He wanted to race up the stairs, out the front door, and tell those two guards what he had found. That was the right thing to do. He knew it. But it also would lead to trouble for him, lots of trouble, answering questions and explaining. They would try to blame him, the same way that sheriff had grabbed his daddy when somebody had raped a white girl back home in Hattiesburg. His daddy had been gone for a whole month. They beat his daddy almost to death until a white man raped somebody else, and they caught him and charged him with both crimes. Sure, this was Washington, not Mississippi, but he couldn't take the chance. He decided to take the safe way out. He retraced his steps to the back door, pretending he had never seen a thing.

Chapter 2

"No . . . No . . . No." Ann Winthrop shot to her feet in the center of the darkened theater, throwing her hands into the air. "Linda, you can't play the mother as some sweet old biddy. The woman's a monster. Her daughter's going to kill her, for chrissake. You need to show that the daughter's justified in doing it. Otherwise, this whole play is crap!"

Ann's outburst produced an awkward silence. Though she was the chairman of the board of the Dolly Madison Theatre and the producer of this production of *Beauty Queen of Leenane,* no one other than the director ever interrupted the actors during a dress rehearsal. Sitting next to Ann, Jennifer Moore was embarrassed for her friend. She stood up next to Ann, providing moral support. From the corner of her eye she saw Del Weber, the director, jump up in the first row, clutching a clipboard tightly in his hand. He stormed over and in a single swift motion flung it to the ground, narrowly missing Ann's feet. "You want to direct it yourself?" he shouted at Ann. "Then it's all yours. I'm gone."

As he charged toward the door, Jennifer circled behind the seats and cut him off at the back of the theater. Grabbing his arm, she said, "Look, Del . . ."

Del was furious. "Who the fuck does she think she is?"

"She's got a point. After all, if a character's going to the extreme of killing someone, especially her mother, the audience has to see that her motivation is strong enough."

"C'mon, Jennifer. Don't get lawyerly with me. You used to be in the theater. You know damn well if Ann had a gripe, she should have told me privately. That's the way it's done."

Del was right, and Jennifer knew that. But the show was opening Wednesday evening, and she didn't want him to quit. "Listen," she said, lowering her voice, "cut her a little slack, would you? It has been a tough time for her."

"Why the hell should I?"

Jennifer stared hard at him and said, "Think about it, Del." She didn't have to spell it out: Ann had given Del a chance after he had come out of drug rehab.

The director started calming down as Ann approached, carrying his clipboard. She handed it to him and said, "Sorry, Del. You're in charge. I'm leaving. Let's go, Jenny."

Five minutes later, with Jennifer behind the wheel of her red Saab convertible pulling out of the garage, Ann blurted out, "What's Linda's problem? Didn't she read the script?"

Jennifer didn't respond. After a few moments of riding in silence, Ann, sounding defensive, said, "I was right about the way Linda played the mother, wasn't I, Jenny?"

"Of course you were right. You dragged me along today to give you some notes. My main thought was that I couldn't buy why the daughter would kill her. I mean, the way Linda was playing the part. But . . ." Jennifer had to make a difficult left turn. She used that as an excuse to stop before her next sentence popped out of her mouth.

"You don't have to lecture me," Ann said wearily. "I know I should have held it back for Del till later. But I'm getting damned tired of doing what other people want."

They rode in silence for several minutes. Then Jennifer said, "What's wrong?"

"What makes you think something's wrong?"

"C'mon, Ann, I've known you for twelve years. Since that darkened theater in New York, when you called to a frightened kid at an audition for *Picnic*, 'Will you step forward?'" Jennifer took a deep breath. "I know something's bothering you. Is it Robert?" She turned and drove north on Connecticut Avenue, away from downtown Washington, in the flow of the late–Saturday afternoon traffic.

"Look, Jenny," Ann said. "You're young and you're drop-dead gorgeous. You've had your pick of men. I wasn't in a good bargaining position when Robert came along."

Jennifer touched her honey blond hair, making certain it was pulled tightly back and locked in place. Then she laughed sardonically. "Yeah, I had my pick of men, okay, and I took Craig. I know that I was on the rebound from that two-timing Ben. I wanted to forget I ever met the crumb, but I still should have had more sense than landing in Craig's arms." Jennifer didn't conceal the anger that crept into her voice when she thought about Craig and their marriage that had lasted two years to the day, because he chose their anniversary to head west into the wilds of Colorado with a nubile nineteen-year-old with big boobs to write the great American novel. That was only eight months ago. Their divorce was final three months after he left. God, it seemed like years. At least there weren't any children. "I don't even have an excuse. For me, it's just poor judgment in picking men."

"Sorry, Jenny, that was insensitive of me."

"Ah, forget it. It's all ancient history by now."

"With a little luck, I'll be able to say the same about me and Robert." She paused and then added the words, "One day."

Anxious to change the subject, Jennifer said, "When you get home, maybe you should give Del a call and go over all of your notes from the rehearsal."

Ann thought about it for a moment and said, "Yeah, you're right. He thinks he's an artist. I'd better smooth those ruffled feathers."

She turned and stared out of the window, deep in thought the rest of the way home. Jennifer decided to leave her alone. On Linean Court, Jennifer eased to a stop behind the navy Crown Vic that belonged to the Office of Diplomatic Security.

Nodding to Mac, standing next to the car, Ann said to Jennifer, "You want to come in for a drink?"

"I think I'll pass. Grace Hargadon and I are going to the Kennedy Center tonight to see Verdi's *Luisa Miller*."

"Just a quick one. You have time."

The urgency in Ann's voice made Jennifer reconsider, but she really didn't have time. "Sorry, it's a seven-o'clock curtain, and we have reservations for an early dinner."

Ann sighed in resignation. "Then why don't you come by tomorrow morning, say around ten? We'll have a light brunch before I go back to the theater for rehearsal."

"Won't Robert be home?"

"Even prisoners are allowed to have visitors."

"No, I meant—"

"I know what you meant. He'll be at Camp David with Philip. Just the two of them. Pretty heady stuff. I heard him talking on the phone to Philip last night. Robert says he's got something important to tell Philip that affects both of them, but as usual he wouldn't tell me. Says he doesn't want me leaking it to the press, which is bullshit, because I've never done that to him, despite everything he's done to me." Ann climbed out of the car. "See you tomorrow."

Driving away, Jennifer thought about Ann's husband. What a prick! For a few minutes, she wound around the tree-lined streets with large, expensive homes. At the corner of Connecticut Avenue, Jennifer slowed at the stop sign. Suddenly, the car phone rang. "Jennifer here."

"It's Robert," Ann screamed hysterically. "He's dead! Somebody shot him! You've got to help me!"

The shock of the news paralyzed Jennifer for an

instant, but she recovered fast. "Call nine-one-one right now. I'm on my way back."

"Oh, God!"

As the news sank in, Jennifer didn't shed any tears. Why should she? She was glad the bastard was dead. "Go out front and tell the guards. And don't touch a thing."

She drove the maroon Ford Taurus into the entrance of Washington's Reagan National Airport, taking care to avoid being stopped in the speed trap set to catch travelers late for a plane. Everything was proceeding like clockwork. While the two guards had seen her leave the house, they had never seen her pull away in the Taurus because she had parked around the corner. She had immediately driven into Rock Creek Park. Inside the car, in a deserted parking lot for a picnic grove, she had peeled off the cap, wig, tie and trench coat. The man's outfit was replaced by a maroon skirt and pale pink blouse that she had hidden under the car seat.

She had been dressed as a woman when she stepped out of the car in that picnic grove, but it didn't matter. No one was around to see her. She opened the trunk and put on the camel's-hair coat that was inside. Then she carefully placed the man's clothes, the gun, and the briefcase in the green trash bag in the trunk.

Now, twenty minutes later, she was in the flow of traffic moving toward the main terminal. Not nervous or tense, but horny as hell. Killing always did that to her. She had seriously thought of fucking Winthrop first, maybe even strangling him after she came and just when he was in the throes of orgasm, but she didn't dare take the chance of leaving bodily traces behind. DNA and other types of medical testing were too sophisticated these days. She would like to have called Chip Donovan. An hour in his bed would have been great, but she couldn't risk that either. They had trained her too well to behave stupidly.

So she followed the plan like a good soldier. She

parked the Taurus on the first level of the garage. It was Saturday, and with the garage half-empty, she had no difficulty finding a space against the back wall, as she had been instructed. She left the parking ticket in the glove compartment. Later, the car would be removed, but that didn't concern her. At the Delta Shuttle counter, she paid cash for a ticket to New York, using the name Nancy Burroughs and a phony driver's license.

Waiting for the plane to board, she rewarded herself for a job well done with a double Absolut Citron on the rocks. The alcohol felt good going down. It deadened her senses, took her mind off sex. "I'll be back in Washington soon, Chip," she thought. "I'll call you then."

After takeoff, she reviewed the evening ahead. She'd exit the plane at LaGuardia, looking like a member of the Westport Junior League, which she was, and pick up her Jeep Cherokee. The traffic would be light heading back to Connecticut on the Merritt. She'd be home in time to join Paul for dinner at the Bradleys'.

After that, there'd be bridge, with Paul bidding aggressively as usual, and she, the conservative member of the team, taking very little in the way of risks. "It's just a game, Gwen," Paul frequently lectured her. "You should gamble a little. You're too risk-averse."

At eleven o'clock, Peggy Bradley would turn on the news, because she always did that. And no one would have any idea that their little suburban housewife neighbor was responsible for "the hour's top story."

Chaos was giving way to order. Ann was upstairs recovering in bed. Jennifer had managed to reach Ann and Robert's son in San Francisco and their daughter in Philadelphia. Both were now en route to Washington. She had tried to call President Brewster with the news, but the closest she got was Jim Slater, his chief of staff.

With Ann resting, Jennifer went downstairs to the

den and watched with curiosity as Arthur Campbell, senior detective with the District of Columbia metropolitan police force, a tall, thin black man dressed in a gray flannel sport jacket and tie, went about his business with quiet efficiency. He had finished taking statements from the guards in front of the house, and now he was supervising half a dozen uniformed D.C. police and forensics experts. At Campbell's direction, they were dusting for fingerprints, looking for footprints and any other evidence.

Jennifer had second-chaired a half dozen murder cases when she had worked in the criminal division at Justice. She knew top-notch police work when she saw it. Campbell was very good at his job.

"I'm ready for you now," Campbell said to Jennifer. He pointed her to a sofa and sat down in a leather wing-back chair across from her in the living room, then removed a small steno pad from his pocket and said, "Now tell me, who are you?" He cocked his head, looking at her oddly.

"I'm Jennifer Moore, a friend of Ann Winthrop's."

Campell was still staring, slightly nodding his head. "Do I know you from somewhere?"

"I don't think so."

"Well, maybe not. How'd you happen to be here this afternoon?" His tone was pleasant but formal.

As a trial lawyer, it was weird to Jennifer to be on the receiving end of an interview. "Ann and I spent the afternoon together at the Dolly Madison Theatre downtown. She's producing a play that's in rehearsal now."

"Are you in the theater?"

"Once upon a time, in a different life."

"Ah, that's it," Campbell said, grinning because he now knew where he had seen her before. "Several years ago. There was a TV movie called *The Models*. You played Kelly, the good-looking blonde. You were pretty good, too."

"Yep. That was me."

"So why'd you give it up?"

"Like you just said. I was the good-looking one who was only pretty good."

He was chagrined. "I didn't mean that." Just then he remembered something else. "Hey, wait a minute, weren't you in a couple of kung-fu movies? I think *Attack Girl* was one."

She was never going to live it down. "You're kidding. I didn't know they released those in the U.S."

"Yeah, they did. Helluva kick you had. When one of those kicks landed, every man in the theater cringed. Seriously, why'd you give up acting?"

She smiled. "It's a long story, but anyhow now I'm a lawyer in Washington."

At the change in subject, his enthusiasm dimmed. He went back to business.

"How well do you know Mrs. Winthrop?"

"Ann's one of my best friends. We've known each other for twelve years. In the last three, since she and her husband moved to Washington, we've spent a lot of time together. As you might expect, he's away or tied up a great deal, and I'm not married. So there you are."

"Do you know why there wasn't a maid or any other domestic staff in the house today? Don't they have people who manage this house?"

"They have a live-in couple who work in the house, but they're away for the weekend."

"There were some hundred-dollar bills on the stairs when I got here. Do you know why?"

"I would guess that whoever killed him stole some money and dropped them."

Campbell was looking down, tapping his pad. "Why does a secretary of state have so much cash in his house that a burglar can't even hold it all?"

Jennifer shook her head. "I don't know. My friendship is with her. I didn't know him very well."

"Maybe somebody wanted it to look like a burglary."

"If that's your theory, then you'll be happy to know that nothing was taken from upstairs."

He eyed her with suspicion. "How do you know that?"

"I asked Ann to check her jewelry and other things."

He smiled. "Helping me do my work?"

"I told you, I'm a lawyer."

Campbell barked an order to one of his forensic people: "Do a thorough job upstairs as well." Then he turned back to Jennifer. "What else did Mrs. Winthrop do upstairs?"

"She told me to call her daughter in Philadelphia and her son in San Francisco. They're on their way."

"Does Mrs. Winthrop have a job?"

"As I mentioned, she's a theater producer. Sometimes she directs. She's also the CEO of the Dolly Madison Theatre downtown, which she started two years ago."

"Did Mr. Winthrop have any enemies?"

"I didn't know him well enough to say. As I told you, my friendship was with her, but just reading the newspaper tells me he had lots of enemies."

He looked puzzled. "What do you mean?"

"The militant Arabs were angry about his efforts to combat Middle East terrorism. The Russians were madder'n hell that he wouldn't support an aid package until they coughed up their nuclear weapons. The Japanese were disturbed because of his opposition to their new Asia trade alliance, and the Chinese were furious that he wanted to sell arms to Taiwan. Together, those groups make up more than half the world."

"You think some foreign terrorist killed him?"

"I don't think anything. I'm just trying to answer your questions."

"Does the name George Nesbitt mean anything to you?"

She stopped to think about it for a few moments. "Not a thing. Who is he?"

Campbell kept on boring in. "To your knowledge,"

he said sharply, "did the secretary of state have sexual relations with men?"

"You mean, was he gay?"

Campbell nodded.

"I didn't get that impression from Ann, but we never discussed their sex life together."

"You think they had a happy marriage?"

Jennifer decided not to share her opinions on this subject with Campbell. Instinctively, she wanted to protect Ann. "I don't know. Her husband was busy. He traveled a lot. She made her own life. In that way, they were like most other important couples in this town. Their marriage didn't come first. But why are you asking me all of this?"

"Did Mrs. Winthrop have a hysterectomy?"

"Why the hell should I tell you that?"

His expression and voice turned harder. "I can easily get it from routine medical records."

"But why do you even care?"

"Because I saw a wet spot in the front of his pants. I've got to wait for the lab analysis, but that fluid tells me that he was getting ready to have sex with somebody, or at least thinking about it."

Mystified, she wondered what was going on here. "Maybe he just urinated."

"Then tell me why he had four dozen condoms hidden in a red file jacket in one of the drawers of a chest downstairs," he said, pointing in that direction. "Most married couples in their fifties aren't worried about birth control, and if they are, they keep whatever they use in a bathroom near their bedroom."

Hearing about so many condoms stunned Jennifer. "Ann had a hysterectomy about six years ago," she said weakly.

Campbell paused to jot some notes in the steno book. When he was finished, he said, "I think I'd better talk to Mrs. Winthrop."

Instinctively Jennifer tried to intervene. "Do you have to do that right now? She's had quite a shock."

The detective disregarded that idea completely. "The events are fresh. Now's the best time."

"Why don't you wait until the FBI gets here? They'll be running the show. Why make her do it twice?"

He bristled. "What makes you such an expert?"

"I spent two years working at Justice."

"Then you'll be happy to know that we're cooperating more these days. The D.C. police and the FBI operate as equal members of a team in a case like this. They won't make her tell her story a second time."

Was Campbell serious? Did he really believe the public announcements that White House officials were making about increased cooperation with the D.C. police? "You're kidding yourself. I called to make sure the President knew what happened to Robert. He wasn't merely the President's closest friend. He was a member of the cabinet. Killing him is a federal crime, as well as a local one. In this case, the FBI will never trust the D.C. police to do a good enough job."

Her words struck a sensitive nerve. "Well, they're wrong," Campbell snapped, "and until they get here, I'll do it my way."

She shrugged. Further discussion was obviously useless. "You're in charge for now. I'll get Ann, but please, can you avoid exposing her to all the blood and the odor downstairs? I don't think that would serve any useful purpose."

That caught him up short. Then he nodded at her request. "Of course."

As Jennifer reached the bottom of the stairs to the second floor, Ann was starting down. Her gray hair was tousled wildly on her head. Her skirt and blouse were rumpled.

"I'm sorry to bother you now, Mrs. Winthrop," Campbell said politely.

"You have to do your job." She led the way to the dining room table, and the three of them sat down.

"Thanks for your help," Campbell said. "I know

how difficult this is for you." He glanced over his note-pad. "What time did you leave the house today?"

"Jennifer picked me up around eleven."

"Anybody else here at the time?"

"Just Robert and the gardener."

"You have a name and address?"

Ann crossed into the kitchen and returned with a brown address book. "Clyde Gillis," she said. "Six-fifteen Quincy Street, Southeast Washington, 555-1249."

"How long has he worked for you?"

"Ever since we came to Washington. Nice man."

"Do you know a George Nesbitt?"

She shook her head.

Campbell gazed at Ann sympathetically. She had had a real shock. He didn't want to badger her. "Did your husband have any enemies?"

Ann scowled. "I have no idea."

Her harsh tone made him pause. Then he pressed on. "Were you aware of any threats that might have been made on his life recently?"

"A couple of nights ago, a man with a foreign-sounding voice called. He asked me if my husband was home. When I said no, he said to tell him that Hammas will kill him if he doesn't change his policy toward Israel."

"Did you tell Mr. Winthrop?"

She nodded. "He laughed about it and said prank calls like that went with the job."

That was about the way Campbell figured it, too, and he shrugged. "To your knowledge, what was taken from the house this afternoon?"

"I didn't see anything."

"Jewelry?"

She glanced at Jennifer. "I checked. It's all here."

"What about cash?"

For the first time, a question seemed to trouble Ann, Jennifer thought. Campbell had the same reaction.

"None of mine. I don't keep much in the house."

"And Mr. Winthrop?"

"He liked to keep a fair amount of cash. I don't know what was taken."

Campbell's instincts told him that the cash was an important point. At last, he might be getting somewhere. "Why did he keep so much cash? In his position that's odd."

"He said it made him feel comfortable to be ready for any emergency."

· The flat way she said it told him this was the party line. Campbell stopped to review his notes, to figure out another way to get at her.

"Do you think you'll be able to find out who killed my husband?" asked Ann, also without emotion.

"We'll sure try, but I have to tell you there were nine hundred and twelve homicides in the District last year. Most were related to drugs one way or another. Unfortunately, we don't have the resources to solve every one of them, but you can bet we'll put everything we have into solving this one."

Campbell didn't say that with pride. It was clear what he meant. An innocent kid on the way home from school in a black area gets caught in a drug cross fire, and he becomes a statistic. A secretary of state, who happens to be from a wealthy New York WASP family and a friend of the President, gets shot, and the mayor would tell Campbell to pull out all the stops. The city's reputation as the murder capital of the world was about to take a giant boost when the secretary of state's death made headlines in every Sunday paper around the globe tomorrow.

Campbell was getting ready to frame his next question when two men came barreling through the front door. One, in his late forties, looking like a former football player, with a blond crew cut, was wearing a brown polyester sports jacket, a white shirt, and a tie. The other one, not even thirty-five, was shorter, a little under six feet, thin and wiry, dressed in an Italian designer suit. He had gray metal-framed glasses and wavy thick brown hair.

"Where's Detective Campbell?" the polyester jacket asked.

"I'm Campbell," the detective said, rising to his feet. "Who are you?"

"FBI Special Agent Bill Traynor, and he's Ed Fulton, who's working with me at Director Murtaugh's request."

The younger man seized his cue. Fulton broke in. "The feds have taken over the investigation," he announced. "Half a dozen FBI forensic people are on the way. You can have your people wait outside."

"Now, hold on a minute," Campbell replied. "It's a homicide committed in the District. We always work together in a case like this."

"Not this time, bud," Fulton snapped. "Not when the victim is the secretary of state."

Looking pained, Ann got up and left the room. Nobody seemed to notice her. Jennifer was too intrigued by the Washington infighting to move.

Campbell walked over to the phone. "I'm calling the police chief," he said. "He'll go right to the White House."

"You're too late," Fulton shot back. "Director Murtaugh has already spoken to the mayor. The truth is that she was very pleased to be rid of this hot potato."

If Fulton thought that invoking Murtaugh's name would make Campbell more malleable, he was wrong. It further enraged the detective. He bit down hard on his lower lip as he picked up the phone. It took him three calls until he found Malcolm Lowry, the chief of police, at a daughter's house. After listening for a minute, he slammed the phone down in disgust.

"Fine, it's all yours," he said. He pointed his finger at Fulton and Traynor. "I hope you two geniuses choke on it."

Fulton wasn't the least bit intimidated. "You don't have to get pissed," he said in a condescending tone. "The secretary of state was a good friend of the President's. This development shouldn't surprise you."

Bill Traynor looked at Campbell sympathetically.

"C'mon, we're all in the same business," he said, trying to smooth things over. "Why don't you start by telling us what you've learned so far?"

Campbell's mouth was set in a firm line. "How could I learn anything if I'm so stupid?"

"Hey, I didn't say that," Fulton replied. "I just wanted to make it clear who's in charge."

This young twerp was pissing him off. "Well, you could have said that we were working together."

"Look, we don't need this crap," Fulton said, now sounding furious himself. "As far as I'm concerned, you can tell us what you learned, pull your people, and hit the road."

Campbell put the notebook in his pocket. He moved in close to Fulton, his fists clenched. For an instant Jennifer thought he was going to punch him out. "You've got an attitude problem," he said. Then he pulled away with dignity, as if he had decided that the satisfaction of smacking Fulton around wasn't worth losing his job. "I've got nothing to tell you, smart ass. The security guards who were out in front this afternoon are still here. Mrs. Winthrop is in the house and"—he suddenly became aware of Jennifer listening with an amused expression on her face—"and Ms. Moore, who brought Mrs. Winthrop home from the theater, is right here. Your forensic people can get any prints or other stuff from my people. I'm out of here."

Campbell shoved his hands into his pockets and stormed out of the house, taking half of his people with him.

"You got anything special to contribute right now?" Fulton asked Jennifer. His tone was haughty. To have gotten his job, this guy must have one helluva résumé, Jennifer thought. She had rarely met anyone who enraged people so easily—including her.

Yeah, I've got something to contribute, Jennifer told herself. A lesson for you in how to talk to people. "Not a thing," she replied coldly. "As Detective Campbell already told you, I brought Ann Winthrop home. If you don't mind, I'll wait with her until her daughter gets here, and then I'll leave. You can find me in the Washington phone book at Blank and Foster law firm on Monday, if you need me."

"By Monday we'll have this crime solved," Fulton said with confidence. "We'll have the man who killed Winthrop behind bars."

Chapter 3

It was almost eleven on Sunday morning and Ben Hartwell, dressed in a fifteen-year-old Yale Law sweatshirt, was trying to teach Amy, his four-year-old daughter, how to operate a scooter. They were on the flagstone patio in the back of his Newark Street house in the Cleveland Park section of Washington, and under his breath Ben was cursing his stupidity in acceding to Amy's repeated pleas for a lightweight aluminum scooter as a birthday gift. Dexterity and balance weren't his strong suits, and he had never ridden a scooter in his life. Plus, Amy was too young for it. She was going to kill herself.

But Amy had said at least ten times, "Really, Daddy, everybody in the preschool has one except me." With the guilt he felt as a single parent, he had yielded. Even after reading the owner's manual, though, he wasn't much help, other than holding the scooter and reminding her about the warnings that were plastered on it. The helmet had been easy. Amy had readily agreed to that. The elbow and knee pads proved to be a sticking point. "Karen and Emily don't wear them, and I don't wanna. I'm no baby."

"They're not for babies," he said, trying to be calm and patient. "They protect your knees. If I were going to ride a scooter, I'd wear knee pads."

She laughed. "You'd look stupid in them."

"But you won't."

"No, Daddy, no," she cried, her eyes filling up with

tears. In the end, he caved. "Only this first time. After today, no knee pads, no scooter."

After ten or fifteen minutes, she told him he could let go. Dressed in a pale pink sweatshirt and red corduroy slacks, Amy, who had practiced on her friends' scooters, was soon zipping around the patio.

While watching Amy, Ben let his mind wander. At some point today he had to prepare his summary of the evidence in the Young case. He kept hearing in his mind the words Senator Young had shouted at him when he was questioning Young yesterday afternoon: "You're just a mad-dog prosecutor." The words had stung so badly that Ben had picked up a paper cup half-full of tepid coffee. He was within a hair of flinging it at the senator and scoring a bull's-eye in the middle of Young's white shirt and expensive silk tie. He didn't have to take crap like that from a senator who had accepted secret payoffs from a Mexican drug cartel. The senator had been trying to get his goat with that "mad-dog prosecutor" charge. It wasn't true.

Suddenly, he heard the pager on his belt beep. It was the phone number of Al Hennessey's house in Georgetown. Oh, shit, he thought. His boss, the U.S. Attorney, never worked or called on the weekend. It had to be something urgent. Ben's guess was that Young had complained about Ben's aggressive interrogation. Might as well get it over with fast, Ben decided. "C'mon, Amy," he said, "let's go inside for a little bit."

"But I want to ride my scooter."

"Just for a few minutes, honey, while I make a phone call. You can play with your Barbies. Then we'll come back out. I promise."

In his first-floor study, Ben dialed Hennessey's number. "It is Sunday," Ben said. "I didn't get my days mixed up."

"That's very funny. Real funny."

His boss did not have a sense of humor. Only that practiced politician's tone. "What's up, Al?"

"I was sitting here having brunch when Jim Slater called from the White House."

"And?" Ben held his breath.

"Slater wants us to hold up thirty days taking the Young case to the grand jury."

"And I hope you told him no fuckin' way."

"You don't tell the President that."

"Jim Slater's not the President."

"He speaks for Brewster. There's no doubt that on most issues, Brewster will do what Jim tells him."

"I thought we're a democracy. Nobody elected Jim Slater."

"Listen, Ben, you know what the score is in this town. Young is a powerful Democratic senator. You're getting ready to cut off both his nuts and stick them in his mouth. If Jim Slater tells me to delay thirty days taking the case to the grand jury, how can I tell him no?"

Ben resisted the urge to shout. "Why does he want the thirty days?"

"They want to make their own independent review of the evidence."

That was total bullshit, as Hennessey well knew. "I'll be working on the summary today. I can have a packet to him in a couple of days. He should be able to review it in a few hours."

"It's more than that."

"Even I could figure that out."

"They want Young's vote on the Tax Reform Act, which is scheduled for December first. Once you go before the grand jury, they're afraid the investigation will leak to the press. Young will be so pissed that he'll work against the Tax Reform Act. Brewster's whole economic program will go down the tubes."

"But if I delay thirty days, there could be a leak, and my witnesses will end up in Lake Michigan wearing concrete shoes."

"I told Slater that."

"And?"

"He doesn't give a shit. He's got one interest in life—helping Brewster. He could care less about anything else."

Ben felt his face getting red with rage. He was sick and tired of White House interference in criminal investigations. It always happened, no matter who was president. "Then call Slater back," he told Hennessey, "and tell him to stick it up his ass. We're doing the jobs we're paid to do."

"Take it easy, Ben," Hennessey said.

Those words fueled Ben's anger. Hennessey was such a wimp. Why didn't he stand up to Slater?

"I hate it when somebody tells me that."

"Don't be so damn emotional. We're talking about a thirty-day delay for chrissake." Hennessey was sounding exasperated. "This is no big deal. You don't always have to do things your own way."

"Why don't you and I go to Ches Hawthorne? The AG will back us in a fight with Slater. There's no love lost there."

"The AG's in Tokyo for a conference on law enforcement in the Pacific Rim. He won't be back until next weekend."

"Then call Slater back and tell him that we want a personal briefing with the President on the issue."

"You don't have a choice," Hennessey said. His sharp, emphatic tone let Ben clearly know that Hennessey was in charge and that he could and would fire Ben if Ben didn't follow his orders.

The message came through loud and clear to Ben, who shook his head in disbelief. For three years Hennessey had done everything the White House had wanted, without a demur, in the hope that he would be nominated for a judgeship on the court of appeals in Washington. So far, all that ass kissing hadn't gotten Hennessey his prize, even though two vacancies on the court had been filled by Brewster in his first three years in office. There was another vacancy now, and Hennessey had redoubled his efforts.

"All right," Ben said, resigned. "Your eggs are getting cold. I'll wait the thirty days. Slater will have a summary of the evidence by five on Tuesday afternoon."

"Thanks, I appreciate that. But don't hang up. Slater raised something else that concerns you as well."

Ben saw Amy walk across the living room, dressed in one of the long black dresses Nan had used for piano recitals, with her mother's lipstick caked across her mouth.

"Will I like this one any better?" Ben asked.

"I don't think so."

Amy was sitting down at the baby grand piano in the living room. "I'll be right there," he called to her.

"What'd you say?" Hennessey asked.

"I was talking to Amy. What did you want?"

"Slater says Brewster's all worked up about the Winthrop killing."

"Based on what I read in the morning *Post,* he should be. It doesn't say much for his anticrime program if the President's best friend, and this country's secretary of state, is murdered in his own house."

Ben heard the piano. Out of the corner of his eye, he saw Amy's little fingers, not pounding, but dancing and gliding on the piano, as Nan had taught her.

"The FBI's going to need help from our office," Hennessey said, "and Slater made me promise to give it to my best lawyer. I immediately thought of you, of course."

"I'm flattered, but then you remembered that I'm working full-time, seven days a week on the Young investigation. So you went to second best."

"Fortunately, I didn't have to because Young's gone on hold for thirty days. Remember?"

Ben thought Hennessey was being ridiculous. He had tried cases. He knew how much work there was to do in a big case like the Young prosecution. "Don't you think I'm going to want to use the thirty days to interview witnesses in Chicago?"

"Pete Hamell in the U.S. Attorney's office in Chi-

cago can do the witness interviews. Don't forget, I
pulled plenty of strings to get Hamell assigned to you
full-time on Young."

Hamell was a second-rate lawyer who had the worst
trial record in Chicago. Ben said tiredly, "You must
want to be a judge on the court of appeals badly."

Hennessey ignored the comment. "It's a little more
complicated than I've said."

"Meaning what?"

Hennessey hesitated, then said, "Jim Slater asked
for you personally on the Winthrop case."

Ben was surprised. "Slater doesn't even know
me . . . although I expect that to change when he gets
my summary of the Young evidence."

"Sure he does. You did, after all, receive the attorney general's award last year. And you have a reputation as a tough prosecutor with the highest conviction
rate in the office."

Ben shook his head at the none too subtle flattery.
"Okay, now that I'm properly buttered up, tell me
what you want me to do in the Winthrop case."

"Get a conviction as quickly as possible and wrap
it up."

"Do they even have a suspect?"

"The gardener working at the house."

"That sounds awfully convenient. Who's on the
case?"

"Bill Traynor's spearheading it for the FBI. He's
one of the Bureau's top people, and he's reporting
right to the director."

"I know Bill. We've done a couple of cases together." What Ben didn't say was that Traynor had
made it clear to Ben that he was anxious to finish up
his twenty-five years in the Bureau, which should be
next year, then cash in by getting a top security job
in industry. He wouldn't be hustling on this or any
case. His primary objective would be to avoid of-
fending the FBI director, Ken Murtaugh, so he could
disappear over the hill with full accolades.

Hennessey added, a bit too smoothly, "Bill's got a

young lawyer on Jim Slater's staff working with him to make sure every possible resource of the government is made available. Ed Fulton's his name. His title for this case is special assistant to Director Murtaugh. He's supposed to help clear roadblocks."

"While supposedly keeping the White House out of a law enforcement matter," Ben said cynically.

"No comment."

"None was required." Ben scribbled Ed Fulton's name on a piece of paper near the phone. "Just what I need. Toilet training some hotshot kid trying to make an instant name for himself in the White House."

Hennessey tried to sound optimistic. "Maybe you'll like this Fulton kid."

"You want to bet on that?"

"I told Slater that you'd call Bill at the Hoover Building as soon as we're done. They need help getting a search warrant this afternoon."

Ben raised his hand, as if Hennessey were in the room. "Hold it a second. Time out. I've got other plans this afternoon."

"Like what?"

"With my daughter, Amy."

"Can't the nanny take her?"

"It's Elana's day off. I'm allowed to be a father one day a week."

"God, Ben, isn't there any way you can rearrange things? We're talking about the murder of the secretary of state, for chrissake. If it's a sitter you need, my daughter's sixteen, and she's—"

"Go back to your brunch, Al. I'll handle it."

"I'll owe you for this."

As Ben put the phone down, renewed energy was surging through his body. He didn't give a shit about Al Hennessey or even Jim Slater. The Winthrop case was high visibility. Killing a cabinet officer was a capital crime. And Hennessey was right about one thing. Of all the people in the office, he had the best chance of getting a conviction.

Okay, so that meant he had to bail out on Amy. First, Ben reached Elana at her sister's, in Adams Morgan. She promised to come within the hour. Then he went into the living room, where Amy was playing the piano with intensity in her deep brown eyes. He sat down next to her on the bench and gently touched a couple of keys. Not that it mattered, because Ben was tone-deaf. Happily, Amy had inherited her mother's ear for music, and "much more natural talent than I ever had," Nan used to say.

Amy stopped playing and started to cry. Gently, Ben picked her up and put her on his knee. She turned and threw her arms around him. As the tears rolled down her tiny face, he felt a familiar ache in his stomach.

"Why did Mommy have to die?" Amy asked.

The question stunned Ben, as it always did, notwithstanding the canned answer that Amy's psychiatrist had suggested. How did you explain to a four-year-old what lymphoma was? How could he say to her, "Sorry, kiddo, you got a bad break. You lost the loving, caring parent and ended up with your workaholic dad—the mad-dog prosecutor?"

But Ben didn't say that. He held her tight. In silence, he waited for her to stop crying. Ben's eyes looked over Amy's curly brown hair to the photograph resting on the piano. He and Nan were standing behind Amy while she blew out the candles on the cake from her third birthday. She might have inherited her mother's ear for music, but unfortunately for Amy, she had inherited Ben's looks. Nan was a ravishing black-haired beauty with coal-black eyes, an exotic, glamorous look, and a perfect nose and set of teeth. Ben had brown hair and eyes, and a square jaw with a double chin at the bottom of a face that usually looked like he needed a shave. Well, at least he and Amy had perfect eyesight, while Nan wore contacts.

Two weeks after that picture was taken, Nan was diagnosed with lymphoma. Ten months later she died. Looking at the picture, Ben was tempted to think that

he and Nan had been happy in those days. But that
would have been revisionist history. They had never
been in love. Their marriage satisfied mutual needs
each had: for some companionship that didn't threaten
career plans; for sex; and for the semblance of a family
life. They were like thousands of other busy Washingtonians in this regard. For Ben, there was something
else as well. He had been on the rebound when he
met Nan. His marriage with the well-known pianist
was a way of sticking it to that bitch who broke up
with him. The marriage would have lasted, though,
because even after Amy was born, they never spent
enough time together to grow weary of each other.

When the well ran dry, Ben brushed back Amy's
hair. He wiped her tears with his handkerchief. Then
he kissed her on the forehead and said, "Listen, kiddo,
I have to change the plans a little today."

She opened her eyes wide and looked at him
suspiciously.

"Suppose Elana takes you to the library for the
story hour and then to Ben and Jerry's. You can have
a hot-fudge sundae with two chocolate-chip cookies.
What do you think of that?"

"But I want to go with you, Daddy," she said.
"Elana always takes me."

"Suppose Elana takes you today, and next Sunday
we practice the scooter and I take you to the movies.
How's that sound?"

Suddenly, she understood. "You have to work again
today," she said dejectedly.

"Yeah, I'm sorry. It's something very important that
just came up."

"Why do you always have to work, Daddy, even on
Sunday? None of the other kids' daddies work on
Sunday."

He was feeling guilty for letting her down, but he
didn't have a choice. The secretary of state had been
murdered. "It's just a busy time. I'm real sorry."

"Well, that's okay," she said, leaning into his
shoulder.

"I'll make it up to you, Amy; I promise."

"You always say that," she replied softly, her words cutting through him like a knife.

He broke away from, her, feeling like crap. "Now you go up and change into your own clothes and play with your Barbies. I'll get the scooter and put it away."

"I want it in my room."

"Somebody could get hurt. It's better in the garage."

She pounded her fists on the piano bench. "No, Daddy. No. I want it in my room."

Ben didn't want to argue with her, and he gave in. "Just keep it in the closet, honey."

In short order, Ben showered and dressed. When he walked into her room to put the scooter away, Amy was dressing her Barbies in fancy clothes and high-heeled shoes. She looked so sad that Ben wanted to cry. Ben ran his hand through his hair, trying to decide how he could remedy the situation. Suddenly he had an idea. The summer before Nan was diagnosed with cancer, she had been invited to play at the Aspen Music Festival. He had loved the town and spending long hours alone with Amy, without the press of legal business. It had been a marvelous two weeks.

"Do you remember Aspen?" he asked Amy.

She perked up instantly. "We went in a raft. We went to concerts. It was fun."

"Right. Over Christmas we'll go to Aspen. Just the two of us. I'll teach you how to ski."

"Wow." Her eyes sparkled with enthusiasm. "For sure, Daddy?"

"For sure, honey."

"Like they ski on television?" She moved her hand across the air. "Whoosh . . . whoosh . . . whoosh."

"Well, maybe you won't go that fast in the beginning, but you'll learn."

Amy got up, raced over, and jumped into his arms. "That's a great idea, Daddy."

Ben wasn't quite sure how he'd manage to get the time away in late December between the Young and Winthrop cases, but he would. He was going to do everything possible to avoid disappointing Amy again.

Chapter 4

Marshall Cunningham, the secretary of defense, sipped coffee on the redwood deck of his estate in Great Falls, overlooking the Potomac River. He was deep in thought, pondering events of the last twenty-four hours and trying to guess what Liu, the Chinese ambassador, would have to say when he arrived in a few minutes.

His wife, Betty Sue, had gone inside to work out on the treadmill. On the table lay the morning *Washington Post*. Not surprisingly, Robert Winthrop's death dominated the front page. The articles about what had happened were filled with speculation, but little in the way of facts. Half a dozen groups claimed credit, including radical Arabs, Serbs, and Kurds. The basic biographical information was straightforward. Cunningham picked up the paper and reread the article.

Robert Winthrop was fifty-four years old. He was born in Darien, Connecticut, the first son of distinguished Wall Street lawyer Albert Winthrop. His mother, Harmonia, was from the socially prominent Dalton family in New York City. Winthrop graduated from Exeter Academy, Princeton University, and the Harvard Law School. Following graduation from law school, he enlisted in the air force, serving during the Vietnam War, with distinction in the Judge Advocate General's office in Washington. He then joined his father's law firm, Spencer, Winthrop, and Brooks.

He was a member of the prestigious Council of Foreign Relations, the New York Athletic Club, the Century Society, and the Cosmos Club in Washington. He was a good friend of President Brewster for many years, and he had been an informal adviser to Philip Brewster when he was still senator, before his election to the presidency.

Cunningham reached into his pants pocket and pulled out two tickets for the Redskins-Dallas game. The Cowboys' owner had invited him and Betty Sue to sit in a box with them, along with half a dozen of the Dallas business elite, who had been friends of Cunningham's when he had been president of Blue Point Industries before he moved to Washington with Betty Sue to take the DOD job. He really wanted to go to the game to see all those people, but he didn't know if he could.

The housekeeper came out and said, "The Chinese ambassador is here."

"Bring him out," he said.

Liu Zhen was a man, like Cunningham, with a cold, impassive look, whose heavily creased face and dark brown eyes, behind thick, black-framed glasses, had been trained to divulge nothing of his inner thoughts—unless, of course, he wanted them to show. As he walked out to the deck and shook Cunningham's hand, they didn't disclose a thing.

Cunningham didn't bother to offer Liu tea. He knew the Chinese ambassador well enough to know that his preference was for strong black coffee. When Cunningham pointed to the thermos on the table, Liu said, "A cup of coffee would be lovely." His English was spoken with a clipped British accent, the result of a Cambridge education at a convenient time to be away from China, when the cultural revolution was going full blast. Liu sat down in a wrought-iron chair at the table and looked out toward the river. "It's a great view of the Potomac and the Maryland side," Liu said.

"Only after the trees shed their leaves," Cunningham muttered. He didn't like small talk.

"I appreciate your seeing me on short notice," Liu said. "Can we speak frankly?"

"Absolutely," Cunningham looked across the table at Liu and gave him a wry smile. "You don't even have to worry about video or recording equipment out here."

Liu didn't appreciate Cunningham's effort at humor. "Then I'll skip telling you that I and my government are sorry that Secretary Winthrop is dead."

Cunningham shrugged. "I wouldn't have believed you if you had. I knew that wasn't why you wanted to see me." The American kept himself in check. There were some questions he wanted to put to Liu, but he decided to wait, letting the Chinese ambassador set the pace of the meeting. Cunningham studied Liu as his visitor sipped coffee. The man's face told him nothing.

Finally, the Chinese ambassador put down his Wedgwood cup and said, "We had nothing to do with the secretary of state's death. I wanted you to know that."

Cunningham refused to tell Liu that he believed the denial. He stared at his visitor, waiting for Liu to continue.

"However, my government hopes that Secretary Winthrop's death will lead to a reexamination of the President's decision to submit the massive arms request for Taiwan to Congress in January. Specifically, we want the four destroyers equipped with Aegis battle-management radar, the army's PAC-3 missile defense system, and the diesel-powered submarines all removed from the package of weapons being sold to Taiwan."

Cunningham took a deep breath, trying one final time to formulate his position on this issue, which had been running through his mind ever since he had heard the news reports of Winthrop's death. "Let's review the bidding. Shall we?"

"As you wish."

"Two months ago when you first heard that Robert Winthrop had persuaded the President to submit the Taiwan arms package to Congress in January, you came to me in the hope that I would persuade Brewster to reverse his decision."

"That's correct. I know that you agree with my government's position on the matter of Taiwan."

"The word 'agree' is an understatement. From the time I've spent in Vietnam and Japan, I understand how significant the issue of Taiwan is to Beijing and how it might become the spark which ignites a full-scale war in Asia. I know that a war like that wouldn't benefit this country."

"But it would benefit big arms manufacturers like Blue Point Industries, who would make the sales to Taiwan."

Cunningham shrugged. "I'm not working for them any longer. You know that doesn't enter into my thinking. I've got one interest now. That's doing what's best for this country. Because of that, I'm willing to accede to your country's position on the undesirability of such an extensive arms package for Taiwan in order to avoid a war. So you could say that we wanted the same thing, you and I. As we both know, Winthrop had a different position."

At the mention of the secretary of state, Liu pursed his lips together.

Certain that the Chinese ambassador was cursing under his breath, Cunningham continued. "Winthrop believed that the people of Taiwan have a right to their independence, that the United States has made commitments for their integrity for many years that should be honored, and that particularly after Tiananmen Square, your government shouldn't be placated by appeasement."

Liu was furious. "All of which is absurd. Taiwan is a part of China."

"Regardless of who's right, Winthrop convinced the President to accept his position. And I gave you my commitment that I would attempt to persuade the President not to submit that arms request for Taiwan to Congress. I was hopeful that I would succeed. Am I correct?"

Liu nodded.

"That's where we stood at the end of October, when your government decided to take matters into its own hands with that London video and everything that followed."

Despite his iron self-control, Liu felt a tiny amount of perspiration breaking out on his upper lip. The London video had been his idea. Beijing didn't know about it. He had put his career and his life on the line with that decision. "We were doubtful that in a matter of foreign policy, you could prevail in view of the President's close relationship with Secretary Winthrop. We decided to provide you with some assistance."

"This was help I didn't need, because it complicates the basic issue. If the video is discovered, there will be a full investigation. Someone will attempt to tie your government to Winthrop's death."

"The video won't be discovered." Liu paused and emitted a short hissing sound. "And we had nothing to do with the death of the secretary of state."

Cunningham selected his next words carefully. "That may be," he said in a tone intended to show Liu that he wasn't convinced. "However, the London video makes it more difficult for me to persuade the President to reverse a decision that Winthrop favored so strongly. For all I know, Winthrop told the President about the video and what you'd done."

Liu pulled back. He hadn't considered that possibility. "You're not serious."

"I don't know. As you said, they were very close."

His face showing displeasure, Liu said, "Are you telling me that you'll no longer work for a reversal of the decision on the Taiwan arms package?"

Cunningham paused for a second, trying to frame his words carefully, wanting to make certain Liu understood. "What I'm saying is that until the case is closed on Winthrop's murder, I'm limited in what I can do on this issue. You've got to understand that."

"I see," Liu said.

Cunningham knew he didn't see at all.

When Liu left, Cunningham went to the edge of the patio, next to the railing, and looked at the Potomac below. Dammit. The meeting hadn't gone the way he'd thought. He wasn't certain that the Chinese would wait for him to obtain a reversal of the Taiwan arms proposal. They might take a more aggressive position on the ground with their military. That would enrage Brewster. Cunningham knew how the President would react. He'd say nobody threatened the United States. He'd increase the arms request for Taiwan and put American military forces in the Pacific on alert. Events would spin out of control faster than a runaway truck on a mountain road. He couldn't let that happen. He'd have to regain control over this situation.

Betty Sue called him from the doorway. "Hey, c'mon, it's time to get dressed or we'll miss the kickoff."

He couldn't afford to be out-of-pocket for the next four or five hours. Too much was going on. He had too much at stake. In fact, as he thought about it, he'd better be with the President this afternoon. No telling what Jim Slater would do on his own. "Listen," he said gingerly, knowing that his next words would produce a violent response. Ah, well, that came with marrying a general's daughter. "With Winthrop's death, it would be unseemly for me to be at a football game."

She snarled at him. "You fucking hypocrite. You couldn't stand the man."

"I know that, but—"

"Oh, for chrissake," she shouted. "Give me the tickets. I'll call Mary Jo and I'll go with her. I can't believe you'd pass up the Dallas game for a man you described as 'a pompous, self-important jerk, and the President's albatross.' "

"Shh, keep your voice down. It's not right to talk that way about the dearly departed." He laughed and she did too. "Did I really use all of those words?" he said.

"Yeah. And you also called him a despicable, whoring peckerhead."

Chip Donovan sipped scotch and ran his hand through his thick gray hair. From his suite in the sophisticated and luxurious Ritz Landis Hotel, he overlooked downtown Taipei. It was already thirty minutes past midnight. Chen Heng was half an hour late. Was it possible he wouldn't show?

It was ridiculous for Donovan to have made the trip from Washington. This wasn't a journey for the head of special operations at the CIA. It was a job for someone on his staff. Sherman, who operated throughout Asia under the cover of a representative of a high-tech venture capitalist, was the logical choice. Sherman had helped plan Operation Matchstick. Donovan should have insisted that Sherman cover this meeting.

As those thoughts ran through his mind, Donovan knew why he had to come. He had recruited Chen more than a decade ago at the time of the protests in support of the students in Tiananmen Square. Chen needed delicate handling, and he was the one to whom Chen responded. Now that they were close to launching Operation Matchstick, Chen would be having anxiety attacks, and for good reason. Only Donovan could keep Chen on board.

Donovan heard a sudden knock at the door. Tensing, he reached for his gun. "Who's there?" he called.

"It's Chen."

Donovan relaxed. Dressed in his usual black suit with a black turtleneck shirt, he crossed the room and opened the door. "You're late."

"I'm sorry. My father insisted that I come to his

house this evening. He wanted to give me more instructions about the plant in Shanghai."

Alarmed, Donovan said, "He doesn't know you're working with me, does he?"

"No, of course not. He wants to know when I'm ready to go over."

"What'd you say?"

"I dodged the question. I was ready to go last week. Then I got your fax, telling me the purchase order was on hold until further notice."

"It was."

"And now?"

Donovan looked around the room. He had swept it for bugs. Still, he didn't want to say anything too explicit. "Operation Matchstick is back on. How soon can you leave for Shanghai?"

Worry lines appeared on Chen's forehead. "Not tomorrow. My older son, Teddy, has a championship baseball game. He's pitching." Chen sighed in resignation. "I guess I can go on Monday."

"Monday is good."

"Will you be able to reassemble the other pieces in time?"

"Everything will be set. Assume that Monday is day one and count from then on the original schedule."

"What about the Chinese army units?"

Donovan answered tersely, "I told you, everything will be set."

Chen responded by taking off his wire-framed glasses and cleaning them with a handkerchief. He didn't have to say a word. Donovan knew that he was trying to decide whether to tell Donovan to shove it and return to his normal life.

Afraid of losing him, Donovan softened. "It's important for your people, what you're doing." He had to keep reminding himself that Chen wasn't a professional. This was Chen's first operation. He was putting his life on the line.

After more work on him, emphasizing the value of the operation to the people of Taiwan, Chen yielded.

They sealed their agreement with a drink. Operation Matchstick was back on track.

After Chen left, Donovan waited a full hour to exit the hotel. He walked a half dozen blocks before ducking into a dimly lit bar. It took a few moments of peering and looking around the smoke-filled room where bar girls entertained their customers before he recognized the man he was looking for—Peng, a senior member of the Taiwanese intelligence service. Peng worked out of a trade mission in Paris, but had flown home at Donovan's request. The two men had collaborated on a number of operations aimed at China over the last decade.

Peng was sitting in an almost pitch-dark corner of the room, drinking beer from a glass and smoking a cigarette. After nodding to him, Donovan stopped at the bar, picked up a scotch straight up, and took the chair next to Peng.

"Thanks for coming here to meet me," Donovan said.

"I was due home for other matters. The timing was good."

Donovan smiled faintly. Peng was letting him know that he wasn't at Donovan's beck and call. "Operation Matchstick is on again," Donovan said.

A smile formed at the edges of Peng's mouth. "When?"

"Subject leaves Monday for Shanghai. I'm worried about leaks."

"No one knows you're here except for me and the director. You don't have to worry about us. I'll let the director know."

"I appreciate that."

"Your timing couldn't be better."

Donovan was nonplussed. "What do you mean?"

"The Chinese have begun significant troop movements toward the Strait of Taiwan in the last couple of days."

Surprise registered on Donovan's face. "To my

knowledge, we haven't picked up anything on our satellites yet. How do you know that?"

By way of answer, Peng calmly blew smoke rings into the air.

Donovan pressed. "I've been open with you about Operation Matchstick."

"You're right," Peng said finally. "Our source is one of our moles in the Chinese intelligence service."

"Are these troop movements the usual saber rattling from Beijing?"

Peng paused to sip his beer. "We don't think so. It's more heavy equipment, including landing craft, trucks, and heavy weapons, as well as infantry. Precisely what's needed to launch an attack on Taiwan."

"Jesus, why do you think they're doing it now?"

Peng shrugged. "It could be Beijing's response to the Winthrop arms package for Taiwan."

"But Winthrop's dead."

"That fact is being celebrated in Beijing. Meantime, Brewster hasn't said he'll modify the Taiwan arms package. My guess is," Peng said sourly, "they're thinking about a preemptive strike."

Chapter 5

"Damage control," Jim Slater, the President's chief of staff, said aloud as he paced in his White House office early that afternoon. Winthrop's murder could easily derail Brewster's reelection next year, and Slater was determined to stop that from happening.

Aside from the three hours he had tossed in bed last night, hoping to sleep, he had spent every minute since he and Brewster had returned from Camp David, once they heard the news of Winthrop's death, engaged in damage control. He had met with newspaper reporters and given television interviews. He had assigned Ed Fulton on his staff to the investigation, and Fulton had kept him informed of every development. In the cold light of the morning, Slater knew very well that only one thing would solve the problem—a fast arrest and conviction. But that required a suspect.

For the first time he was beginning to breathe a sigh of relief. The law enforcement net had snared the gardener. It might be possible to close out the case in record time.

Slater heard a phone ringing on his desk. He expected it to be the President's secretary telling him that Brewster had returned to the White House after a condolence call on Ann Winthrop. Instead, it was his private phone, which he snatched on the first ring.

Slater heard a melodious woman's voice. "Jim, I've

been out. I just listened to the message on the special cell phone you left me."

"I'm real sorry I can't make it tonight."

"I could meet you earlier or later. Whatever works for you."

Slater hesitated. God, with all of the tension, what he most needed was an hour in bed with her tonight. Slater glanced at the grandfather clock standing against the wall across the room, next to a picture of Slater on a horse with the Oxford University polo team taken thirty-five years ago.

As hard as he tried, Slater couldn't rationalize leaving this building until well after midnight again. Nothing was more important right now than steering a path through this morass so that Brewster was still standing politically when it was all over—which meant that Slater would be alive as well. "Just can't do it tonight. I'm so sorry."

"Is your wife in town?" she said.

He knew her well enough to tell she was pouting. Trying to cheer her up, he laughed. "If Alice were here, she wouldn't stop me for a minute. I'm afraid that I'm chained to my desk on account of Winthrop's death."

"Oh. I guess I can understand that. I saw you on *Headlines* last night. You sounded good, although your shirt was wrinkled."

Slater laughed again. "I've got no one to iron for me."

This time she laughed with him. "That won't be me. I don't iron."

"I didn't think so. You know that I'll see you as soon as I can."

"I know that, Jim."

"Meantime, we'll talk."

When he hung up the phone, Slater resumed pacing. He was a tall, handsome man, with a well-conditioned, athletic look that made him seem younger than his fifty-five years. Dressed in a dapper double-breasted gray pinstripe suit from Gieves & Hawkes on Savile

Row—where he shopped twice a year—navy suspenders,
and a monogrammed bold striped shirt that had become
his trademark, topped off with gold presidential-seal cuff
links, he was an imposing figure. With his thick head
of dark brown hair parted in the center and pasted
down, he looked very much like the New York investment banker he had been as chairman of Bullman
and Glass, one of the largest investment banking
firms in the world, before Brewster selected him to
be secretary of the treasury two years ago. He exuded
confidence and success. His appearance had contributed to the adjective "unflappable" that was frequently used to describe Slater in the Washington
press.

Last year, when a rash of scandals brought the
Brewster administration to its low point of a thirty
percent approval rating, the President had moved
Slater from the treasury to White House chief of staff.
Slowly but surely, under Slater's cool stewardship, the
President's standing had risen in the polls. Congressional Democrats had applauded Slater's efforts,
thrilled that someone with a sharp analytical mind and
not merely a political hack occupied that critical position in the White House. Increasingly, Slater was
being mentioned as the next chairman of the Federal
Reserve Board, which he viewed as the most important office in Washington next to being president. Now
all of that was at risk.

In New York, Slater had prided himself on being
able to find a way to do any deal and solve any
problem. He had brought that ability with him when
he came to Washington. He would find a way to deal
with this situation. He would steer Brewster through
this minefield, just as he had steered the CEOs of so
many Fortune 500 companies through their mine-
fields.

The phone rang again. This time it was Ed Fulton
on Slater's office phone. "Is this a good time for a
progress report, Mr. Slater?" Fulton asked.

"Fire away," Slater said in the curt voice he used with subordinates.

"The prosecutor you wanted, Ben Hartwell, will be here soon to help us get the search warrant."

"Do you and Traynor still think that the gardener killed Winthrop?"

"We're sure of it."

"What was his motive?"

"Robbery. Gillis needed cash. Winthrop had plenty of it in the house."

Slater tapped his manicured fingers on the desk. "Before you arrest this gardener, you'd better have an ironclad case. Am I making myself clear?" Slater imagined Fulton trembling at the other end of the phone.

"Yes, sir. You are."

"Because you know what would hurt President Brewster next November even worse than Winthrop's death don't you?"

"Yes, sir. Arresting the wrong man."

"No, arresting an African American who was the wrong man."

"I got that, sir."

"But if you and Traynor tell me after you do the search that he's the one, I won't second-guess you. I'll make sure that we nail his ass. Are you getting me?"

"Yes, sir, Mr. Slater. Loud and clear."

Before going to the FBI to meet Fulton and Traynor, Ben stopped at his own office in the U.S. Courthouse, a few blocks away. From the bookshelf he pulled down a large dark green volume—this year's issue of *Lawyers in U.S. Government Service*. Edward Fulton's entry was brief. It told Ben that Fulton was only thirty-two years old.

He had been born in Kalamazoo, Michigan, and he had been a super achiever in school, graduating summa cum laude and Phi Beta Kappa from Michigan, with a major in political science. Following graduation,

he had enlisted in the marines, a fact that surprised
Ben, and he rose to the rank of captain. Three years
later, he entered Harvard Law School, where Fulton
was editor-in-chief of the *Harvard Law Review,* graduating first in his class—a lot better than I did at Yale,
thought Ben. But I managed to have a good time,
unlike those geeks who studied night and day. He
doubted whether Fulton had played as many poker
games during his three years in law school. After graduation, Fulton had clerked for a U.S. court of appeals
judge in Ohio and then for the chief justice of the
Supreme Court. Two years ago, he had gone right
from his clerkship to Jim Slater's staff as an assistant
White House counsel. That didn't happen on merit
alone. Somebody in the family or a friend must have
had a connection with Slater or the president's party.
Maybe a big contributor. Fulton was married and had
two children.

From the bio, Ben could complete the picture. Fulton was not only bright, but incredibly ambitious and
hardworking. Even driven. On the fastest possible
track for success. Probably arrogant as well. His family
would never stop him from getting ahead. They would
either support him or be brushed aside. Ben had
known plenty of Washington types like Ed Fulton. It
was a lonely ride.

Ben decided to walk down Pennsylvania Avenue to
the FBI building. He was only a couple of pounds
overweight on his nearly six-foot frame, but he could
feel himself getting flabby. In response, for his fortieth
birthday in April, he had bought a treadmill. So far
he had used it only twice. Between his job and Amy,
there was never time for exercise.

Fifteen minutes later and out of breath, Ben arrived at the FBI. Quickly, he surveyed the scene in
the fifth-floor conference room. Fulton and Traynor
were sitting across a table that held a dozen half-
empty cups of cold coffee and some doughnuts that
were quickly going stale. Though both of them had

glazed, bloodshot eyes, there was a difference in their appearances. Traynor's shirtsleeves were rolled up to the elbows, his collar was open at the neck, and his tie and jacket had been tossed on a chair in the corner. Fulton was still dressed smartly in a white shirt and a jacket and tie. He was tired, but he looked neat. That was the way Nan had always wanted him to look, Ben thought, but he rarely achieved that standard. Usually, he looked the way he did today: rumpled suit badly in need of a pressing and a food-stained tie.

Traynor introduced Ben to Fulton, then said, "Sorry for what I look like. We've been up all night."

"I figured as much. You guys have anything to show for it?"

"We've found the killer," Fulton announced with pride. "We just need you to get us a search warrant."

Fulton exuded the arrogance Ben had been expecting. "Why don't you tell me exactly what you've found?" he said to Traynor.

Fulton didn't like being ignored. "Get us the search warrant now before he gets rid of the evidence. We'll give you the details later."

"Wrong," Ben shot back. "It doesn't work that way. Malcolm Penn's the judge on emergency duty today. He won't sign a simple extension of time, much less a search warrant, without the whole story."

Involuntarily, Fulton's eyes began blinking. He turned to Traynor. "I thought you said we'd be able to work with this guy. Right out of the chute, he's yanking our dicks around."

Traynor looked at Ben and gave a slight shrug. What do you want me to do? was what it conveyed to Ben, which wasn't very helpful. Oh, well, Ben was willing to do battle alone.

Once Traynor saw the fire flaring in Ben's eyes, he reassessed and decided to mediate, to head off a fight. "Listen, Ed, let's take a few minutes and tell Ben what we know."

"And after that, we're doing things my way," Fulton replied. "Otherwise, I'll get Mr. Slater to call Hennessey and straighten it out."

Ben was ready to pack up and head back to his office. Seeing this, Traynor held up his head. "Let's take a break," he said coolly, "and go to the men's room."

On the way, Traynor filled Ben in. "The kid's new. He's smart, but he's young and inexperienced. He's landed this big job on Slater's staff, and he wants to make a good impression. Get ahead fast. You know what I mean. Let him talk. We'll ignore him and do it our way."

That was a ludicrous proposal, coming from a guy who knows better, Ben thought. How bad could somebody want to retire? "That's a great way to approach a major case."

Traynor winced. "We don't have a choice. I don't like it any better than you. Please, we've got to work with him."

Ben didn't respond until they were alone in the bathroom washing their hands. "Is this hotshot naturally so obnoxious, or does he work at being that way?"

"Please, Ben, as a personal favor to me, try to work with him. This case is so high-profile that my ass is now on the line if something doesn't happen soon. You can't believe the heat we're getting from the White House."

Back in the conference room, Traynor went over to Fulton and persuaded him that they should give Ben a summary of what they'd found. Over a fresh cup of coffee, Traynor started talking. "Here's what we know so far. The secretary of state was home alone with two guards out in front of his house on Linean Court. At two o'clock, he had a visitor for a scheduled meeting. State Department business. A George Nesbitt, who showed a California driver's license for ID. We haven't been able to locate Nesbitt."

Traynor paused to sip some coffee. "There was a

gardener, Clyde Gillis, working in the yard in the afternoon, raking leaves. Gillis's first story was that he was never in the house. He told us that about seven last evening. Since we had fingerprints and shoe prints in the house, we took samples from Gillis."

"And?"

"We made a positive ID about midnight, including a fingerprint on Winthrop's chest and another one on his wrist. So we went back to Gillis and told him that."

That wasn't the way the FBI operated. They gathered all of the evidence in a methodical way before confronting a suspect. It was obvious to Ben that Fulton had been calling the shots.

"And?" Ben asked.

"At about four A.M. we got story number two from Gillis. He entered the house to collect a check for his work. He found Winthrop's dead body, got scared, and ran away without telling anyone what he saw."

Gillis's story sounded plausible to Ben. "Where is he now?"

"At home in southeast Washington. We asked him not to leave his house for the next six hours. He agreed. We've got two agents out in front to follow him if he runs."

"You asked him not to leave his house, and he voluntarily agreed?" Ben asked skeptically.

"Yeah, that's right," Fulton responded.

Traynor looked embarrassed. He knew that they weren't following standard FBI procedures.

Ben said, "Tell me what happened."

"We leaned on him pretty hard. We told him if he set foot out of the house or used the telephone, we would immediately arrest him."

Ben shook his head in disgust. "For which you didn't have probable cause. So you decided to place him under virtual house arrest, and I assume that when you asked him for the prints, you told him that he had a right to counsel and that he didn't have to talk to you or anyone without first consulting a lawyer."

A heavy silence hung over the room. "I decided not to," Fulton replied defiantly.

Ben was stunned. "You ever take a course in criminal procedure? You ever hear about the Fifth Amendment?"

"Don't be a wise guy," Fulton said, though he began fiddling with his college ring engraved with fraternity initials. "I want him to talk. I don't want him clamming up."

"Why didn't you hook electrodes up to his nuts?" Ben's voice was hard, showing the cold fury he felt. "That works even better."

"I'll forget you said that."

"But I'll remind you if I can't use the key evidence, and the judge throws out our case against Gillis because you deprived him of his rights." Incredulous, Ben turned to Traynor. "Jesus, Bill. You know better than that. You're a pro in this business, not like our hotshot friend here from the White House."

Traynor looked down at his hands. "The director made it clear to me at the beginning. Ed here is in charge. The order came right from Slater at the White House."

Ben shook his head. Traynor was so eager to please, he wasn't doing his job. He turned back to Fulton. "The only thing that surprises me, hotshot, is that you called for help from the U.S. Attorney's office."

Unchastened, Fulton glared at Ben. "We need a search warrant."

"I assume you're a member of the bar. Go get one."

"Judge Penn insisted that the application come from an assistant U.S. attorney."

Now Ben saw how this had all played out. "And you couldn't cow the judge by invoking the name of Jim Slater and the White House?"

Fulton didn't respond.

"What a shame," Ben added. "That's the trouble with having federal judges appointed for life. You guys in the White House can't push them around."

"If you've had your fun," Fulton replied sharply,

"can we stop farting around and go get the warrant? We want to search Gillis's house and the truck that he uses to haul leaves."

"What are you looking for?" Ben directed the question to Bill Traynor.

"A gun. Money that was taken from the house. We think lots of money was taken. There might be other evidence."

"You guys really think Gillis did it?"

Traynor looked at his notepad. "He has a sick kid. He needs money for medical treatments. It certainly looks like robbery."

"Why not Nesbitt? You haven't been able to find him."

Traynor hesitated. "The time sequence fits Gillis better."

He said it in a halting voice that made Ben wonder if he really believed it. "What do you mean?"

Traynor glanced back at his notes. "According to the guards in front of the house, Nesbitt arrived at two in the afternoon and left at two-thirty. Gillis was there from eleven to four. The FBI lab puts the time of death at three-fifteen."

"How precise is that time of death?"

Traynor held out his hands. "It's an estimate. You know how they do these things. They check body temperature. It's got a margin of error."

"We had the best guy in the FBI lab look at the information," Fulton interjected. "We found him at the Kennedy Center last night and brought him to check over everything."

Ben couldn't believe this moron. "I am so impressed. And you no doubt love his answer."

"What's your trouble, mister?" Fulton said. "You got a soft spot for gardeners? Gillis did it just as sure as God made little green apples. He looks and sounds guilty, and he's changed his story."

Ben shrugged in agreement. "You're probably right. He probably is guilty. But that's not what it's all about, hotshot."

"I don't like being called that."

"I didn't think so. That's why I keep doing it," Ben said, boring in. "The point is, when we get to trial, the issue won't be whether Gillis did it or not. The issue will be whether I can put on an airtight case without getting my evidence tossed on a technicality. They taught me that at the Yale Law School, and I'll bet they even taught it to you at Harvard."

Fulton shot Ben a surly look. "Oh, fuck off."

Ben advanced on him. "Look, asshole, I'm on your side. I've got other things I'd rather be doing right now than screwing around with this case, but the only way I'm going to get back to them is by getting a conviction that sends Gillis to the electric chair, if he's guilty, which is likely. That means putting on evidence that won't get excluded. That means tying up every loose end. Now, what's the deal on Nesbitt, Bill?"

"We're still looking for him," Traynor said, again uncertainly.

Ben knew that he had found the weak link in the case against Gillis. "Look harder. I want to be able to tell the judge that we left no stone unturned."

"I've got a straight line to Director Murtaugh on this case. I'll ask him to double our search team."

Ben was pleased to hear that. If the FBI put on a full court press, he was confident that they'd find Nesbitt.

"Did you find any other prints in that part of the Winthrops' house?"

"Nothing. Other than Winthrop's."

"Who found the body?"

"Mrs. Winthrop."

"When?"

"At about four-thirty yesterday afternoon."

"What'd she do first? Call the police? Or notify the guards in front of the house?"

Bill Traynor rubbed the weariness from his eyes before responding. "Her first call was actually to a friend who brought her home from the theater. Then Mrs.

Winthrop called the police. The friend got to the house about fifteen minutes before the police."

"What's the name of the friend?"

"She's a lawyer. Jennifer Moore is her name."

Startled, Ben drew back sharply. He hadn't seen Jennifer since she had walked out on him more than five years ago. There was a long silence as Traynor's words hung in the air like an awful ghost. Ben finally said, "Well, isn't that nice?" He still winced in pain when he thought about her, but he had no intention of running away from the case. It was time, he decided, to excise this dybbuk once and for all. "Get me a secretary," he barked to Traynor. "I'm ready to dictate the application for a search warrant."

Marshall Cunningham was determined to see the President as soon as he returned with the First Lady from paying a condolence call on Ann Winthrop. He remained in telephone contact with one of the Secret Service agents in the presidential motorcade. As soon as the cars crossed K Street, Cunningham walked upstairs to the President's living quarters.

Moments later they arrived.

He had known Brewster for ten years, and he had never seen the President or the First Lady so emotionally shaken. Beverly's face was red from crying. She immediately headed off to their bedroom, without even saying hello.

The President's jaw was set in a somber expression. The lines in his craggy face were more pronounced. His usually carefully combed gray hair was mussed in the way it was when he became upset and he ran his hands through it. His eyes had a glazed look. "I never drink before the sun goes down," he said. "You know that. But I sure as hell am going to make an exception today."

"It's horrible," Cunningham responded, wanting to sound sympathetic. "Absolutely horrible. I can't tell you how badly I feel for you and Beverly."

"I appreciate your saying that. Your opinion means

a lot to me. Next to Robert, you're my oldest and closest friend in the administration. I know that the two of you didn't always see eye to eye."

A veil of sadness covered Cunningham's face. "Those were policy differences. On a personal level, we always got along, and I knew how much his friendship meant to you."

Walking over to the tea wagon, the President asked, "You want one?"

The last thing Cunningham wanted now was a drink, but he didn't want to refuse the President. "Whatever you're having, Philip."

Brewster poured two fingers of Jack Daniel's into a couple of glasses and added some ice. After handing one to Cunningham, who put it down on an end table, Brewster sat on a sofa and sipped the drink slowly. "Robert and I went back so far. Christ, he was my catcher when I pitched at Exeter. He fixed me and Beverly up on our first date."

Cunningham sat impassively and let Brewster rattle on. He shared none of his leader's sentiments. As far as he was concerned, it was a miracle that Winthrop didn't die in the sack with some bimbo, setting off a major scandal that would have doomed Brewster's chances for reelection. It was a classic case of how badly things can turn out if a president appointed unqualified cronies to top-level jobs in the government. Family money and connections had been enough to get a partnership for Winthrop in a New York law firm. That was right where Brewster should have left him after being elected president—unless, of course, he wanted to name his friend to an ambassadorship in a nonsensitive country.

"What a shame," Brewster continued. "He was a good man. He had so much to offer the country and the world. I'm going to miss his counsel."

Jim Slater appeared in the doorway to the room. "I couldn't agree with you more," Slater said, "but we'll find out who did this horrible deed and bring him to justice. I promise you that, Philip."

"Have you spoken to Murtaugh?" Brewster asked.

"Several times. I'm on it myself, working with him and his best people at the FBI. We're going to catch the bastard fast and go for the death penalty."

"Robert deserves that much."

Slater nodded. "It's a real blow for all of us. How's Ann taking it?"

"Like a trooper. The funeral's in New York tomorrow. Their kids are on their way there now. Ann's flying up early this evening. Fortunately, the press left her house when I did. She should be able to get some rest."

Ignoring Cunningham, Slater continued talking as if he and Brewster were the only ones in the room. "Well, the reporters sure aren't leaving you alone. There are a shitload of them downstairs, and they want you to make a statement about the search for Robert's killer."

"What'd you tell them?"

"I didn't. I've got a tentative hold on network time tonight at eight o'clock, after the football games. My thought is that you would just make a short statement here in this room in front of the fireplace. No question-and-answers. I figure you can use Robert's death to blast the Republicans for holding up your crime bill in the Senate. You can gain some points politically by showing how we're on top of this investigation."

"You think that's smart?" Cunningham said. "Using Robert's death for political purposes?"

Slater glared at him. "That's not the point. People are worried about crime. If this could happen to the secretary of state, then they're not safe in their own homes. They've got to be reassured."

"What do I tell them?" the President asked.

Slater reached into his jacket pocket and pulled out a piece of paper. "I've got two people working on a draft right now. Let me read you a paragraph I wrote for them to include."

Brewster nodded, and Slater began reading. " 'I

want to assure each and every American that no effort
will be spared to find the perpetrators of this heinous
crime and to bring them to justice. It is but one more
example of why the Congress should promptly enact
the administration's crime bill, S.83. Violent crime is
a plague gripping America. A cancer in the heart of
our great country. We must strike back, declaring war
on crime in a way that will finally eradicate it from
our midst. What yesterday's tragic events demonstrate
is that unfortunately no American citizen is safe in his
own home—regardless of where he lives and even if
he's the secretary of state. We must stop talking and
act to ensure the most basic of all protections to all
of the American people.' "

"That's not bad. When will you have the draft?"

"In about an hour. We'll describe how extensive the
FBI search is. We'll tell them that we already have a
number of leads, and we may even have an arrest
within twenty-four hours."

Cunningham pulled back in surprise. "Is that true?"

"Absolutely. I've got a kid on my staff, Ed Fulton,
working with one of the top guys in the FBI, who's
reporting directly to Murtaugh. Fulton just called and
told me it was a simple robbery gone wrong. An inside
job. Not terrorists and not hardened criminals."

"Who was it?" Cunningham asked, pressing for
more information.

"The gardener at the Winthrops' house. They're
moving fast to build an airtight case and make an
arrest."

"That would be good news," Brewster said.

"Very good."

Cunningham eyed Slater with hostility. "What's
Ches say about the idea of the television statement?"

Slater was annoyed. Dealing with Winthrop's murder wasn't the purview of the secretary of defense.
Cunningham was using his friendship with the President to gain a foothold on Slater's turf. "I haven't
called yet. I figured we'd call him now."

The President glanced at his watch, then picked up

the phone and told his secretary, "Get me Attorney General Hawthorne. Try the Okura Hotel in Tokyo."

A few minutes later, Ches Hawthorne was on the speakerphone. "Jim wants me to go on TV tonight to talk about Robert's death," Brewster said. "What do you think, Ches?"

It was the middle of the night in Tokyo. The call had awakened Hawthorne, who had had too much sake at dinner, out of a sound sleep. "What would you say?"

Slater repeated his summary of the proposed television address. There was a long silence while Hawthorne tried to think it through. "It's probably a good idea," he finally said, "How soon can I see a copy of the statement?"

"I'll fax it to you within the hour."

"I think I should come home tomorrow," Hawthorne said, "and personally take charge of the Winthrop investigation."

Slater decided he'd better jump in fast. He didn't want Hawthorne getting a lot of publicity and looking like a hero when there was an early arrest. "That's a terrible idea," he replied. "You're attending an international conference devoted to crime control and law enforcement. We'll look like idiots if you have to rush home because of a murder. Besides, Murtaugh has his top people involved. No offense, Ches, but what would you add being here that you can't contribute by phone and e-mail?"

"There may be legal decisions to be made."

Cunningham was amused by the infighting between Slater and Hawthorne. Pleased that the gardener's arrest was imminent, Cunningham didn't care who took credit for it.

"I got Al Hennessey to give us the best man in his office," Slater said.

"What do you think, Philip?" Hawthorne asked the President.

"It's your call, Ches, but I think Jim makes some good points."

"All right, I'm convinced. I'll have Sarah Van Buren, the head of the criminal division at Justice, keep me informed."

When they hung up the phone, Cunningham thought about telling the President about his meeting with the Chinese ambassador that morning, but decided against it. In Brewster's emotional state, his knee-jerk reaction would be to blow up at the Chinese and take some action against them. Maybe even increase Winthrop's proposed arms package for Taiwan. It would be a poor decision, because Cunningham was convinced that, if pushed, Beijing would attack Taiwan. No, he had to gamble that Winthrop hadn't told Brewster about the meeting at Winthrop's house on November first and the London video.

Free! Free at last! Ann thought as she leaned back in the warm bubble bath. Finally, the frenzied activity of the last twenty-four hours was over, and the house was empty. They all meant well, so genuine in their concern for the grieving widow. God, if they only knew how she felt.

And what about Matt and Gerry? How did they feel about their father's death? Neither of the children had been close with Robert. When they were young, she had tried to be both mother and father—making up for Robert's indifference that frequently descended into unreasonable commands and destructive criticism. The petty tyrant making arbitrary demands on his subjects. Of course, it was inevitable that neither of them would measure up to his standards, and so Matt had a job as the editor of a small literary magazine in San Francisco, about as far as he could go physically and spiritually to escape from his father without leaving the continental United States. And Gerry had set aside her Ph.D. in history to teach fourth grade in an inner-city school. Both drifted away, coming home as little as possible because of Robert, while blaming her for not giving them more support in battles with their father. It left her with a gaping hole that she had tried to fill with Jenny, her surrogate daughter, whose own mother had hit the road and left Jenny with her father when she was only four.

So why did you marry him? she thought to herself.

And the answer came out the same as it always did: Respectability, Dr. Freud . . . I was craving respectability once again.

But it was a futile hope. Like virginity, once lost, it couldn't be recaptured.

Ah, the world before Robert. Those were marvelous times. The late sixties, the early seventies. "Armies of the night," Norman Mailer had called them. We acted. We seized control. We shaped our country's path. The people ruled. Justice was on our side. After so many years, the embers from that conflagration still glowed deep inside of Ann. They were remnants from the greatest time of all for her.

God, she was happy.

Free! Free at last!

Suddenly, she was startled by a sound from downstairs. It was a short, muffled cough, coming from someone in the living room. She bolted upright in the tub and climbed out. Grabbing her white terrycloth robe, she instinctively drew the belt tight around her waist. For an instant she thought of calling the police, but decided they would never arrive in time to help her. She looked around the bedroom for a weapon.

Nothing!

But in the closet of Matt's old bedroom there was a baseball bat he had used in Little League and refused to toss out.

Taking care not to make a sound, she retrieved the bat. Gripping it tightly in her right hand, she quietly descended the carpeted staircase. Halfway down, she stopped and peeked over the banister. The living room was empty, but a man had been there. The scent of a man's cheap cologne drifted up to her nose.

There was noise coming from the den, adjacent to the living room. The television was playing softly. Why on earth would a burglar be watching TV? She remained frozen to the spot and listened. He was inserting videotapes into the VCR, playing a little of each tape, then tossing it on the floor.

Continuing down the stairs, she trod softly, her damp, bare feet silent on the thick blue carpet. Then she raced across the living room and stopped behind the louvered door that connected the two rooms. A tape of a football game was playing. The man's back was facing her as he looked at the television screen. He was short and muscular—built like a tank, dressed in a gray sports jacket. His skin was dark and swarthy. A Spaniard or an Arab, she guessed. There was a bulge at his waist that might be a gun in a hip holster. She was about to sneak up on him when she realized that he would see her reflection in the television screen. So she waited. Finally, he ejected the football tape and squatted down, looking through their collection of a few dozen tapes in the cabinet below the television. That was when she made her move, stalking across the Oriental carpet, raising the baseball bat high.

She swung the bat forward with all the strength she could muster, aiming for his head to knock him out. At the last second he heard her and stood up. The bat struck him square in the rib cage. She heard his bones crack.

He screamed in pain and then fell to the ground, landing on his front with his face on the parquet floor beyond the edge of the Oriental. She let go of the baseball bat and jumped on his back. Ferociously, she grabbed his hair in both her hands and pulled his head back.

"What are you looking for? Who sent you?" she shouted at him. "You invaded my house. Who sent you?"

He didn't answer.

She smashed his head forward, driving his face against the hard wooden floor. His nose broke. Blood poured from his face, down through his thick, dark beard. She pulled his head back again.

"Who sent you?"

Suddenly, she felt a tremor under her. He had been holding his body still, summoning his reserves of energy. Now he pushed up off the floor with martial-arts force. He flipped her off his back, and she flew halfway across the room. In an instant, he was on his feet, dashing toward the living room and the front door. She gathered herself and grabbed the baseball bat. By the time she ran out of the house, though, he was driving away in a maroon Toyota Camry.

She spent several minutes cleaning the blood from the floor, the living room carpet, and the front of the house. All the while she thought about why he had come. He had been looking for a videotape. Finally she realized it must be the one that the Chinese ambassador had given to Robert. But who had sent this man? The ambassador? Or someone else? It didn't matter for now. The critical fact was that he had left empty-handed. That meant he would be back.

Trembling from what had just happened, she sat in the living room, trying to decide what to do. After she calmed down, she picked up the phone and called the White House. Being the widow of the President's best friend had some advantages. She got through to President Brewster in record time. "Sorry to bother you, Philip, but you asked me to call if I needed anything."

"And I meant it. What can I do for you?"

"I may be imagining it, but I think some people are wandering around outside. Nothing to worry about. Just tourists, acting as if this house were the newest monument in town."

"People can be so cruel."

"Unfortunately, you're right. I was wondering if you could station a couple of Secret Service people here for about a week or so."

"Absolutely. I should have thought of it myself. They'll be there within thirty minutes. Also, the plane's waiting for you at Andrews. Whenever you're ready, let me know and I'll send a car and driver."

"I really appreciate it."

"Call me if you need anything else."

Ann's second call was to Jennifer. "I need a favor, Jenny. A big one. I hate to ask you, but—"

"I'd do anything for you. You know that."

"The funeral's in New York tomorrow morning. Matt and Gerry are already there. I needed time to pull myself together. Besides, they're in their own worlds, as you might expect, and of little help to me. Any chance you can go up with me this afternoon and stay over?"

Jennifer's mind was racing, thinking about the law firm work she had planned to do at home today. She could take it with her to New York. "All right. How soon do you want me to pick you up?"

"How about in an hour?"

"I'll be there."

"I'm warning you. It's going to be a mess for me with his mother, Harmonia, and the rest of his family."

"That bad?"

"Unfortunately, yes. Whoever said WASPs don't show emotion? Harmonia always hated my guts. She viewed my mother's being Jewish as a personal slap in the face. Now she's not above using Robert's death to get one up with me, but guess what? I don't give a shit. I withdrew from the competition. She can do whatever she wants for her son's funeral."

"I'll do what I can to help."

"Oh, and there's one other thing," Ann hesitated. "Once you told me that you had a gun."

Jennifer was alarmed. "I still do. I have a permit. No single woman should live alone without one, but why do you ask?"

"Would you mind bringing it along?"

Jennifer's voice became spiked with anxiety. "Is something wrong?"

"I'm just edgy after what happened to Robert yesterday."

"I'll never be able to get it on the plane."

Ann laughed. "Oh, don't worry about that. The President has Air Force One waiting for me at Andrews. They wouldn't dare put me and my friend through a metal detector. Let's meet there in two hours."

Chapter 6

Ben stood behind the battered wooden table in interrogation room number two and waited for Clyde
Gillis. The clock hanging on the dirty beige wall
showed it was already five minutes after nine on Sunday night. Ben was enjoying the respite of solitude,
having spent most of the last hour battling with Fulton, who wanted to participate in questioning Gillis.
It had taken a bitter argument, but Ben finally had
persuaded Fulton that he should do the questioning
alone, with Fulton and Traynor observing behind the
one-way glass wall. When Gillis was ready to confess,
Ben would buzz for Traynor, who would then be a
witness.

Fulton had yielded to this approach only after Ben
had cried, "Look, you asshole, you want a confession.
One-on-one I'll probably be able to get it. We load
up on him, and he'll clam up. You can make book
on that."

Traynor had agreed with Ben, arguing to Fulton
that, based upon his own experience, Ben was right.
In the end Fulton backed off.

Two guards led Gillis into the room, dressed in
prison blues and handcuffed.

"Take off the cuffs," Ben ordered the guards.

"We'll wait in the corner," one of the guards said
as he unlocked the cuffs.

"Nope. You're out of here."

Puzzled, they looked at each other. "Don't worry,"

Ben said. "I know where the buttons are in this room to call for help, but I won't need them."

Ben turned to Gillis, who was rubbing his sore wrists. "You want some coffee?"

"Yes, please."

Ben filled two Styrofoam cups from a thermos. Then he sat down across the table from Gillis and handed one to him. "My name's Ben Hartwell."

Ben looked up at the clock again and noted the time on the yellow legal pad resting on the table. Nine-fifteen. One hour was all it should take, he decided. In an hour he would have his confession, and he could get back to Senator Young.

Gillis was watching Ben carefully, waiting for him to begin.

"You don't have to talk to me," Ben said.

"I want to talk," Gillis said, though he looked scared to death.

"I mean, legally you have a right to a lawyer and to have your lawyer here when I question you."

"I didn't do anything wrong."

He sounded beaten down, not defiant. Ben gave him a long, measuring look. There was neither the awkward shifting and looking down at the floor, nor the blatant hostility that Ben usually saw in those who committed a serious crime and found themselves snared in the net of the criminal justice system. "It's still good to have a lawyer. I wouldn't talk to the police or a prosecutor without having a lawyer present if I were charged with a crime."

"I didn't do anything wrong," Gillis maintained.

"That's not the point. Our system's not so great. You need to be protected."

Gillis put his hands on the table and squeezed them together. The man displayed a quiet, resolute dignity, Ben thought. His black hands were callused from hard work, but he sat up straight and stared back at Ben, his eyes showing his determination.

"I can't afford a lawyer."

"The court will appoint one."

Gillis stared at Ben for several seconds and then down at his hands again, thinking. Finally he said, "I've got nothing to hide. I want to talk to you because I think I can trust you. Maybe you'll help me get out of here."

"That's not likely."

Ben said it calmly, and Gillis's eyes showed a spark of hope. "I'll take my chances."

"You'll have to sign a statement saying that I offered you a lawyer and you refused."

"I'll sign it."

Ben produced a waiver form from his briefcase, which Gillis read carefully while Ben sat watching him, trying to form an opinion from the man's face. Ben couldn't help but think that he looked honest and sincere. Finally, Gillis signed it.

For several minutes Ben sat across the small wooden table staring at Gillis, without saying a single word. He imagined that Ed Fulton, on the other side of the one-way glass, was ready to explode. But this was part of Ben's standard technique in questioning a suspect—letting him wait and letting the pressure build. That made it easier to obtain a confession, which was precisely what Ben was looking for tonight—an early confession, followed by prompt sentencing.

Ben pointed at the tape recorder resting on the table. "I'm going to record our discussion," he said. Gillis nodded.

Ben had him state his name, and address, and the fact he worked as a gardener for the Winthrops.

"What time did you arrive there yesterday?"

"Eleven o'clock in the morning. Like always."

Ben kept the questions coming, to get Gillis talking. "What did you do when you arrived?"

"Went to work raking leaves."

"When did you stop raking?"

"About four o'clock. Then I went home."

"What about lunch?"

"I had a sandwich in my truck. Ate it about noon."

"During that entire time period from eleven to four, did you talk to anyone?"

"Sometime around noon Mrs. Winthrop came outside. She asked me about my boy, Clyde, Jr."

Gillis was speaking softly, and Ben said, "You'll have to speak up. What about your child?"

"He's sick with a kidney disease. He needs dialysis."

"Who pays for that?"

"Insurance pays for some. I have to pay for the rest."

"And it's expensive?"

Gillis nodded. "Yes, sir. I have bills at home."

Ben knew all of this. Now it was time to dig a little deeper. "How much do the Winthrops pay you?"

"Five hundred dollars a week year-round. I come twice a week. Wednesday and Saturday. I take care of everything in the yard."

"Do they pay you with a check or cash?"

"By check."

"Always?"

"Yes, always."

"They have never paid you in cash?"

He thought about it for a moment. "No, never."

Ben rapidly changed subjects, to get Gillis off balance. "Did you see anyone enter the house?"

"About two o'clock a man came. I saw him talking to the guards in front."

"What did this man look like?"

Gillis shrugged. "I was busy with my work. I never got a good enough look to describe him. About all I remember is a brown coat."

"Did you see him leave?"

"No, sir. I didn't."

"While you were working in the yard on Saturday, did you happen to look through a window and see anything unusual in the house?"

Gillis shook his head.

"Please give me a verbal answer."

"I'm sorry. The answer is no."

"Did you see anyone else in the house besides Mr. and Mrs. Winthrop?"

Gillis paused. "At around two o'clock, I saw a light go on in the downstairs room in the back."

"What else did you see?"

"That's all. The curtains were drawn. I saw the light appear through a crack in the curtains."

"So, about four o'clock you stopped raking?"

Gillis nodded. "Yes," he added.

"And?"

"I went inside to get my check from Mr. Winthrop."

"What happened then?"

Gillis hesitated. "I went downstairs looking for Mr. Winthrop."

Ben wanted to put him on the defensive, to see how he'd respond. "Isn't that unusual to have a gardener roaming though the house?"

"Mrs. Winthrop told me it was all right, and I always come in on Saturdays, even when she's not home."

"And then?"

"I found Mr. Winthrop's body." Gillis closed his eyes, recalling the horrible sight.

"And you saw some hundred-dollar bills on the stairs. Right?"

Gillis nodded. "Yes."

"What did you do then?"

"I touched Mr. Winthrop's chest and felt his pulse to see if he was still alive, but he wasn't."

"And then?"

He looked down at his hands. "I left the house without telling anyone. I know now that was the wrong thing to do."

"So why'd you do it?"

"I was afraid that somebody might think . . ." He stopped midsentence.

"That you killed him?" Ben asked.

Gillis nodded again.

"Did you kill Mr. Winthrop?"

"No, I did not."

"Who killed him?"

"I have no idea."

"Did you take any of the money that was on the stairs?"

"I didn't take anything."

Ben rose to his feet. The nice-guy routine was over. "You already lied to the FBI once," he said, shifting to a sharp, confrontational tone. "Why should I believe you now?"

Gillis's jaw became stubborn. "I didn't kill Mr. Winthrop."

"Yesterday, you said that you were never in the house. Didn't you?"

Gillis nodded, then said, "Yes."

"And you were lying."

"I was scared."

"When they found your fingerprints and footprints in the house, you changed your story. Right?"

Gillis nodded his head miserably. "I told the truth. I didn't kill Mr. Winthrop."

"You're lying again," Ben fired at him. "Now we've got some new evidence. It's time for you to change your story again. Isn't it? To tell me another lie?"

"What new evidence?" he asked nervously.

"Do you know what we found in your truck, hidden under the seat?"

Gillis shook his head.

"Really?" Ben said. "It's the stuff you put there."

"What stuff?"

Ben was watching him carefully to see how he would take the news he would receive next. "About five thousand dollars in hundred-dollar bills, and the gun that was used to kill Mr. Winthrop. The results of the ballistics test are clear."

Gillis looked like he'd been punched hard in the gut. "That can't be," he said weakly.

Ben paced for a few seconds, letting the news sink in. Then he pressed the off button on the tape recorder. He didn't want a defense lawyer claiming that what came next amounted to a coerced confession. "Let me tell you where we are now," Ben said calmly. "I've got the evidence to get a first-degree murder conviction. You were in the house before Saturday. You knew Mr. Winthrop kept lots of cash in the house. So on Saturday you planned to rob Mr. Winthrop. You brought a gun with you. You went into the house to get the cash. Mr. Winthrop surprised you, and you shot him. That's how it happened."

Wide-eyed, Gillis stared at Ben in disbelief.

"You know what?" Ben added. "When I get my first-degree murder conviction, you're going to the electric chair, because you killed the wrong man. And I'm not kidding about the electric chair. When Congress passed the Crime Bill in 1994, they specifically made it a capital crime to kill a cabinet member. So I'm not conning you."

"I didn't kill him," Gillis mumbled softly.

"Yeah, sure. In this town you can kill just about anybody any day of the week, and you get a couple of years in jail. Five if your lawyer screws up. But when you kill the secretary of state, who happens to be a close buddy of the President, we have to make an example of you. That's the way the system works."

Ben saw beads of perspiration breaking out on Gillis's forehead. His blue prison shirt was wet under the arms. Ben was getting to him now. He always liked to lay out his best evidence and the worst penalty. That technique usually worked to obtain a confession. When people asked how he could do this for a living, he responded, "Because more than ninety-nine percent of the people who get to this point in our system are guilty, and I'm doing a public service by getting them off the streets." Now he would move in for the kill.

"You've got a choice," he said softly. "It doesn't have to be the electric chair."

Gillis looked up.

"If you play ball with me and you confess, I won't go for the max. I'll go for a lesser charge. No trial.

No electric chair. It's as simple as that. I'll be on your side. I'll sell it to the judge. Five years in jail. Max. With good behavior, you'll be out in two. What do you say?"

"I didn't kill him," Gillis said stubbornly.

"Right. And a little birdie flew into your truck and put the money and gun under the seat."

Gillis looked bewildered. "I don't know how they got there."

"A judge and jury will know." Ben went for the jugular. "You're dead meat. You don't have a prayer. That electric chair's bolted down to the floor, and they tie you in real tight. 'Cause otherwise, you'd fly up to the ceiling when they turn on the juice. Your flesh will fry. Your eyes will pop out of your head. You know what that feels like?"

Gillis was terrified. "I didn't kill anybody."

"And I play quarterback for the Washington Redskins."

Feeling helpless, frightened to death, Gillis leaned over and put his head into his hands. Ben paced back and forth across the room. "It's entirely your choice," he said, sounding indifferent. "The easy way or the hard. For me, it's just another case. For you, it's your life on the line. You want to be around to watch your kids grow up, or have them toss flowers on your grave?"

Suddenly, it all became too much for Gillis. With his head still in his hands, he began to cry—first muffled sobs and then racking cries of anguish. The sounds pierced the stillness of the room and made Ben shudder. He waited for Gillis to finish.

When Gillis finally looked up at him through tear-stained, bloodshot eyes, Ben said calmly, "I want to be your friend. I can help you. All you've got to do is confess."

"But I didn't kill Mr. Winthrop," Gillis said weakly.

"Sorry, bud," Ben said in contempt. "You've lied to me once too often. You just lost my friendship. You're on your own now."

Ben looked at the second hand on the clock. He let

the room remain in total silence for a full sixty
seconds.

"Last chance," he said grimly.

"I didn't do it."

Ben hit the buzzer on the wall. The interview was
over.

"You fucked up," Fulton said to Ben. "You quit
too soon. You had him on the ropes. You could have
put him away and gotten a confession."

Along with Traynor, they were back in Ben's office.

Traynor was ready to jump to Ben's defense, but
Ben cut him off. "How many suspects have you ever
interrogated, hotshot?"

Fulton's face showed righteous indignation. "That's
not the point."

"It is the point. I've seen your résumé. The answer
is not a single fucking one."

"I'm a good judge of people."

Ben moved in close, madder than hell. "You're a
kid who's wet behind the ears. Go back to the White
House, for chrissake. Let Bill and me do our jobs."

Fulton extended his first two fingers and jabbed
them against Ben's chest. "You're wrong."

Ben savagely pushed Fulton back by the shoulders,
knocking him against the wall. "Don't you ever touch
me again."

Traynor moved in quickly and put himself between
the two. "Hey, c'mon, we're all on the same side."

"I want an apology from him, or I'm out of here,"
Ben said.

Turning to Fulton, Traynor said patiently, "He's interrogated hundreds of witnesses. We have to rely on
his instincts. Slater asked for him specifically on the
case, because of his record. We've got to work with
him."

Invoking Slater's name had the desired effect. The
rigidness went out of him. His face changed from
bright red to a mottled pink. "Okay, I'm sorry, Ben,"

Fulton said reluctantly. "Maybe I got a little carried away. I thought you were so close. I wanted a confession."

Ben wasn't listening. Instead he was thinking about Gillis crying with his head in his hands. "You guys are going to hate this," he said, "but there's another possibility. That Gillis didn't kill Winthrop."

"Are you out of your fucking mind?" Fulton said. "Did you forget what we found in the truck?"

That was powerful evidence, Ben thought, which couldn't be dismissed. "They could have been planted," he said, speaking softly because he knew he was on shaky ground.

"Oh, yeah? Who planted them?"

Ben was trying to put it all together in his mind. "I don't have any idea."

"I don't fucking believe I'm hearing this."

"Then go get your ears checked," Ben snapped. "Regardless of what I think about Gillis's guilt, I'm not ready to file charges against him. With what we have now, if a decent defense counsel puts Gillis on the stand, he'll come off credible to a jury in this town and walk. They'll use the absence of Nesbitt to find reasonable doubt."

Getting red in the face again, Fulton could barely contain himself. "Well, I'm sure as hell not going to let you release Gillis," he cried. "I'll go to Mr. Slater, and he'll—"

"Save your big guns, hotshot. I don't want to release Gillis right now, anyhow, because of what we found in his truck."

"Then what the hell do you want to do?"

Ignoring him, Ben checked to see if he had any coffee left in his cup. There were only the dregs. Finally he said, "We'll hold Gillis in jail as long as we can without filing charges. That'll sweat him. Meantime, we try to find George Nesbitt. We need him to explain what happened at his meeting with Winthrop. We need him to convince us that Winthrop was alive and well when he left the house." Ben turned to Traynor. "Get the Bureau to pull out all the stops on finding George Nesbitt. Here and in California."

Traynor nodded, glad to get to a practical course of action. "What else do you want me to do, Ben?"

"Have a couple of your best people canvass Gillis's neighborhood. See if one of the neighbors saw anyone approach Gillis's truck Saturday night or Sunday morning, before you found the money and the gun. It's possible somebody planted that stuff in his truck."

"Will do."

Fulton was shaking his head in disbelief. "And what happens if we don't find Nesbitt? What then?"

This guy would step on his grandmother's face to get ahead, Ben thought. "We'll cross that bridge when we get to it."

Chapter 7

Jennifer was alone in the suite Ann had reserved for her at the Mayfair Regent, overlooking Madison Avenue. Her head ached as she glanced at the desk cluttered with papers. It was a helluva way to spend a Sunday evening in New York, trying to complete a brief on behalf of KRC Industries, a large conglomerate charged with a criminal violation of the Clean Air Act for improperly emitting chemicals into the air at a plant it owned in West Virginia. State officials had informally authorized continued operations to keep employees working while complex pollution-control issues were being resolved. Unfortunately, the U.S. EPA didn't like the deal and took the case to a grand jury, which approved the filing of criminal charges. Jennifer was staring at a trial date the first week in January. After rubbing her head for several moments, she walked over to her suitcase in search of a bottle of Advil. Suddenly, the phone rang.

"Did I wake you?" Ann asked.

"I wish."

"We have to talk."

Ann sounded distraught, and Jennifer quickly replied, "I'll be right there."

"No, meet me downstairs at the bar."

"Are you up to that?"

"At this hour it's sure to be deserted."

* * *

They sat at a small round table in a corner of the nearly empty room. A sad-looking, gray-haired black pianist was finishing up his final set of the evening. "Those were the days, my friend, we thought they'd never end. . . ."

The waiter deposited two glasses of Grand Marnier and quickly departed.

"I just heard the news on television," Ann blurted out. "They arrested Clyde Gillis, my gardener, for killing Robert."

"This fast? That's pretty good police work."

Ann shook her head, looking somber and intense. "But he didn't do it."

"How do you know that?"

She stiffened in her seat, outraged. "I've known Clyde Gillis for years. He's honest. He's devout. He would never do something like that."

"You can't always tell what another person will do. Even if you think you know him."

"Don't you understand?" Ann insisted. "They want a scapegoat to reassure people. To show that the administration's on top of things. Clyde Gillis happened to be there."

"You don't know what evidence they have," Jennifer said carefully.

"I know he didn't do it." Her eyes were sparkling with certainty.

"You want to tell me how you know that?"

Ann ignored the question. "I want you to represent Clyde Gillis," she announced.

Jennifer was startled. That was about the last thing she had expected to hear. "You can't be serious."

"Why not?"

"The man's charged with killing your husband."

Ann snorted. "Clyde Gillis is a decent human being. Robert was an SOB."

Jennifer couldn't figure out where Ann was coming from. She had a crazed look in her eyes. Was she losing it? "I can't do it, Ann."

Ann leaned forward, touching Jennifer's wrist. "I'll

pay whatever fee you want. About an hour ago the estate lawyer who handled Robert's business affairs stopped by. He told me that I'm going to inherit a couple of houses and about sixty-two million after taxes."

"C'mon, you know money's not the issue. You paid my way through law school, for God's sake. When I offered to pay you back, you refused to take it, telling me that you might need a good lawyer one day. Even without all of that, I'd do anything for you."

"Then why won't you take the case?"

"I'd love to," she said, knowing full well how liberal Ann was. "I went to law school to help people and to cure injustice. I'm not exactly getting job satisfaction from representing corporate polluters, but . . ." She hesitated.

"But what?"

"I participated in a number of murder cases when I was at Justice. But I was never lead counsel." She could see Ann was unmoved. "I'll get one of my partners to do it. Jimmy Elkins does stuff like this every day of the week. And he's a good lawyer."

"I don't know Jimmy Elkins, but I know you. You're a terrific lawyer. You've always been a star in court—when you were at the Justice Department and in private law practice." Ann paused to sip her drink. "Sorry, Jenny, it has to be you. I'm asking you to do it as a favor. Because we're friends. I need you."

"But why? I don't understand."

Ann took a deep breath. "I've got to tell you something, and when you hear it, you will change your mind."

She took another sip before beginning, putting Jennifer on the edge of her chair. What mystery was she about to learn?

"For about the last three years," Ann began slowly in a hushed, conspiratorial tone, "I suspected that Robert was frequently sleeping with other women, but I couldn't prove it. So I didn't confront him. We had no real marriage. Oh, we had sex, sometimes frequently, but I didn't enjoy it. I didn't care. I was seriously thinking of divorce. Then about two weeks ago—it was November the first, I remember the date—we were having dinner at home one evening, and he got an emergency call from Liu, the Chinese ambassador."

"How'd you know it was the Chinese ambassador?"

"Maria answered the phone, came into the dining room, and announced Robert had a call. At first he didn't take it. He told her to take a message and to say he would call back."

"Then what happened?"

"She returned a few minutes later and said that it was the Chinese ambassador calling on an urgent personal matter."

"This time he took the call?"

"Right. He was talking in the other room. I couldn't hear anything he was saying. When he returned to the dining room, he was shaken. Really shaken."

"That doesn't sound like Robert."

"Exactly. That's why I was stunned to see him. I don't think he's ever been so upset. I mean, his face was as white as chalk. Well, anyhow, he said that Ambassador Liu would be coming to the house in about two hours. He would be meeting with Liu in his study downstairs, and under no circumstances was he to be disturbed. I knew that Robert had been locked in a bitter battle with the Chinese government for several months because he wanted the President to authorize a huge arms sale to Taiwan. Beijing was adamantly opposed to the sale. So my guess from the way he seemed, all agitated, was that the Chinese government had something to use against him and get their way on the sale. I wanted to know what it was myself because I figured it might help me to get a divorce."

"So what'd you do?"

"When Robert went up to dress, I went downstairs to his study. I planted a small, unobtrusive recorder that looks like a paperweight on one of the bookcases. I use it sometimes during a rehearsal when I'm directing," she explained. "The actors have no idea that they're being recorded, so they're not inhibited. Later, I can listen to the recording and pick up things I may have missed."

Ann paused to finish her drink. She signaled to the waiter for another and didn't continue until he had replaced her drink and departed.

"Anyhow," she continued, "Ambassador Liu came and stayed about an hour. Robert made sure that Maria and I were upstairs. I peeked out from the top of the stairs and saw the ambassador when he arrived, but he couldn't see me. Then I waited until Robert left for the office the next day to play the tape."

"What'd Liu say?"

"When Robert had been in London two weeks earlier, for a meeting with the Chinese foreign minister, he used a woman in London named Peg Barton to arrange an evening for him with two prostitutes, together in bed at the same time. The Chinese knew about this. They had the whole thing on video. Liu gave Robert a copy of the video, and told him that they had another copy. He also told Robert that they knew he hired prostitutes in many other places as well. Then very smoothly Liu turned to the decision on arms for Taiwan. He gave Robert a choice. Robert had thirty days to change his position on the arms sale or resign as secretary of state. Either way, the video would be forgotten. But if he didn't do either by December the first, then Beijing would act in a manner that 'would embarrass' Robert personally. Those were the ambassador's words. To me, it meant they would go public with the video."

Jennifer let out a low involuntary whistle.

"Yeah, that is a mouthful. Isn't it?"

"So what'd you do?"

"Well, the next day I found the video in one of Robert's desk drawers. I played it, which made me slightly ill. I mean, I'm not exactly a prude when it comes to sex, but Jesus, the three of them were doing about everything you could imagine. Well, anyhow, I

made copies of both the video and the audiotape,
opened a new safe-deposit box at Bank of America
across from the treasury, and locked them inside. I
returned the video to Robert's desk, and that night I
confronted him."

"How'd he respond?"

"As you might imagine, he was plenty pissed that
I'd recorded his conversation with Liu. I told him that
I wanted a divorce without a penny of his money. If
I didn't get it, I would leak the story of his London
fun and games to the press."

"Good move."

"I thought so, too. He agreed to the divorce, if I
never mentioned the video to anyone and waited a
year until after Brewster's reelection. His proposal was
that we continue to live together in the house, keeping
up appearances. He wouldn't make any demands on
me, sexual or otherwise. That was good enough for
me." She paused. "Then someone killed him. So here
I am," she added in a caustic tone, "the happy and
wealthy widow."

"But what does this have to do with his death?"
Jennifer asked.

Ann swallowed hard and said, "I think the Chinese
government arranged for Robert's death to change the
administration's decision on the Taiwan arms deal
when he wouldn't do what they wanted. That's why I
know Clyde Gillis didn't do it."

Jennifer's eyes opened wide. "That's a mighty big
jump from what you've told me so far."

"Then add this. Yesterday, Ambassador Liu sent
somebody to break into my house and steal back the
video he left with Robert."

Jennifer was shocked. "How do you know Liu was
responsible for that?"

"C'mon, Jennifer. The intruder was trying out tapes
in the television when I confronted him. Who else
could it have been?"

"What happened?"

Ann tapped her fist on the table and smiled. "I hit

him with an old baseball bat of Matt's, but my swing didn't do the job. He got away from me. I chased him out of the house, but I was too slow. He drove away in a maroon Toyota Camry. I couldn't get a license plate number."

Jennifer couldn't believe Ann sounded so cavalier about what had happened. First her husband had been murdered in the house, then the intruder. It all sounded incredibly frightening. "Did he get the video?"

"No. After Robert was killed, I put the original the ambassador gave Robert in the safe upstairs in the bedroom where I keep my jewelry. And as I told you, I have a copy of the video in a bank downtown."

"What about the police? Did you call them, or the FBI?"

"I thought about it, but rejected it. At the time, I didn't think the attempt to steal the video was connected to Robert's death, and I didn't want my personal life dragged into it."

"And now?"

"I can't tell them because I'm convinced the Chinese government was responsible for Robert's death. Clyde's arrest tells me that somebody in the administration knows that and wants to cover it up. Besides, you saw Ed Fulton. That guy's something else."

"Regardless of whom that character in the maroon Toyota is working for, you know he'll be back to get that video."

Ann nodded. "The President has guards watching my house. That's why I asked you to bring your gun to New York."

Jennifer tightly clutched her purse holding the loaded .22 and looked around nervously.

"So what should I do about the video?" Ann asked.

Jennifer smoothed down her hair, pondering the question. The pianist was loading his music into a leather folder. Jennifer had an idea. "Let me talk to a PI here. Mark Bonner's a former New York City cop. He'll know what we should do."

"This is all so personally sensitive to me," Ann said.

"That's why it's important to have you represent Clyde and not anyone else. Even one of your partners. You're my friend. You'll minimize any embarrassment to me."

"I understand that, but I'm not persuaded from what you've told me that the Chinese government arranged for Robert's death. Maybe they did, and maybe they didn't. Clyde Gillis could have killed him too. That's another possibility."

"Does that mean you won't represent Clyde?"

"I'm still afraid that Clyde Gillis won't get the best possible defense if I'm doing it."

Ann took a deep breath. "Then let me give you one more reason."

Jennifer looked at Ann expectantly.

"On the television news, they said that Ben Hartwell's the prosecutor on the case. Wouldn't you like a chance to beat him?"

Jennifer blinked in shock, then nodded. It was logical they'd bring him in.

Ann was right, of course. She'd do anything to get even with that cheating bastard.

"Okay, you've hooked your fish," Jennifer said. "But don't get your hopes up about the chances of getting Clyde Gillis off. Your Chinese ambassador story doesn't give me much to go on."

As soon as she left Ann in the elevator and returned to her own suite in the hotel, Jennifer picked up the phone. She stared at it for a few moments, wondering why she was making this call in the middle of the night. Why was she so anxious to talk to Ben? Was it just because of Clyde Gillis, or were some bitter embers from their relationship still glowing?

Hoping that the telephone number was the same as the one he had had five years ago, her own home phone number for the ten months she had lived with him, she punched out the buttons rapidly. If the number wasn't still the same, she'd be in trouble. Ben always had an unlisted number to minimize the number of threatening calls that went with his job.

"Ben Hartwell here," a sleepy voice said.

"It's a voice from your past."

She heard him shuffling as he sat up in bed and turned on a light. She wondered if it was the same Tiffany lamp that he had bought on one of their weekend trips to the Eastern Shore. "Jenny, how good to hear from you," he said sourly.

Listening to him, she'd have thought that she was the one who had run off to California for a lover, rather than the other way around. "Right out of a bad nightmare, huh?"

"You had no right to just pack up and go, leaving me that stupid note."

She smiled, thinking about the stinging missive she had left under the box containing the engagement ring: *I always knew you were a workaholic. That was strike one. And you had no soul. Strike two. Now I know you cheat on me. You've struck out.*

Ben was fully awake. "That note was total bullshit. I worked hard. I wasn't a workaholic. I don't know what the hell you meant by no soul, but it pissed me off."

"I meant that you didn't care about the guilt or innocence of any defendant. Each conviction was just another notch in your belt. Actually, I thought the note was very accurate."

"And I never cheated on you," he protested. "I could have explained everything about Los Angeles. You never gave me a chance."

Oh, please, what did he take her for? "I didn't want to listen to more lies."

"I heard you had a great marriage to a *Washington Post* reporter. Short and not so sweet."

"That was nasty."

"Unlike me, I heard that he really was cheating on you. So maybe you didn't do yourself a favor by walking out on me, Jenny."

"I'm glad to hear you're as arrogant and conceited as ever. And don't call me Jenny. My name's Jennifer." Except for Ben, when they were dating, Ann was the only one whom she permitted to call her Jenny.

Ben let out a long sigh. "Is this a bad dream, or are we really having this conversation? I never wanted it to end, you know that."

She softened for a moment. "Okay, I don't want to rehash our past either. I'm actually calling about a professional matter."

He was happy to hear that she sounded like the old Jenny. God, he hoped that she hadn't been brought in as part of Senator Young's legal defense team. "Which case?"

"I'm representing Clyde Gillis."

Ben sounded flabbergasted. "You've got to be kidding. How could you defend Gillis? You're a close friend of Winthrop's wife."

"Yeah, I know it's odd. But Ann is positive that Clyde Gillis didn't kill her husband." She imagined his forehead wrinkling, as it did when Ben, who liked to be in control, had to deal with something that flew in from left field.

The prosecutor's voice took over. "You want to tell me how you know that? Maybe I'll turn him loose."

She laughed. "Good try, but I think I'll wait for trial to present my case."

Ben rubbed his eyes, trying to make sense out of what he was hearing. "You can't be his lawyer. You brought her home. You could be a witness."

She wondered what was running through his mind. Was he sorry that she was representing Gillis, rather than a pubic defender, because his case would be more difficult? Or was he hoping that by calling in the middle of the night she was opening the door for him to revive their relationship?

"I don't think so," Jennifer said. "What would I testify to?"

She waited for him to respond. When he remained silent, she couldn't help picturing him in that bed.

They had always slept naked together. She quickly shook that thought out of her mind.

He yawned. "Listen, Jenny, I love being able to talk to you after five years, but couldn't we have done this in the morning?"

He was right. She could have waited, but she didn't want to admit that. "Actually, I called tonight for a reason."

"What's that?"

"I don't want you interviewing my client without my being present."

"Sorry, you're too late. I already talked to him. I'll be happy to give you a tape of the interview," he offered.

"You recorded the whole thing?"

He chuckled. "Funny thing happened. The machine stopped recording in the middle."

All of her old anger flared up inside her. "You bastard. You haven't changed at all."

"You don't sound much different either. Where are you now? At home?"

"I'm in New York."

"For the funeral of the man your client murdered. How touching."

Jennifer didn't respond, but she was fuming.

"When you get back to town, call me," Ben said acidly. "I think we should talk. I know that you'd like to whip my ass in court, but don't let that conflict with what's in your client's best interest. When I tell you about the evidence, I think you'll want to plead this one."

"I doubt that."

"I'm going for the death penalty."

"Yeah? Well, you'll have to get a conviction first."

Chapter 8

"I was expecting you to call again," Ben said as he woke out of a sound sleep. The red digital alarm next to his bed read 6:02. He wasn't surprised that it was so early. Jenny was a morning person. It was one of the ways in which their lifestyles hadn't meshed.

"You're becoming psychic," Al Hennessey said. "I'm impressed."

"Oh, it's you."

"Thanks a lot. I expected some gratitude. I'm calling with the opportunity of a lifetime."

"C'mon, it's too early for this horseshit."

"You and I have been invited to watch the sunrise through the windows of the White House."

"You're kidding."

"I wish I were. Slater wants us in his office at seven for a briefing about the Winthrop case. Sarah Van Buren from Justice will be there."

"Seven? Did I hear you right?"

"Slater wants to do it before he leaves for New York and Winthrop's funeral."

Ben threw his legs over the side of the bed and sat up. "You want to tell me what prompted this meeting?"

"I think you should tell me," Hennessey said in a tone now rough and angry, devoid of any jocularity. "Start by telling me what you did to Ed Fulton."

Ben had known this was coming. "You mean he went crying to the teacher?"

"Something like that."

"I've been trying to get him to make noises like a lawyer."

"Well, he told Slater you're incompetent, and I should take you off the Winthrop case."

Furious, Ben jumped out of bed with the phone in his hand. "That bastard."

"Was that your game plan?" Hennessey asked sharply. "To fuck Fulton over so badly that I'd have to yank you, and you'd be able to go back to the Young case full-time? Because if it was, I'm going to ream your ass. It makes me look like a fool. I don't like anybody questioning the competence of one of my people, or how I run this office."

Ben was surprised that Hennessey was coming on so strong. Slater must have turned up the heat on him full blast. "That wasn't my plan, I swear it. Fulton doesn't like me because he's a control freak, and I won't let him run things. Besides, he wants to file charges quickly so he can show his boss how great he is. He doesn't know what type of evidence you need to file a case like this."

"Be ready at six-thirty. I'll swing by and pick you up."

"Why don't we meet there? I don't jump through hoops without a cup of coffee."

"I'll have it for you in the car. Hot and strong. What you really need is a little rehearsal with me so you don't get us both fired."

As Ben put the phone down, he wasn't surprised that they'd been summoned. In America's great legal system, the White House was supposed to keep out of criminal prosecution in individual cases, but every time he'd been involved in a case with highly charged political fallout, sooner or later he ended up at 1600 Pennsylvania Avenue for what was typically billed as an informational briefing.

Ben scribbled a note for Elana, telling her that he wouldn't be able to have breakfast with Amy, which he rarely missed. Before leaving, he looked into

Amy's room. She was sleeping peacefully in her little bed with her right thumb in her mouth—a habit she had once abandoned but resumed after Nan's death, along with occasional bed-wetting. Ben wanted to walk over to kiss her, and remove that thumb, but he was afraid of waking her. Lately, she'd had trouble sleeping and woke up with nightmares. So he settled for watching her. She was so cute with her curly brown hair falling over her face.

It was a strange sensation for Ben—the love he felt for Amy. Before Nan died, he hated to admit, he had felt little, if any, emotional attachment to Amy. Since then he was finding that he loved her in a way that he hadn't thought he was capable of. Maybe he could have had that type of relationship with his own father, if only . . .

He heard a horn honking on the street. That must be Hennessey. He headed quickly downstairs and out the front door.

"Do me a personal favor," Hennessey said to Ben as they walked from the car to the White House. "Even if you think Fulton's an idiot, try to keep your views to yourself. Slater's high on that kid."

"C'mon, Al. You know Fulton's a total ass."

Hennessey sighed with resignation. Ben's independent streak drove him crazy from time to time. Living with it was the price he had to pay for Ben's terrific ability as a trial lawyer. Yet there were times that he wasn't certain he wanted to pay it any longer. "Please, just treat him with some respect."

"That genius will get the respect he deserves."

"Great," he said wearily. "At least I keep my résumé current for days like this."

When they arrived at Slater's office, Fulton and Sarah Van Buren were seated at a conference table that occupied one corner of the spacious room. Slater was on his phone, pacing while he talked, barking orders to White House staff members about the President's schedule for the day and where he should be at every minute during the morning trip to New York. "Make sure Air Force One is ready for a nine A.M. takeoff. I'll have the President and Mrs. Brewster there. Marshall Cunningham and his wife will be the two other passengers." Ben nodded curtly to Fulton, whose smug expression warned him it was going to be a rough ride this morning.

The minute Slater hung up the phone, Hennessey introduced Ben to the White House chief of staff, who looked dapper in a blue-and-white-striped shirt and navy suspenders. His suit was double-breasted dark blue, Ben could tell from the jacket hanging behind the door. Ben wasn't an expert on men's clothes, but it looked expensive to him, the sort of thing Slater might have worn as a partner in a big New York investment-banking house. It made Ben feel self-conscious about his own crumpled charcoal-gray suit. He should get it cleaned and pressed on the weekend, he told himself, especially if he was going to be seeing Jennifer.

Still pacing around the office while the others sat at the table, Slater said to Ben, "I hear you're the best man in the U.S. Attorney's office in Washington." His tone was smooth. "I'm looking forward to seeing your package of evidence against Senator Young to-morrow."

Ben was immediately on guard. When people in Slater's position gave out compliments, they wanted something in return. "Yeah, well," Ben said, "I've won a few cases over the years."

"No need for false modesty. I know all about your record. That's why I wanted you on the Winthrop case. President Brewster cares a lot about this one. As you may know, the secretary of state was his close friend. And you know what else?"

"No, what?"

"We need a quick conviction of Winthrop's killer to show the country that we can control crime. It's a question of public confidence. We don't want people thinking they're not safe in their own homes."

"All of that's fine with me," Ben replied calmly, "but we also have to be sure we have a case that we can win before a jury."

Slater nodded his head. "Amen. I couldn't agree more. But, with the evidence against that gardener, you don't have a question, do you?"

"Actually, I've got a big question."

Slater looked mystified, as if Ben had said pigs could fly. "Well, that's real funny, because when I heard from Ed about the evidence you've got in this case, I thought it's a slam dunk. You should file charges today for murder one against that gardener—" He looked at Fulton. "What's his name?"

"Clyde Gillis," Fulton responded meekly, keeping a low profile in the presence of his boss.

"Yeah, Clyde Gillis."

Hennessey glowered at Ben, who was avoiding eye contact.

Ben said, "My gut tells me that if we did that with what we have now, we'd run a serious risk of losing before a D.C. jury."

Slater moved up close to Ben and said in total disbelief, "You're telling me that the gardener didn't do it?"

Is he serious, or is this an act? Ben wondered. Standing his ground, Ben didn't care. "As a matter of fact, I think he probably did do it, but that's not the point. I'm not interested in determining guilt or innocence. That's up to a jury and God. My job's to build a case. If I can't march George Nesbitt into that courtroom and put him on the stand to testify credibly that when he left, Winthrop was alive and well, then I've got a huge hole in my case that any good counsel will drive a truck through to establish reasonable doubt."

Slater scoffed. "What are the chances of the gardener hiring a good lawyer? Won't he get one of those public-defender kids right out of law school? You ought to be able to handle him easily."

"Unfortunately for us, Gillis already has a damn

good lawyer." He glanced over at Van Buren. "She used to work at the criminal division of DOJ."

Van Buren looked up. "Who?"

"Jennifer Moore."

Sarah knew all about Ben and Jennifer, but she didn't say a word. Nor did her face betray any emotion.

"Who's paying for this *good* lawyer?" Slater asked.

"Jennifer's a friend of Ann Winthrop. My guess is that Ann thinks Gillis is innocent, and she's bankrolling his defense."

Taken by surprise, Slater looked at Van Buren. "Is that ethical?"

"I'm afraid so."

Slater paused to regroup mentally. This wasn't how he had expected this to play out. "Let's assume this Jennifer Moore's the world's greatest lawyer. How's she going to explain the evidence? The money and gun in the gardener's trunk?"

"She'll say that somebody planted them."

"Will she have any basis for that conclusion?"

Ben shrugged his shoulders. "Beats the shit out of me at this point. But I sure hope to know the answer to that question before I go to trial."

Slater sneered. "So is it fair to say that we're talking about a defense lawyer blowing smoke against the city's best prosecutor and some pretty strong evidence?"

"You could put it that way," Ben said guardedly.

"Well, I'm not a lawyer. Thank God for that. But when I was an investment banker in New York, I employed lots of lawyers. Some pretty good ones. Some not so good. The good ones always relied on facts, lots of facts, to justify their conclusions, and that's how we acted."

It must have been a real treat being his lawyer, Ben thought. Even at a thousand dollars an hour or whatever those guys got, definitely hard work. "Sometimes you don't have facts. You've got to rely on what

your instinct tells you, aided by experience. That's
where I am right now. My gut tells me that we'd better
find George Nesbitt before we file charges against
Gillis."

"Then we've got a problem, Ben," Slater said, dripping condescension. "You and I have a problem because your gut conclusion won't be good enough for
Philip Brewster, and he happens to be the President
of the United States. Brewster needs a conviction right
now. He wants to move ahead with this case against
that gardener ASAP. He's the man we all work for.
So that pretty well settles it."

It took all of Ben's self-control to avoid laughing
out loud. He'd learned long ago how staff people in-
voked their great leader's name when the great leader
might not even be aware of the issue being discussed.
It was a wonderful Washington ploy. But Ben was
prepared to play the game on terms like these. Slow
and easy, he cautioned himself before he began talking. Don't explode. He wants you to do that. Do it
the way he does, no emotion, calm and reasonable.

"Now, I've been around Washington a long time,"
Ben said. "I can see that for political reasons you guys
up here want to get a quick arrest and conviction and
show that you're tough on crime. On the other hand,
the President won't be happy if we charge the black
gardener, Clyde Gillis, and then later on we find this
white guy, George Nesbitt, and it turns out Nesbitt
really killed him. That won't play well in the inner
cities next November. I'd hate to see the man whom
we all work for"—he caught Slater's eye—"get hurt
by that."

His words made an impression on Slater. As always,
potential adverse political consequences commanded
attention at 1600 Pennsylvania Avenue.

"How's the search coming for Nesbitt?" Slater
asked Fulton, who sprang to his feet.

"One of the two guards who saw Nesbitt—Jeb
Hines—is in California now. They started with fifty-
eight possibles with that name. Using age and photo

IDs on driver's licenses, they narrowed the universe to twenty-six possibles. Now they're using phone calls and personal visits to contact the twenty-six. It's slow going. As of an hour ago, four have been eliminated. That means there are still twenty-two possibles."

Slater stood next to the window and looked out at the White House lawn below for several moments, evaluating the alternatives. Finally he turned around. "Ed, you tell Murtaugh that I want every conceivable resource used in the search for Nesbitt, and I want it completed by four o'clock P.M. Wednesday, Washington time." He glanced over at Van Buren. "I assume we can say that Ches is on board with this approach?"

"Absolutely. I talked to him before coming over here. He agrees that priority number one is finding George Nesbitt. 'No stone unturned' were the words the AG used."

"What happens Wednesday at four o'clock?" Ben asked.

"That's when you file charges against the gardener for murder one and the death penalty."

"That may not be enough time," Ben protested. "Suppose they haven't found Nesbitt by then?"

Slater's face screwed up in anger. He didn't like being challenged by underlings. He was willing to listen to reason, but once he made a decision, the discussion was over. "Well, it's all the time you've got, pal." Reasonableness was gone. Iron was in. "Four o'clock Wednesday. You got that?"

"Just in time to make the evening news," Ben said.

"Oh, really," Slater said sarcastically. "Gee, I hadn't thought about that. You're obviously as smart as your résumé indicates."

"I want two more days," Ben replied stubbornly, keeping himself under control. "Till the end of the week."

"Well, you can't have them. This isn't an ordinary case. Robert's death coming now is, to say the least, awkward for the President. It's less than a year until the voters decide on his reelection. Crime's a major issue with the people. Maybe the most important one of all. The political fallout from this crime could be devastating unless we can show that there's prompt and severe punishment."

"But—" Ben continued.

Slater cut him off. "Let me be real clear about where I'm coming from, pal. Yeah, in general I'd like to be certain we charge the right man with Winthrop's murder, but in the confines of this room, I'll be blunt about it. That's not my primary concern. I've got to help the President run this country. That means making people feel safe in their own homes. And I've got to ensure the President's reelection, which will be a tough battle next year. Now, I hate to put it this way, but those two objectives are more important to me than the life of one gardener. Am I getting through to you?"

"Loud and clear," Ben replied.

Then the chief of staff turned to Hennessey. "You tell your boy here that it's four o'clock Wednesday afternoon, or he's off the case. Start looking for somebody else who won't give us this shit."

Looking squarely at Ben, Hennessey said, "It will be filed by four on Wednesday. If Ben won't do it, someone else in the office will."

Ben glared at Hennessey. The goddamn gutless swine, Ben thought. He won't even say a word to help me out. He's letting me swing in the breeze. And Van Buren's no better. She knows damn well I'm right.

Ben reviewed his options. It was a tough call. On a personal level, he wanted to tell Slater to piss up a rope, but then they'd find someone else, someone not as good, to do their bidding. This case was high-profile. It was the kind of case prosecutors would give anything to have, with daily press and television coverage. He wasn't letting go of it. Besides, if Clyde Gillis was innocent and they were trying to railroad him, Ben might be in a position to stop them as long as it was his case. Jennifer was wrong in that note she had sent him. He did have a soul. Every conviction wasn't just a notch in his belt. "Four o'clock Wednesday," Ben said reluctantly.

I'm signing my own death warrant, Chen thought as he sat in the garden of his large villa in Taipei and looked at the stars in the dark sky, as if they could soothe his anxieties.

"Where are you?" his wife Mary Ann called in English, with a British accent, from inside the house.

"Out here."

"What's wrong?"

"Nothing."

"It's the middle of the night. You climb out of bed to sit outside, and you tell me nothing's wrong."

"I didn't want to disturb you."

Wearing a thin powder blue cotton robe, she came out carrying two snifters of cognac and handed him one. "I figured this should help."

"It won't hurt."

"You're worried about your trip tomorrow and the next month in Shanghai?"

"I'm not sure why I offered to go. It's ridiculous that I can't even fly there. That I have to go through Hong Kong. He was stupid to put a plant there."

"You were trying to be the good son. The plant's in trouble."

"That's an understatement. The notebook computer line has been down for weeks. He should never have put a plant on the mainland."

She shook her head at him. "You've been like this for days. First I thought you were worried they might arrest you for your protest activities in the United States at the time of Tiananmen, but I decided that's too long ago. Besides, they want the Shanghai branch of Diamond Computer Company too much to hassle you over that. Then I started thinking." She paused to sip some cognac.

The shrewd look in her eye put him on the edge of his chair.

"The gray-haired man who came to see you a couple of months ago. The one you introduced as a professor from MIT. He wasn't that, was he?"

Chen wasn't surprised that she had figured it out. The first time he had met Mary Ann at a lecture at Harvard, when he had been a student at MIT, he had been struck by her intelligence. She was a junior at the time. Born in Hong Kong, she had lived there with her parents, both British, who knew that once the Chinese took over the island, their golden life as expats in paradise was over. He met her a year after Tiananmen when they killed Mai, the woman he had been in love with, who had gone home to Beijing for the protests.

"What does he have you doing over there?"

"Who?"

"The gray-haired man."

He met her gaze head-on. "I won't lie to you. But I can't talk about it."

She reached over and put her hand on his. "I won't tell you what to do. You've got your own devils driving you. What happened to Mai is part of it. I know that. But think about us. Think about our life. Our children. Trying to get even with them isn't worth it."

He sighed. "It's not just getting even. We live in a world where money rules. People, like my father, who gave up everything and fled here with Chiang Kaishek are now ready to surrender their freedom for cheap labor and greater profits for the computer company."

"Aren't you being unfair?"

"I don't think so. If they get the confederation with the mainland they want, our freedom will be gone in a few short years."

"So we'll go back to England or the United States."

"The trouble is, I like our life here."

She shook her head and finished her drink. There was no point arguing. She wouldn't be able to change his mind. From the time she had met him, she knew there was a part of him she would never be able to reach.

She finished the cognac, which suddenly tasted bitter. "Let's go back to bed," she said.

They made love. Afterward, she began sobbing. "Be careful. Whatever you do. Please. I want you to return."

Her words shook him. Was he being a fool? Six months after Tiananmen, Donovan, the gray-haired man, had arranged a meeting with Chen at a Boston bar. His proposal had been simple—If you want to strike a blow against Beijing, tell people back home you're spending the summer at a U.S. high-tech firm and let the Company, as he euphemistically referred to the CIA, give you some training. "A sort of summer camp in the mountains. We'll pay you what you'd make at a high-tech firm. Then at some time in the future, we may call on you and ask you to do something for Taiwan, to strike a blow against Beijing. Of course, you'll be able to refuse. It'll be your choice."

In fairness to Donovan, it had been his choice to participate in Operation Matchstick. Donovan never pressed him. Donovan laid out the diagram for the operation, and said, "It's up to you, Chen. Are you in or out?"

Donovan was clever, Chen had to admit. Even in his choice of a name for the operation. If you thought about those missiles across the strait aimed at the heart of Taiwan, aimed at his house, they were like matchsticks. Deadly matchsticks poised to snuff out their lives.

Chen didn't view himself as a hero. He was an ordinary man, who had been drawn by stages into something larger than his own life.

Would he affect the course of his people's future by slowing down the rush to embrace Beijing for economic reasons?

Would he be remembered as a hero? Or as a fool and a stooge for the American devil?

Chapter 9

Ann asked Jennifer if she would walk with her from the hotel to Adams Chapel on Madison. Irreverent as always, Ann whispered to Jennifer that she was wearing a thick black veil because she didn't want anyone to notice if she broke out in a smile. Gerry, with her husband, walked on the other side of her mother, and Matt, accompanied by his wife, was two steps behind, deep in thought, undoubtedly of unfinished business with his father. Neither of the couples had children because they were concentrating on their careers—a fact that displeased Ann, who wanted grandchildren.

As she walked, Jennifer's thoughts turned toward her brother, Gabe, as they always did when she attended a funeral.

They had been children of privilege, born to a surgeon and his beautiful wife, Valerie, in tony Winnetka in the gold coast suburbs of Chicago. It was a world that might have satisfied most of its residents, but not the restless Val, who took off one day without any warning, leaving behind a four-year-old daughter and two-year-old son, on a quest for the mystic life in Nepal, from where she never returned. From then on, it was just Jenny and Gabe against the rest of the world. They were doing reasonably well, she thought, until their father moved his new wife into the house with her own three children. That was October of Gabe's freshman year in high school. Two months later, her brother died from an overdose of drugs he had purchased on the school grounds.

A part of Jennifer died that day as well. What was left she threw into the theater and acting as a way of escaping from reality. With the aid of Miss Cohen, a marvelous drama teacher, who not only coached her at school but got her a summer apprenticeship at the Goodman Theatre and later a scholarship to Carnegie Mellon, Jennifer's escape from reality became a reason for living.

Blaming her father for what had happened to Gabe, she hadn't spoken to him since she left for college. After many years of bitterness, it was Ben who had helped her come to grips with what happened. He had persuaded her that it was time to bury the past in a distant place in her mind and to move on. Only at funerals did those memories come flowing back and rip her apart. There she was at the cemetery outside of Winnetka screaming, "No, no, no!" and holding on to Gabe's coffin so tightly that her father had to pull her away in order for it to be lowered into the ground.

As soon as they entered the Adams Chapel, the Secret Service was in evidence along each wall, anticipating the arrival of President Brewster. Outside, reporters were milling around like sharks waiting for someone to toss a blood-soaked body from a boat.

Three minutes before eleven, the precise time on the day's schedule Slater had set for the President, a sleek, bulletproof black Cadillac limousine pulled up in front of the chapel. Out stepped the President, accompanied by his wife, Beverly, and Jim Slater. A second car traveling behind carried the Cunninghams.

Philip Brewster might not be the best president this country ever had, but he was a gracious, decent man, Jennifer thought. Robert Winthrop had been his close friend since school days and his political adviser for almost two decades. When he stopped and told Ann

in a halting voice that choked back tears how sorry
he was, there was no doubt that he meant it. "We'll
find out who did this," he vowed.

As soon as the President sat down, the organ began
playing. Ann gripped Jennifer's arm hard, digging her
nails into her skin. The sudden intensity of Ann's emotion startled her.

Twenty minutes later, President Brewster climbed
the steps to the podium to speak. "When I first arrived
at Phillips Exeter Academy forty-one years ago, one
boy stood out among all others in our class. He had
maturity, intelligence, and a zest for life beyond his
age of thirteen years. He . . ."

Jennifer stopped listening. If the President only
knew. Her mind began wandering, thinking about
what Ann had told her last evening. It was Jennifer's
guess that Ambassador Liu hadn't taken his video to
the Oval Office. The President, standing up there in-
toning piously about his friend, didn't realize that he
had been spared a major scandal.

Jennifer wasn't the only one who had tuned out the
President. Jim Slater turned his head ever so slightly,
looking unobtrusively out of the corner of his eye.
Ann Winthrop was sitting on the center aisle. To her
left was Jennifer Moore, whom he had met just before
the ceremony, with Ann providing the introduction.
Jennifer was properly dressed in black. With her legs
crossed, her skirt had ridden up a little. She was showing an awful lot of gorgeous leg.

That wasn't all Slater liked about Jennifer. He had
received an e-mail from Fulton on Air Force One en
route to New York, pulling together her bio at Slater's
request following the morning meeting with Ben.
From it, Slater learned that Jennifer had graduated
from Carnegie Mellon eleven years ago, which made
her about thirty-two now. She had gone off to New
York for a career in the theater. After a year of waiting tables and taking bit parts way off-Broadway on
the second floor of warehouses, she had gotten her

big break. In an article attached to the e-mail, the *New York Times* had covered in detail the story of how Jennifer, as a young understudy in a Broadway revival of *Picnic,* directed by Ann Winthrop, had been propelled into the lead midway through a performance. Trent McCall, while standing and kissing Denise Waller onstage, the star whom he'd been trying unsuccessfully to sleep with ever since rehearsals had begun, grabbed her buttocks and pressed her close to his erection, grinding his body against her. Irate and red-faced, Denise had pulled away and shouted, "You groped me, you asshole!" Then she slapped his face and stormed off the stage.

While the stunned audience murmured in their seats, Ann pleaded with Denise to go back on. "It's him or me," she shouted at Ann. "You can't have both of us." For Ann, that was no choice. Denise's understudy, Jennifer Moore, was ready to go. Ann went to the center of the stage in front of the curtain and announced, "Give us ten minutes and the performance will continue with Jennifer Moore in the role of Madge Owens." Jennifer had received the audience's goodwill, followed by good reviews, and she finished out the run.

Other Broadway parts followed, but they were too few and far between for the actress to live decently, so, armed with introductions from Ann to some key Hollywood players, she set out for Tinsel Town. After a couple of minor roles in feature films, a few television movies-of-the-week, and lots of prime-time guest appearances, something happened that made Jennifer return east to attend Columbia Law School. Fulton hadn't been able to find out what that something was.

Following graduation, she came to Washington. In the criminal division of the Justice Department, she was viewed as a rising star, but after three years she gave it up, joining the Washington law firm of Blank & Foster. Last year she had become a partner, specializing in litigation. She was a member of the board of the Dolly Madison Theatre, the Washington Opera,

and the Women's Legal Defense Fund. So why the
hell is she defending Clyde Gillis, the gardener?
Slater wondered.

The longer he looked at her, the more he started
thinking about her in ways that had nothing to do
with Clyde Gillis or the case. There was something
enticing and sexually provocative about her—even
dressed for a funeral—with her honey blond hair
pulled back tightly.

As the President sat down and the minister moved
back to the lectern, Slater sneaked a look at his watch.
God, how much longer is this crap going to continue?
I've got so much to do back in Washington.

Mercifully, the service ended fifteen minutes later.
With the crowd milling around and gradually drifting
out, Slater approached Ann. "If you're going back to
Washington, you're welcome to join us on Air Force
One. Marshall and Betty Sue are staying in New York.
So we've got room for you and your kids or anyone
else you want." He was hoping that she'd bring
Jennifer.

"My children are heading back to San Francisco and
Philadelphia," she said in a tone of resignation, sorry
that neither one offered to spend time with her. Sad
that they didn't have any semblance of a family. "It's
just me and Jenny."

"I think I can handle that," Slater said, concealing
his delight.

"You have some visitors," was all the guard told
Clyde Gillis.

Uncertain what to expect and beaten down after
Ben's effort at intimidation the night before, Gillis
walked with hesitancy out to the central visiting area
in the jail. It was a single room with twenty wooden
tables and benches scattered around. Half a dozen
armed guards constantly patrolled the perimeter,
watching for any exchanges between the prisoners and
their guests—each of whom had passed through
metal detectors.

When he walked through the doorway of the room, he saw them seated on one bench. His wife, Lucinda, in the center, Naomi and Ruth, ages twelve and seven, on one side of her, and Rachel and Clyde Junior, ages eight and seven, on the other. Gillis threw his shoulders back and raised his head. He forced a smile onto his face.

Once they saw him approaching, the two older girls waved. Little Rachel, the smallest and shiest, clutched her mother's hand tightly and pressed her body close to Lucinda. Clyde Junior slipped off the bench and ran over to take his daddy's hand. When Gillis sat down across from Lucinda, Clyde Junior remained at his side.

"How are you doing?" she asked.

"Okay so far," Gillis said. "I told the prosecutor what happened. I think he believed me that it was all a mistake."

The two girls moved over next to their father. Ruth squeezed his hand.

"It wasn't a mistake at all," Lucinda said. "It's just some more injustice that white folks push on us."

"I know it's not fair, but . . ."

Lucinda had a look of rage in her eyes. "It's more than just unfair. I'm working to get you a lawyer. Not just any lawyer, but a good lawyer. Only they want so much money, and I can barely make his next treatment."

Gillis put his arm around his son. "How's he feeling?"

"I'm okay, Daddy," Clyde Junior blurted out. "Mama says I'm the man of the house now, so I should act like it."

Naomi began to laugh. Lucinda shot her a look. "That's enough."

"God will take care of me," Gillis said with deep conviction. "C'mon, let's all pray."

Lucinda didn't object to praying with her husband, but she still wanted a good lawyer to help do the Lord's work.

As they leaned in toward the center of the table, he began to recite, "The Lord is my rock, and my fortress, and my deliverer. . . ."

On the plane, Ann went to the back with Philip and Beverly Brewster in the presidential compartment. Slater sat down next to Jennifer, who thought he looked debonair dressed in shirtsleeves, blue striped and monogrammed on the pocket, navy blue suspenders, gold cuff links with the presidential seal, and a red silk Hermès tie with gray sheep. She liked how stylish he looked—unlike some men, such as Ben.

As they taxied out toward the runway, a marine officer asked them, "Would you like something to drink?"

"Black coffee for me," Jennifer replied.

"The same," Slater said. Then he turned to Jennifer. "Did you know Robert well?"

"Not really. My friendship has been with Ann. She's a classy lady."

"He and Philip were such close friends. Go figure."

This remark made her pause, but then she said, "I've often wondered about that myself. They seem so different."

Slater shrugged. "Sometimes you develop friendships as children. I guess they stick with you."

She nodded. "That's about as good an explanation as any."

Air Force One roared down the runway. When they leveled off, the marine served the two cups of coffee.

"It's been a long time since I've been with a famous actress," Slater said.

She smoothed down the side of her hair. "What do you mean?"

"I saw you in *Picnic* on Broadway. You played Madge, right?"

She was pleased. "I got lucky landing that part."

"That was a helluva story. I remember reading it in the *Times*. With Trent McCall groping that actress. What was her name?"

"Denise Waller."

"Yeah. See? You made me forget her. And as for your being lucky landing the part, life's full of chance events. It's always that way. So why'd you give up the acting biz and go to law school?"

She paused to sip some coffee. "You really want to know? I had a lock on a starring role in a good feature film. My agent sent me out to the director's house in Malibu one Sunday for lunch, to get acquainted. Just the two of us."

"So what happened?"

She looked irate. Just thinking about it rankled her. "The old Hollywood casting couch. We finished lunch. We were sunning on the deck, and he dropped his pants. Real subtle."

He shook his head and snarled, matching her anger. "That's disgusting. So what'd you do?"

"I told him to stuff it into a piece of liver."

He burst out laughing. *Portnoy's Complaint.*"

"Yeah. Well, anyhow, the next day, my agent called to say I blew it. I'd lost the part. He was plenty pissed at me. He was even more pissed when I told him what happened. 'Why didn't you just fuck the guy?' my agent said. 'What's the big deal? You're no virgin, for chrissake.' "

"So you went to see a lawyer," Slater said.

She was surprised. The guy was smart, thinking on his feet. "How'd you guess?"

"I feel as if I know you. I can understand how your mind works."

She smiled, liking him more and more. "So you tell me what happened."

He finished his coffee, touched her arm ever so gently with his left hand—which didn't have a wedding band, she noticed—and then removed it. "The lawyer told you that you'd never get any legal relief because of the director's power."

"Precisely."

"So you decided to go to law school and then to the Justice Department to do something for other women caught in this situation. Cases involving battered women were one of your specialties."

She was stunned that he had guessed so much about her. "So what about you, Jim? Let me take a stab in the dark like you did. Poor kid from the wrong side of the tracks someplace like Pittsburgh. Scholarship to Yale, MBA at Wharton, and with your drive you blow them away on Wall Street."

He laughed easily. "Close, but no cigar. I'm the black sheep in an old ranching family from California, near Santa Barbara. My dad was ready to disinherit me when I refused to go home after Stanford and join him in the family business. I got a Rhodes, Harvard MBA, then Wall Street. He learned to love me again when he needed financing about ten years ago."

"So why'd you cash in your chips on the Street and come down to D.C.?"

He laughed. "You must be a good trial lawyer. You know how to bore into the key question quickly."

She smiled at the compliment.

"I wanted to serve my country," he said, echoing the standard line heard from high-level appointees in Washington. "Give back some of what I've gotten."

She laughed. "Are you trying to kid me or yourself?"

He looked hurt. "I was being sincere, and you don't believe me."

"Poor baby." Jennifer poked him playfully. "You came down because you figured that you're smarter and can do things a lot better than the dopes running around our town."

Now it was Slater's turn to be surprised. She was plenty sharp, this Jennifer Moore. "How'd you know that?"

She gave him a devilish smile. "I've been around Washington a while."

Their laughter was drowned out by the whine of landing gear being lowered. Jennifer couldn't believe that they were already descending toward Andrews Air Force Base. Jim Slater must have been good company. It was the quickest New York–to-Washington flight she ever remembered.

"My jaw hurts from saying the appropriate grieving-widow phrases." Ann lifted her chin, turning it to and fro. "As for Philip, he's an ass to be so torn up about Robert's death. He should be damn glad Robert didn't bring the whole administration crashing down on his head."

A light mist was beginning to fall as Jennifer pulled onto the beltway, turned on the radar detector, and gunned the engine. "I doubt if Jim Slater shares the President's grief," she said.

"Well, well." Ann winked at her. "I could see that you made a new friend on the plane."

"What do you think of him?"

"I don't know him that well, but he disliked Robert, so he can't be all bad."

The radar detector started to beep, and Jennifer cut her speed to sixty-four. "Is there a Mrs. Slater?"

"Alice, the equestrian queen," Ann said dryly. I've met her a couple of times. Spends her life riding and worrying about her horses. They have a big horse farm in Rancho Santa Fe near La Jolla and a place in Westchester. She refused to move to Washington. As far as I can tell, they've got a marriage in name only. Parallel play. He does what he wants. She does too. Which mostly involves horses."

Jennifer was pleased by what she had just heard. "Any children?"

"My understanding from cocktail-party gossip is that early on in their marriage they couldn't have any. They never tried very hard." ·Ann's expression darkened. "You seem awfully interested."

"Just curious."

Ann gave Jennifer a stern protective look. "Be careful, Jenny."

Jennifer understood exactly what was running through Ann's mind. "Yes, Mom," Jennifer said laughingly. "What am I missing?"

"As long as he's still married, you don't want to be the other woman. It's not a good part to play in Washington. Rarely brings happiness and joy, or even a long run."

Jennifer winced. "Aren't you getting ahead of me here?"

Ann said earnestly, "I know you. I also know that Jim's smart, sophisticated, and suave. Twenty years younger and unmarried, he might be worth a careful look."

"I gather that he and Robert weren't exactly the best of buddies."

"That has to be one of the great understatements of all time. Robert said that Jim was unprincipled. Totally amoral."

Jennifer burst out laughing. "You mean as opposed to Robert?"

Ann laughed too, but said, "Actually, this may sound funny, and believe me, I'm not getting soft on my late husband, but while he was a disgusting human being personally, in matters of state he had some principles. That's what got him into trouble with the Chinese government. He believed we had made commitments to Taiwan, and we had an obligation to honor them. Not to toss them aside for pragmatic Machiavellian reasons. He was convinced that nothing had changed since Tiananmen Square. He detested the ruling regime in Beijing." Ann reflected for a moment. "Of course, there was the personal jealousy factor. Jim resented Robert's close friendship with Philip, and Robert saw Jim as an evil influence corrupting Philip's decency. Call it sibling rivalry. So they battled over every decision."

"Sounds like a great way to run a government."

"Oh, it was. And don't forget Marshall Cunningham. He despised both of them. Thought he was the most astute politically among the three of them. The one who was best able to make judgments on foreign policy issues because of his military-defense-contractor background."

She paused and shook her head. "I used to call them the Venomous Triumvirate. That's probably unfair to Marshall, who's really not so bad." She stopped to think about what she had just said. "No, I take that back. He is just as bad. He's totally results-oriented. When he sets off on a course, he won't quit until he succeeds, regardless of the cost. He loves exercising all the power he has. He uses people to get what he wants. Jim's the same way. You know how I hate crap like that."

"In that way he's like half the people in this town."

"I know, but I don't have to like it."

Jennifer pulled off the beltway. They started driving south on Connecticut Avenue, heading toward Ann's house.

"Did you get a chance to talk to your PI friend, this Mark Bonner?" Ann asked, knowing that the answer would be yes because Jennifer always did what she promised.

Jennifer looked a little sheepish. She should have told Ann first thing this morning, but she decided to leave it alone until after the funeral. Then there was the whole Slater business on the plane. "I called him at home in New York late last night."

"What does he think I should do about the video in my house?"

"Mark's got a great plan."

Ann looked at Jennifer with confidence, knowing that her friend had found a solution to her problem. "You want to let me in on it?"

Jennifer returned Ann's look. "You bet. Mark's theory is that if your intruder friend can't get into your house because of the security people the President sent, he'll go after you personally until he gets what he wants."

"That's a pretty frightening thought. So what should I do?"

Jennifer spoke softly, sounding mysterious. "Make yourself the bait."

* * *

The State Department occupies a sprawling, dull gray, eight-story, nondescript building in a part of Washington known as Foggy Bottom, which acquired its name in the days when Washington was still a small southern town built on a swamp. Fulton and Traynor barged in unannounced to the secretary's suite on the top floor. With Hazel and Doreen, Winthrop's two longtime secretaries, in New York for the funeral, there was no one to provide resistance. Certainly not the temp manning the phones, who moved out of the way as soon as Traynor flashed his FBI badge. The game plan Fulton had developed was simple. They were each carrying empty briefcases. Traynor would look through the file cabinets in the outer office, while Fulton went alone into Winthrop's inner sanctum. What Traynor thought they were searching for was any information that could lead them to George Nesbitt. Fulton, though, had a second objective in mind. As soon as he locked the door to Winthrop's office, Fulton began a careful search through every desk drawer and cabinet for any evidence of Winthrop's extracurricular sexual activities or anything else that could damage the administration.

Fulton found diaries for each of the last three years, since Winthrop came to Washington, with curious evening entries that had to be some code for Winthrop's sexual assignations. He stuffed all of the diaries into his briefcase, along with Winthrop's little black book of telephone numbers and addresses, again written in some type of code, because all the names were men's names. Fulton guessed that Jack must mean Jacqueline; Alex, Alexandra; and so forth.

Once Fulton had sanitized the office, he opened the door and met Traynor back in the outer office. "Any useful info?" Traynor asked.

"Not a thing," Fulton replied, lying without any qualms. He rationalized that what he had taken was irrelevant to the Winthrop murder. During the secretary's life, his whoring around had been one of Washington's best-kept secrets. With his death, it couldn't be permitted to rise up and bite Brewster and the administration on the ass.

Three blocks from Ann's house, she said to Jennifer, "Don't stop and look, but on the right, there's a maroon Camry parked. I'll bet it's my visitor from yesterday."

As they drove by, Jennifer glanced at the man behind the wheel, whose nose was heavily bandaged.

"Did you do that to him?" she asked.

"Damn right. I was furious. If he wasn't so strong, I'd have killed him."

Jennifer let out a long, low whistle. "He's obviously learned how to breathe through his mouth. I'm glad I'm on your side."

Ann looked fierce. "I'm ready for the second act, as you put it a few minutes ago."

"He's not Chinese."

"I didn't say he was. I said the Chinese government sent him."

"You may be right, but we've got to know for sure."

Ann stopped to talk to the two armed agents from the Secret Service in front of her house. Then she and Jennifer went inside. They stayed only five minutes— long enough for Ann to get the videotape from the safe upstairs and for Jennifer to call Mark in his car. "You in place?" she asked.

"A-okay," he answered in a curt military voice.

"The Camry's there too. Three blocks up on Ellicott."

"I know. I've got a bead on him."

"We're leaving in about five minutes."

"Gotcha."

Jennifer hung up the phone. Ann came into the room, nervously clutching the video in her hand. "You sure this is going to work?"

Jennifer looked confident. "Mark's good. He's never let me down yet."

"There's always a first time."

They climbed into Jennifer's car and drove back

up Ellicott toward Connecticut Avenue. Through the rearview mirror, Jennifer watched the Camry turn around quickly and fall in behind them. She couldn't see behind the Camry. She was hoping that Mark's rental car was back there somewhere. Thinking about it, she realized that she shouldn't expect to see him, because he wouldn't want the driver of the Camry to know he was there. At Connecticut Avenue she turned left, and then a few blocks later left again and into the parking lot for a strip mall that included City Video Center, with a sign that said, *Tapes Rented. Tapes Sold. Tapes Duplicated.*

The parking lot was only about a third full. Jennifer parked twenty yards from the entrance to the video store. She took the loaded .22 from her purse and slipped it into the pocket of her gray raincoat. She had last fired the gun at a practice range two months ago. She could use it if she had to. Then she looked at Ann. "Showtime. You ready?"

Ann emerged from the passenger side holding the video in her right hand, where it was visible. Jennifer kept her hands in her coat pockets. Side by side they walked toward the entrance of the video store. A light, cold drizzle was falling. When they were halfway there, Jennifer saw a white-bandaged face approaching to cut them off. Jennifer waited until he was ten feet away to pull out the gun. "What do you want with us?" she demanded.

He sneered. "Don't play games with me. I want the video."

"You can't have it," Ann said. "So fuck off."

He was seriously considering forgetting about his assignment, just for the pleasure of killing this bitch.

"You know I'll get it sooner or later. Once you leave it in the shop, it's as good as mine. The kids who work here won't risk a scratch for your video. If you take it home, I'll make your life miserable until I get it."

Ann was nervous, feeling uneasy about Jennifer's plan. This was taking so long. Each second increased the risk that this goon would blow up and try to get even with her.

Sensing Ann's anxiety, Jennifer glanced over the man's shoulder. Mark's car was in place. By now he had to be snapping away on his Nikon. She'd better move things along before they took an unexpected turn. She nodded to Ann.

"Let's take it back home," Ann said to Jennifer, following the script.

"Ah, screw it," Jennifer said forcefully, not giving away how she felt inside. Her hair was getting wet. A trickle of water was dripping down the side of her face. "It's not worth it. Give him the damn thing. You've got to get on with your life."

Ann hesitated. "Maybe you're right."

He took a step toward them.

"Stop right there," Jennifer barked, drawing and aiming the gun. "Toss it to him," she said to Ann.

Ann lobbed the tape in an underhand throwing motion. The man caught it with both hands.

"You got what you wanted," Jennifer said. "Now get the hell out of here fast, before I take target practice on what's left of your face."

He looked furiously at the two women. When Jennifer tightened her grip hard on the pistol, though, he reconsidered. He turned and ran toward the Camry. In an instant, he was roaring out of the parking lot.

Mark rolled down his window, gave them a quick thumbs-up sign, and drove after the Camry.

Back at Ann's house, they changed into dry clothes and waited by the phone. It was almost two hours before Mark called from the cell phone in his car. Jennifer grabbed it on the first ring.

"Your boyfriend made his delivery."

"Where?" she asked anxiously.

"Slow down. They're too professional to deliver straight there. He walked into Farragut Square with a white plastic bag in his hand. Left it under a park bench and sat there in the rain until the pickup man came."

"What happened then?"

"Patience, Jennifer. Patience," Mark barked, sounding like a drill sergeant. "The pickup man got into a car with diplomatic plates. He drove back to the Chinese embassy up on Connecticut Avenue."

A huge smile lit up her face. "Beautiful. I love you, Mark."

"I aim to please."

"And you got all of this on film?"

"I'm insulted that you asked. That's what you're paying me for."

"What's the number on the plates?"

"It'll be on your e-mail this afternoon along with the photographs, but I already checked. The car's registered to the Chinese embassy."

"Thanks, Mark. Great job."

Jennifer put the phone down. "Mission accomplished," she said to Ann. "You got that creep out of your life, and we know that you were right. He was working for the Chinese government." Her mind shifted gears to the Gillis defense. "Tomorrow, I want you to go down to that bank vault, take out the video, make a copy, which you'll drop off at my office, and return the original to the vault."

Ann's eyes sparkled with satisfaction. "You're going to use the tape in Clyde's defense. You do believe me that the Chinese killed Robert."

"Absolutely. I don't intend to let Clyde Gillis take the fall for it."

"Ann Winthrop asked me to represent you," Jennifer said to Clyde Gillis. They were alone in an interview room at the D.C. jail.

Before she said another word, Gillis blurted out, "I didn't kill Mr. Winthrop. I hope she believes that."

As Jennifer looked into his eyes, she was convinced that he was telling the truth. "Ann knows you didn't do it, and I believe you. We just have to convince some other people."

"You mean like that Ben Hartwell?" Gillis made no effort to conceal his animosity.

Jesus, Ben must have put a full court press on Gillis. She knew how frightening he could be to a defendant. "Convincing a judge and a jury," she said soothingly, "will be much more important." She reached into her briefcase and extracted a yellow legal pad and a pencil. "Okay, start at the beginning," she said. "Everything that happened to you from Saturday morning until this minute."

As he spoke, she took copious notes. His account of Saturday's events confirmed her belief in his innocence. His description of the jail interview with Ben infuriated her. It had been an effort at intimidation, plain and simple.

When Gillis finished his story, she dropped her pen on the table and squeezed her fingers, which were stiff from writing. Gillis sipped a glass of water as she leafed back through her notes, looking for any clarifying questions to ask.

He was feeling less nervous than when she had arrived, because she seemed to know what she was doing. Still, he didn't know what to make of this situation. It was odd that Mrs. Winthrop, whose husband died, had hired a lawyer for him. He felt as if he were a pawn being manipulated by so many forces. Nothing that happened now would surprise him.

"Go back to Saturday," Jennifer said. "Did you see anyone else go into the house?"

"Around two o'clock a funny-looking man in a brown raincoat."

"What do you mean, 'funny-looking'?"

He shrugged. "I don't know. Sort of looked like a woman."

"Tall? Short?"

"Average."

"Did you see him in the house with Winthrop? I mean, through the windows?"

"Not really."

"What's that mean?"

"Through a crack in the curtains in the back room downstairs . . ."

"The room in which he was killed?"

"Yeah. That one. I saw a light go on a little after this man came, but that's all I saw."

As she leafed through her notes, what repeatedly jumped out at her was the money and the gun in Gillis's truck. That was powerful evidence someone had planted. But who? Somebody working for the Chinese government? That certainly seemed like a possibility after everything else that had happened today.

Did they have Ben on their payroll too? She dismissed that idea instantly. There was plenty that she disliked about him, but he'd never do anything like that. On the other hand, if he was being duped by the planted evidence, he'd do everything he could to persuade Gillis to confess.

Now that she had heard about this two-o'clock visitor to Winthrop's house, she was feeling more bullish about her case. Somebody else had been in the house at the time. She'd find out who he was and zero in on him. Of course, she still had the gun and the money from Gillis's truck to deal with, but all she had to do was create enough reasonable doubt for one juror to hold out.

"One other question about this two-o'clock visitor," she said.

Gillis gave her a pained look. "I didn't see him that well."

"White man or black?"

"White," he answered.

Good, she thought. If I zero in on this visitor, a mostly black D.C. jury will get the picture. It's the same old story: A black man's being nailed to cover up for a white crime. You're dead meat, Ben Hartwell.

As she thought about him, she looked up at Gillis again. "If that Ben Hartwell comes back, or one of his people, don't you talk to him."

He gaped. "You mean I don't have to?"

"That's exactly right."

"Good. I won't do it." He hesitated, then asked, "Are you going to get me out of here?"

"I'm sure going to do my best," she said. She stuck out her hand for him to shake. "And I'm feeling a lot better about the case now than when I got here."

Chapter 10

She was asleep in her spacious Westport house when the phone rang in the den. Even though it was two-fifteen in the morning, she heard it immediately. All of those years working in the field had taught her to be a light sleeper. Her life had depended on it. Paul didn't stir as she slid out of bed. In her bare feet she raced lightly across the cold wooden floor. Goose bumps broke out all over her naked body.

She brushed back her long blond hair as she picked up the phone.

"Is this Nancy Burroughs?" the caller asked. The words were chopped and broken. From her training she knew they were using a voice scrambler again. That didn't bother her. People calling her had a right to protect themselves and their identity.

"It's a very proper British name," she responded in the prearranged code.

"We need your help again. Our business isn't finished. Washington has gotten more complicated."

"It always does."

"Reservations have been made for you at the Shoreham Hotel. Check in before nine o'clock this morning. Somebody will contact you. You'll get your instructions then."

"Understood."

The phone suddenly emitted a dial tone.

Gwen stood for a couple of minutes in the den looking at the sliver of moon outside, deciding how to get to Washington. Driving was clearly much better because she could transport her own guns and other equipment, but any car—even a rental car—could be traced. So she decided to fly unarmed. They would provide the equipment she needed. If it wasn't up to her standards, well, she loved shopping in Washington.

She went back to bed, but she couldn't fall asleep. Excitement was surging through her. She was like a warrior thrilled to be going back into battle. The suburban life was just a way to pass time. She lived for days like this.

Thinking about it made her feel randy. She considered waking Paul, but he was sleeping so soundly. Besides, she wasn't sure that he would be up to it without a major effort on her part. That was a price she had decided to pay when she married for financial security. So she reached into the night table on her side and removed the dildo. She inserted it with her left hand and massaged her clitoris with her right. To stifle her cries when she came, she bit her lower lip. Afterward, she lapsed into a deep sleep.

Two hours later, she woke up ahead of the alarm. Before leaving for LaGuardia and the seven o'clock shuttle, she left Paul a note on the kitchen table. "I had to go for a couple of days for business—Love, Gwen."

Paul wouldn't complain. And he wouldn't ask her any questions. That, too, was part of their agreement. He knew that she would be back.

Believing that Cunningham was too soft on the Chinese, Chip Donovan persuaded Margaret Joyner, the director of the CIA, to invite Admiral Hawkins, the chairman of the Joint Chiefs, to the meeting dealing with Chinese troop movements. Donovan also knew that there was no love lost between Hawkins and Secretary of Defense Cunningham. When Cunningham had been passed over for chairman of the Joint Chiefs by Brewster's predecessor in favor of Hawkins, Cunningham had resigned from his position as a general in the army to become CEO of Blue Point Industries. The four of them were gathered around a table in the back of Cunningham's office.

With a silver-tipped pointer in his right hand, Donovan, dressed in his usual black suit and black turtleneck, was pointing at a map of China on the wall and explaining what the agency's spotters, including Sherman, had observed on the ground in China, what Peng had reported, and what satellite pictures showed. "The conclusions from all of these are the same," Donovan said. "This is the largest Chinese military buildup toward Taiwan that we've ever seen."

"And you think that Beijing is getting ready to launch an attack?" Hawkins asked.

"That's the conclusion I would draw. I think—"

Cunningham interrupted Donovan in midsentence and turned to Joyner. "You don't share that view. Do you, Margaret?"

She took off her glasses and tossed them on the table. "I can never predict what they're up to. If it's a bluff, toward what end? Unless . . ." She hesitated, uncertain whether she wanted to complete her thought. In the dispute between Winthrop and Cunningham about the President's decision on the Taiwan arms package, she had supported Winthrop when asked by the President. Now she didn't want to give Cunningham the satisfaction of conceding that the Taiwan arms package might be producing the result he had predicted. A month ago, she had believed that Beijing would move on Taiwan when they were ready to do so, regardless of what Washington did, and at least Taipei should be in a position to defend itself. She was no longer sure.

"Unless what?" Cunningham pressed.

She wiggled out of presenting her thoughts. "Unless Beijing's trying to create a foreign policy diversion to take the focus away from another round of domestic unrest."

"What's Taiwan doing in response?" Cunningham asked.

"Mobilizing their forces. Acting as if there will be war this time."

Cunningham grimaced. He hated to see both sides go down this path. One spark could ignite the whole thing.

"I think we'd better take the issue to the President," Joyner said.

"Not without a detailed recommendation from this group," Cunningham responded, unwilling to take a chance that Brewster, who sometimes shot from the hip, would call Beijing's bluff and start a war in Asia. "He's absorbed by economic matters, putting together the tax-cut package and the upcoming European economic summit. Also, he's only operating at half speed these days. He hasn't recovered fully from Robert's death. You should know that. If we leave him on his own, there's no telling which way he'll jump."

"Fine," Joyner said. "Then my suggestion is that we recommend to the President that he call Ambassador Liu. Tell him what we have seen and demand that Beijing pull back their forces."

Donovan looked at Hawkins, egging him on with his eyes. The admiral took the cue. "At the same time, we should begin moving our own forces in the Pacific toward Taiwan, letting Beijing know that we take our commitments to Taiwan seriously. We have three aircraft carriers in the region. I say we put them on a course for the Strait of Taiwan."

Cunningham raised his eyebrows. "You're ready to go to war for Taiwan?" he asked, sounding incredulous. His intention was to make Hawkins feel like a fool, but it didn't work. The admiral wasn't intimidated.

"I wouldn't put it that way."

"Then how would you put it?"

"I want the Chinese to know that we honor our commitments. With your West Point and military background, you of all people should understand that sometimes we have to resort to force in support of principle."

Cunningham held his ground. "I also understand the horrible toll on those involved. And"—he raised his voice for emphasis—"the limits of American military power in Asia. By making the military moves you suggested, we're playing a dangerous game."

Joyner interjected. "It's a dangerous part of the world. Now, do we have a recommendation to take to the President, based on what Admiral Hawkins and I proposed?"

Cunningham was afraid to disagree. He didn't like the Joyner-Hawkins position, which the President would accept if it came from this group. But he was worried that opening up the issue before Brewster would produce an even more militant decision.

With a sly smile on his face, Donovan watched Cunningham squirm. You can suck up to Liu all you want, he thought. When Beijing sees those aircraft carriers moving toward the Strait of Taiwan, they'll get the picture. And at the same time we'll hit them with Operation Matchstick. Boom. Boom.

Gwen parked the battered dark blue Honda Civic on the street about two blocks from the D.C. jail. Before getting out of the car, she paused to check herself in the rearview mirror. The brown contact lenses masked her blue eyes. The long brown wig, aided by facial makeup, made her a brunette. She had rounded off her face with large tortoiseshell glasses, with plain glass, to complete the bookish, serious look that she wanted.

Her clothes matched that image. Under her old cloth coat she wore a simple gray suit and white blouse. The top two buttons were left undone. A little of her lacy bra showed through, and some cleavage as well. She put on pale lipstick and looked at herself again.

Satisfied with what she saw, she picked up the worn leather briefcase from the car seat, slung it over her shoulder, and headed out of the car. The sky was dark and threatening. Rain was predicted, but that wouldn't come until this afternoon.

A few blocks away she saw the outline of RFK Stadium, its charcoal-colored light towers rising to blend into the dense gray sky. It was cold, and she walked quickly. Approaching a twenty-foot fence, she looked up at the coiled barbed wire on top, running around the perimeter of the old redbrick building. Just above the main gate was a guardhouse, and two men, one gripping a machine gun, watched her carefully.

She stopped at the gate and rang the bell.

"Identify yourself," a man's voice announced through an intercom.

"Estelle Marino, public defender. I'm here to see Clyde Gillis."

There was a long silence while whoever was in the charge studied the list of approved visitors for the day. Gwen maintained a confident look. She had been assured that her name would be on that list.

She could feel a slight moisture under her arms. Jails did that to her. It was the one thing in life she feared. Not just the confinement, but the torture that went with it almost everywhere in the world. And you were helpless, so damned helpless. She had Saddam Hussein to thank for her fear of jails. The bastard. If she had her way, he'd have been rotting in the ground long ago.

A buzzer sounded, and the gate opened by remote control.

"Proceed to the front door of the building, Miss Marino," the voice said.

She walked slowly across the deserted path that led to the front door, knowing that countless eyes were watching her from the barred windows that made up the top three floors of the building. Her walk wasn't provocative or sensual. It was professional, that of a harried, overworked, and underpaid public defender.

Inside the front door, a heavyset white man of about fifty with red hair, cut short, and a grizzled, pock-

marked face sat behind a thick piece of plate glass.
The badge on his khaki prison guard's uniform said
Harvey "Red" Dougherty.

"Your ID," he barked into a microphone. She
passed him the photo ID that showed her as an attorney with the District of Columbia Public Defender's
Office.

He studied it for a moment, then looked at a computer printout resting on the desk in front of him. He
nodded and slid it back to her. "Pass through the
metal detector," he said, pointing.

She met with Clyde Gillis in a small interview room
near cell block four. They made her wait alone for
fifteen minutes before they brought him into the room
in handcuffs. A different guard—not Dougherty—was
with him. Gillis looked weak and tired. His eyes were
bloodshot and unfocused as he sat down across the
table from her. In the center of the table, her briefcase
sat open with the row of six identical-looking pens
arranged on top of a yellow legal pad.

Gwen waited until the guard left the room and
slammed the door.

"I'm with the Public Defender's Office," Gwen said.
"I'm helping your lawyer, Jennifer Moore. Estelle Marino's my name."

"I already told my story to Miss Moore."

"She wanted me to hear it again. To see if there
are any inconsistencies."

Gillis studied Gwen for a moment. It didn't sound
right to him, but he didn't know how lawyers operated. So he summarized his discussion Sunday evening
with Ben. While he talked, she listened intently. There
was no need to take notes. Her mind had been trained
for total recall if she simply listened carefully enough.
She felt no emotion for Clyde's plight. He was a small
fish who happened to be in the wrong place when a
predator had dropped a net. Life was like that. It happened to people like Clyde Gillis all the time. Still,
when he was finished talking, she feigned the sympa-

thy she didn't feel. She glanced down at her hands, pretending to be weighing his words.

Then she looked up abruptly. "You're not going to like what I have to tell you."

He stared at her through those bloodshot eyes.

"Jennifer's right," Gwen said.

"Right about what?"

"Before I came over today, she said that you should do what Ben Hartwell told you to do. Plead guilty." She sounded like a doctor recommending surgery to cure a condition. "With the evidence they have, we'll never be able to beat the death penalty if we go to trial. If you plead, we can get you off with five years max. You'll be out in twelve months with good behavior." She reached into the briefcase and pulled out the yellow pad and one of her pens, making sure she had an unarmed one. Then she handed it to him along with the pad. "I think you should write out a confession, then ask the guards to deliver it to Hartwell. Don't tell him I told you to do it. Pretend that you thought some more about what he said, and that now you agree he's right. Jennifer and I know him. You're lucky you drew Ben Hartwell. Once he has your confession, he'll settle for a light sentence."

He picked up the pen but didn't go any further. "I didn't kill Mr. Winthrop," he said stubbornly.

"You can't beat the system."

He thought about his daddy being beaten nearly to death in that Mississippi prison. Yet with all of that, he'd refused to confess to a crime he hadn't committed. Clyde wouldn't either.

He shook his head.

She studied him carefully and decided that this tactic wouldn't work. She shifted her approach.

"There are powerful people," she said pleasantly, "who would like you to confess. They're prepared to pay you two million dollars if you do that. It'll be deposited in a bank in Switzerland. The interest on the money, ten thousand a month, will be deposited in your bank account here in Washington. With this money, you'll have enough to pay for your little boy's dialysis even if you lose your insurance, which will happen before long."

Clyde pulled back with a start. "Please say that again."

She repeated her words.

When she was finished, he said, "You're not my lawyer. Who are you?"

She wondered why it had taken him so long to catch on. "That's not important. If you don't trust me, I'll be able to give you proof that the first ten thousand dollars has been deposited into your Washington bank before you write out your confession."

He didn't respond, eyeing her distrustfully.

"Two million dollars," she said, "for one year in prison. That works out to more than five thousand dollars a day. Not a bad deal, I'd say, considering that if you don't take it, you're certain to end up in the electric chair."

"But I didn't kill Mr. Winthrop. God knows that. He won't let me be convicted." He nodded.

"Since you believe in God, let me quote you a passage from the Bible: 'And, behold, there came a great wind from across the wilderness, and smote the four corners of the house, and it fell upon the young people and they are dead.' That's from the book of Job, chapter one, verse nineteen. Those were the messenger's words when he told Job that all of his children had been killed.' It's very relevant to you—because if you don't confess and take the two million dollars, I'm going to kill your children one by one."

She reached over to the briefcase and pulled out another ballpoint pen. She pressed down with her thumb and a stiletto blade sprang out through the bottom. Gwen picked up the yellow pad, held the blade against it, and sliced clean through the paper.

Clyde shrank back, trembling with fear.

"I'm going to kill them one by one," she repeated calmly. "And then your wife. And each time a typed note's going to arrive in your prison mail quoting that passage from the book of Job."

Terrified, he sat motionless and watched her.

She stood up, still with the stiletto in her hand, and shrugged her shoulders. "It's all the same to me. You decide."

When he didn't respond, she closed up the stiletto, put the pens and paper in her briefcase, and slammed it shut.

"Think about everything I've said," she told him. "You'll never see me again, but if I hear that you've confessed in the next two days, the money will be deposited in that Swiss bank. If not, I'll have to take the other approach to get what I want. God help you and your family, Clyde Gillis."

Chapter 11

"What do I tell Jim Slater if he asks about the Winthrop investigation?" Al Hennessey asked Ben.

It was five minutes to five. Ben had just handed his summary of the evidence concerning Senator Young to Hennessey, who wanted to deliver it personally to Slater at the White House.

"Tell him that nothing's changed since Monday morning. The FBI's still looking for George Nesbitt."

"Any leads?"

"Fulton and Traynor are coming over in a few minutes to brief me. You want to stick around?"

"Sorry. Roz and I have a black-tie dinner party at David Kelso's house."

"Life's tough among the Georgetown elite," Ben remarked. "You need a strong liver just to survive the nightly onslaught of alcohol."

Hennessey didn't appreciate Ben's constant barbs. "Did I ever tell you that you're not very funny?"

Ben chuckled. "All the time."

When he returned to his office, he found Fulton and Traynor waiting for him, standing amid the piles of paper on his desk, both chairs, and even the sofa.

"You guys can sit down."

"There's no place to sit," Fulton said, looking around in disgust. "This office is a mess."

"Then move the papers onto the floor, hotshot."

He grunted as he moved a gigantic pile. "How can

you get anything done in a pigsty like this?" he muttered.

Ben decided to laugh it off. "I know where everything is. That's the point. I'll bet your office is as clean as a whistle."

"You're damn right," the former marine said.

How did the saying go, about clean desks and empty minds? Ben turned to Traynor. "Where are we?"

"The interviews in Clyde Gillis's neighborhood didn't produce a thing," Bill replied. "Zippo."

Ben was disappointed. In an inner-city area like that, people were out on the street, looking out of windows, at all hours of the day. If the gun and money had been planted, someone should have seen it. He was beginning to doubt his instincts. Perhaps Gillis had killed Winthrop. "You're sure nobody saw or heard anything?"

"One of the neighbors thought she heard some noise around eleven o'clock Saturday evening. She looked out of the window. Couldn't see a thing."

Ben filed that away. "OK, what about the search for George Nesbitt?"

"We're down to six possibles," Traynor said. "But one's a very good lead."

"Tell me about him."

"VP for marketing for a San Jose semiconductor company that did one-point-two billion dollars in sales last year—mostly in the Far East and former Soviet empire."

Ben was buoyed by the news. This might be a lead. "So he'd have a reason to meet with Winthrop."

"Exactly," Traynor said. "And his wife thinks he was in Washington over the weekend."

That struck an odd note. "What do you mean, 'she thinks'?"

"He travels a lot on business. She can't keep track of him. From the driver's license photo ID on file in Sacramento, Hines says he could be the man."

"So where is mystery man now?"

"Nobody seems to know. We're working on it

through his wife and his office. We've got wiretaps on both of his phones."

Ben snapped to attention. "Authorized?"

Traynor shook his head slightly. "You don't want to know. We're willing to lose the conversations. We just want to find him."

Mystified, Ben tried to add up what Traynor had said. "That's weird for a big company VP not to be tied to his phones."

"Unless, of course, he's killed the secretary of state, and he's in hiding." Traynor replied.

Ben didn't want to go down that road. "Remember, in the search for Nesbitt, we're looking for a witness, not a killer. We already have Gillis. We just need to confirm that Nesbitt met with Winthrop Saturday, and that our former secretary of state was alive and well when Nesbitt left." He turned to Fulton. "What do you think, hotshot?"

Fulton was doing a slow burn inside at Ben's reference to him as "hotshot," but he didn't want to give Ben the satisfaction of admitting it. "I think this George Nesbitt had his meeting with Winthrop, left the secretary of state alive and well, as you just put it, and is spending a few days shacked up with his mistress. He's still in Washington."

"Are we checking hotels here?"

"We've done every last one. Not a trace of our Mr. Nesbitt."

Ben looked at Traynor for confirmation, and he nodded. "The mistress could have an apartment."

Fulton jumped in, wanting to be the one reporting the news. "We've gotten a list of his credit cards. In about an hour we'll have all of his charges in the last week. Meantime, Jeb Hines is in California working with the FBI out there, running down the other five possible George Nesbitts."

The telephone rang. At first Ben ignored it, wanting his secretary to answer. Then he remembered she had gone for the day. He picked it up.

"Okay, Ben," Jennifer shouted so loudly that he

pulled the phone away from his ear. "Tell me what you did to him."

"Did to whom?"

"To my client, Clyde Gillis."

From their time together, Ben knew that Jenny had degrees of anger. Right now she was in the "bright red zone." "I didn't do anything. What are you talking about?"

"I went to the jail to talk to him this afternoon."

Ben couldn't resist the temptation to wisecrack, "That's generally a good idea when you're building a case." Yet he felt stupid for making the comment, and he immediately backtracked, trying to sound sympathetic. "So what happened?"

"Monday he was fine, protesting his innocence loud and clear, even after your little effort at intimidation. Today he won't even talk to me. Just sat there for thirty minutes staring down at the table. He's out to Mars. I figure that you or one of your thugs slipped some drugs into his food."

Ben was alarmed. Jenny wouldn't be imagining this. "You can't be serious."

"Oh, c'mon, Ben. The heat's turned up full blast on this case. Clyde Gillis is a scapegoat."

"If you know who the real killers are, let me know. Then I can release your client and go after them."

"Stick around for the trial," she said harshly, "and you'll find out."

"I can't believe that you would make such an outrageous charge against me," he said, being honest. "I play hard to win, but you know damn well that I'd never be a part of anything like that."

There was a long pause. "Yeah, I guess you're right," she said, her voice lower. "But somebody else could have drugged Clyde Gillis. Suppose they're hiding it from you?"

"You know what I think of conspiracy theories like that. This is starting to sound like a discussion you and I had one evening at Obelisk about Martha Mitchell, and whether the Nixon gang did her in."

"Yeah, well, everybody in Washington's not as honorable as you are."

"I guess that's a compliment."

She softened her tone. "Actually, it was meant to be. Uh, look, Ben, I want to see a copy of the FBI report on the Winthrop murder."

Ben had been expecting her to get to this issue. "Sorry, Jenny, I can't give you any gifts. The case is too high-profile. The FBI report hasn't been released to the public. We haven't charged your client yet. You'll get it when either of those happens."

More stiffly she said, "Then at least I want a copy of the tape you made of the interview with Gillis on Sunday."

"Same answer."

"C'mon, Ben. It's my client's statement. Either I get it, or I'll go to a judge in the morning."

Ben hesitated. He wanted to wait until four tomorrow afternoon, Slater's deadline, to delay filing charges in the hopes they could find Nesbitt. He didn't want to risk judicial interference earlier in the day. On the other hand, he'd had the tape transcribed this morning. He'd read the transcription. It didn't give anything away.

"I'll have a copy of the transcript delivered to your office by nine tomorrow morning," he said, being agreeable. "But let me tell you something. We found money, lots of money, in his truck, and the gun that FBI ballistics says killed Winthrop. I'm being real serious when I say that you might want to cut a deal in this case rather than take it to trial."

Her answer was immediate, as he should have known it would be. "No deal. I've got an innocent client."

"All defense counsel tell me that. Then right before trial they want to talk." He wasn't telling her anything she didn't know. "But you've got a special problem here. I'm afraid that once the ball starts rolling, with all the publicity, I may not be able to cut a deal for you. So if you want to avoid murder one and the electric chair, you'd better talk to me early, Jenny.''

She knew that he was leveling with her, and she appreciated it. "Can you tell me when you're going to file charges, or are you taking this to a grand jury?''

The prosecutor's wall went back up. "We haven't decided.''

"I'm not going to let you hold him indefinitely without being charged.''

"I didn't think so.''

"Thanks, Ben.'' Her end clicked off abruptly.

Ben put the phone down and looked at Fulton and Traynor.

"She's not going to make our life any easier.''

What he didn't tell them was that on the phone, he had glibly brushed off Jennifer's charge that somebody had gotten to Clyde Gillis in jail. Deep down, however, he was worried about it. Somebody was playing hardball on this case, using him in the process. He wasn't sure who or why, but he didn't like being manipulated. He intended to find out what was going on.

It was almost eight o'clock when Ben got home. Amy was sitting next to Elana at the kitchen table, sipping hot chocolate.

As soon as she saw him, she ran across the room crying. He picked her up and hugged her.

"What happened?" he asked Elana.

"She's had a bad day. One of the girls at school said some things that upset her. She hasn't been able to sleep. So I got her up. I thought some hot chocolate would be good, and maybe you'd be home soon. I hope you don't mind.''

"No, of course not.''

He carried Amy upstairs and held her in the rocker in her room. Her arms went around his neck, squeezing him as tightly as she could. Rocking gently, he said, "You want to tell me what that mean girl said?''

"It was Didi," she blurted out. "She said Mommy

ran away because I was a bad girl, and then she started singing real loud, 'I have a mommy and you don't. . . . I have a mommy and you don't.' " She burst into tears again, her little body convulsing.

Ben was furious. This was the third time it had happened. Tomorrow morning, after the kids went to school, he'd call that little shit Didi's mother. Hopefully, he could appeal to her as a human being to stop her daughter from doing this.

When Amy had calmed down, he said to her, "You believe me, don't you?"

"Uh-huh."

"And what did I tell you?"

"That Mommy got sick with a very bad disease, and she died."

"That's right. And that was nobody's fault. And Mommy loved you very much because you were always a good girl."

With eyes wide open, Amy looked at him beseechingly. "Where did Mommy go?"

"She passed into another world, honey. Where she's resting peacefully."

"Why didn't she want to be with me?"

He felt a great wave of sadness, and he blinked back tears. "She couldn't help it."

She clutched him tightly. "Daddy, will you die and leave me, too?"

God, this was harder than any judge's interrogation. "No," he said with all the confidence he could muster. "I won't die and leave you."

"Will I die and go into another world like Mommy?"

"Not for a very long time." He pushed forward in the chair and stood up. He carried her over to her bed. "Come on, you've got to get some sleep."

She wasn't willing to let go yet, though. "Will you play something for me, Daddy?"

"Of course, honey." Ben went to the study for his guitar. When he returned, he played an old Spanish love song for Amy—the same one he had played for

Jenny the first night they made love in this same house. Before he was finished, Amy was asleep sucking her thumb.

Exhausted, Ben went back to his own bedroom and tried to sleep. It was hopeless again tonight. He tossed and turned in bed—the bed he had shared with Jenny for almost a year. Thinking about her, remembering her next to him, her smell, her taste. He could see her walking out of the bathroom with droplets of water from the shower glistening on her skin, with only a towel wrapped around her head, turban-style. She would sashay around the bedroom, tantalizing him as he lay in bed trying to read a brief. In a matter of seconds, he would toss the brief on the floor, and she would crawl into bed with him. All those nights came back vividly. Her favorite position was sitting on him, because she said that let him penetrate the deepest. He loved it that way too, loved watching her move up and down on him, her hands behind her on the bed, her breasts bouncing in the air. She would become so aroused sometimes that sweat would pour down the front of her body and onto his chest. And when she finally came, she screamed it out. He usually came right after, and they'd collapse together on the bed, with her head resting on his shoulder, the way she liked to do. God, he hadn't thought about her like this for years. Talking to her again on the Gillis case had unleashed the feelings that had never died.

They had met on one of those stifling hot July days that remind Washingtonians that their city is really a southern town, which could never have developed into a major population center if not for air-conditioning. The city had been in the throes of a record heat wave. Those who could had exited for temporary refuge at one of the beaches in Rehoboth, Ocean City, or Nags Head, or in the mountains. The heat wasn't slowing Ben down, though. He had assembled the evidence on his latest case. He was ready to go to the grand jury with charges that the secretary of the interior, Nick Malvern, had raped one of the administrative assistants in his office and attempted to rape another. The day before, Ben had gotten a call summoning him and Al Hennessey to the office of Sarah Van Buren, the head of the criminal division at DOJ. To Ben there were two possibilities. Either DOJ was going to take over the trial of his case, or he would be directed to drop the charges.

Walking across Pennsylvania Avenue to main Justice, Ben tried to strengthen Al Hennessey's backbone, to resist any involvement by DOJ in the case. This meeting, though, had something totally unexpected in store for Ben. Minutes after he and Al had arrived in the fifth-floor conference room, the team of DOJ lawyers Van Buren had assembled to review the case filed in. Included in that team was a woman so striking that Ben couldn't take his eyes off her. She was tall and lithe, just an inch or two under six feet. She had honey-blond hair tied up in a bun, and her wire-framed glasses didn't conceal the most beautiful face he had ever seen. Her nose and mouth were perfectly proportioned, with full, round lips. Her blue-green eyes sparkled. Her skin was so fresh and clean that it almost glowed. She was small-busted with a narrow waist. Even dressed in a proper lawyer's navy blue suit, she carried herself with grace and elegance. She's a goddess, Ben thought. There was no other way to describe her.

The meeting started promptly, with Hennessey summarizing their case and Ben trying to establish eye contact with her, as she could easily tell, because she appeared to be ignoring him, while giving him an occasional smile. She was smart, too. Ben knew that as soon as she opened her mouth. Where have you been my whole life, Jennifer Moore? he wanted to say.

He was so taken with her that he changed his strategy. As long as he would be lead trial lawyer, which was justified from his experience and the work he had done on the case, he'd take Jennifer on as second chair at trial, and DOJ could have a say in all of the strategy discussions. A startled Al Hennessey couldn't believe that was the deal Ben was cutting.

After the meeting, Ben told Jennifer he'd start briefing her. At lunch at the Old Ebbitt Grill, Ben's initial impression of Jennifer was confirmed. She was everything he could have imagined in a woman. She wasn't even involved with anyone else in a serious relationship. He suggested dinner that evening at Equinox, hoping to snow her with the elegant food.

They had such a great time at dinner that when the waitress asked them about dessert, Ben looked at Jenny hopefully and said, "Thanks, but we have something at my place." As soon as they were inside the door, they started kissing passionately, touching each other all over, ripping off their clothes like a couple of teenagers. When they were naked, Ben picked her up and carried her up the stairs.

In this same bed, they went at each other most of the night. For Ben, it had never been like that before. When the morning sunlight broke through the curtains, Ben was dead tired and very much in love. He slipped out of bed, turned on the coffee downstairs, and returned moments later with his guitar. As she began to stir, he serenaded her with an old Spanish love song that he had learned at Berkeley.

Their cooperation in the Malvern prosecution never amounted to much because the defendant copped a plea to assault and resigned from his cabinet post a week later. A few weeks after that, Jennifer moved into his house. They were the happiest months of his life. Besides the fabulous sex, he loved doing things, going places with her, sampling the myriad ethnic restaurants in Adams-Morgan, watching old foreign films in tiny theaters near Dupont Circle.

On New Year's Eve, he proposed to her, presenting her with a gorgeous diamond solitaire ring from Tiffany's. They set a date for a June wedding because

Jennifer wanted to make sure they really knew each other before making a lifetime commitment. Ben would have gotten married sooner, but she was adamant.

We almost made it to June, he thought, turning over again in bed. God, I don't need her back in my life. Not now. If I had any sense, I'd pack my bags in the morning and head out with Amy to Aspen. They must have snow there already. Beautiful, beautiful Jenny. The goddess of love. The purveyor of misery.

Was I insane? Jennifer thought, accepting Marianne Kelso's last-minute invitation to a black-tie dinner at her house in Georgetown this evening with all the work I have to do on the Gillis defense and the West Virginia pollution case for KRC Industries?

The message had been waiting on Jennifer's voice mail at the office late in the afternoon. "It's Marianne Kelso; I desperately need a favor. I had a last-minute cancellation. I need an extra woman. Please don't let me down. Please. It's black-tie. Cocktails at eight o'clock. Chamber music at nine o'clock. Dinner at ten o'clock."

Marianne was the largest contributor to the Women's Legal Defense Fund, and a member of its board, for which Jennifer served as general counsel. Marianne had been a great source of comfort for Jennifer when Craig had hit the road for Colorado. So Jennifer didn't want to turn down the request. Also, she knew that Marianne liked everything to be perfect for her dinner parties. An imbalance of men and women would make her very unhappy. But Jennifer's motive in accepting wasn't totally selfless. She needed a few hours off from work, and an invitation to one of the Kelsos' dinners was among the most prized in Washington. Besides the people and the food, they had a collection of art including a Renoir, a Monet, and two Chagalls.

Still, by seven o'clock, with tons of legal research

to do for Clyde Gillis's defense, she was sorry she had agreed to go. She finally reached a compromise—she'd skip the cocktails and most of the chamber music. As long as she was in her assigned seat at one of the dinner tables, Marianne would be pleased.

In the closet in her office, Jennifer kept a short black dress with thin straps that would work. At eight-thirty she showered, then changed clothes and jumped into a cab so she wouldn't have to waste time getting her car from the garage.

Her timing was perfect. The string quartet was ready to begin its final piece—a Bach sonata—when she arrived. As she tried to slip unobtrusively into an empty chair in the last row, next to Marianne, many of the forty or so heads turned toward her. "You look great," Marianne whispered. "Thanks for coming."

"Sorry I'm late. The cabdriver was clueless."

Marianne raised an eyebrow. "You haven't missed a thing."

Seated two rows in front of Jennifer was Jim Slater, who didn't bother to turn around when she entered. He heard their words and smiled to himself. She'd see him when he sat next to her at dinner. She'd no doubt guess that he had arranged for her to be here.

Across town at a reception for Jacques Morot, the visiting French foreign minister, at the magnificent residence of the French ambassador, Liu pulled Cunningham aside and took him out onto the spacious flagstone patio that overlooked Rock Creek Park. They each held a glass of 1985 Clos La Roche by Dujac.

Liu looked at Cunningham sternly. "I didn't appreciate the message President Brewster gave me today to deliver to Beijing. I'm even more unhappy about your three aircraft carriers."

Cunningham placed his hand on Liu's arm, signaling the need for restraint. "I did what I could to soften my government's response. Admiral Hawkins and others wanted to take far stronger action. Beijing's troop deployments toward Taiwan have made people here upset."

Liu pulled his arm away from Cunningham. "Then we're even, because the Winthrop arms package for Taiwan has people in my government outraged. With good reason, as I've been telling you for some time."

"I understand that. I'm trying to get it reversed."

"The leadership in Beijing won't wait forever for you to accomplish that. At some point, before long, we'll have to act on our own."

"This issue's too important for riddles. What are you saying?"

Mystified, as always, why subtlety didn't work with Americans, Liu took a sip of the excellent wine, trying to frame his words with care. "Unless you inform me by December first that your President will not submit the Winthrop arms package for Taiwan to Congress, then we intend to take action shortly after that date to unify the island of Taiwan with the People's Republic of China, using all available means."

Liu's words shook Cunningham to the core. "Then your government is intending to go to war?" he asked in disbelief.

Liu had a trace of a sinister smile. "We can't wait indefinitely for unification while you continue to arm Taiwan in a way that will make its liberation increasingly costly."

Cunningham looked out over the park below, watching cars wending their way over its narrow roads, as he thought about what Liu had just said. "I've told you before," Cunningham finally replied. "I'm prepared to support unification and to urge President Brewster to support it by diplomatic means. Not by threats of war."

Liu shrugged. "The decisions are being made in Beijing. They're not mine to revise. We prefer that you view our troop deployments as an incentive rather than a threat to change the Winthrop arms package by December first."

Cunningham studied Liu's face in the patio lights. It told him nothing. "That's not enough time. Winthrop's death is a complication. Tell Beijing to slow down on the troop deployment we're seeing. Tell them that I need until December seventh to achieve the policy reversal you want."

The choice of the date wasn't lost on Liu. He chuckled. "You have a sense of humor."

Cunningham hadn't intended to make a joke. He saw nothing humorous in this situation. "There's still one more important condition to my getting this done."

Liu's back stiffened. He hadn't told Beijing about other conditions. "What do you mean?"

"It assumes that you and your government are not implicated in certain criminal matters in the United States."

"We won't be. You don't have to worry."

"You sound so confident now. It's a big change from Sunday."

Liu lowered his voice to a whisper. "The video has been retrieved. No one will be able to connect us to Winthrop's murder."

When the concert ended, Slater huddled with Senator Burgess from Ohio, chairman of the Senate Judiciary Committee, tipping him off that charges would be filed against Clyde Gillis tomorrow afternoon. Watching through the corner of his eye, Slater waited until she was at the table before walking over.

As he held out her chair, he said, "Well, well, isn't this a pleasant surprise."

She looked at him and shook her head in disbelief. "I should have guessed you were responsible for my being here."

"David's a good friend."

"And like you, he was also a big fund-raiser for President Brewster."

He laughed easily. "Was he really? I hadn't heard that. But more important, you look smashing tonight. Generally, I don't find black to be a flattering color for women. It works for you."

She was pleased by the compliment, showing it with a warm smile. "Well, thank you."

"But I think most colors would work."

As they chatted through the first course, a delicious squash soup, Slater tried different subjects, looking for something they had in common. Before the waiter cleared the bowls, he found it: They were both Anglophiles. Attending Oxford, he had gained an appreciation for England, particularly London.

"During those three years," he said, "I spent every hour I didn't have to study exploring the countryside or running around London."

Her face lit up. "Really? It's my favorite city in the world, with all that theater. Once I finished school, whenever I could scrape together the plane fare, I was off for London. Not just the West End. I particularly loved the fringe shows. You know, above a pub."

He placed a hand on hers for an instant and then removed it. "I hit quite a few of those when I was at Oxford. Mostly, though, I liked the West End and the action there."

She nodded. "In my acting days, I had enough theater contacts to get somebody to comp me a ticket for most shows."

A waiter served rack of veal and ratatouille. "I even lived in London for three years," Slater said, "running our office there during the go-go years of the late nineties."

Slater paused to sip some wine. It was an elegant 1982 Château L'Evangile. "Great wine," he said.

She tried it and agreed. "I'm not such a connoisseur, but I'd like to learn."

"If you ever want a teacher, give me a call."

She gave him a coy look. "You're a collector?"

"I have a modest cellar."

"What, a thousand bottles?"

"Try two."

She laughed softly.

When the waiters were clearing the dishes, David Kelso came over. "She's Marianne's good friend," he said to Slater, tongue in cheek. "You'd better be taking good care of her."

"I'm trying to, but since I left New York, I lost all my people skills. All I do is work down here."

David burst into laughter. "That'll be the day. With the power you now have, there must be a dozen young people eager to do your bidding. In fact, you should bring Jennifer, here, into the White House."

Slater looked at her longingly and nodded his head. Now, there's an idea, he thought. "Um, I don't know, David. She's making too much of a financial killing in private law practice."

Jennifer laughed. "Not quite."

Kelso drifted away, his mission accomplished. Slater picked up his glass of red wine and sipped it slowly. Just then the pager in the vest pocket of Slater's jacket vibrated. He took it out and checked the number. "It's the President calling," he told her. From the sparkle in her eyes, he could tell she was impressed.

Slater excused himself, went into a deserted book-lined study, and called the White House on his cell phone.

"Where are you on the Winthrop case?" Brewster asked.

Oh, goddamn it, Slater cursed under his breath, it was eleven-thirty. Why the hell was Brewster pestering him about this now? Still, he couldn't very well tell the President of the United States what he was thinking. "We're on course for filing charges against the gardener Wednesday at four P.M."

"Did he do it?" Brewster asked.

"That's what the guy in my office, Ed Fulton, is telling me. He's been on the case since day one. Also,

I've got the best guy in Al Hennessey's office on the case. He wouldn't file if he didn't think we had the right man."

"All right, let me know tomorrow as soon as the charges are filed."

"I'll be sure to do that."

Before returning to his seat at the table, Slater stopped in the doorway and gazed at Jennifer. She was engrossed in an animated conversation with Senator Burgess on her other side. He watched the lovely way in which she moved her hands, pushed back her hair, and laughed easily with the senator. She had a grace, style, and intellectual sophistication that went beyond her looks. Sure, she was twenty or so years younger than he ~~~s, but he could handle her.

He suddenly remembered that Ed Fulton was waiting outside in Slater's car, planning to brief him on the way home. He dialed Fulton's cell phone number. "Listen, Ed, something came up for me here tonight. Why don't you take a cab home?"

"Will do, Mr. Slater."

"What about the search for George Nesbitt?" he asked Fulton.

"They're down to three possibles."

"And the one from San Jose?"

"Still can't find him."

"Tell Murtaugh I want ten more agents put on it."

"I'll call the director first thing in the morning, sir," he said.

When Slater returned, the party was breaking up. "Can I offer you a ride home?" Slater asked Jennifer.

"I'm in upper northwest. If that's out of your way, I could take a cab."

"Nothing's out of my way," he said.

As the limo pulled away from the Kelsos' house, Jennifer and Slater leaned back in the plush leather seat. She gave the driver her address on Livingston Street. "Where do you live?" she asked.

"I've got a small house down here on Tracey Place in Kalorama." He gave her a knowing look. "My real home is in Chappaqua, up in Westchester. I've also got places in Rancho Santa Fe and Aspen."

"So where is Mrs. Slater tonight?" she asked. "Doesn't she like parties?"

Seeing the doubt in her face, he decided to take the bull by the horns. "I am married, but we have a rather unusual arrangement. Alice lives where she wants. I do the same." When Jennifer didn't respond, he added, "You probably wonder why we stay married."

"Yes, I was thinking that."

He shrugged. "I guess neither of us have had any reason to make a change. Alice made it very clear a long time ago that she prefers her horses to me."

"Whatever works," Jennifer replied. Despite Ann's warning clanging in her head, she had to admit she was very interested in this man.

When they pulled up in front of her house, he climbed out of the car and walked her to the front door. Watching her fiddle with the key, he wondered if she'd ask him to come in, but she didn't. So he kissed her once on each cheek and headed back to the car. He was pleased with how it had gone tonight. He had no doubt that she was as taken with him as he was with her. With this one, he'd move slowly. Anything worth having was worth waiting for, and she was clearly worth having.

"Has the package arrived yet from Alpha Materials in Japan?" Chen asked the secretary in the director's office of Diamond Computers in Shanghai, while trying to conceal the anxiety in his voice.

"Not yet, Master Chen," she replied. "We're looking for it carefully. Every day you ask, and I tell you that."

Chen was furious at himself. He was too anxious about the package. If she became suspicious, she'd report him to one of the party big shots in Shanghai. They'd begin watching him around the clock.

"Well, a few more days doesn't matter," he said. "But I would like to show my father that I can get the notebook computer line running and make the production projections for my month over here."

She smiled. "Ah, Master Chen. Now I understand. My brother always had to prove things to our father, too. With fathers and sons it's always the same."

Relieved that he had allayed her suspicions, he went down to the factory floor and watched the assembling of computers. It was truly an incredible operation. The raw materials cost nickels and dimes. The labor was dirt-cheap. Assembly was simple. And at the end of the day some of the world's giant computer companies would stamp their names on these little black boxes and charge thousands of dollars for them. It was no wonder the world's economy went into a nosedive when people held on to their old computers and delayed spending money on newer, marginally improved models. The whole high-tech business was one giant money-recycling machine, Chen decided.

At noon he left the factory, heading for a luncheon meeting of a computer manufacturers group. Shanghai, the pearl of the Orient, was the commercial heart of modern China, a city of sixteen million people, where the pace was frantic. Yet as Chen walked into the hotel ballroom where the luncheon was taking place, he found a subdued crowd.

Rumors were rife that Chinese troops were on the move toward the Strait of Taiwan. Something was happening with Taiwan. Nobody at the luncheon knew precisely what it was, but everyone was convinced it would be bad for business.

Chen listened to the worried patter, but he wasn't thinking about business. The war talk reminded him of that damned package. He used the emergency number Donovan had given him to call Roger Sherman, his contact in Shanghai. With Sherman's cover as the representative of a high-tech venture capitalist, a meeting between the two men wouldn't look suspicious. Sherman offered to come to Chen's hotel, the Pudong Shangri-La, for dinner at the hotel's Cantonese restaurant.

When Chen arrived, he found Sherman in a booth in a corner that ensured privacy, far from the security men at the door. Anticipating Chen's concern about Operation Matchstick, Sherman said, "The package was shipped this afternoon from Osaka. You'll have it day after next."

"What about assembly?"

"There are directions inside. Very simple for someone like you with an engineering degree. Make sure you're at least a hundred yards away when you press the detonator. It's a delayed action. You'll have plenty of time to get out of the area."

"Understood."

A waitress approached with heaping plates of scallops and shrimp. Sherman signaled to Chen to stop talking until she was gone.

Chen moved some food around with his chopsticks, not sure how to broach the reason he had called Sherman for the meeting. Finally, he dove in. "I've heard today," Chen said nervously, "that Chinese troops are heading toward the Strait of Taiwan. What's happening?"

Sherman was uncertain how much to tell Chen. He had been following the Chinese troop movements for the last couple of days. This morning he sent a coded message to San Francisco, where his phony venture capital firm had its headquarters. From there, the message would be sent to Langley. The situation was serious. More than serious. It was grim. He put the chances at seventy-five percent that China would attack Taiwan.

"Just another flap between Washington and Beijing over arms for Taiwan," Sherman said. "They happen every couple of years. Lots of saber rattling on both sides. Nothing will come of it."

Chen wasn't fully satisfied. His eyes were blinking involuntarily, and his hand was shaking. "What about the army unit I'm supposed to meet?"

"Their location hasn't changed. If anything, this should help you. There are so many troop movements these days, nobody can keep track of them. Operation Matchstick is even more important now."

"Why so?"

"It'll send a message to Beijing that they don't have free play in this part of the world. It'll make them pull back from their war threats."

"Or encourage them to attack," Chen said soberly.

Chapter 12

Gwen didn't like jogging in a warm-up suit. She preferred the feeling of perspiring freely, her bare skin against the natural elements. Even on a raw, blustery cold morning like today, she left the Shoreham dressed only in black runner's shorts and a white T-shirt with the Washington Wizards logo that she had purchased yesterday in the hotel gift shop. As always, she was braless, and as soon as she hit the chilly air, her nipples hardened and protruded against the tight cotton shirt. She knew that she made a sensual picture, that someone who didn't know her would say that she was asking for trouble alone on a jogging path through the woods. That didn't concern Gwen. Once a creep had tried to attack her. She could have easily eluded him by running away, but instead she broke his right arm at the elbow. She left him crumpled by the path, screaming in pain.

From the hotel she ran downhill into Rock Creek Park, running hard, pushing herself for a full thirty minutes. A glimmer of a bright red sun was starting to appear in the eastern sky as she ran along the Potomac toward the Lincoln Memorial. The reflecting pool was nearly deserted at this hour. Gwen slowed to a trot as she climbed the steps, following the path of thousands of tourists who came each year to pay a visit to Honest Abe. Gwen had insisted they meet at the Lincoln Memorial. There was absolutely no way anyone could set a trap for her there.

A figure in a long black coat was waiting for her at the top of the stairs, facing away from Gwen, standing at the base of the massive marble feet. When Gwen's sneakers tapped against the stairs, the figure wheeled around quickly and stared at Gwen, the wet T-shirt plastered against her body.

"The gardener hasn't confessed yet."

"I didn't think he would."

"What now?"

"You don't have to know the details. You hired me. It's my job to get the result you wanted. I'll decide on what happens next. Do you have what I asked for?"

By way of reply, a white envelope was extracted from a pocket in the long black coat and handed over to Gwen. Quickly, she tore open the flap and looked at the single picture.

"It's Clyde Gillis's wife, Lucinda, and their four children. Address and telephone number on the back."

"And the money?" Gwen asked.

"Five million U.S. will be deposited in Credit Suisse on the Bahnhofstrasse in Zurich within the hour. The contact there is Heinrich Winkler."

From the other pocket of the long black coat came a small piece of paper with an account number, W32A27LGR42, which Gwen looked at and returned.

"That's for you."

"I don't need it," Gwen said. "The number's committed to memory."

As Gwen knew it would, her words produced admiration and fear.

"What about the other materials I wanted?" Gwen demanded.

"Are you sure that you need them?"

Gwen was irritated. "I told you when you hired me. If you want me to do a job, I do it my way. If that doesn't suit you, then get someone else."

"I didn't mean—"

"Then give me the stuff." Gwen mentally counted to ten, and when there was no response, she moved up quickly and slammed her contact hard up against the marble base of Lincoln's statue.

"Look here," she said. "My ass is on the line as well as yours. The stuff I asked you for is what I need to save both of us."

Her actions produced the desired result. This time a brown envelope came out of the coat pocket. Inside were two photographs. One was a man around forty, Gwen guessed. He wasn't bad-looking, but what struck her most about him was the intensity in his dark brown eyes. She knew that look. Like her, he was driven and purposeful. He couldn't be underestimated. It was a small bonus for her that he was a lawyer. She hated lawyers.

Gwen looked at the second photograph. It depicted a girl about four years old with curly brown hair and crooked baby teeth. She was sitting on a swing and waving at the camera. Gwen glanced down at the stairs, making sure that the area was still deserted. It was too early for tourists. The sun was beginning its slow ascent. The water of the reflecting pool was beginning to sparkle.

"The man's name is Ben Hartwell. His daughter is Amy. There's a piece of paper in the envelope with his home address and telephone number. Also the address of Amy's preschool group."

Gwen nodded, then stuffed the contents of the two envelopes into a pocket in the back of her shorts. "Don't worry. You'll get the result you want. And unless something goes wrong, which it shouldn't, this is our last meeting."

They were back in the conference room at the FBI. Bill Traynor, a piece of chalk in his hand, was standing in front of a blackboard. Ben, Ed Fulton, and Director Murtaugh were watching him carefully.

On the board was a list of six George Nesbitts, each with a number of identifying facts. The last six possibles. Lines had been drawn through four of the six George Nesbitts.

"Last night at ten-thirty, Pacific time," Traynor said, "we took Jeb Hines to the town of Montecito, outside of Santa Barbara, where he confronted the fifth George Nesbitt at his home. Jeb's convinced he's not the man."

With a flourish, Traynor drew a line through number five. He was playing it up for Murtaugh, emphasizing what a thorough manhunt he had directed.

Ben said, "Number six is our San Jose computer VP, right?"

Traynor nodded.

"The guy we haven't been able to find?"

"We found him."

Ben looked up. "Well?" he said anxiously.

"He called his home late last night, and we traced the call. It was made from the Trade Winds Hotel along Mission Bay in San Diego. Yesterday around six in the evening Nesbitt checked into the hotel."

"Alone?"

"Accompanied by another man. They took one room with a king-size bed. Room 807."

"Has Hines seen the man?"

"Not yet."

Fulton jumped in, "What do you mean, not yet?"

With Director Murtaugh now personally involved, Traynor was determined to play it by the book. "They showed the room clerk the artist's sketch of Nesbitt. He says the guy in 807 could very well be our man, but we're not going in without a warrant. The magistrate should have signed it at seven o'clock Pacific time this morning." Traynor glanced at his watch. "Ten minutes ago."

Ed added, "And suppose Nesbitt got away while your guys were fucking around with the magistrate?"

Ben smiled. At least this guy was consistent.

"There's no chance of that," Traynor said, proud of how he'd handled it. "Once we established that they were in the room, we've had someone outside in the corridor all night. No one came in. No one went out."

"What happens now?"

Traynor eyed the phone. "They'll call us here in a few minutes with a report."

Jeb Hines, accompanied by two members of the FBI's San Diego office, raced with guns drawn into the lobby of the Trade Winds Hotel along Mission Bay. Chuck Connor, the head of the local FBI office, flashed his badge at the startled desk clerk. Half a dozen hotel guests immediately scattered.

"We're going up to eight-oh-seven," Connor said to the desk clerk.

In the elevator he reached into his pocket and extracted a pair of metal cutters. "I can get through a chain in twenty seconds," he boasted to Hines. Then he reached into another jacket pocket and waved the search warrant he had gotten minutes earlier. "I was told to play it by the book," he said, and laughed.

On the eighth floor, Connor nodded to the agents at each end of the corridor. With Hines in tow, Connor walked up to room 807. "You stay here and cover me," Connor said, handing the warrant to Hines. "Christ, I hate faggots."

Connor never gave a warning. With a gun in his right hand and metal cutters in his left, he smashed his shoulder, driven with all the force that his two-hundred-forty-five-pound body could muster, against the door to room 807, directly above the doorknob. The thin wooden door shattered as the chain ripped out of the frame. Connor dropped the metal cutters and ran into the room.

Startled out of a deep sleep, two naked men bolted upright to a sitting position in the king-size bed.

"What the fuck is this?" one of them screamed angrily.

Connor flashed his badge. "FBI. We're looking for George Nesbitt."

"Yeah, well, I'm George Nesbitt," the other man said defiantly. He wrapped the sheet around his lower body and stood up. That left his partner, naked and exposed, grabbing a pillow to cover his privates.

"Just stop right there," Connor said, pointing the gun threateningly at Nesbitt. "Jeb, get in here," he called over his shoulder.

Hines ran into the room carrying his own gun.

"What do you think?" Connor asked him.

Hines looked carefully at the man and then at his friend, still sitting in bed. "Negative," he said, not concealing his disappointment.

"Sorry, guys," Connor said. "The wrong George Nesbitt."

He turned and started to leave.

"Are you out of your fucking mind?" Nesbitt screamed at him. "Breaking in like this? You ever heard of the Constitution? I'll sue you and the FBI for so much money that you'll be cleaning out toilets the rest of your life."

Connor wheeled around. "We had a search warrant. Besides," he said, pointing at the sheet, "I doubt that your wife and kids would enjoy a lawsuit like that."

Dejectedly, Bill Traynor listened on the phone to Connor's report. The others in the room quickly deduced what had occurred.

"What do we do now?" Traynor asked Ben when he hung up the phone.

Before he could respond, Fulton chimed in, "We've got our marching orders. We file charges against Clyde Gillis."

"We?" Ben said. "Don't forget, hotshot, I'm the only one here who can file that case. I haven't decided what I'm going to do."

"Then I guess you need your ears checked, because I sure as hell heard Mr. Slater order you to file those charges by four today, regardless of what happened with George Nesbitt."

Ben's face turned stony. "You may not believe this, but Jim Slater can't order me to do squat."

"Now, that's a novel view of the executive branch of the government."

"Stick around. You'll learn all sorts of new things."

Ben felt better yanking Fulton's chain. In reality he knew Fulton was right. Ben had the grand jury primed and ready to rubber-stamp an indictment charging Clyde Gillis with first-degree murder. From the evidence, he thought he had no choice, apart from his own nagging doubts. Al Hennessey would be able to announce to the world at four o'clock today that charges had been filed. Ben knew damn well that if he refused to sign the indictment, any of the other assistant U.S. Attorneys would be eager to add their names. The ball was rolling.

Chapter 13

Jennifer shut the door of her office and told her secretary to hold all of her calls. She needed time to think about the Clyde Gillis case.

How could she represent a client who wouldn't talk to her?

She kept asking herself, Did Gillis kill Winthrop? Is that why he wouldn't talk to me?

She refused to believe that. Earlier this morning she had met with Gillis's wife, Lucinda, who affirmed her husband's innocence in the strongest terms. "You've got to help my Clyde," she had pleaded. "The Lord knows he didn't kill anybody."

So like any good criminal lawyer, Jennifer pushed aside any doubts about what her client did or didn't do, pressing ahead to prepare a defense. Her objective was to build a solid enough case that the Chinese government had hired George Nesbitt to kill Winthrop, and that the administration, to avoid a foreign policy brouhaha, was engaged in a massive cover-up, with Clyde Gillis taking the fall. Once she had her case built, she intended to present it to Ben. He'd realize how well it would play before a D.C. jury. She was also confident that her position would work its way up to Sarah Van Buren, the AG, and maybe even the President, because of the foreign policy and political implications of her going forward with this explosive story. Of course, if it was White House intervention she was looking for, she could pick up the phone and call Jim Slater. She considered and rejected that possibility in a nanosecond. Her relationship with Jim was already too complicated.

Jennifer realized that while her plan made sense in theory, she was missing a major ingredient. Her case against the Chinese government was anything but solid. The idea of George Nesbitt as a hired assassin lost credibility when she thought about what Detective Campbell had told her at Ann's house on Saturday. If Campbell was right that the stain on the front of Winthrop's pants was precoital fluid, that suggested Nesbitt had come for a sexual encounter. Was Robert Winthrop bisexual? If he was, then had Nesbitt tried to exploit that fact to blackmail him? Or had they planned a homosexual encounter that produced an argument, which led to Nesbitt's shooting Winthrop? Suppose Nesbitt wouldn't do it with Winthrop for some reason. Winthrop got angry. Winthrop threatened Nesbitt to get him to change his mind. He refused. Winthrop kept pressing. Finally Nesbitt killed Winthrop. Leaving the house, he tossed some money and the gun into Clyde Gillis's truck when the guards weren't looking. It seemed plausible.

Or maybe Clyde Gillis really did kill Winthrop.

So how could she build her case?

"Facts," she remembered her criminal law professor had taught her. "You always start with facts."

The fluid Campbell had observed in front of Winthrop's pants was a fact. The file folder stuffed with condoms downstairs in Winthrop's house was a fact. Winthrop's liaisons with prostitutes had given the Chinese ambassador the ammunition to blackmail the secretary of state. That was a fact. The common ingredient in all of these was Winthrop's sexual behavior. Somewhere in that behavior was the key to unlocking the puzzle of his death. She had to find that key.

Jennifer hit the intercom button on her telephone. "Kathy," she said to her secretary, "please get me Dr. Grace Hargadon at NIMH."

"A messenger just arrived with something for you, Miss Moore."

"Will you bring it in?"

Kathy entered a moment later carrying the largest floral arrangement Jennifer had ever seen. She put the flowers down on a credenza and handed Jennifer a small envelope. Inside, the note read, *I enjoyed being with you at dinner last evening—Jim.*

Kathy looked at her expectantly. "A new boyfriend, Miss Moore?"

Jennifer blushed. "Nothing of the sort. Now get me Dr. Hargadon on the phone."

Grace was able to see Jennifer in an hour. While packing up her briefcase to head out to NIH, Jennifer stopped and stared at the flowers. The arrangement was quite magnificent. He was entitled to a thank-you. She checked her directory of government telephone numbers and dialed 284-2000.

It was impressive to hear the operator announce, "This is the White House."

"Jim Slater, please."

A secretary picked up. "Mr. Slater's office. Who's calling?"

"Jennifer Moore."

"Please hold. . . ."

There was a long pause while the secretary asked Slater if he could take the call. It'll be just as well if he doesn't, Jennifer thought. I'll just leave the thank-you message with her and be done with it.

But Slater picked up. "Well, hello, there, Jennifer. Great evening at the Kelsos'. What can I do for you?" He sounded relaxed and self-confident.

"I want to know if you bought out the flower shop."

Acting surprised, he laughed. "Oh, they came."

"Jim, they're incredible. Thanks so much."

"Happy to hear you like them. Nosegay does a great job."

She wanted him to know how much she appreciated the thought. "They've certainly made my day."

"Listen, I've got an offer for you. Tomorrow evening the Washington Opera's doing *Luisa Miller*. I could probably scrounge up a couple of tickets for the presidential box. How about that and a late dinner somewhere?"

"How'd you know I like opera?"

"Well, you are on the opera board. That gave me a hint."

She was pleased that he was obviously doing some checking on her. Then she thought about Ann's advice that getting started with any married man, even one as attractive as Slater, was a mistake. She could tell him that she was supposed to see *Luisa Miller* next week, which was true, of course, because she had missed the performance last Saturday when Robert died, to spend time with Ann.

From her silence, he sensed her hesitation. "It is Verdi. Nothing wrong with seeing it twice in a season."

"Great. I'd love to," she replied.

"I'll leave your ticket at the box office."

Chip Donovan sat at his desk and examined the message, now decoded, that Sherman had sent from Shanghai via the venture capital firm in San Francisco. Chinese troop movements had advanced. The President's warning to Liu yesterday, following the consensus reached at the meeting Donovan had attended with Hawkins, Cunningham, and Joyner, had done nothing to slow down the Chinese deployment toward the Strait of Taiwan.

Let them keep coming, Donovan thought. Unlike Cunningham, President Brewster had balls. If the Chinese dared to attack Taiwan, and Donovan hoped they would, he was confident that Brewster would respond with force. Now was the time to fight that battle. The United States couldn't afford to wait much longer for the inevitable battle over Taiwan. Not at the rate the Chinese military machine was developing.

But would the Chinese attack?

That was why Operation Matchstick was so important. If Chen succeeded, and Donovan was confident he would, that would be the spark that would force the Chinese to attack.

As Donovan reread Sherman's report, there was one fact in it that disturbed him. "Extremely nervous" was how Sherman described Chen. Jesus, I hope he doesn't bail out on me now, Donovan thought. Everything's in place. Don't let me down.

Jennifer briskly climbed the concrete stairs in front of building ten of the National Institute of Mental Health, one of the largest in the NIH complex in Bethesda. She averted her eyes from the sun reflecting off the black glass windows.

Walking through the main corridor to the elevators, she passed a display heralding innovations in medicine and science. People were milling around in the lobby near the bank of elevators. One young doctor, in a white lab coat, after glancing impatiently at his watch, muttered something inaudible and headed for the staircase.

On the fourth floor, she exited the elevator and followed the signs for the north hallway in search of 4N 257. Having never been in the building before, she was surprised at how small and close together the offices were as she walked down the long corridor. Here, the great scientific minds of the world were working in offices the size of closets.

Finally, she reached her destination. A small sign with black block letters on a white background read AFFECTIVE DISORDERS, CHIEF GRACE HARGADON. She headed toward the left looking through open office doors until she spotted Grace. A tiny, slight woman in her late fifties, whose size concealed a powerful analytical mind, she was hunched over her computer ferociously typing. Reports as well as her various articles were piled haphazardly on the floor and a table that was too large for the room, giving the office a cluttered look. Before Jennifer could say a word, Dr. Hargadon wheeled around and curtly said, "I'll be with you in one second." She resumed typing to complete her thought.

Looking at the scientist, Jennifer couldn't help but smile. Unlike most casually dressed researchers, who wore slacks, shirts, and white jackets, Dr. Hargadon was, as usual, dressed in a Chanel suit—this one in pinks and muted greens. Having inherited a fortune from her father, who owned a score of cable TV stations in the Pacific Northwest, she could easily afford to wear three-thousand-dollar suits. Jennifer had first met her several years ago when Jennifer was still at the Justice Department, and a defense lawyer used Grace as his expert to persuade a jury that the defendant's abusive behavior toward women was so compulsive that he should be deemed to be temporarily insane rather than prosecuted. Dr. Hargadon was simply the best psychiatric witness Jennifer had ever encountered. After the trial, Jennifer made it a point of getting to know her. Over lunch at the prestigious Cosmos Club, where the scientist was a member, they found they shared another interest—opera. Since Grace's husband, a physician, found it boring, she and Jennifer had taken a subscription to the Washington Opera each of the last several years.

Dr. Hargadon finished typing, spun around in her chair, and pushed her brown designer glasses up on her head. "You missed a good opera Saturday. It was the best *Luisa Miller* I've ever seen."

"I didn't want to leave Ann until her daughter got there."

"How's she doing?"

"That's what I wanted to talk to you about. Ann leaned on me to defend Clyde Gillis, the gardener who—"

"I know who he is," she said in her brusque professional tone, one that bore no resemblance to her friendly manner when she was off duty. "With all the media attention the case is getting, I'd have to be living on the moon not to know." She suddenly stopped. Something hadn't computed. "Most widows don't hire a defense lawyer for their husband's alleged killer."

"This isn't a typical case."

Grace refilled the large mug on her desk from a sterling silver thermos and pointed to the chair next to her desk. Jennifer sat down.

"You've got my attention."

Jennifer didn't hesitated to talk to Dr. Hargadon. She knew the scientist would keep everything in confidence. "Our distinguished former secretary of state had some problems. He had a compulsive sexual desire, an abnormal sexual drive."

Dr. Hargadon smiled. "Aren't I supposed to be the one making the diagnosis?"

Jennifer laughed easily. "Good point."

"You stick to the symptoms. Tell me what you mean by abnormal?"

"There was an underside to his behavior. Whenever he traveled, which was often, he arranged for call girls. Sometimes more than one. To me, that's abnormal behavior."

"So he liked women. Lots of men do. Why do you think it's abnormal?"

"It made him the target for blackmail."

"But even if that's the case, how does that help you?"

"I want to understand him. I'm hoping that I'll be able to find the key to who killed him."

"What else do you know about him?"

"He was AC/DC as well."

"You know that for sure?"

"On Saturday afternoon, the day he was killed, a man visited him. He came for sex with Winthrop."

Dr. Hargadon raised her eyebrows. "A man?"

"His name was George Nesbitt."

"How do you know the visitor came for sex?"

"A detective observed fluid on the front of Winthrop's pants. It wasn't urine. Money was thrown around."

The scientist scratched her head in puzzlement. "I

think I'd better talk to your friend Ann. When can I see her?"

Jennifer glanced up at the clock on the wall. "I thought you'd never ask. I wanted some time alone to give you the background. She'll be here any minute."

"You're one step ahead of me, as always."

Sure enough, they heard footsteps in the hallway and Ann appeared in the doorway. The two women had met a couple of times before at Jennifer's house.

Dr. Hargadon plunged right in with her usual directness. "I want to help if I can, but we'll have to talk frankly about your husband and your sex life with him. Can you handle that, Ann?"

"With pleasure," Ann quickly replied.

Dr. Hargadon picked up a white pad. With the Cross pen on her desk, she jotted a few notes. "Let's talk about Robert during a defined period of time," she began. "Say the last three years, since you moved to Washington and he was secretary of state."

Ann nodded.

Dr. Hargadon continued, "Describe his mood."

"What do you mean?"

"Was he sometimes irritable and sometimes euphoric?"

"More of the latter. For several days at a time he would be wildly euphoric, gloating to me and others about all the great things he was accomplishing at the State Department. Once I accused him of taking uppers. He laughed at me and called me a sullen bitch."

"Focus on these periods of emotional high. What else did he do that was unusual?"

There was a long silence. Ann was thinking.

While waiting, Dr. Hargadon doodled on the pad, which she frequently did. Jennifer had always had a vague urge to have another psychiatrist analyze those markings.

Ann looked up. "He had almost unlimited energy during these periods, and he rarely slept. He'd sleep three hours, play tennis, and run everybody ragged in the office with all sorts of brilliant new ideas."

"What about sexual activity?"

"He'd go after me like a wild man for days at a time. Then he'd settle down to two or so times a week. When he was in a high like that, he'd want me as much as five times in a twenty-four-hour period. He didn't care that I wasn't getting a thing out of it. In jest, I once told him to go stuff it somewhere else. Obviously, he did just that."

"How often did he have these euphoric states?"

"More in the last year. Near the end, almost on a weekly basis."

"Did he ever indicate that he felt larger than life?"

Ann thought about the question for a minute. "I don't know if this is what you mean, but he always seemed to think that he was invincible. He would dream that he was president. He would even tell me what the reporters would write about—how incredible he was. Again, I usually tuned him out when he went into this routine. I thought his ego was superinflated. He sounded like such a jerk." A look of skepticism came over Ann's face. "Is any of this relevant to Robert's death?"

"Bear with me a little longer," Dr. Hargadon replied, pausing to make a note. "To your knowledge, was he taking any drugs or medication?"

"He hated taking an aspirin, let alone any mood-altering substances. Increasingly, he was against putting foreign substances in his body."

Dr. Hargadon stopped talking and looked over her notes.

"Where are we, Doctor?" Ann asked her.

Dr. Hargadon took a deep breath and said, "Your husband probably had what we call hypomanic episodes."

"In English, please."

"It's a mood disorder. With more severe behavior, he would be manic. But in contrast, hypomanic episodes aren't severe enough to cause impairment in social or occupational function or to require hospitalization. But they're still a problem. With counseling or even, if necessary, medication, we might have been able to control it."

"And the sex with prostitutes?"

"That's all part of the hypomanic profile. Typically, hypomanic people have periods of time when they are full of energy and euphoric, involving themselves in pleasurable activities, with sex usually being at the top of the list."

"Should I feel better that my husband was a nut instead of being a philanderer?"

"The characterization doesn't matter. The bottom line is that you've confirmed what I suspected while talking to Jennifer. Robert was engaged in self-destructive behavior that he may not have been able to control."

Ann retorted, "But none of that psycho stuff is particularly helpful now. Is it?"

Jennifer caught Dr. Hargadon's eye and silently mouthed the words, "George Nesbitt."

"There's one other matter. Jennifer has the idea that somebody named George Nesbitt showed up for a homosexual encounter with your husband on that Saturday afternoon."

Ann looked at Jennifer incredulously. "That's ridiculous. Robert wasn't gay."

"How can you be sure?" Dr. Hargadon said. "Plenty of wives—"

"He was homophobic, for God's sake."

"How do you know that?"

"When he was at Exeter, another boy once came into his bed when he was sleeping and began fondling him. Robert woke up and punched the kid so hard that the boy's face was a bloody pulp. It took seventeen stitches to sew him up. If Philip Brewster in the next room hadn't intervened in response to the screams, then Robert probably would have killed him. The other boy was expelled and the incident was hushed up. Robert told me about it with pride."

"How did the subject happen to come up?"

"About two years ago I learned from a news source that under Robert, there was an unwritten rule at the State Department—don't hire any men who seem gay. It was illegal as hell. Once I confronted him with it. Publicly, he said, of course, he would deny it if anyone put it into print, but privately he confirmed it was true. He told me about the Exeter incident and said gays were unreliable and could be blackmailed by foreigners, which is pretty hypocritical given what happened to him. He was a liberal on just about every topic except gays. But there you are. My husband wasn't a very nice man, which is why I'm damn happy he's dead."

Jennifer decided to break in. "Couldn't this loud expression of homophobia have been a cover for his latent homosexuality?"

Grace looked at her thoughtfully. "In my opinion, clearly not on the facts Ann just told us. He seemed too repulsed and acted too violently for that."

"But George Nesbitt was a man."

"Really? What makes you so sure George Nesbitt was a man?" Dr. Hargadon said flatly.

"What?" Ann blurted out. "The guards in front of the house said he was a man."

Jennifer, too, was flabbergasted. "Run that by me again."

"My opinion," Dr. Hargadon said slowly but confidently, "is that George Nesbitt was a woman disguised as a man. Actors do it to play a part. The two of you certainly know that. It was a great way for a woman who arranged to have sex with Robert to gain access to him in the house."

"You really think so?"

"Go back to the lab people. Have them check the house and all of Winthrop's clothes. Maybe you'll find a woman's hair somewhere that's not Ann's or the maid's. And maybe it came from George Nesbitt."

"What makes you think so?"

"Let's assume that Winthrop was compulsive about sex with call girls, which you've told me is a fact. He can't have a prostitute show up at his house Saturday afternoon. So he tells her to dress like a man."

"And she kills him."

"Maybe."

"Why? Because he didn't pay her enough?"

"Quite the opposite. She was probably paid plenty by somebody else to kill him."

"And that somebody knew how to gain access to Winthrop."

"Precisely."

Jennifer immediately thought of the Chinese ambassador. Winthrop wouldn't resign, so had Liu arranged to kill him? "Now all I have to do is find that somebody."

"Find out who supplied Winthrop with prostitutes. There's your missing link."

In the parking lot at NIH, as they were separating, Jennifer told Ann, "Pull together every letter, personal paper, cancelled check, or any other document that belonged to Robert and pile them up in one of the second-floor rooms in your house. Also, go down to his office at State. Clean out his desk and personal files."

"I'll have it all by tomorrow afternoon."

"Great. When it's ready, call a young lawyer in my office, Louise Jenson. She'll hustle out to your house."

"But why do you want all that stuff?"

"Dr. Hargadon may be right. Whoever supplied Robert with prostitutes might be the key we're searching for."

With her cell phone, Jennifer called Detective Campbell. He was located at Theodore Roosevelt High School on 13th Street, where a sixth-grader had just gunned down a classmate who tried to steal a pair of sneakers from his locker. Campbell was too angry about the high school case to talk to her on the phone. "Write me a letter," he barked loudly and hung up.

She raced across East-West Highway, hoping to reach Roosevelt before Campbell left. She narrowly succeeded. The detective was getting into his car, notepad in hand, when she pulled up in front of the school. He climbed back out of his car and slammed the door.

"Sorry I was rude to you," he said. "It's not your fault."

"I need your help," Jennifer said meekly.

He paused to pull on his cigarette. "You've got a poor memory. I checked out of the Winthrop case."

"Clyde Gillis needs your help."

He gave her a curious look. "That's right. I heard you were representing him. The whole thing's got me a little puzzled."

"Don't try to figure it out. Just help me."

But Campbell was still replaying the events inside the school. "That crazy fucker was only twelve years old," he exclaimed. "He bought the gun himself with money he made hustling drugs. All that for a pair of Nikes. Goddamn, what are we going to do? When I played basketball at Georgetown, I didn't care what kind of shoes I had. Now these punks need the best shoes to waltz up and down the street. What will the next generation be like?" The detective looked back at Jennifer and sighed. "What do you need, Miss Moore?"

"I'd like to get a copy of your report on the Winthrop investigation."

"I wasn't kidding. I didn't file one."

"You know that fluid you saw on the front of his pants?"

He looked at her warily. "Uh-huh."

"Is it discussed in the FBI report?"

He smiled. "I think the Bureau missed it."

"Yeah, right. Who did their work?"

"Henry Langston in the Bureau lab."

"C'mon, those FBI people are too good to miss something like that."

Now she had his attention. He tapped his fingers on the hood of his car and looked at her quizzically.

"There could be a lot of other possible explanations for its omission."

"Such as?"

"Langston was planning to test Winthrop's pants, but before he had a chance, somebody in the government, maybe a top dog at the Bureau, called and told him to skip it because it was irrelevant and could only embarrass Mrs. Winthrop."

"Is that what happened?"

He didn't seem to think so either. "I'm just saying it's a possibility."

Yet someone might have made another request. "Who made the call, you think?"

"Langston wouldn't say, but he'll tell you the truth when you get him under oath and cross-examine him at trial. Henry's the kind of guy who won't risk perjury for any reason."

"I have another question. How thoroughly did they examine Winthrop's body for foreign hairs?"

"With a fine-tooth comb. They'd have given anything to come up with one from an African American, but they didn't."

"What about the carpet in the room in which Winthrop was killed? Did they check that carefully as well?"

He regarded her with a new respect. "I don't know. I doubt it. Bill Traynor was pushing the investigating unit to get done and get out."

"I have a proposition for you. How would you like to go back with your lab people quietly and do a thorough job on the carpet in that room? I'll arrange for Ann to give you access to the house."

He liked this idea a lot. "What am I looking for?"

"A hair. A woman's hair."

"Ann's hair?" he asked, puzzled.

"No, a hair that might be from George Nesbitt."

"But you said . . ." He suddenly started to laugh. "If we found something, that would really show the Feds who's competent and who's not."

"And it would strengthen my case on reasonable doubt."

He tossed the cigarette to the ground and crushed it out with his foot. "There's one thing you've got to understand," he warned her. "I'm a police detective. I'm not a PI. If I find anything, I'll give it to the government's trial team as well as to you."

She had been hoping to surprise Ben before the judge, at a pretrial hearing, or maybe even at trial. "Suppose you hold up talking to them for a while?"

"No way. It's my job."

She thought for an instant about having Mark Bonner arrange for the testing, but quickly rejected it. If Campbell found anything, his police credentials would make him a much more effective witness. Besides, Ben couldn't do a damn thing with the test results except read them and weep. "Go check the carpet," she said. "I'm going to blow Ben right out of the water."

He wrinkled his nose. He was impressed with Jennifer and wanted to help her out, but this was taking a turn he didn't like. "Careful, now; Ben's a personal friend."

"Then if you find anything, you can deliver the bad news to him yourself."

Chapter 14

Clutching a thin briefcase in his hand, Chip Donovan walked out of the main entrance of the agency's headquarters in Langley and into his waiting limousine. "The Westin Hotel on Mass Ave. in Washington," he said to his driver. "I have a lunch meeting. Wait for me there. Afterward, we're going up to the Hill."

The black Lincoln Town Car pulled away from the curb, and the last of America's superspies from the Cold War days snapped open the briefcase resting on the backseat and pulled out a thin brown envelope. Inside there was a pad with Donovan's scribbling that would have been unintelligible to anyone else. To him, whose mind functioned better with a pencil in his hand, they were the conception of a follow-up mission in China after Operation Matchstick succeeded. This time it would be a massive explosion in Tiananmen Square, taking the battle right to the party elders. And at the heart of his plan was one of his own seasoned pros.

He wanted to move while there was still a void at State. He had no idea whom Brewster would pick to be the new secretary, but it was likely that Donovan would never get support for his approach in Foggy Bottom. This morning, Donovan had been in his office trying to fill in some of the blanks in the new proposal when the private telephone in his desk drawer rang. As soon as he heard the voice at the other end, he knew how he could fill in one of the key blanks.

"Do they still have grilled Dover sole for lunch?" were Gwen's first words.

"What a nice surprise," he had replied.

"One o'clock today. Our usual place. Is the suite still eight-oh-three?"

He glanced at the calendar on his desk. He was supposed to be lunching with Senator Hanlon up on the Hill.

"How do you know I'm free?" he had asked her. "Maybe I'm busy."

"Because for me, you'll cancel anything on your calendar."

She gave that deep sensual laugh of hers, and he smiled. Of course, she was right. He didn't have to eat with Senator Hanlon. A late-afternoon meeting would work just as well.

In the back of the car, he closed his eyes and thought about her. He had met Gwen almost twenty years ago. At the time he was the head of naval intelligence, operating in Boston and planning to move to the CIA. One morning a report of a bizarre case came across his desk. A drunken sailor had picked up a hooker in the combat zone in Boston and had gone home with her. He strangled her and then fell asleep. At about four A.M. her fourteen-year-old daughter, who was also turning tricks on the street, came home alone and surveyed the scene. She picked up a two-by-four, and with repeated blows smashed in the sailor's skull. Then she took a kitchen knife and cut up the rest of his body savagely. She put his sexual organs into an envelope and mailed it to the U.S. naval headquarters in Boston.

Donovan had gone to see her at the Waltham School for girls, where she was incarcerated. From the court files, he knew that she had no idea who her father was. It took three visits before she would even talk to him. Yet he knew that he had found what he was searching for: a totally amoral human being devoid of human emotion, precisely what he wanted to be part of a new elite unit of anti-terrorist killers that

he planned to organize at the CIA. Donovan's theory
was that the only way to stop terrorists was by training
people who operated the way they did. It took him
three more visits to recruit her with the promise of a
new life if she let him and the agency people train
her. A single call from Langley to the governor of
Massachusetts secured her release.

Fourteen years later, he couldn't blame her for leaving the agency after Operation Desert Storm. She
could have killed Saddam six months before Iraq invaded Kuwait if the first Bush White House had only
given her a green light. Though Donovan had repeatedly offered to divorce his wife and marry her, Gwen
had told him, "You're for love and fun. When I get
married, it'll be for money." Following her plan, she
married Paul, who had started a highly successful computer support business, and got his money out by
going public, leaving the suckers who bought in holding the bag in the now defunct company. How could
Donovan ever be angry at her? He had created her.
She was what he had made her.

They crossed the Potomac on the Teddy Roosevelt
Bridge, hit downtown, and got stuck in a massive traffic jam caused by blocking off Pennsylvania Avenue
to cars. What's this country coming to? Donovan
thought. We can't even protect our President.

"Use the siren," he ordered his driver.

"Yes, sir," the stocky former army sergeant said.
He slapped a red gum ball up on the roof, hit the
siren button, and drove through a narrow lane that
opened for the Town Car.

Donovan was ten minutes late. She was already in
the suite when he arrived. He could smell her before
he could see her. He should have guessed that she
wouldn't wait for him. She was trained to pick any
lock.

He followed her scent through the living room into
the bedroom, where she was stretched out naked on
top of the floral bedspread, her head resting against a
cluster of pillows, her legs spread. He walked over and

kissed her long and hard, and she pulled him down onto the bed, clothes and all. Then she pushed him away and began undressing him, tossing his clothes on the floor as she went.

"I was glad you called me," he said. "I was hoping that you might need something from me."

"Yeah, I need something from you. Nobody goes down on me like you do. That's what I need."

When he was undressed, he began kissing her body slowly and methodically, using his tongue to play with her breasts while his left hand stroked her soft, wet vagina. When he buried his head between her legs, licking her engorged clitoris, her whole body began to tremble. Finally, she grabbed his head with both of her hands and pulled his face down hard against her. "Oh, God, yes, you bastard," she cried out in pleasure. Moments later, she spun her body around and went to work on him with her mouth.

After an hour of making love, they both lay back exhausted. Gwen laid her head on his chest, full of graying hairs that gave away his sixty years. "Should I order lunch?" he asked.

"I did when I arrived." She glanced at the digital clock next to the bed. "It'll be here in about twenty minutes."

She climbed out of bed, ran the bathwater, and threw in some bubble bath. When it was full, they sat in the tub together with her leaning back against his chest.

"What brings you to Washington?" he asked.

"Just passing through on my way back from Europe," she lied easily. "I decided to stop over and break up the trip. I like to see you when I can."

"Thanks," he said dryly. "Everybody should have something he's really good at. How's Paul?"

She kicked her feet, splashing the water. "He's Paul. I have everything I could want, and my freedom too. It's perfect. Well, almost."

"What do you mean?"

"He doesn't like oral sex." She laughed.

He played with her breasts, massaging the nipples between his thumbs and forefingers until they grew taut. "You working much?"

"Freelancing for some foreign governments." She flicked a glance around the room. It was the agency's suite. She knew he regularly swept it for bugs, but technology was getting so sophisticated you could never be sure. Besides, he didn't need to know about her current project in Washington. "You don't want to know more than that," she added, "but I do need a favor from you."

He kissed her lightly on the back of her neck. "I'd do anything for you, Gwen. You know that."

"I want to do a little shopping while I'm in Washington. Any suggestions?"

He stiffened slightly behind her. "What are you looking for?"

"The usual," she said casually. "Surveillance equipment. Weapons. And so forth."

"Go to 1285 Seventh Street Northwest. Ask for Big Bob, and tell him it's company account 762. Pay him in cash. He won't ask you for an ID."

She nuzzled her cheek against his. "You're so good to me."

"I try," he said lightly. "People call me from time to time asking for a recommendation. You're the first name I always give them."

She reached behind her buttocks and cupped his balls in her hands. "Thanks, Chip. I like working. Not for the money, of course. I don't need that, but for the fun of it."

He smiled and shook his head. He truly had created a monster.

She could feel his dick growing, and she wrapped her hand around it. "I'm such a psychopath. You ever worried that I'll kill you?"

He chuckled. "No way. Not until you find somebody to make you feel good like I just did."

She twisted her head around and kissed him. "You conceited bastard."

The doorbell rang. They heard a man call, "Room service." She stood up and tossed him a terry-cloth robe. "Put a tent over your pole."

She refused to let the waiter fillet her Dover sole. Donovan watched her devour the fish voraciously and then use her teeth to pick any meat off the bones.

"I see that you're still wearing your black uniform," Gwen said. "You promised to tell me why one day."

A large smile lit up his face. He ran his hand through his thick gray hair. "It's not that exciting."

"I've always wanted to know about it."

He got up and fixed himself a glass of scotch and a vodka for her. "I went to a Jesuit school for college. St. Vincent in western Pennsylvania. I wanted to be a priest."

She burst out laughing. "You, a priest?"

He looked offended. "I had a cherubic face in those days."

"You still do. And you probably loved to eat pussy then. Was that legal? I mean, for somebody who was studying to be a priest?"

"The answer's no, and that came later. Well, anyhow, it was the height of the war in Vietnam, and I stopped believing in God, which made it hard to be a priest. But something else happened. When I saw kids burning the flag and pissing on it, I got really outraged. This country's not perfect, but it's the best there is. So the U.S. became my god. I started wearing the black suit and black turtleneck—my uniform, as you put it—because it made me feel like a priest in my own order. Call it Saint George, as in George Washington, if you'd like. So there you have it."

She loved the story. Smiling, she asked, "How's the work going for you in your religion these days?"

"I'm developing a new project, as a matter of fact. You interested in doing something with me again?"

"Didn't we just do something?"

It was his turn to smile. "I mean professionally."

"I won't come back to the agency and all that bureaucratic horseshit."

"I wouldn't ask you to. I mean as an independent contractor. It'll involve travel to the Far East."

Her eyes gleamed with interest. "I could handle that. The only place Paul likes to go is Europe. Talk to me when you're ready."

"I hope to. Things may change with Winthrop gone."

"Yeah, it was too bad about him. Washington's getting to be a dangerous town." Careful, she told herself, once the words were out of her mouth. He's smart, and he knows your body language very well. Don't give away too much.

"They arrested Winthrop's gardener," he said.

"I saw that in the newspaper. Did he really do it?"

Donovan shrugged. "I'm not involved. It's Murtaugh's baby. As usual, the FBI is clueless."

She laughed. The rivalry between the two agencies hadn't changed.

"Actually, it is funny," he said, "Murtaugh couldn't find Winthrop's killer if his life depended on it. I sure as hell am not going to use any of our people to bail him out."

The way he said it made her hesitate. "If it wasn't the gardener, then who do you think did it?"

"I just know what I hear on the street."

"Which is?"

He kept his face bland, but he was staring at her intently. "A foreign government's involved. Maybe even a big one in Asia. The biggest one of all."

"Really? Isn't that nice."

Her innocent act didn't fool him. "Did you ever hear of a book called *The Peter Principle*?"

She shook her head.

"One of the author's theories is that a person can be really good at one job, but when he gets promoted to planning and management responsibilities, he runs into trouble."

She looked at him with a worried frown. "What are you trying to tell me?"

"Just watch your back. I'd hate to have anything happen to you."

"I got a call from Mrs. Winthrop telling me that she got you a good lawyer," Lucinda said to Gillis. "Jennifer Moore is her name."

Wanting to talk more about his situation, she had come alone to visit him this time. They were sitting across from each other at one of the wooden tables in the visiting room.

When Gillis didn't respond but looked into space with a blank stare, Lucinda said, "Did you hear what I just told you? Did this Jennifer Moore call you?"

"It won't make any difference," he said weakly.

"What do you mean?" She leaned across and shook his arm, which brought a guard scurrying over. She quickly pulled back. "What are you talking about?"

"Nothing will matter." He sounded so beaten down and despondent. She had never known him to be like this, not even when doctors had diagnosed Clyde Junior's kidney disease.

"What's wrong?" she asked, concerned.

He didn't respond.

"I know there's something wrong. Please talk to me, Clyde."

He shook his head sadly and looked down at his hands, refusing to say another word until visiting time was over.

From a pay phone in the visitors lounge, Lucinda called Jennifer and told her what happened.

Jennifer knew exactly what she was talking about, which was a source of some relief to Lucinda.

"They did something to him," Jennifer said.

Lucinda was puzzled. "Who did what?"

"I don't know," Jennifer answered determinedly. "But I intend to find out."

Chapter 15

At three o'clock, Ben took a copy of the indictment of Clyde Gillis up to Al Hennessey's office on the fifth floor. Outside, a gloomy sky had overtaken the early morning sun. It matched his mood. Drafting the indictment, which the grand jury had rubber-stamped, had been painful. With each line, he had more and more doubts as to whether Gillis had in fact killed Winthrop. There was nothing specific he could point to, just his instinct as a prosecutor. Still he plowed on, like a good soldier, for all the considerations he had weighed in his mind in Slater's office on Monday morning, but feeling antsy all the while.

The moment Ben walked into his office, Hennessey barked at Liz, "Hold all my calls."

"Except if Jim Slater calls from the White House," Ben shot back.

Ben's quip infuriated Hennessey. "Jesus, you got an attitude."

"I think we should be lawyers, not political hacks."

Hennessey scowled. He was getting tired of Ben's pious carping. They weren't operating in an independent sphere. They were part of the government. "Life's never that easy for prosecutors. We work for the President, remember?"

"Yeah, but who elected Jim Slater?"

Hennessey wanted to give Ben a tongue-lashing, yet right now there was a more important matter than that. "I assume that you're ready to file against Gillis on the Winthrop murder," Hennessey said.

Without responding, Ben handed him a copy of the indictment charging Gillis with first-degree murder and seeking the death penalty.

Hennessey sat down at his desk and read it slowly. Hoping that the weakness in their case, the inability to locate Nesbitt, would be obvious from the document, Ben waited until Hennessey was finished to make one more try. "I don't think we should file it," Ben said. "If we can't produce George Nesbitt at trial, Jennifer and the press will tear us apart."

Hennessey tapped his fingers nervously on his desk. He thought once again, as he had repeatedly since Jim Slater had spoken to him during cocktails at David Kelso's house last evening, about the vacancy on the court of appeals. Slater had said that he wanted to put Hennessey's name on a short list for the appointment. "And by the way, I assume that indictment will be filed by four tomorrow afternoon." Hennessey could practically see himself in judge's black robes. He wasn't going to risk losing that prize over the Clyde Gillis case.

"That's not an option," Hennessey said flatly. He gave Ben a hard stare. "This indictment's going to be filed. I hate to put it this way, but if you can't live with that, you'll have to resign from the office. It's that simple."

From Hennessey's cold tone, Ben knew that further discussion was useless. He wasn't willing to give up his job over this issue. Even after the indictment was filed, he told himself, he could manage the case so Gillis wouldn't be railroaded. Annoyed, he watched Hennessey remove a gold-plated pen from the desk holder and add his signature above Ben's with a flourish. Even the way Hennessey signed his name annoyed Ben. Then Hennessey snatched the phone from its cradle and called Malcolm Wyatt, the chief judge on the district court.

"Malcolm," Hennessey said, "we're filing charges

against Clyde Gillis for the murder of the secretary of state. In the interest of avoiding a media circus, I think this case justifies a special assignment. You wouldn't want a fiasco like the O.J. trial in your court. Would you?"

There was a long pause. Ben knew what was running through Wyatt's mind. The district court had a lottery system for assigning judges to cases, and the chief was always reluctant to depart from that procedure.

Wyatt said something Ben couldn't hear. Then Hennessey responded, "How about Judge Hogan?"

Astounded, Ben raised his eyebrows. Lucille "Hang 'Em High" Hogan was viewed as a prosecutor's dream. She was the toughest sentencer on the court. "The judge from hell," a defense lawyer had once named her. Ben had tried a score of cases before her, and he'd won all of them. He also knew, however, that in those rare instances that she thought an innocent person was being charged, she could turn into a prosecutor's nightmare.

To Ben's surprise, Hennessey must have gotten his request. The next words out of his boss's mouth were, "Will you ask Judge Hogan if she'll set arraignment at ten tomorrow morning? We want to move this case."

Hennessey coughed nervously. "Well, give it a shot."

He put the phone down, cut across his office, and dropped the indictment on Liz's desk. "File it yourself," he said to her. "Give Burton in the public affairs office a copy. He can release it to the press. Also, schedule a press conference in about an hour. I'll be down then."

He turned back to Ben. "You want to join me at the press conference?"

"That's OK," Ben said, keeping his voice neutral. "You can take full credit for this one."

The judicial express train had left the station. God help Clyde Gillis, Ben thought.

He returned to his office and was still brooding

about the case an hour later when the phone rang. It was Ed Fulton.

"Now that you've filed," Fulton said. "I want to apologize for how I've been acting, and turn over a new leaf."

Ben's suspicions were immediately raised. "What prompted this, hotshot?"

"You've got a lot of experience," Fulton said, as pleasant as could be. "I want to learn from you when you get the case ready for trial. I won't get in your way. I promise."

Ben shook his head in disbelief. He couldn't figure this kid out. "And you'll stop behaving like such an asshole?"

Across the phone line, Ben heard Ed muttering with anger. "Yeah, and you'll stop calling me hotshot?"

Ben didn't really want to give that one up, but he said, "It's a deal."

"Good, then how's about coming out to the house with me for dinner tonight? My wife Theo's a great cook."

The offer surprised Ben, and he reluctantly agreed. As long as he had to work with Fulton, maybe they could find a way to be decent to each other.

"I'll swing by and pick you up at seven," Fulton said.

Ben watched Al Hennessey's press conference on the television set in his office with a sullen expression. Hennessey was smart. He was sticking to the indictment, not giving their case away. Still, he gave the impression that Clyde Gillis was guilty beyond a shadow of a doubt. Hennessey handled the questions well, making a nice appearance in his neatly pressed gray Oxxford suit. Ben had seen enough labels on Hennessey's jackets to know what he wore. None of the reporters asked about George Nesbitt, but that wouldn't last. Before long, Jennifer would be leaking to the press all of the facts about Winthrop's missing visitor. Ben would be left to pick up the pieces. If the case against Clyde Gillis went south, as Ben expected, Hennessey would be holed up in his office while Ben, in his wrinkled suit, would have to take the heat before the television cameras.

At the conclusion of the press conference, Ben called Jennifer.

"We filed," he said glumly.

"I saw the press conference," she said crisply. "Thanks for the advance notice. Were you that worried about a response by me?"

Ben sighed, wishing he could tell her it wasn't his idea. "You know how these things go."

"Only too well when you're involved."

Her dig burned him. In a flat voice he informed her, "Judge Hogan has the case."

"Don't tell me you guys let it go on the wheel and I got an unlucky draw."

Ben didn't say anything. He didn't want to lie to her.

"Thanks at least for that," she said.

"The judge wants to do arraignment tomorrow at ten. Can you be ready?"

"It doesn't take long to prepare for saying 'not guilty.'"

She was being hostile, and he didn't want that. He had called to see if she'd consider a deal. "Look, Jennifer, I think we should talk about the case."

"Why?"

"I want to talk in person. Can you come over here?"

"Nope. Neutral territory only."

"How about the Old Ebbitt Grill in thirty minutes?"

For a moment, the professional voice softened. The restaurant, the scene of their first meal together, had been a favorite meeting place of theirs for drinks after a long day. "You still a regular there?" she asked.

Ben's answer was gentler as well. "I'm not much different from the guy you used to know."

"Yeah, that's the problem. Oh, and I'll buy my own drink." She wasn't being nasty or unpleasant. It was a simple reaffirmation of a message she had delivered to him after they were a couple—we're equals, Ben; don't try to control me.

He laughed. At least that part about her hadn't changed. "Heck, you can buy mine as well."

Ben got to the restaurant before Jennifer, and he was seated in a corner booth sipping a beer when she walked in, swinging a briefcase in her hand. It had been five years since he had last seen her. As he watched her approach, he realized that she was even more strikingly beautiful than he remembered. Her facial features were perfectly sculpted. She had lost none of her grace and elegance.

A waiter rushed over. Jennifer asked him for a club soda. "I'm working tonight," she informed Ben.

"You look good," he said.

He had not intended to make this comment. It just came out. She smiled, knowing it was an instinctive reaction. That pleased her.

As the waiter placed the drink in front of her, she took a sip to cover her momentary confusion. "You wanted to talk about Clyde Gillis?" she said.

To his regret, he saw the gates close. "Yeah. Listen, suppose I could eliminate the death penalty. Would you be willing to plead him to murder one?"

"Sorry, Ben. No way," she said firmly. "Clyde Gillis didn't do it."

He hesitated, thinking of another angle. "I doubt if I could ever get approval, but suppose, just suppose, we were willing to drop down to murder two?"

Jennifer kept her face deadpan, but inside she was tingling with excitement. She knew Ben so well. He was giving a lot away. The self-confident expression was a mask he put on for all meetings with defense counsel, but his words were signaling that he knew his case had serious problems. If it didn't, he would never have made the offer she had just heard. Later, when Gillis came around, they could discuss a possible deal. She was certain that anything Ben offered now would remain on the table.

A good-looking blonde dressed in a short black miniskirt and a scoop-neck blue sweater came into the restaurant and sat down at the bar. Ben followed the sway of her sensual body with his eyes. Subtly, he thought, but not subtly enough.

"You haven't changed at all," Jennifer said, startled at the sudden flash of jealousy she felt.

Ben saw it too, and he seized it as the opening he had been looking for. "You know, you never gave me a chance to explain. Would you like to know what really happened when I went to California?"

"I don't want to talk about it." She couldn't afford to be distracted. Not now. Clyde Gillis's life was on the line. "But I do have a counterproposal."

"What's that?"

She ignored his hopeful face. "We do our best to forget our past, and we behave like two professionals who have difficult jobs. We cut the sarcasm and wise-guy comments. We behave civilly to each other. How's that?"

Maybe he had been too eager to explain about California. "I think that's a great idea, as long as I get to call you Jenny again."

She smiled. "Okay, Ben, if it means that much to you."

That was progress. He could explain about California later. For now, though, he had to return to the business at hand. "Tell me what kind of deal you want."

"A dismissal."

Ben leaned back. "Are you serious?"

"I'm dead serious. I'm convinced you've got the wrong man."

He frowned. She knew he couldn't go that far. "Jenny, that's what defense lawyers always tell me about their clients. Can you give me something more to go on?"

"I think that George Nesbitt killed the secretary of state. You guys can't find Nesbitt. So you grabbed the first likely suspect."

Ben bit his lip. "Since we're now behaving like a couple of professionals, I have to tell you, not for attribution, of course, that I'm worried about everything you just said. The trouble is, I can't explain away the evidence we found in Gillis's truck."

"It could have been a plant. But in any event, you can't rely on that evidence as a trial lawyer. I doubt if you'll even be able to get it in. Fruits of a poisonous tree. You guys violated his rights before the search."

He waggled his hand, palm side down. "You might or might not keep it out. Lucille's not fond of motions like that. However, let's put that aside for now. If you really believe that Gillis didn't kill Winthrop, then who did?"

"From everything I've seen, I think that agents of a foreign government hired Nesbitt to kill him."

Ben recoiled in surprise. "You want to tell me which government?"

She was silent for a moment. "Right now I can't say any more on that subject. But I will tell you one other thing. Winthrop was a slimeball. He went to bed with everything in a skirt."

Ben smiled tightly. "And that'll be your defense? It's okay to kill philanderers?"

"Maybe."

"To me, that sounds like Ann Winthrop's line. That's not going to do you any good. But please, can't you tell me about these agents of a foreign government?"

"I'm glad I've got your interest," she said lightly. "I think I'd better wait for Judge Hogan."

Jennifer felt her old attraction to Ben returning, and she wasn't certain she liked that. It was time to go. "See you in the morning." She finished her drink, placed five dollars on the table, and got up to leave the restaurant.

Ben returned her awkward good-bye and watched Jenny walk away. God, she was much more self-confident than he remembered. As the door closed behind her, he noticed the blonde at the bar was giving him the eye. She was alone. The chair on either side of her was empty. He couldn't even remember the last time he had had sex. Between his job and trying to be a good father to Amy, there never seemed to be time for sexual relationships, not even a one-night stand. Being with Jenny had strongly reminded him of this gaping void.

There was no harm in trying. He stood up and walked toward the bar. Then he suddenly remembered he had promised to come to Fulton's house for dinner. "Theo's a great cook," Fulton had said. The guy's wife was probably slaving away in the kitchen now, to serve her lord and master.

Ben didn't want to disappoint her. Five paces before the bar, he cut a sharp right toward the door.

Gwen swung around on her bar stool and watched him walk away. As she had listened to his approaching footsteps, she knew that the fish had taken the bait. There was no hurry. He wasn't going anywhere. She was now in control. She could reel him in later.

Chapter 16

Ed Fulton was waiting for Ben when he returned to his office. "Where were you?" he asked.

Ben had been thinking about Jenny on his walk back from the restaurant, and Fulton's words hit him like a bucket of ice water.

"I didn't realize that I reported to you."

"When it comes to the Gillis case, I'm supposed to be an equal partner."

"You may not believe it, but the Gillis case isn't the only thing I'm working on." Ben caught himself and eased up. "Besides, I thought you and I were supposed to be turning over a new leaf."

Fulton remained as antagonistic as before. "We were, but you should have told me that you had a relationship with Gillis's lawyer. I shouldn't have had to hear it from Sarah Van Buren."

Ben could feel his anger rising. "I have two answers to that. The first is that it was in the past. And the second is that it's none of your fucking business."

Fulton wasn't going to let it go. "But it is my business. If you've still got a thing for her, then we've got a major problem."

"Yeah, we've got a problem, all right," Ben shot back, "because you interrogated Clyde Gillis at his house in a way that violated his constitutional rights. If the judge throws out the evidence we later got from his truck as the fruit of a poisonous tree, then our whole case goes down the drain." Ben made a sucking noise with his mouth. "Just like that."

At this thought Fulton blanched. "Judge Hogan will never do that."

"What makes you so sure? The many cases you've tried before her?"

When Fulton didn't respond, Ben pressed on. "If you're thinking that one of your buddies in the White House can put the fix in with the judge, forget it. Aides to presidents with more clout than Brewster have tried that before, and the iron lady turned them in to the disciplinary panel of the D.C. bar."

Ben thought for an instant of relating what Jenny had told him about agents of a foreign government being involved, but decided to hold it back. She might just be probing and bluffing. No point sending the hotshot into orbit unless it was absolutely necessary.

"Is she any good?" Fulton asked.

"Who?"

"Your old girlfriend."

"Look, asshole—"

"I mean, as a lawyer."

"She's damn good. Watch her. You'll round out your education. Someday when you grow up and get to court yourself, you can use her as a role model." Ben suddenly stopped and smiled disarmingly. "Look, Ed, I don't mean to be nasty. Somehow you just bring it out in me."

The ex-marine's face unclenched a notch. "It's my fault. I shouldn't have busted your chops about Jennifer Moore. Let's head out to my house for dinner."

Jennifer sat in her seat in the last row of the sold-out Dolly Madison Theatre and watched the curtain going up on the premiere of *Beauty Queen of Leenane*. Yet she wasn't focused on the show. She was mapping out in her mind the motions she wanted to file to strengthen her position in the Gillis case, plus the research that she and Louise, the young associate working with her, had to do. She was going to make sure she looked good in front of Bén in that courtroom tomorrow.

For Jennifer, the play couldn't end soon enough, but she refused to leave early. She had come for Ann, who was standing behind Jennifer with her back to the door, her eyes riveted on the stage. She would stay until her friend was ready to go home. Then she would return to the law firm for several more hours of work.

Mercifully, the play, performed without an intermission, was short. Jennifer jumped to her feet to join the rest of the audience in the standing ovation that was typical in Washington, regardless of how good the performance was.

"They really liked it," Jennifer said to Ann a few minutes later when they stopped at a bar next door for a glass of champagne—their traditional drink when one of Ann's shows opened.

"Linda still isn't playing the part right," Ann said with a snarl.

"She was a lot better than Saturday."

Ann pressed her lips together. "Del knew I was right. He could have shaped her up, but he didn't. He wanted to show me who's the creative boss."

"You really think that?"

"I know it." She ordered a second glass of champagne. "You, too, Jenny?"

"No. I'm okay."

"You going back to work tonight?"

"Unfortunately, yes. Some motions for Clyde Gillis's arraignment tomorrow."

"Of course. I should have remembered." She placed her hand on Jennifer's wrist. "You shouldn't have come tonight."

"I wouldn't have missed it for the world. Besides," she added wryly, "who needs sleep?"

"How are you coming with Clyde's defense?"

Jennifer's thoughts flashed to the meeting with Ben that afternoon. "We're doing fine. Thanks to you and the Chinese connection, I've got something. I'll be able to blow a lot of smoke."

"I gather that you didn't sleep much last night either."

"What do you mean?"

Ann looked worried. "I heard about Marianne Kelso's party."

"Did you hear I misbehaved?"

"Not from Marianne. Jim Slater called me."

Jennifer unconsciously patted her hair. "What'd he want?"

"Oh, he pretended to be calling to see how I was doing after Robert's death. In reality, I think he was digging for intelligence about you."

Jennifer was pleased and flattered. "Really?"

Ann narrowed her eyes. "You sure you want to get involved with him?"

Jennifer could see how genuine Ann's concern for her was. "The truth is, I don't know. I honestly don't know."

"I just don't want you to get hurt."

Jennifer hesitated and then said, "Suppose I told you that I like spending time with him?"

Ann sighed. "I can see why. He has a lot going for him."

"And one very big negative."

"You said it. Not me."

Ed Fulton lived in a comfortable two-story colonial just off Western Avenue on the D.C. side of Chevy Chase, close to Rock Creek Park. He didn't get this house on his salary, Ben thought. There's got to be some family money. The trees towering over the house had shed a blanket of leaves that covered the yard. A large deer with antlers cut across the road, startling Ben.

Fulton smiled. "We see them all the time."

Ben expected Fulton's wife to be a small, mousy-looking woman who saw herself as an appendage of her hard-driving, ambitious husband. Instead, Theo-

dora was a tall, striking brunette with haunting chest-
nut eyes and magnificent clear skin with a touch of
olive that told of her Mediterranean roots. Wearing a
navy skirt and a powder-blue sweater that was flattering on her full-bosomed figure, she had a clean,
fresh look, as if she had just stepped out of the
shower. Ben smelled the scent of a luxurious perfume
when she shook his hand at the door. "I'm always
pleased to meet one of Eddie's colleagues," she said,
sounding as if she meant it.

The children, whom Fulton had told Ben about,
were a boy, five, and a girl, three. The instant the
door closed they raced away from the nanny, a Latina
woman in her twenties, and greeted their father with
wild shouts and cries until he took turns picking them
up. Proud of his children, Fulton introduced them to
Ben, then said, "You have to excuse me. I gotta get
these guys to bed." With Kirstin over his shoulder,
Kevin tugging on his hand, and the nanny following
behind, Fulton made his way up the stairs.

Without asking what he wanted, Theo handed Ben
a glass of sparkling wine. "Spumante," she said, "from
the lake country of northern Italy. Make yourself at
home. I have to do a couple of things for dinner."

Ben wandered into the den, paneled in a rich
cherry, and gazed at the pictures and plaques that
lined the walls. One wall was devoted to Theo's family
and the other to Ed. The first picture that caught
Ben's eye was Theo in a graduation cap and gown
surrounded by her parents and holding up a diploma
from the University of Michigan that read CUM LAUDE.
Her mother's face closely resembled Theo's.

On the left was a picture of her father in a tuxedo
and shaking hands with President Brewster. They were
standing at the podium of what must have been a
Detroit political fund-raiser, from the sign in the background. The handwritten inscription read, *Without
your help, Carl, I would never have carried Michigan.*
Above that picture was one of her father standing in
front of a factory building, dressed in a suit and tie

and wearing a hard hat. A little girl, who must have been Theo, with a hard hat covering her eyes, was holding on to his hand. In the background the sign on the building read ERICSON FASTENER COMPANY. And above that was a photo of Theo holding a gavel and sitting at a table with a sign that said ALPHA PHI SORORITY.

Wanting to understand Fulton better, Ben moved to the other wall. There were the pictures he expected to see, namely Fulton with the chief justice of the Supreme Court, for whom he had clerked; with Jim Slater; and finally with President Brewster and an inscription that read *To Ed, in appreciation for all of your fine work.* Ben expected to see all of those photographs, as well as Fulton's diplomas from college and law school—summa cum laude. They were par for the course on a Washington wall. What Ben didn't expect to see was a framed newspaper article from the *Kalamazoo Times* that was captioned, *Third-Generation marine inducted.*

The article recited the fact that Fulton's grandfather, a captain in the marines, had died in the battle of Okinawa. His father, who left his job in a Kalamazoo foundry to enlist in the marines, had died in the highland jungles of Vietnam. Next to that article was a picture of a little boy standing close to a woman with a tear-stained face, dressed shabbily but holding herself with resolute dignity as a marine officer handed her a folded flag. The boy, no doubt little Ed, was saluting the officer.

All of these items reinforced Ben's view of Fulton— from a modest background, but very bright, hardworking, and ambitious to the point of being driven. He had become tremendously successful for his age, and he was now on a classic Washington PET—Power Ego Trip.

Ben became aware of the scent of perfume. He wheeled around to find Theo holding a glass of sparkling wine and watching him from the doorway to the den.

"Quite a story, isn't it?" she said. "Eddie was a patriot before it became fashionable."

"That's true," he said easily. "How'd you meet him?"

"Fraternity-sorority mixer my freshman year. His junior. After that night neither of us ever dated anyone else. He was so much different from the Grosse Point boys I'd grown up with. Nobody had ever given him anything. Everything he had, even tuition and expenses, he earned working and with scholarships. He was not only superbright and ambitious, but sensitive and caring. Good to his mother, whom he supported. Even a star pitcher in the IF League. He made me feel special. It was love on the first date, for both of us."

The happy recollection made Ben feel sad. He had always wanted a relationship like that with someone.

"You married, Ben?"

"I was once. She died."

"I'm sorry."

"Thanks. The good news is that I've got a little girl, Amy. A great kid."

"You should bring her out to play with Kirstin and Kevin sometime."

Suddenly there was a pounding on the ceiling above them. Ben looked alarmed, but Theo waved her arm upward and smiled. "Don't worry; they're just jumping around up there. They're good kids, but they're wild when they see Eddie, because he's almost never home. That's why I was delighted when he called to say he was bringing you for dinner. Otherwise, I wouldn't have seen him until midnight."

She said it in a cheerful voice, which surprised Ben. He had expected to hear a tinge of resentment, and he wouldn't have blamed her. This couldn't have been what she had bargained for when she agreed they should stay in Washington after Ed's Supreme Court clerkship. Still, the drift of the discussion made Ben feel uneasy. He changed the subject, pointing to the picture of Theo with her father in front of the factory. "What kind of fasteners did they make?"

"My grandfather started the company," she said with pride. "They didn't make the screws and bolts you buy at a hardware store. In the early days, it was fasteners for automobile frames and parts. Then they shifted to high tech, precision, finely machined and calibrated fasteners for spaceships, airplanes, and other sophisticated uses. Daddy, who's running the company now, sells to Boeing, Lockheed-Martin, Northrop Grumman—all of them. People have been trying to buy him out for years, but he won't give it up."

So that's where the money came from. "I'll bet you have a brother who's in the business."

"Nope. I'm an only child. Since it looked like I was going to be the only one, based on what the doctors said, and I wasn't going to be Ted, the son he wanted, he called me Theo. He still figures that one day we'll come back to Detroit, that Eddie will practice law, and I'll run the business."

"Not much chance of that, is there?"

She nodded. "Eddie's always had a rapport with Daddy, but Detroit's not in the cards. Not the way Eddie's been making a name for himself here."

There were several responses that Ben wanted to make to that comment, but he decided they were all insulting to his host, and he didn't want to do that as a guest in the house. He took a sip of his drink, trying to decide how to respond. At that moment, Fulton appeared behind Theo and said, "Let's eat, guys."

They sat down at the table, set with beautiful blue and white Limoges china and Baccarat crystal. Fulton and Theo sat across from each other with Ben between them. Fulton bowed his head and said, "We thank you, dear Lord, for all of the generous bounty that you have provided for us."

Theo got up and returned carrying homemade ravioli stuffed with wild mushrooms, while Fulton poured a deep red wine.

Ben was blown away by the ravioli, which was simply the best pasta he had ever eaten. He asked Theo, "You made this yourself?"

"From scratch, Ben. I take it that you like it?"

"Like it? I love it. Where'd you ever learn to cook?"

"Well, I had a long year after graduation from college and before we got married while Eddie was stationed in Macedonia on a peacekeeping mission. So I went back to the land of my mother's family, in a hill town of Tuscany called Rada. There I took several cooking courses to pass the time between Eddie's leave periods. Then we'd set off for the lake country, or Venice, or Barcelona, depending on how much time we had. When Eddie had only a couple of days, we never left the villa."

Fulton blushed, while Theo had a starry look in her eyes, as if she were longing for those days, when they made love morning, noon, and night.

When Theo got up to clear the pasta and bring on the main course, Ben sipped some wine, which was fabulous. "What are we drinking?" he asked, not that it would have made any difference to him, because he knew nothing about wine.

Fulton shouted to Theo through the swinging door that led to the kitchen, "Ben wants to know what's the wine, hon."

She shouted back, "Tell him it's 1990 Brunello de Montalcino from Altesino."

Fulton winked at Ben and said in a low voice, "You got that?"

Ben nodded. She returned with osso buco in a blue pot, which proved to be spectacular. You're a lucky man, Ben thought.

As they ate, they talked about Europe, with Theo doing most of the talking. Ben, who had never been outside of the United States, listened eagerly. They had traveled widely in Italy, Switzerland, France, and Spain. Next to Tuscany, Theo loved northern Italy and the small towns in Provence.

Midway through the osso buco, she pointed to the credenza and a second unopened bottle of the Barello, or whatever it was—Ben couldn't remember—and said, "Eddie, why don't you open that other one?"

Fulton dutifully complied and refilled their glasses, although he was drinking very little himself. Ben, who didn't usually drink wine at dinner, was enjoying this one, keeping pace with Theo.

Following the main course, Theo disappeared into the kitchen for several minutes. Ben thought he heard a hand beater scraping against a metal bowl. It was a good guess. Desert was zabaglione spiked with Frangelico and accompanied by Vin Santi and homemade biscotti.

When they had finished, she asked Ben, "How about some espresso?"

She probably made great espresso as well. "Sounds like the perfect way to end a perfect meal."

She was heading back into the kitchen when the phone rang. "I'll bet I know who that is," she said, winking at Ben. "Listen, Eddie, why don't I answer and tell Mr. Slater that you decided to take the evening off?"

Fulton glared at her and raced into the kitchen to grab the phone before she could.

"You can go into the den," Theo said to Ben. "I'll bring your espresso."

At this point, sensing the marital tension that Slater's calls created, Ben would have preferred to go home. The problem was that Theo had worked so hard. He couldn't be rude to her. All of that was true, but he had to admit there was something else keeping him. She was a very foxy lady. In his current horny state he enjoyed looking at her and talking with her. "Sure. Sounds good," he said.

A couple of minutes later, she joined him in the den carrying two cups of espresso. "Welcome to the Fulton household," she said, sounding amused rather than bitter. She sat down on the sofa. "It's like this every night Eddie manages to make it home."

Ben found himself in the odd position of defending Fulton. "He's in a tough position, working for someone as demanding as Jim Slater."

She laughed. "Eddie loves every minute of it. Carrying the great man's briefcase and doing his bidding. He'll do anything to get a higher mark from Jim Slater. Anything at all."

The conversation struck Ben as very odd. She didn't sound as if she resented her husband and Slater. Was it that her Eddie was getting ahead in Washington? Ben ran with that idea. "He's just starting out. He wants to succeed."

"And he's doing a good job at it, though there's a price to pay."

Ben felt awkward. He didn't know what to say.

Realizing this, she added, "I shouldn't be saying these things to a stranger, but it's funny. I feel as if I can talk to you."

Ben smiled. "I sometimes have that effect on people. I guess it comes from questioning witnesses all the time."

She drained her espresso and put her feet up on the sofa under her, letting her skirt ride up high on her thighs. She wasn't wearing panty hose, and Ben could see the pale yellow of her bikini panties and a little of her dark brown bush peeking out on the edges. It was a provocative position and she knew it. She watched him watching her and smiled at him. I'd better get out of here, Ben thought.

She resumed talking as if nothing had happened. "Eddie didn't used to be like he is now. When I first met him in college, he was sensitive and caring. Ambitious but not driven to succeed at any cost. If he had been that way, I would never have married him."

Ben had seen it happen again and again. Young men and women like Fulton came to the nation's capital in droves at the beginning of every new administration. Power for them was the ultimate aphrodisiac, to become players in Washington. Very few succeeded. And those who did often surrendered a part of themselves in a Faustian bargain. He tried to sound constructive. "Washington sometimes does that to people. It puts them over the edge. They get caught up in making it big here." He shrugged. "Sometimes they do."

"Meaning that usually they don't."

As Ben was framing his response, Fulton reappeared.

"My master returns," she said, pulling down her skirt and lowering her feet to the floor.

Ben had had enough of both of them. This could get ugly. He stood up, holding his hands in front of his pants to cover the bulge. Theo noticed it with an amused expression, but Fulton was oblivious. "I'd better be going. Let me call a cab."

"Don't be silly. I'll drive you home," Fulton said. "Besides, I've got to go back to the office now. You're on the way."

At the door, Theo gave Ben each of her cheeks for a perfunctory farewell kiss, European style, and said, "Ciao," then quickly disappeared.

"Sorry to leave you alone so long with Theo," Fulton said as he started the engine. "I hope she didn't bore you to tears."

"No apologies are necessary. She's good company." A lot more fun to be with than you are, Ben thought.

"I'm sure she's plenty pissed at me," he said, backing out of the driveway, "but how can I not take a call from Mr. Slater? How can I not go back to the office and prepare the things he needs first thing in the morning?"

Fulton was very happy, Ben decided, that the call had come. It showed how important he was. "You have to do what you have to do."

"Part of the phone call dealt with you," Fulton told Ben.

Ben was thinking Fulton was nuts to leave his sexy wife in that lonely house. Still, he asked, "Oh, and what did your fearless leader have to say about me?"

"I gave him a status report on the Gillis case. He

was pleased that you've got an early arraignment and that Hogan's the judge. He's met her a few times. Wants to know if he can do anything to help."

"Tell him," he snapped, "the last thing I want is White House interference." He didn't have to behave like a good guest any longer. "Tell him to stay out of my way so I can get the case ready for trial."

Fulton was shocked. "Oh, I'd never talk to Mr. Slater that way."

"Well, you'd be doing him a favor if you did."

"It's a matter of respect and loyalty. I mean, how I talk to somebody like Mr. Slater."

"Jesus, you were in the marines too long." It was an unkind comment, knowing what had happened to Fulton's father and grandfather, but Ben didn't care.

Fulton clutched the steering wheel tightly to control his anger. "You obviously don't believe in serving your country."

Ben could feel his blood pressure rising as well. "I've spent my whole career in public service. I've had lots of high-paying offers from law firms, but I've turned them down."

"So why do you keep doing what you're doing?"

"It's a long story."

"We have time until we drop you off."

"We do," Ben said. He closed his eyes, not wanting to talk to Fulton, to Theo, or to anyone else for the rest of the night. "But we're not going to talk about it."

Amy was sleeping peacefully when Ben got home. He sat in the rocker in her darkened room and watched her. "So why do you keep doing what you're doing?" Fulton had asked him in the car.

It was a story he had told very few people—only Jenny and Nan. When the tragedy occurred, he was too young to comprehend it. Years later, when he had been a student at Berkeley, he had been obsessed with finding out what had happened to his father. Doggedly, he had pursued the events of more than a decade earlier, until he had pieced the story together from newspaper articles and interviews.

In the late fifties, when he was born, it had been a time of great growth in San Francisco. With limited land available, city council approvals for building projects were critical. With what was at stake, it was perhaps inevitable that there should be widescale corruption in the city government. Still, what Ben's father, Morris Hartwell, a young assistant district attorney, found exceeded what anyone had thought. Builders and developers were making massive payoffs into a slush fund. The open question was which city officials had masterminded this scheme and who were its beneficiaries. The public and the newspapers were clamoring for an end to the corruption and punishment for wrongdoers. Morris Hartwell, an ambitious young prosecutor, followed a paper trail that led him to Curt Richardson, a city council member who was clearly living well beyond his public salary. Following a sensational, headline-grabbing trial, Morris got his conviction and Richardson went to jail for twenty years. After a year Richardson was stabbed to death in the prison exercise yard. Then additional facts came out about the former councilman's life and his sources of income from a private investment in a Tahoe gambling casino. As Morris kept digging, he realized that Richardson had been set up with false evidence, and the young prosecutor had been duped by the false trail. Slowly, without any of the press fanfare that accompanied the earlier case, he began building a case against two other city councilmen. He was on the verge of taking his new evidence to a grand jury when a truck smashed head-on into his Ford Fairlane on a fog-shrouded road outside of the city. Morris and his wife, Nell, were killed instantly. Their five-year-old son, Ben, was at home with a baby-sitter at the time.

Ben was raised by Muriel and Stanley Walton. Stanley was a friend and colleague of Ben's father in the DA's office. He concluded that Morris's accident was a homicide, but he lacked the courage to pick up the torch. So he raised Morris Hartwell's son instead. The Waltons had a daughter, Terry, about Ben's age. They took him into their house, raising him as if he were Terry's brother, although their relationship became much more complex once they began dating as students at Berkeley.

Once Ben pieced the story together, he vowed that he would spend his life prosecuting the corrupt, particularly where a homicide or public officials were involved. That commitment led him to law school and then to the prosecutor's office in Washington. With each conviction, he felt he was avenging the wrong that had been done to his father and to him.

As the awful memories faded, Ben got up from the rocker and kissed the sleeping Amy gently. She turned over in her bed, pulled the thumb out of her mouth, and said, "I love you, Daddy."

"I love you too, honey," he whispered.

"Your package from Japan has arrived, Master Chen," the director's secretary said.

"Have them bring it up to my office," Chen replied, tingling with excitement. When the delivery man tossed the cardboard box on the floor, Chen wanted to scream, "Careful or we'll all be blown sky-high!" But he held his tongue and bit his lower lip.

That evening, Chen pretended to be working at his desk until the factory workers had gone home and the office was deserted. Then he reached into the closet in his office and pulled out the empty brown leather suitcase he had brought in last week. It was precisely the right size to hold the package from Alpha Industries.

The contents were all plastic. Nothing metal. Still, the suitcase was heavy with the package inside. Chen began perspiring as he lugged it down three flights of stairs and two blocks until he found a taxi.

Back in his room at the Shangri-La Hotel, Chen closed the curtains. After putting out the DO NOT DISTURB sign, he threw the dead bolt on the door and hooked the chain for good measure.

Carefully, he slit open the top of the cardboard box, using a penknife he had in his shaving kit. With his engineer's training, he inspected the contents packed in bubble wrap. He studied the directions and examined each part. Sherman had been right: For a trained engineer like Chen, assembling it would be a piece of cake. Satisfied that he would be able to put it together and get out fast, he repacked everything as it had been in the box, then returned it to the suitcase. Tomorrow he would call in sick. He had no intention of leaving the hotel room until he received the signal from Sherman.

Chapter 17

While munching on a bagel with strong black coffee, Jennifer glanced at the front page of the morning *Washington Post* to check the coverage of the Clyde Gillis case. There was a factual article about the charges that had been filed and this morning's arraignment. Nothing inflammatory from Hennessey or Ben.

At least Ben's keeping his mouth shut and not trying to prejudice prospective jurors, she thought with relief. God, she felt tired. She had been at the office until three A.M. doing legal research and drafting motions for Clyde Gillis. After only three hours of sleep she was gulping down coffee to sharpen her mind. She paused to rub her tired eyes. When she opened them and turned back to the newspaper, she saw a news analysis by Jim Revere, a *Post* staff writer, beginning in the bottom center of the front page, which focused on the question of who had the greatest influence on the President now that his friend and closest confidant was dead.

There's a logjam on the White House switchboard these days because of the huge number of incoming calls for Jim Slater. The trend that began with Slater's shift from treasury to the White House has snowballed with Robert Winthrop's death. Everyone in official Washington now realizes that the former New York investment banker is the second most powerful man in America.

Senator Rick Turner of Michigan said, "We all know how important Jim is. He's the one making the trains run now, putting it all together, the politics, the strategy on issues and policy, and the key appointments. He's the focal point of this administration."

Though Slater has been in Washington only three years, he has already created a mighty cone of influence. "Access to the President runs through Slater's office. And you'd better not try an end run," one senior official said, "or you'll be banished to political Siberia for the next year—and the four after that if Slater manages to engineer a reelection for President Brewster."

It was a heady thought for Jennifer to realize that "the second most powerful man in America" was courting her.

Everything was suddenly happening too fast. She was in the middle of the most important case of her life. Ben was back. He had been so sharp with her sometimes, but she realized that was only a defensive response on his part because that was how she had begun with him on the telephone Sunday night. He made it clear at the Old Ebbitt Grill that if she changed her approach and softened, he'd do the same in a minute. He had never forgotten what they'd had together any more than she had. But did she want Ben again? More than the intriguing, exciting Jim Slater?

Ben snapped the seat belt tight against Amy's lap in the front seat of his Volvo wagon, closed the door, and strode quickly around the back of the car to the driver's side. Since it was Thursday morning, they were on their way to Dr. Van Holland's office for Amy's weekly eight-o'clock appointment with the child psychiatrist. Even if Van Holland was on time, it would be tight to deliver her to preschool after the session and make it to court for Clyde Gillis's ten-o'clock arraignment. Ben was willing to risk it, though. He couldn't let her miss an appointment, and he couldn't ask Elana to take Amy because the doctor required at least one parent to come. Beyond all that, Ben knew that it was important for him to talk with Amy afterward, on the ride to preschool, about what had happened with the doctor.

He started the car and pulled away from the curb, deep in thought about whether these sessions really did Amy any good. He didn't see the blue Chevy that pulled out of a parking space behind him. It followed the Volvo at a steady fifty-yard distance.

Glancing over at Amy, he saw her clutching the old battered yellow metal lunch box with Barbie on the front. The damned thing was rusty on the corners, and he decided to make one more try at getting rid of it. "Saturday I'll buy you a new lunch box," he said.

She held it tightly against her chest. "No, Daddy. I like this one."

"But it's old, honey. The corners are sharp. You could get cut."

"Mommy bought me this lunch box. I want to keep it."

"But they have beautiful—"

"No, Daddy. I want this one."

He sighed and gave up. At Wisconsin Avenue, he turned right, moving into the heavy morning traffic of one of the main north-south corridors in Washington.

In the Chevy, Gwen lost sight of Ben's car, but she didn't care. Early this morning she had hooked to the underside of the Volvo's rear bumper the transmitter of a sophisticated homing device that Big Bob had sold her yesterday. The miniscreen on her car seat showed precisely where he was.

An hour later, when Ben pulled out of the parking garage of the Foxhall Medical Center on New Mexico Avenue, Gwen was waiting for him in the Chevy. She gave him a head start of fifty yards before pulling in behind him.

In front of the preschool, she watched him kiss Amy and then wait while the child scrambled into the small redbrick building with the yellow Barbie lunch box in her hand and a tiny backpack over her shoulders. Her hair was longer, but the child looked just like the picture Gwen had been given yesterday at the Lincoln Memorial. Through a pair of binoculars, she studied the girl's face while Ben kissed her good-bye, committing it to memory. Now she could easily pick Amy out of a crowd of children on a playground through a rifle scope.

Ambassador Liu walked diagonally across Franklin Square from the corner of 13th and K, in downtown Washington, carrying a Starbucks bag. Across the square, he saw a maroon Camry parked and a man with a bandage on his face behind the wheel.

The park service was late in raking this year, and the grass was strewn with leaves. As Liu walked, pigeons scattered from the path. He sat down on a bench near the center of the square and removed a cup of coffee from the bag. As he sipped it, he tried not to notice the man with the bandage approaching. Liu waited until he was seated on the bench to look around. No one was within listening range.

"You wanted to see me," the man said.

"After thinking about it, I'm worried that she may have made copies of the video."

"You want me to go back and visit her again?" the man said, relishing the chance of working over that bitch Ann Winthrop. Maybe he'd even get lucky and find that good-looking piece from the parking lot in the house as well. He became aroused just thinking about what he'd do to her.

Sensing his reaction, Liu said, "I just want you to get all the other copies of the video. You can't harm her or anyone with her, and don't take anything from her house."

When the man didn't respond, Liu added, "The fee's the same as before. There's twenty-five percent

in cash in the Starbucks bag. The rest you'll get when
the job's done. But I won't pay you if anybody gets
hurt. Is that clear?''

Grumbling, the man nodded.

Liu knew he had made a mistake not considering
copies of the video earlier. What had turned him in
this direction was the relative ease with which Ann
had surrendered the one she had. He was convinced
that scene had been staged, that Ann had at least one
more copy stashed somewhere, and he had to get back
all of the copies. If his government ever found out
that he had done this to Winthrop on his own, he
would be brought home to Beijing and summarily exe-
cuted. But it was imperative that Ann not be injured.
The Clyde Gillis prosecution was roaring along. He
didn't want to do anything to sidetrack it.

There was a carnival atmosphere, the usual Washington media feeding frenzy, on Constitution Avenue
in front of the U.S. Courthouse when Jennifer arrived
at nine-thirty. The TV cameras were already disgorg-
ing the footage they had just shot of Clyde Gillis
entering the courthouse through a side entrance. Run-
ners were standing by to get it to the network studios
ASAP. Those print reporters who hadn't received an
entrance pass in the day's press lottery were kibitzing
on the sidewalk, smoking cigarettes and drinking luke-
warm coffee. None of them had the faintest idea that
Jennifer had anything to do with the case, and she
walked undisturbed into the six-story boxlike struc-
ture, briefcase in hand. Her anonymity would end with
this morning's hearing.

In the courtroom, Jennifer set up her papers at
the defendants' counsel table and closed her eyes
for a minute, thinking about how this was likely to
play out. When she opened them, she found the
prosecution table was still empty. What had happened to Ben?

Her surprise became Judge Hogan's dismay when
the judge took the bench and Ben still hadn't arrived.

"Why don't you move to dismiss for failure to prosecute, Miss Moore?" the judge said facetiously.

Before Jennifer could respond, Ben raced into the courtroom.

"Ah, Mr. Hartwell," Judge Hogan greeted him. "I see that you decided to honor us with your presence this morning."

There were titters of laughter in the packed courtroom, which Ed Fulton, seated in the last row, didn't appreciate in the slightest.

Cutting through the center aisle in the gallery, Ben glanced up at the bench and the judge's pale white face, with its black half-moon glasses, thin, narrow lips, and thick mop of gray hair. He gave her a wry smile. "I'm sorry, Your Honor." He had tried too many cases before Judge Hogan to be intimidated by her grandstanding manner. Besides, even in a large city court system like Washington's, a camaraderie existed between judges and the prosecutors who appeared before them regularly.

Judge Hogan glanced over to her right. "Bailiff, get the defendant."

They brought in Clyde Gillis, dressed in prison blues, a tired-looking, beaten-down shell of the man who had raked leaves at the Winthrop's house only five days ago. Jennifer moved forward to the lectern to stand beside her client. Her courtroom manner, Ben decided, was far more polished than he remembered. She displayed greater self-assurance as she touched her honey-blond hair, which was tied back tightly, waiting for Judge Hogan to address a question to her.

"Does the defendant waive the reading of the charges?" the judge asked.

"Yes, Your Honor," Jennifer said.

"And how does the defendant plead?"

"Not guilty," Jennifer replied firmly. Then she held her breath. Even this morning Gillis had refused to talk to her. She had no idea what was running through his mind. She just hoped that he didn't speak up now and challenge her plea. Happily, he didn't.

The judge looked down at her calendar. "Trial thirty days from today, Friday, December seventeenth," she said sharply, giving the defendant the absolute minimum time.

"Your Honor," Jennifer replied, "this is a complex case. I was just recently brought in. I really think—"

"How much time would you like?"

"I need sixty days at least."

"That's too long. I'll give you until January third. That's it. No more delays. Don't even consider asking for a further extension."

"I understand, Your Honor."

The judge looked at Ben. "What about bail? What's the position of the United States?"

Ben didn't hear the question. He was still thinking about the trial date. He had made reservations yesterday to fly with Amy to Aspen on the twenty-third of December. If this case went to trial on January third, then—

"Mr. Hartwell," the judge snapped, "are you with us?"

Embarrassed, Ben jumped to his feet. "Sorry, Your Honor."

"Let the record reflect Mr. Hartwell is still alive."

There was laughter in the courtroom.

"Now, would you care to enlighten us about the position of the United States on bail? That's when the defendant goes free until trial."

More laughter.

Ben's face turned red with embarrassment. He recovered quickly, though. "It would be highly inappropriate to let the defendant out under any circumstances. It's a capital crime. He's only lived in this community a short while. The whole world is watching this case. We can't run the risk of having the defendant skip out."

"Miss Moore, what's your position?"

"Mr. Gillis has no prior arrests. A perfectly clean record. He's the sole source of support for a wife and four young children—one of whom is quite ill and needs costly treatments. If you keep him locked up and he can't work, it will be impossible for them to survive."

Jennifer's plea made the judge stop and think. She took off her glasses and held them in her hand, looking pensive. "So what do you want?"

"Release him on his own recognizance."

The judge was willing to consider a reasonable request, but this was too much. "Are you serious?"

Jennifer knew from the sound of her voice where the judge was headed. Lacking a reasonable compromise, Jennifer was stuck. "Yes, Your Honor, and I believe that under the law with no prior arrests—"

Judge Hogan interrupted, "Bail denied."

"But, Your Honor—"

"Next, pretrial motions. Will you have any, Miss Moore?"

"Yes, Your Honor. We have serious constitutional violations. For the first interrogation of the defendant, he was placed under house arrest without being apprised of any of his rights. Facts were coerced from the defendant. He wasn't informed of his right to counsel. All of the government's evidence is the fruit of that poisonous tree. I'll be moving to dismiss."

"Mr. Hartwell, what do you have to say about this?"

"It's ridiculous. We—"

"That's what I thought you'd say. File your motion in one week, Miss Moore," the judge said sharply. "Response due four days later. I'll hear it in two weeks. What about discovery, Miss Moore? I assume you'll want some."

Jennifer responded to the no-nonsense judge, "I'll have my motion in one week."

"We'll give her the stuff a week later and file any opposition then," Ben said.

"Anything else?" Judge Hogan asked.

"No, Your Honor," Ben and Jennifer said in unison.

"This court is now adjourned."

The bailiff led Clyde Gillis out through a side door. Judge Hogan followed minutes later. That was the signal for the reporters to descend on Ben and Jennifer like an avalanche. Ben spotted Art Campbell in the back of the courtroom, but Ben couldn't get through the mob of reporters to talk to him. Then Campbell was gone.

None of the reporters paid any attention to the tall, broad-shouldered black woman sitting in the front row, dressed in a navy blue suit that she wore to church on Sundays. Standing up, Lucinda Gillis suddenly felt light-headed. Instinctively, she reached her hand out to her daughters Naomi and Ruth, but to no avail. She fainted dead away. Mercifully, her head landed on the bench rather than the hard stone floor.

As soon as she collapsed, Jennifer raced over. She told Ruth to go to the ladies' room and get paper towels dipped in cold water. Jennifer brought Lucinda around quickly, and then led her out of the courtroom accompanied by her four children. Tears were streaming down all of their faces. As Jennifer helped them into a cab and paid the driver, she said to Lucinda, "Don't worry. I'm going to get Clyde out of this."

"It's a crime," Lucinda said. "They've got the wrong man."

Lucinda was home ten minutes when the telephone rang. "It's for you, Mama," Ruth said. "Some woman."

"I don't want to talk to anyone."

"I told her that. She said she has to talk to you. It's important, and it's about Daddy."

With an effort, Lucinda dragged herself from the bed, where she had been trying to rest. All she could do was think about Clyde. He didn't kill anybody. This was all some white man's doing; she was sure of it. But Clyde would get the white man's justice. And what about her and the kids? How would they ever manage without him? She would never go on welfare. She was too proud for that.

She staggered to the telephone.

"I think I can help you," the woman said.

Lucinda was immediately wary. Was this a trick, or a joke? "Who are you?"

"We have to talk in person."

Lucinda wasn't budging. "Don't fool with me."

"I'm not fooling with you, I promise."

"How can you help me?"

"The people I work for know that Clyde didn't kill Winthrop. That he was framed with phony evidence. He's being used to take the fall for some powerful people."

That made sense to Lucinda. "But what can you do about it?"

"There's a way to fix it so it goes easy on Clyde and your family's taken care of."

Clyde had looked so dreadful in court that Lucinda was willing to at least listen. "Yeah, how are you going to do that?" she asked.

"I can't tell you over the phone. Take the red line Metro to the Van Ness station. Then take the exit for the west side of Connecticut Avenue. Ride the escalator to the top. I'll be waiting for you there. And you must come by yourself, or I won't stick around."

Lucinda was torn. She had learned long ago, when men tried to lure her into a car with promises of money, that gifts didn't fall out of the sky. But if powerful people were really involved, she couldn't pass up any chances. Clyde had worked for the secretary of state, after all. "How will I know you?" Lucinda asked.

"You won't," Gwen said, "but I'll know you."

Believing that she was safe after the video had been turned over, Ann had asked Brewster to remove the guards from the front of her house a day after Robert's funeral. Now, as she opened the front door with a bag of groceries in one hand and stepped inside, she was sorry. Right away she detected the scent of a man's cheap cologne, the same odor that she had smelled on Sunday when the intruder was in the house. She turned to bolt, but he had been waiting for her behind the door. Moving fast, he grabbed her around the waist, pulled her back inside the house, and kicked the door shut. When she struggled, he pulled a heavy rope from his pocket and looped it around her body, pressing her arms against her sides. Like a sack of potatoes, he picked her up and tossed her over his shoulder, kicking and screaming, as he carried her upstairs. Her screams didn't bother him. The house was sufficiently isolated so no one could hear her.

Once they reached the master bedroom, he flung her down on a chair in a sitting position. Then he tied her ankles together, sat down on the bed, and removed a gun from his pocket.

There was terror in her eyes. "What do you want?" she asked.

"Is that any way to greet an old friend?"

"If you want money or jewelry, you can have them."

He laughed harshly. "You can't buy your way out of this."

"Then what do you want?"

"I want all of the other copies you made of the video."

"There are none. You got the only one."

He sneered. "You take us for fools."

She wondered who "us" was but didn't ask. Her situation was already dire enough. She couldn't risk saying anything to persuade him that she knew so much that he should kill her, regardless of whether he got the video. "No, I don't. I never made a copy."

He was idly examining his gun. "Are you ready to tell me the truth?"

"I did tell you the truth."

"I'm going to take a little target practice," he said, enjoying himself. "First your right kneecap. Then the left one. After what you did to my face, I won't mind if I miss on the first couple of shots. Eventually, I'll hit the target."

Ann was more scared than she had ever been in

her life. The fear was threatening to shut down her mind. She had to think.

He took a silencer out of his pocket and attached it to the gun, which he pointed at her. Then he pulled his finger away from the gun. He made a motion as if he were pulling the trigger. "Pow. Pow. Last chance."

Ann's brain began working. She had to find a way out of this mess. He'd never have to know Jennifer had a copy of the video.

"Okay, you'll get what you want," she said, sounding reluctant. "There is one other copy, in a bank vault downtown."

He nodded. "That's a start."

"What do you mean, a start?"

"I want all the copies."

Okay, Ann, she told herself. You're in the theater. Be convincing. "That's the only one."

"You're lying."

Her strength and determination were overcoming her fear. "Think about it," she said. "Why would I possibly make more than one copy? It doesn't make sense. I made an insurance copy. I didn't make two insurance copies." When his face didn't show any reaction, she added, "Search the house if you want to."

He nodded, considering her words. To satisfy himself, he got up and went through a couple of her dresser drawers. When he didn't find anything, he said, "All right. You're going to that bank vault now to get me the video."

"Whatever you want."

They drove in his maroon Camry. Repeatedly, he warned her that the loaded gun was in his pocket and he would kill her if she did anything suspicious to get help. She cowered against the door of the car.

They parked in front of the bank on Pennsylvania Avenue. Inside, he walked with her to the vault area and then to a small room, where she extracted the video from the metal box and handed it to him.

She wanted him to leave her in front of the bank, but he insisted on her getting back into the car.

"Please," she said, "you've gotten what you wanted. Leave me alone."

"Get in the car, or I'll kill you."

She spotted a policeman about fifty yards away. For an instant she considered screaming. Then better judgment prevailed. No point to that, she decided. He'd shoot her and then escape.

When he drove into Rock Creek Park, she became frightened again. What did he plan to do with her now? Rape her? Then kill her? She shuddered, imagining the possibilities.

He stopped in a deserted picnic grove. "Give me your purse," he said.

After she complied, he searched inside. Once he found her cell phone, he shoved that into his jacket pocket and returned the purse.

"Get out," he said. He'd be well out of sight by the time she found a car to stop. He wasn't worried about her seeing the license plates of the maroon Camry. It had been stolen in Ohio. The plates were phonies. As a precaution, he'd abandon the car in a deserted area of rural Virginia, where nobody would notice it.

Watching him pull away, Ann breathed a large sigh of relief. Ten minutes later, just as it was starting to rain, she flagged down a cab with a passenger who was willing to help her out when she said she had had a fight with her boyfriend, who had driven off, leaving her in the park.

All the way back, she couldn't stop trembling. She had to call Jennifer as soon as she got home.

Chapter 18

Ben's secretary handed him a white envelope with his name scrawled on the front. "Somebody slid this under the door," she said, puzzled.

Ben tore open the envelope. As he began reading the barely legible handwriting, a stunned look formed on his face.

> Dear Mr. Hartwell:
> I confess to the murder of Robert Winthrop. I killed him just like you said, to get the money. I brought a gun with me on Saturday. I knew where Mr. Winthrop kept money in his house. He surprised me when I was taking the money. So I shot him. I am sorry I did this bad thing. Please tell the judge that I want to change my plea to guilty.

It was signed, *Clyde Gillis.*

Ben read the letter again. Then, deep in thought, he let it drop to his desk. He should be jumping up and down for joy. The case he had never wanted was over. He had another notch in his prosecutor's belt, as Jenny had put it to him on Sunday night. He could go back to the Young investigation full-time. He'd be able to take Amy to Aspen for Christmas. So why wasn't he happy?

Because Clyde Gillis's confession didn't make sense. In all of Ben's experience as a prosecutor, no defendant had confessed right after entering a not-guilty plea. And no defendant represented by counsel had confessed without first making a deal on sentencing. It was obvious that Gillis hadn't consulted Jennifer. Ben was certain that she had no idea about the confession. Christ, he could take this confession and go for the death penalty. If Jenny was right that he had no soul, and he was anxious to get even with her, that was what he would do.

Ben picked up the phone and called Ed Fulton's office.

"He's up on the Hill with Senator Wallingford on the tax bill," Fulton's secretary said. "He asked me not to disturb him unless it was an emergency."

"Have him call me when he gets back," Ben said, happy that he could have some additional time to mull over the confession before talking to Fulton, who no doubt would want Ben to race back in to Judge Hogan this afternoon.

Ben reached for the phone to call Jennifer. Then he hesitated, thinking over what had happened. Why had Gillis decided suddenly to confess? Was he guilty, and he decided he could get a lesser sentence? Was he trying to clear his conscience? Neither of those fit the man he had interviewed Sunday night.

Then what? Had someone coerced him into confessing? Who? Why? Or paid him off? Jenny had said a foreign government was involved. Were they behind all of this?

He picked up the phone and called the jail. "Check today's visitors log," he said to the clerk on duty, "for Clyde Gillis."

After several minutes Ben heard, "Only visitor today was his wife, Lucinda, at one-ten this afternoon. Left at one-forty."

Ben immediately dialed Jennifer.

"You'd better sit down," he said to her, "and hold on tightly to the arms of your chair. I want to read you something that just arrived in my office."

She didn't say a word while Ben read. She waited

for him to say, "Give me your fax number and I'll shoot over a copy." Then she exploded.

"Okay, Ben," she cried, "what did you guys do to get him to write that document?"

Ben was so indignant that he could barely speak. "I . . . I . . . I had nothing to do with it. I don't know that anybody did anything to your client."

"C'mon, Ben," she said with a snarl. "I wasn't suggesting that you were personally involved, but somebody did something to my client. You know that."

Ben figured she was right. Still he didn't respond. This confession was so unexpected.

"What are you going to do with it?" she asked.

"I don't have any choice, Jenny. I have to take it to Judge Hogan tomorrow morning and ask her to call the defendant back in for another hearing. Then I'll present his confession to the court. If it smells fishy, she'll bear down hard on him with her own interrogation."

Jennifer was still outraged. "I'll be egging her on."

"I figured as much."

"I'll say someone drugged my client. He wouldn't even talk to me."

Suddenly, Ben realized that the hearing before Judge Hogan could be the way to stop the government's railroading of Clyde Gillis. If the gardener didn't kill Winthrop, then whoever was responsible for the secretary of state's death might have made a serious error by obtaining this confession. "Look," Ben said, "suppose I offer to cut you a deal. The same deal you could have had before the confession."

Without hesitating, Jennifer responded, "No deal. My client didn't do it. I read the transcript of the tape of your interview with him, or at least the part of it you gave me. It confirms for me that Clyde's innocent. If you go before the judge tomorrow, you'd better bring the tape of that interview, because I want the judge to hear it. She'll know something funny's going on. Lucille may be the judge from hell for guilty defendants, but she also has a deep sense of fairness for innocent ones. She'll do her job conscientiously. You know that damn well. Personally, I think you guys screwed yourselves when you rigged the system to get her."

Ben had to agree with her on Judge Hogan. Hennessey hadn't consulted him before he made that call. He didn't know the judges nearly as well as Ben because he hardly tried cases anymore himself. He relied on the rumor mill. He wasn't down in the pits with the rubber and the grease.

Ben returned to the transcript of his Sunday interview with Gillis. "Plenty of guilty people have claimed they were innocent in an initial interrogation. That doesn't prove a thing."

"I have other evidence to prove somebody else killed Winthrop. Solid evidence, not conjecture."

Here it was again, this evidence she had. "Please, Jenny, share it with me."

"You'll hear about it in court if you're foolish enough to march to Judge Hogan with that confession."

"C'mon, I don't have any choice."

At last her voice lowered a few decibels. She knew there was no way Ben would ever coerce a phony confession. "My advice is that you sleep on it overnight. Let me know first thing in the morning if you still want to put your head in Lucille Hogan's noose. I'll do my best to help you."

Ben put the phone down and stared at the dirty window in his office for several minutes, idly watching a pigeon contributing to the debris on the ledge. What kind of evidence could Jenny possibly have? She had to be bluffing, stalling for time. Or maybe she wasn't. This case was starting to smell like fish that had been left out all week.

He walked into the outer office, made a copy of the confession, and handed one to his secretary. "It goes to Jennifer Moore at Blank and Foster by fax."

Ben turned around and had started back into his own office when he heard a man calling him from the corridor, through the open door. "Ben, I have to talk to you."

Immediately, he recognized Art Campbell's voice. Ben wheeled around and approached his visitor. "How are you, pal?"

"Pretty good for an old man with six grandchildren," Campbell replied, and then laughed.

Prosecutors and detectives often developed a bond from working together over the years, as the prosecutors depended upon the detectives for their testimony that was so critical at trial. But for Ben, his relationship with Campbell went deeper. The experienced detective was someone Ben had learned to trust. He was not only professional, but totally honest. Unlike many of his colleagues, he would never fudge the evidence to help get a conviction, even if he was convinced the defendant was guilty. And they had hit it off personally. For years they had lunch every couple of months. They went to a Wizards game together at least twice a year. Campbell, who had once played for Georgetown, would show Ben some of the fine points of the game. In June, Ben had attended the wedding of Campbell's youngest daughter.

Ben grabbed two cans of Coke from the small refrigerator in his outer office and tossed one to Campbell, who snatched it on the fly in his large right hand.

"It's about the Gillis case," Campbell said as he moved a pile of papers from a chair to the floor in Ben's messy office, popped open the can, and sat down.

"Yeah, I saw you in the courtroom today. I wondered why."

Campbell looked at Ben, puzzled. "You don't know?"

"Know what?"

"I was at the crime scene with my people before the FBI arrived."

Ben had raised his can to take a sip. He put it down with a thud, spilling some soda through the top. "I had no idea."

Campbell shook his head. "My fault. I should have figured they'd do it that way and gotten over here myself. I knew what those guys were like."

"Which guys?"

"Ed Fulton and Bill Traynor."

"Oh, them." Ben leaned back in his chair and put his feet up on the desk. "You want to start from the beginning?"

"Saturday, I was the first detective at the murder scene. Just starting my investigation when those two jerks showed up. Said they were running the show. Fulton treated me like I was a piece of dog shit. So I split and took my people with me."

Ben shook his head in disgust. That kid had messed up the case from the very start.

"After Saturday, I was so damn mad," Campbell continued, "that I didn't want to have anything else to do with the case. When I heard about the evidence they found in Clyde Gillis's truck, I figured he was guilty. I didn't think any more about it. Then your old girlfriend came to see me."

Ben bolted upright in his chair. "Jenny? What'd she want?"

"She said she was convinced Clyde Gillis didn't do it. She persuaded me to go back to Winthrop's house to check for additional evidence."

Ben was stunned. "You should have told me. I'm your friend. It was my case."

"With all the heat coming from the White House," Campbell said, looking apologetic, "I figured I'd be doing you a favor not telling you. If I didn't find anything, lots of useless shouting would be avoided. And if I did find something, I told her that I would take it to you as well as to her."

Ben held his breath. "And did you find anything?"

"A blond woman's hair on the blue carpet in the room where Winthrop was killed."

Ben waited for more. When it didn't come, he asked, "What's that prove? It could have been his wife's."

"Ann Winthrop has gray hair."

"Well, it could have been anybody's who visited the house in the recent past." Ben looked at him curiously. "I thought you found some evidence to help us locate George Nesbitt. He's the other suspect I've been worried about. We've moved heaven and earth to find him." He waved his hands, still nettled about the man's disappearance. "The blond hair doesn't do much for me. Did you tell Jennifer about it?"

"She was ecstatic. She has the idea that George Nesbitt was a woman dressed like a man who came ostensibly for sex and then killed Winthrop."

Ben rolled his eyes. "Other than one of Cinderella's blond hairs, does she have anything to back up that fairy tale?"

"She has a guard, Jeb Hines, who thinks Nesbitt looked effeminate. She has the stain on Winthrop's pants and the folder of condoms."

Ben gaped. "What are you talking about? What stain? What condoms?"

Campbell smiled. Usually Ben was the one in the know. "Yeah, that's the second thing that brought me here today. After I found the blond hair, I decided to read the FBI report. It didn't mention the two things I saw before the jerks arrived."

"Which were?"

"In a red file folder in a credenza, Winthrop had about fifty condoms stashed."

"Yeah, so the guy liked to fuck."

"And on the front of his pants, there was a fresh stain. It may have been semen. It could have been precoital fluid."

"Let me guess," Ben said. "The FBI report didn't mention the stain."

Art Campbell cocked his finger at him. "Even for a white boy, you're pretty damn slow, but eventually you get there."

Ben paused to consider these new developments. "Still," he said, "it might not have anything to do with the crime. Maybe Winthrop did have some blond bimbo in for sex, and his friends at the White House wanted to spare Mrs. Winthrop the brutal tabloid treatment. None of this tells me that Clyde Gillis didn't kill Winthrop."

Ben said it with bravado, but he knew the ground had shifted irrevocably. Even if this was the only evidence Jenny had alluded to on the phone, he'd have a problem with Judge Hogan. Plus, she might have something more that Campbell didn't know about.

"Now let me show you something," Ben said. "This seems to be my day for revelations."

He reached across his desk, picked up a copy of the confession, and handed it to the detective.

Campbell took a pair of reading glasses from his pocket, studied it carefully, and returned it to Ben. "I don't believe it."

"Why not?"

"My gut tells me different, along with everything else I now know." Campbell looked at Ben thoughtfully. "We've been friends a long time. So I can be blunt with you. Right?"

Ben nodded.

"I think they're using you in their cover-up. Somebody at the White House. Maybe even Brewster himself. They know Clyde Gillis didn't kill Winthrop because they know who did it. Gillis just happened to be in the wrong place at the wrong time. Otherwise, they would never have even had a suspect. It would have gone down as an unsolved crime."

For a long moment Ben was too stunned to respond. "I don't know," he replied weakly.

"Then let's find out for sure before you take the confession to the judge, and the press gets hold of it."

"How do you propose to do that?"

"Without any fanfare, I'll get Winthrop's pants from the FBI lab and have our chemists analyze them. Then I want to talk to everybody who lives around Gillis's house. Maybe they saw someone plant the gun or money in his truck."

"The FBI already did that. They came up with nothing."

Campbell smiled. "We're talking southeast Washington. I know those people. They don't talk to the FBI. I'll send people they know. People they'll talk to."

"How long will it take?"

"Give me twenty-four hours."

Ben swallowed. "I don't know."

The telephone rang. When Ben ignored it, his secretary buzzed. "It's Ed Fulton on a cell phone up on the Hill. Returning your call."

Ben looked at the confession and then at Campbell's black, crease-lined face before picking up the phone. The moment of truth had come. How could he avoid telling Fulton about the confession?

"What's up?" Ben said casually.

"I'm returning your call."

"I just wanted to check in with you. We didn't have a chance to talk after court. What'd you think?"

"It went great. We've got an early trial date. Mr. Slater's happy. I'm happy. I thought you were calling about some new development in the case."

Ben sucked in his breath. "There hasn't been any new development," he said flatly.

The man whom Jenny said had no soul had just put his entire career on the line. Nervously, he put down the phone and looked at Campbell. "You've got twenty-four hours," he said grimly. "Aside from my secretary, Jennifer's the only other one who knows about the confession. There's no chance they'll tell anyone. But if nothing turns up before tomorrow at four o'clock, I'll have to take the confession to the judge. I'll say I just received it."

Campbell laughed. "You mean you'll lie, and I'll swear to it."

"Yeah, something like that," Ben said, joining in. "Then when we both get fired, we can get season tickets to the Wizards."

After Campbell left his office, Ben sat at his cluttered desk thinking about everything that had just happened. The detective's words, "They're using you in their cover-up . . ." kept popping into his tired brain, and made him feel very uncomfortable. Was he being paranoid? Was Campbell totally off the reservation, and was Clyde Gillis really the killer? He was so confused, he no longer had an opinion.

He remembered the words of Bill Dunn, a former colleague who had gone into private practice and was minting money. Dunn used to say, "When the going gets tough, the tough go for a drink."

Ben turned off his computer and took the elevator to the parking garage in the basement of the building. It was already dark outside, and it was raining again. Not paying attention to traffic and driving west on Pennsylvania Avenue, he almost hit a pedestrian at a crosswalk at Tenth Street. He slammed on the brakes and skidded to a stop just in time. Happily, there were only seven more blocks to the Old Ebbitt Grill. Ben found a parking space on the street and went inside. Maybe I'll get lucky, he thought, after the way the rest of my day's gone. Maybe that blonde will be back.

Jennifer had the copy of Clyde Gillis's confession in her hand when she arrived at the jail.

"What's going on?" she asked her client, who stared up at the ceiling and refused to respond. "Did you actually sign this confession?" she asked, trying to sound sympathetic—which was how she felt, because she was certain someone had gotten to him.

He still wouldn't answer.

She waved the document at him. "Did someone coerce you into signing?"

More blank stares.

She asked the guard to show her the visitors log. At first she was told it would take a court order. Finally, the guard on duty, Harvey "Red" Dougherty, relented and showed her the log. Ben had been there Sunday night, and according to the log, no one else other than Jennifer, Lucinda, and the children had visited Gillis.

As she left the jail, she checked her cell phone, which she had turned off when she had been inside. There was a message from Ann.

As she drove in the pounding rain, she called Ann. "I got your message."

"We have to talk."

Jennifer looked at the clock in the car. Time was tight if she was going to meet Slater for the opera, but her defense of Gillis was now at a critical point. If Ann had something, she'd better hear it. Besides, she wanted to tell her about Gillis's confession.

"How about my house in thirty minutes?"

"I'll be there."

Ann was parked in front of the house when Jennifer arrived. As soon as they were inside, Ann told her what happened with the intruder.

"My God, that's horrible," Jennifer said. "Did you tell the police?"

"I haven't told a soul. I'm afraid if there's a police investigation, it'll come out that you've got a copy of the tape. That'll make you their next target." Ann's hands were shaking.

"You want something to drink?"

"Do you have any sherry?"

Jennifer fixed two glasses with ice and handed one to Ann.

"Where's your copy of the videotape?" Ann asked.

Jennifer pointed to the briefcase she'd been holding when she entered the house. "I've been carrying the video around with me. Never sure when I'll be able to use it."

"Well, watch your back because these people are ruthless. Since you were with me when we turned over the first one, they may go after you next."

Trying to sound brave, Jennifer said, "I've got the gun in my briefcase."

Ann wasn't impressed. "You don't want to mess with them."

"You're right. I'll get another copy of the video made in the morning and lock it up in my office." Jennifer shifted nervously in her chair. This whole mess was getting worse and worse. "I've got a development of my own to report to you," she said.

Ann looked at her with her eyes wide open. "Am I going to like this one any better?"

"I don't think so. Clyde Gillis confessed. He wants to plead guilty."

Ann's head snapped back. "What?"

"You heard me."

"B-but that's impossible," Ann stammered. "You . . . you have evidence linking the Chinese government to the murder. Today's little episode—"

Jennifer interrupted her. "It's all good evidence, but it's circumstantial. With more time, I might be able to get direct evidence establishing that they were responsible for the murder. Unfortunately, time's not something I have. If I go to Ben with what I've got now on the Chinese government, Ben will wave Clyde's confession at me and laugh. I'd do the same if I were in his shoes."

"Jesus, what a mess. Was the confession coerced, or was Clyde paid off to take the fall?"

"Either way. But who's responsible?"

Ann pounced on the question. "How about Ambassador Liu?"

Jennifer removed her glasses and cleaned them with a damp kitchen towel. "That thought has been running through my mind. But how will I ever be able to prove it?" She shook her head. "I feel so bad about Clyde. I can understand what Judge Hogan did, but since I couldn't get him out on bail, how's his family going to get along financially? You told me one of his kids needs expensive medical treatments."

Ann slapped her hand against her forehead. "You're so right. I should have thought about that. I'll call Lucinda tomorrow and offer her some money. I hate it when people give to faceless institutions and ignore people they know. I could kick myself. Thanks for reminding me."

Reminded of something herself, Jennifer glanced at her watch and winced. "I've got the opera tonight." For an instant Jennifer paused, hoping Ann wouldn't ask whom she was going with, but she couldn't mislead her friend. "Actually, I'm going with Jim Slater."

Ann shook her head in disapproval. "The presidential box, no doubt."

"How'd you guess?"

"I figured he'd pull out all of the stops in order to snow you." Her tone was sarcastic.

Jennifer was ashamed to admit that the idea of being in the presidential box with the second most powerful man in the country was quite an aphrodisiac. "C'mon, Ann."

"Sorry, I shouldn't have said that. I guess I'm just jealous no one has wanted to snow me."

Jennifer stared hard at Ann. "I know you too well. You're not jealous at all. You said it because you think I'm making a mistake with Jim, and you're feeling helpless to stop me."

Ann gave a short, sardonic laugh. "Okay. You're right. But you're a big girl. You must know what you're doing."

Ann waved her off. "Why don't you go up and get dressed? I'll drive you to the Kennedy Center. We can talk in the car."

"I was planning to drive myself."

"That's for the peasants," Ann said in a caustic tone. "Jim will no doubt have a car and driver to take you home."

Jennifer dressed quickly. For the evening, she had picked a gorgeous teal dinner dress that was just waiting for an occasion like this. Before going downstairs, she switched her purse for the evening to one large enough to hold the video. After what Ann had said, there was no way she was letting it out of her sight.

"Wow, you look smashing," Ann said to Jennifer as they walked to the car.

Once inside, Jennifer repeated her question. "What's bothering you about Jim?"

"Jim's debonair, suave, and attractive. He's bright and he's fun to be with."

"Sounds good so far," Jennifer quipped.

"He's also married. That's a prescription for disaster, and I care too much about you to want you to be hurt."

For several minutes, they rode in silence. Finally, Jennifer said, "I appreciate your concern, Ann. I really do. And I'll think about what you've said."

"That's all I ask." They were approaching the Kennedy Center. "Have a good time at the opera."

"I will. I love Verdi's music."

"What are you seeing?"

"Luisa Miller."

"Isn't that the one in which the two lovers die at the end?"

"Thank you, Ann."

Ben sat at the bar and sipped a frozen margarita slowly, thinking about everything Campbell had said. The drink tasted bitter, matching his mood. Campbell was probably right, he decided. He was being used by people in the administration as part of a cover-up. That was easy enough to figure out. Much harder was trying to determine who was behind it, and what he could do about it.

A television set was playing above the bar. Two ESPN announcers were prattling on about the Capitals hockey team. Suddenly from his left he heard a woman say, "I want whatever that man's having. It looks good."

He turned his head. It was the blonde, two chairs away. There was an empty chair between them. She was pointing to his glass. She had a warm smile that showed perfect teeth.

The bartender said, "Frozen margarita with salt."

God, she was beautiful, Ben thought. Her long hair hung down straight, kissing her shoulders and the jacket of the smartly tailored gray business suit she was wearing.

Before the bartender made the drink, Ben said, "You look more like the champagne type to me."

"Do you really think so?" she replied. He loved the sound of that voice.

"A glass of champagne for the lady," Ben said, "and a refill for me. Put them both on my tab."

"You don't have to do that."

Ben had a bedroom voice of his own. "With the kind of day I had, I'd like to do something nice for someone."

"Well, gee, thanks."

The bartender brought their drinks and then departed. Ben moved over and sat next to her. "Where you from?" he asked.

"Sunnyvale, California. I'm in the computer software business."

Ben laughed. "Do you know George Nesbitt?"

That came completely out of the blue, but she didn't move a muscle to show her alarm. "No, who's he?"

"That was a joke. He's somebody I almost knew from San Jose. He's in the computer business, too."

He raised his glass and tapped it against hers. "To the computer business."

"Is that what you do too?"

"Nope. I'm a lawyer."

She gave him a warm smile, indicating that pleased her. "I should have guessed that. In Washington, all the men I meet are lawyers."

Ben laughed and held out his hand. "Ben's my name."

She shook it warmly. "I'm Sally."

"You staying near here?"

"Are you kidding?" she said scornfully. "We're just a start-up. I'd never get reimbursed for the high rates in this part of town. I'm out in Virginia near National Airport at one of those no-name motels."

Ben sipped his drink, thinking. He wasn't sure what to do next. He hadn't picked up a girl at a bar since he was in law school. That just wasn't something he did. But there couldn't be any harm in it. There wouldn't be complications. She was probably going home soon. She didn't even know his last name. Finally he said, "What are you doing for dinner this evening?"

"I figured I'd go back to the hotel and order up from room service. I hate eating alone in a restaurant."

Well, that was certainly an encouraging response, he thought. "How about having dinner with me over at the Willard?"

"I'd love to. I'll bet they have great room service there."

Ben was startled. He actually had had the dining room in mind, but he wasn't about to look a gift horse in the mouth. "I've heard they have the best room service in town."

She skipped off the bar stool with her glass in her hand and said, "I've got to go powder my nose."

While she was gone, he thought briefly of Jennifer, then dismissed the idea. He didn't owe her a thing. The way she was acting, he had zero chance of getting back together with her.

A few minutes later when the blonde returned, her glass was empty. She was wearing a tan raincoat and black leather gloves, carrying the glass in her hand, which she deposited on the bar.

Outside, it had stopped raining. They walked the four blocks to the Willard. While he registered for a room, she waited for him near the elevators, out of sight of the desk clerk, who had no interest in Ben or why he needed a room without a reservation. Ben looked respectable. His credit card cleared immediately. That was all the clerk cared about.

A few minutes later, they were in 422, a deluxe room with a queen-size bed. Ben picked up the room service menu and started to open it, but she put a gloved hand over his and said, "Can we wait till later?" There was no doubt what she wanted first. "There's no way to say this, but I'm sexy as hell for you right now."

Ben could hardly believe his ears. Nor could he believe his good luck when she took her hand and fondled his crotch, holding it on his already swelling cock.

"Tell you what," she said, "you get undressed out here. I'll go in the bathroom. Then I'll come out naked as the day I was born."

"You don't have to undress in there. I wouldn't mind watching you."

She giggled. "I'm a little modest about undressing. Once I get my clothes off . . . well, I stop being modest. You'll see for yourself."

She held up a gloved finger to his mouth. He licked it eagerly and tried to embrace her, but she slipped away—heading toward the bathroom.

"You get undressed, too," she called over her shoulder.

Ben quickly tore off his clothes and tossed them on a chair. Naked, he sat down on the edge of the bed, waiting for her.

The bathroom door opened a crack. "Okay, close your eyes," she called through the opening. "I'll tell you when you can look."

Ben did as he was told, trembling with expectation. He couldn't even remember the last time he'd been with a woman.

She didn't tell him he could look, but he could smell her scent. So he opened his eyes anyway. Startled, he recoiled. What the hell? She was still fully dressed in her raincoat and black gloves.

"Hey, what—" he said, standing up.

She drove her fist hard into his stomach. The air sucked out of his body with a great whoosh. As he collapsed to the floor, she reached into her raincoat pocket and extracted a damp cloth, which she held tightly against his mouth and nose while grabbing his head from behind with her other hand. He flailed wildly, trying to grab the cloth and pull it away, but she was too strong. He could feel himself losing consciousness, the strength sapping from his body.

When he came to, he was naked, lying facedown on the bed. Each of his hands and feet was tied to one of the posts of the bed. A piece of duct tape covered his mouth. His face was turned so that he could see her, sitting in a chair dressed in her raincoat and gloves and holding a small cylindrical silver object shaped like a pen.

His first reaction was raw fear. What was she planning to do to him next? His second was anger at himself and his own stupidity in picking up a woman he didn't know in a bar. How could I have done something so idiotic?

"I see that you're finally awake, Ben Hartwell," she said.

He tried to open his mouth, but it was hopeless.

"Sorry, I had to tape your mouth. I didn't want you to be able to scream. Still, that makes it hard for us to have a conversation, so I'll try to anticipate your questions. Right now you're wondering how I know your last name." She flashed an ugly smile. "I know everything about you. I know that you live at Thirty-five-ninety-one Newark Street. I know that your daughter Amy is four years old, a real cute girl with curly dark brown hair the same color as yours. She attends the Cleveland Park Preschool."

Slowly she walked over to the bed and sat down on the edge. She held the silver cylinder in front of his face, pushed down on the top with her thumb, and a stiletto blade shot out of the bottom.

Instinctively, he pulled his face away from the knife that gleamed in the light from the lamp on the bed stand.

"Oh, you don't have to worry about your face," she said, almost purring. "I'm not interested in your face. No, what I'm considering is surgery on another part of your body." She flicked the blade upward. "What I'm going to do is to take this knife and insert it into your ass. Then I'm going to plunge it into your prostate and I'm going to cut away, slicing it like a peach. You won't have to worry about having another child. You'll never be able to have sex with a woman. Now, how's that sound to you?"

He tried to shout, but he couldn't make a sound through the tape. From pure terror, sweat was streaming down his face.

"When I'm finished with you," she said, "I'm going out to your house. I'll find your daughter, Amy, in bed. Then I'll cut her throat. You can bury her when they let you out of the hospital. Do you understand all that?" She touched the steel against his naked buttocks. "Nod if you understand me," she ordered.

He moved his head up and down as best he could.

"Now I'm going to tell you what you can do to avoid all of this," she said. "It's simple. All you have to do is agree to accept Clyde Gillis's confession, accept his guilty plea, take him to the judge, and persuade her to accept it as well. That's all you have to do. That isn't much, is it?"

Ben didn't move.

"Well?" she demanded.

She pressed the blade against his buttocks, breaking the skin. He could feel a trickle of blood oozing down his leg.

"Will you do it?"

He had no doubt that she would do everything she had said. He nodded his head as vigorously as he could.

Satisfied, she got up from the bed and stood about five feet away.

"Before I leave, I want to tell you some things," she said. "First, if you don't do what you just promised, Amy's as good as dead. After that, I'll get you alone again and perform prostate surgery on you. You can bet the house on that," she said, laughing. "Second, I didn't tie the ropes too tight. If you keep twisting and turning, my guess is that you'll get out in about an hour, when I'll be at least fifty miles from here. Third, you don't have to worry about the little scratch on your butt. It'll stop bleeding in a few minutes. Consider it a souvenir of our evening together to remind you to do what you promised."

She turned and walked toward the door. Before opening it, she said, "By the way, Ben, you shouldn't pick up strange women in bars. It's a dangerous thing to do."

Chapter 19

"I'm so glad you could join me this evening," Jim Slater said as she approached.

He was standing in the red-carpeted corridor on the mezzanine of the Kennedy Center Opera House outside of the presidential box, chatting with a man and two women. Good grief, she thought, that can't possibly be Gloria Clurman, the Broadway and movie star.

"Jennifer, have you ever met Gloria Clurman?" Slater asked.

"Never have, but I'm thrilled."

Having been briefed by Slater, Clurman gave Jennifer a warm smile. "Well, I'm happy to meet you as well. I'll never forget how you got the part of Madge in *Picnic*. I understand you did so much with it. Unfortunately, I wasn't in New York at the time. I would have loved seeing you."

Jennifer radiated with pleasure. "That's quite a compliment, coming from you, Ms. Clurman."

"Please call me Gloria."

Slater turned to his other side. "Jennifer, meet Henri DuMont, the French ambassador to Washington, and Mrs. DuMont."

After Jennifer shook Madame DuMont's hand and the ambassador kissed both of her cheeks, Slater said, "The three of them will be joining us for the opera and dinner."

When the lights in the corridor flickered, Slater took her by the arm and led his guests toward the door of the box. Walking quickly by, Senator Blake from Massachusetts stopped to say hello to Slater.

In the orchestra pit below, the musicians were doing their final tuning up. Slater whispered to Jennifer, "I hope you like Verdi as much as I do."

"He's magical."

He touched the tip of her chin. "You're magical."

It took Ben forty-five minutes of frantic twisting and tugging before he freed his right arm. In another ten minutes he unfastened the other three ropes. All he could think about was Amy and whether she was all right.

It was late. Elana should be sleeping, but he had to know. He tried to compose himself enough to call. He was trembling so badly that he dropped the phone twice before he could punch out his home number. It rang three, four times with no answer. He hung up before the answering machine kicked in, then dialed again. "C'mon, Elana, wake up," he muttered, praying that it was only because she was sleeping that she hadn't answered. One, two, three rings. He was getting ready to hang up when he heard her sleepy voice. "Mr. Hartwell's residence."

"Elana, it's Ben. I'm sorry to wake you. I have to know if Amy's okay."

"She sleeping."

"Can you go in and check on her?"

There was no answer. Elana must think he was crazy.

"Please, Elana," he said.

"I go look."

For a minute—which seemed to Ben like an eternity—there was silence at the other end of the phone. He held his breath until she finally returned.

"Amy is sleeping."

Ben breathed a huge sigh of relief. "Thank you, Elana," he said. "Sorry I woke you."

His second call was to Art Campbell at home.

"Something awful's happened," Ben said. "How soon can you get to my house?"

Campbell was instantly alerted by the fear in Ben's voice. "Twenty-five minutes. You want a cruiser sooner?"

Ben tried to make his tense and weary mind work. Amy was all right. The blonde was probably at least fifty miles from here, as she had promised. "Twenty-five minutes will be great," he said. "Come by yourself."

In the mirror, he checked his rear end. The bleeding had stopped, but the two-inch gash looked ugly. He ran some warm bathwater, sat down in it, and soaped the wound. It stung like the devil. He forced himself to sit in the water while he counted to one hundred. Then he dried it off, only to find it had started bleeding again. Ben had a Band-Aid in his wallet and covered the wound awkwardly. Before leaving the hotel room, he stopped to look at his face in the mirror above the bureau. His eyes had a wild look. His hair was messed up. His arms and legs ached. The whole evening had a surreal quality, as if he had been watching himself in a horror movie.

Christ, he was such a fool, picking up the blonde like that. He had nobody to blame but himself. Then his brain unscrambled, and he understood what had happened. No doubt about it, he had made things easier for her, but she would have gotten to him one way or the other. If not at the Willard, then at home— where Amy was. What sadistic games would that killer have played with a four-year-old to persuade him to do what she wanted?

He tried not to think about the answer to that question as he drove home, speeding across the streets, running red lights in his desperation to get to Amy. As soon as he entered the house, he ran up to her room. It was just as Elana had said. She was sound asleep. He sat down on the rocker and watched her, finding comfort in her innocent face as she dreamed.

That was where he was when Campbell arrived ten minutes later. Ben went down and opened the door.

"You look like you just saw a ghost," the detective said.

"Try George Nesbitt. I think I met George Nesbitt."

Campbell felt a surge of adrenaline. He was ready to move. Winthrop's murder, plus the Gillis arrest and his bizarre confession, had been nagging him around the clock. Maybe now they'd get some answers.

"Where is he?"

"You mean she."

Ben's words stopped Campbell in his tracks. He rubbed his eyes, trying to make sense out of what Ben had said. "The blonde?"

"I can't be positive. There's a good chance."

"You want to tell me about it?"

Ben felt the ache in his behind. "Only if you won't think I'm a total fool."

"That bad?"

"Worse."

Ben went into the other room, poured brandy into two snifters, and handed one to Campbell. Sitting across a small glass-topped coffee table from the detective, Ben took a long pull on his drink. God, that felt good. He needed it. His hands had almost stopped shaking.

Slowly, Ben told the story of his evening, pausing from time to time to sip the amber liquid until the glass was empty. As he spoke, relief replaced his anger and outrage at what she had done to him.

Meanwhile, Campbell listened silently, never touching his glass, but jotting in the small notebook that he had extracted from his jacket pocket.

At the end, Ben said, "Okay, now you can tell me I'm the world's biggest fool."

"You're the world's biggest fool. Do you feel better?"

Ben gave a short, nervous laugh. "What do I do now?"

Campbell shifted in his chair, sitting up straight. "You've got a number of choices."

"Such as?"

"You could do what she wants. Accept Clyde Gillis's confession, let him change his plea, and try to persuade the judge to accept it."

That was the last thing Ben was going to do. "I may be a fool, but I'm not a coward. Her attack convinced me that your scenario from this afternoon is right. Gillis didn't kill Winthrop. Somebody else did, and somebody powerful in this town wants Gillis to take the rap. I won't be part of that. How can you even suggest that? You're a cop, for God's sake."

Campbell held his hands up. "I wasn't suggesting it. I was only laying out your options."

"Well, I don't like that one. Give me another one."

"You could withdraw from the case and hope that satisfies her."

"Same answer as the first one. Keep talking."

"Go to Bill Traynor and the FBI, tell them everything that happened, and let them take it from here. It's their case."

Ben had considered that possibility on the way home. "But suppose FBI Director Murtaugh's a part of the cover-up. If I do that, I'll be signing my daughter's death warrant, and mine as well."

"That's possible."

Ben picked up Campbell's untouched glass of brandy and took a long sip. "You got any good choices?"

"Life doesn't always allow for good choices." Campbell wrinkled his brow, thinking. "I could provide police protection for you and Amy. Then you and I could quietly play detective, trying to find out who hired the blonde to kill Winthrop and attack you. Meantime, we don't say a word to the Feds."

"How the hell do we solve the mystery ourselves?"

"You won't like my answer."

"Try me. Right now I'm desperate."

Campbell took a deep breath. "The first thing

you've got to do is bury the hatchet with Jennifer
Moore. Start pooling all of your information with her.
I'm convinced from talking to her earlier today, when
I told her about the blond hair, that she knows some-
thing about Winthrop's death from her friend Ann
that she hasn't shared with either of us."

Ben grimaced. "She would never work with me. We
have too much history."

"I know all about your history. Why not ask her?
Give it a try. You're not a couple of teenagers. You're
both professionals, and you've got a common problem."

Ben knew that his pride was stopping him. After
what she had done, breaking off their engagement un-
justifiably, the last thing he wanted to do was come
pleading to her for help. "There must be another
way," he said.

"If there is, I sure don't see it."

Ben decided to put that idea aside for the moment.
"How good a job could you do protecting Amy and
me?"

As soon as the words were out of his mouth, Ben
realized how stupid the question was. He knew the
answer before Campbell said it.

"There are no guarantees. Our police department's
tight on money. Unlike the Feds, we don't have unlimited resources. On the other hand, the Gillis case is
important to us. I happen to love this city. I hate
seeing its image take a needless pasting. Besides, I'd
like to repay my own debt to Bill Traynor and Fulton.
I'm senior enough. I can get the people I need to do
the job."

"Will they be able to stay in the background? I
don't want to frighten Amy. The kid's already seeing
a shrink once a week."

"I'll use plainclothes people as much as I can. I'll
stay close to it myself." He looked Ben squarely in
the eye. "But even with all of that, there's a risk. I
don't want to mislead you. We're going up against

some powerful people, and we don't even know who they are."

"You think we have any chance of succeeding?"

Campbell had no interest in that sort of question. "We can give it our best shot. That's all we can do. I also learned something that may be worthwhile this evening—while you were trying to get laid."

"Yeah, what?"

"Having my people canvass Clyde Gillis's neighborhood turned up nothing, but I talked to the guards at the jail."

"And?"

"Gillis had only one visitor this afternoon after the arraignment. His wife, Lucinda."

"I knew that," Ben said abruptly.

Campbell gave him a small smile. "But I'll bet you didn't know that when she was with her husband, she handed him a pen and paper. He wrote out something and handed it to her."

Ben pounded his fist on the table. Now they were getting somewhere. "So they got to her, and she convinced him to confess," Ben said, thinking aloud.

Campbell nodded, though he was puzzled. "It sure seems like that to me. I'm going to drop in on Lucinda Gillis for a cup of coffee in the morning and shake that tree."

Ben didn't reply. He was trying to decide what to do. In the last couple of hours, the stakes had escalated enormously. While Ben agonized over his decision, Campbell pulled a package of cigarettes from his pocket and tapped the pack on the arm of the chair. Finally, he broke the silence. "You've run out of time, white boy," he said, smiling at Ben. "What'll it be?"

"We're getting to the bottom of this. I'll call Jennifer right now."

Ben reached for the phone and dialed her home. He got the answering machine. "Jennifer, it's Ben. Please give me a call. It's important that we talk as soon as possible."

He put down the phone.

"She's probably asleep," Campbell said, "and she turned off her phone. You'll hear from her in the morning."

"Either that or she's screening her calls, and she doesn't want to talk to me," he said glumly.

Campbell laughed. "Jesus, you've still got a thing for this woman."

"Oh, go fuck yourself. Stick to being a detective and stop trying to play psychologist."

Suddenly, Campbell leaned across the table and put his two huge basketball player's hands on top of Ben's. His eyes narrowed and he gave Ben a long, hard stare. "I'm your friend. You sure you want to do this?"

Ben wasn't going to flinch. "You didn't give me any better choice."

"You're just a lawyer. You're not a cop. You have a young kid to worry about. This is big. Why not just get out of the way and let it happen without you?"

"After tonight, I'm not sure that's possible. Our blonde—Nesbitt, or whoever she is—may still go after Amy if I don't find out who's pulling her strings first." Ben didn't add that his father's experience was influencing his thinking. His father hadn't let anybody push him around. He had been willing to take risks. "Besides," Ben added, "we're officers of the law. This Winthrop affair's starting to sound like Watergate. I don't want to let it happen."

"That's great in theory, Ben, but it may crush you and me like a couple of paper cups on the beltway."

"I'm willing to take that chance."

Finally satisfied, Campbell leaned back. "All right. Let's get started. I'll get one of the artists we use to come over and make a drawing of the blonde."

"Now?" Ben said, surprised. "It's late."

Campbell grinned. "You'll never sleep tonight anyhow."

Magical was again the word that popped into Jennifer's mind, only this time to describe the whole evening as Ambassador and Madame DuMont pulled away in a car from the Bistro Francais in Georgetown and Gloria Clurman left on foot for the Four Seasons, where she was staying.

It had not only been the best performance of *Luisa Miller* Jennifer had ever seen, but during intermission, in the private VIP lounge on the mezzanine level, she had met all these important people who kept coming up to Gloria and Jim. The two of them were like powerful magnets that attracted everyone in the room. Then at dinner, Henri DuMont was tremendously funny, a marvelous raconteur who loved poking fun at the quirks of people from various European countries. Jim egged Gloria on to regale them with stories of the funniest things that she had seen backstage and on movie sets. As she obliged, they roared with laughter. The wine flowed freely. First Dom Perignon with *moules marniere,* and then with the steak and *frites* a fabulous Bordeaux Jim ordered that Jennifer had never heard of before, except she heard the word Rothschild in the name. They all had too much to eat and drink, but she loved every bite, and especially the chocolate soufflé at the end accompanied by a sauterne.

Occasionally, during dinner, Jennifer felt a little guilty for taking time from her preparation of the Gillis case. She rationalized that she had worked so much the last couple of days that she needed some time off. Besides, she had done everything she could for now. The next move was Ben's with the confession. Thinking of him also caused a nervous twinge, but she shook it off.

She was beginning to think about getting home when the driver of Slater's black Lincoln Town Car raced behind the car and held open the back door for the two of them. As the car pulled away, Jennifer closed her eyes and snuggled up against Slater, who draped his arm around her. "I have a modest proposal," he said.

"What's that?" she replied, her eyes still closed.

"Ever seen a polo match?"

"Can't say that I have."

"Good, because Saturday morning I have a match in Rancho Santa Fe. Fly out with me Friday evening. We'll come back Sunday. It'll give us a chance to get to know each other better." His arm tightened a little more around her. "Also, I want to explore with you the possibility of your coming back into the government at a high level. Maybe I'll create a new position in the White House to deal with women's issues. Health, sexual harassment, and so forth. You're smart and talented. I want the administration to take advantage of that."

His words jolted her. With her eyes opening wide, she pulled away from him. "What about Mrs. Slater? Where will she be?"

He looked nonplussed. "Actually, she'll probably be in Argentina buying horses. What difference does that make?"

Jennifer gave a short, caustic laugh. "Come on, Jim. What is this, the Washington version of the casting couch?"

He smiled at her with a twinkle in his eye. "You know what your trouble is?"

"I don't like any question that begins like that."

"You figure that every man is interested in only one thing." He delivered the words in a smooth, soft voice, suggesting amusement rather than irritation.

As a lawyer, she always enjoyed verbal fencing. Trying to match his tone, she said, "Well, aren't they? Men are all alike. You want one thing. You'll get it any way you can."

In the dim light of the car, she saw that he looked genuinely offended. "I'll bet you have plenty of conquests," she added.

"Actually, I don't, but I don't expect you to believe that. The truth is that I find you exciting and attractive. Not some conquest. But if that's what you think this is all about, an excuse to get into your pants, then you can stay at Rancho Valencia, a gem of a resort close to my place." He laughed. "You can even wear a chastity belt all weekend if that'll make you feel better."

She hadn't meant to come off sounding like such a shrew. To show that she liked him, and was sorry for what she had said, she punched him playfully in the ribs. "But who gets to hold the key?"

"What key?"

"The key to the chastity belt."

He laughed. "I do, of course."

"That's what I thought." She leaned over and kissed him on the lips. "It's a nice invitation, Jim, but I'm afraid I have to work this weekend."

The kiss had made him momentarily hopeful. Her words quickly shattered that. He regrouped, concealing his disappointment. "Ah, well, whatever is worth having is worth waiting for. I assume it's the Gillis case that's keeping you here."

She pulled back, eyeing him sharply. "How did you know that?"

Slater realized he'd better be careful. She couldn't know that Ed Fulton was on his staff, or she'd be sure that his only interest in her was to sabotage Gillis's defense. He'd have to remind Fulton to keep a low profile. Stay in the back of the courtroom. Identify himself as a special assistant to Murtaugh.

Slater pretended total innocence. "You were all over the television news today, after this morning's arraignment. I wondered why you didn't plead him."

Her face had shut down. "I don't think we should talk about it."

Slater said softly, "You mean, because I'm the enemy?"

"Not the enemy. But you happen to work for the man who's the boss of the prosecutors I'm going up against."

"The connection isn't that close," he said mildly. "Although I did meet Ben Hartwell. He's no match for you."

"We really shouldn't talk about it." Her voice was firm, and he backed off.

The car turned onto her street. Earlier, she had wondered what would happen when they got to her house tonight. Despite her hostility about the case, she liked Jim Slater, and she wanted him—wanted him in her bed. Wanted to know if he was as good at sex as he was at everything else. The wine had lowered her usual inhibitions to nearly zero. Why not? she finally decided. But he'd have to make the first move tonight. If he was still in the mood after her challenging him.

At her front door, she inserted the key in the lock, and she waited. He put his arms around her, pulled her close, and kissed her, a long kiss. She felt him pressing against her. She knew that he was aroused. Then he released her.

"Thanks for a great evening," he said. And he walked down the cement steps to his car. Just like that. He had his driver wait until she was inside the house before pulling away.

As she deactivated the house security system, she was pissed at herself for being so defensive in the car. Based on how he did everything else, he would probably be a superb lover. She had no one but herself to blame for the fact that she would be climbing into her bed alone.

As his car sped down Connecticut Avenue, Slater leaned back in the seat and smiled. Tonight he could have had her; he knew that. But she'd have to realize from the start that he'd be calling the shots.

The Shangri-La lobby was air-conditioned to a cool seventy degrees, but Chen was perspiring as he carried the brown suitcase from the elevator to the front entrance. Over his shoulder he had a black duffel bag with clothes for a two-day trip. He knew that the security police stationed guards in the large hotels to watch the foreign devils. With the midday bustle in the hotel, and being Chinese, he hoped they wouldn't pay much attention to him.

A bellman offered to help Chen with the suitcase. He waved the man away, not wanting anyone else to have control of the bag. That was stupid, he decided. It made him look more suspicious.

In the cab on the way to the train station, he asked himself once more whether he wanted to go through with this. There comes a time, he decided, when an individual has to stand up for what he believes. Since the Tiananmen Square protests, the regime had gone on doing what it had done to Mai, arresting and killing innocent people, university professors, students, and anyone who dared to yearn for freedom. Now they were gearing up to use their military might against Taiwan. People like his father had become accomplices in their own destruction. Well, that had to end. The world and the people in Taiwan had to realize that there was nothing inexorable about the growth of Chinese power—any more than Japan's in the 1930s. Operation Matchstick would send a powerful message to all of Asia and the world: Beijing isn't impregnable.

As for the personal risk, he had gone over the operation numerous times with Donovan. Everything had been planned with precision, to the last detail. Nothing could go wrong. No one would ever know he had done it.

The train station was a sea of humanity. After standing in a long line, Chen bought a first-class ticket for a train going southwest to Nanping, in Fujian province, about 230 miles inland from the Strait of Taiwan.

At the entrance to the train track, two policemen carrying clubs stopped him—one tall and thin, the other short and squat.

For what seemed like hours to Chen, the tall one examined his visa and passport.

"The nature of your business in Nanping?" the tall one asked.

"My computer company has one plant in Shanghai. We're considering building a second one in that area."

"Why there?"

"It's close to Taiwan. After unification, there will be transportation across the strait. We want to get there early."

That seemed to satisfy him. One of the goals of the regime was to stimulate new business.

Meantime, his colleague was eyeing Chen's bags suspiciously. "What's in that one?" he asked, pointing to the large brown suitcase.

"Computer parts," Chen said. He held his breath. The contents had been packaged to resemble computer parts, and that was what the writing said. Yet if the policeman began taking the items apart, he'd be able to determine what Chen was carrying. Chen felt the moisture building under his arms and soaking his shirt.

The short policeman pointed to the black duffel bag. "Open that one," he said.

When Chen obliged, he looked inside, examining the contents with care. Chen kept glancing at the large overhead clock. It was getting late. Other passengers were rushing by him, loaded down with bags. If he missed this train, he'd lose his pickup in Nanping and be stranded there.

He had only ten more minutes until the train's departure. Rushing these two policemen was a poor idea, he decided. With difficulty, he kept himself in check.

Sensing Chen's anxiety, the thin man said, "You have plenty of time."

The two policemen took a few steps back. The short one whispered something Chen couldn't hear. Then his colleague looked at Chen for several moments. "You can go," he said.

Chapter 20

"Will you make me French toast for breakfast, Daddy?" Amy said as she scampered into Ben's bedroom and jumped on his bed.

It was a few minutes past seven. Ben was wide-awake, as he had been all night. "I will on one condition," he said.

"What's that?" she said, climbing under the covers. He made sure his pajama bottoms were pulled up and tight around his waist. He didn't want her to see the Band-Aid.

"What condition?" she asked warily. She was used to the little deals Ben made with her to get her to do things.

He smiled. "The condition is, I get a big hug and a kiss."

She was happy to oblige. Holding her tight, Ben thought, God, I love this child so much. I can't let anything happen to her.

"Yuck," she said. "You're all grizzly. You didn't shave."

"Well, I just woke up, silly. Now, you let the French toast man get dressed. He'll meet you in the kitchen."

"I'll get the batter started."

"Easy, kiddo. Wait for me."

"Daddy. I know what to do. I'm no baby."

This morning there wasn't any request of hers he wouldn't grant. "Great, you get started," he said.

Amy knew that she was on a roll. Reading her father's mood, she added, "And I'll make chocolate milk, too."

"Whatever you want," he said as she scooted out of the room.

The French toast was cooking in the pan, and Amy was getting ready to turn it, under Ben's watchful eye, when the phone rang. It was Jennifer.

"Sorry, I got in too late last night to call you back," she said in a brisk tone. "What'd you decide to do about that phony confession?"

"Hang on a sec," he said as he helped Amy turn the French toast. While keeping one eye on the frying pan, he stretched the phone cord as far as it could go into the dining room. Not wanting to alarm Amy, he whispered, "A new development in the Gillis case. It was frightening, believe me. I've got to talk to you. Please, Jenny, it's urgent."

Jennifer knew something was very wrong. "What time would you like me at your office?"

"Forget the office. Come to my house as soon as you can. Bring everything you have that's relevant to Winthrop's murder. And please don't say a word about this to anybody."

They had just hung up when Amy shouted. "It's burning, Daddy!" He ran into the kitchen and snatched the pan from the burner. "Just a little crisp," he said, examining the undersides. "We'll smother it in lots of maple syrup."

That made her very happy. As she ate, he walked to the back of the house, where he unobtrusively glanced out of the kitchen window. A plainclothes D.C. cop was sitting on the bench next to Amy's swing set at the far end of the yard near the garage, watching the house. Ben went back to the front and stood at the picture window looking out. An unmarked car was parked in front with two of Art Campbell's detectives in the front seat.

Ben no longer thought that the blonde was fifty miles away. She was still in Washington. Before long, she would strike again. The only question was whether he and Campbell could find out for whom she was working and end their party before that happened.

When Amy was dressed and ready for school, Ben scooped the child up into his arms and held her tight. "You have a good day, kiddo," he said.

She kissed him. "You, too, kiddo."

Opening the door, Ben heard footsteps. His heart skipped a beat as he glanced through the storm door. With relief, he saw Jennifer walking up the steps, swinging a black briefcase in her hand.

"Time to go," Amy said.

When he put her down, Amy grabbed her old metal lunch box and book bag, then took Elana's hand.

He watched them go down the stairs, passing Jennifer on the way. At the sidewalk, they turned left and headed up the street toward the preschool. Amy was singing a Spanish song Elana had taught her. The police car fell in behind them.

"Cute kid," Jennifer said. With a pang she wondered if she and Ben would have had a child like that if they had gotten married.

"Thanks."

"How old is she?"

"Four. I'll bet you were a beauty when you were four."

She smiled at the compliment. "I was trouble, too."

"So what else is new?"

"One thing that isn't new is that sweatshirt you're wearing," she said in a jocular manner. She tapped him playfully on the shoulder, wanting to make it clear that she was willing to get away from her biting, sarcastic manner.

He eyed the Yale Law School sweatshirt dubiously. "Yeah, you were always after me to toss it. I could lie and say I bought a new one."

"But I'd know that a new one couldn't possibly get so grungy in five years."

"I feel comfortable in it," he said by way of apology. "I do my best work in it."

"So I remember. By the way, I assume those are still the same jeans?"

He smiled. "Regrettably, yes."

Jennifer took off her raincoat and hung it herself in the closet. She was wearing a perfectly pressed Dior gray suit with a thin red stripe and a white blouse. He didn't see how anyone could look so good early in the morning. If she felt awkward being back in the house she had lived in for almost a year, she didn't say anything, although he did watch her woman's eye roaming around, trying to determine what changes had been made since she moved out.

"Let's go back into the kitchen," he said.

He poured two cups of steaming coffee into mugs and sat down across from her, while she waited patiently for him to begin.

"Art Campbell told me about the blond hair," Ben said. "He also told me that you don't think Clyde Gillis killed Winthrop. I want you to tell me what you know."

"Where are you going with this?" Jennifer said evenly. "You've got to let me in on what's happening before you can expect me to lay out my whole case. Really, Ben. I'm not being difficult."

Ben paused to sip some coffee. She was right, of course. He had to tell her everything first, before he could ask her to disclose what she knew.

"I'm convinced," Ben said abruptly, "that Clyde Gillis didn't kill Winthrop."

She straightened up in surprise. "Wow, that's a mouthful." A great load had been taken off her mind. "Then why are we here? Why don't you dismiss the case? We can all go back to what we were doing before last Sunday."

"It's not that simple, I'm afraid."

"You want to tell me why?"

He looked down at the table, ashamed of what he had done, not wanting to admit it to her. "I was threatened last night and nearly killed," he said clumsily.

At first she thought he was kidding, which Ben had had a tendency to do when they were dating. She was ready to laugh. Then she saw the grimness in his face. She thought about the attack on Ann yesterday to get the second copy of the video, and she knew this was no joke.

"That's why we're meeting here, Jenny. Art's got police covering the house."

"Oh, Ben, I'm so sorry," she said.

He knew she meant it. "I appreciate that. I really do."

"What happened?"

He hesitated, not sure how much to tell her. "A blond woman attacked me."

Alarm bells started going off for Jennifer. "Where did this happen?"

Ben squirmed in his chair. At all costs, he refused to tell Jennifer what had happened to him last night. His interest in her was still strong. If she ever found out what he had done, she would probably be so repulsed that any chance of a rekindling on her part would be snuffed out forever.

"The details aren't important," he said, "and it's painful for me to talk about." Which was true, he thought. "The key thing is that the blonde who attacked me has to be our infamous George Nesbitt. When you put that together with the fact that George Nesbitt was a phony name, and my impression from my interrogation of Clyde Gillis at the jail Sunday night, a different scenario spins out."

She was suspicious about the details, but let it go. "Which is?" she asked.

"Art and I figure that somebody in the administration knows who killed Winthrop, and they're trying to cover it up. Your client happened to be in the wrong place at the wrong time. They rigged the evidence to fit him."

That was what she had thought all along. "Then why not release him?"

"These people play for keeps. She threatened to

kill me and Amy." He winced at the memory. "The confession has to be coerced. If I let Gillis out, she'll kill him in a minute and leave a copy of the confession beside the body."

The news of these threats alarmed her. "Then why not go to Director Murtaugh at the FBI, or even the President? Ann can get us into the White House."

He said quietly, "Because I don't know how high up this goes."

She thought he was overreacting. "Brewster's a decent man. He's never been mixed up in anything like this."

"Neither of us knows him that well," he said, frowning. "I can't speak for you, but I'm not prepared to bet my daughter's life on a guess about the integrity of a president I don't know. We've had some beauts in the Oval Office over the years."

"So whom do you trust? What do you plan to do?"

"With Art's help, and hopefully yours, I'll find out who hired the blonde to kill Winthrop. Then I'll go to the President—only after I've set it up so I can say the story goes to the press if anything happens to me."

She nodded her head hesitantly. "That sounds like a good plan."

He saw the doubt on her face. "The trouble is, I don't have much time. On top of that, I don't have the faintest idea who hired the blonde. That's where I'm hoping you might be able to help."

Jennifer studied Ben carefully. In those bloodshot eyes was a fear that she had never seen before. Ben was genuinely afraid for his own life and Amy's. How could she possibly not help him? She wouldn't be compromising the rights of Clyde Gillis. Ben was now in agreement with her that Clyde was innocent. And if Ben was right, Clyde might be murdered unless they found out who was behind Winthrop's death.

She reached into her briefcase on the floor and pulled out a stack of papers. "These motion papers are what I've been working on the last couple of days," she said as she tossed a copy across the table.

Ben studied the headings: *Motion for Temporary Injunction to Prevent the Chinese Ambassador from Leaving the United States; Motion to Depose the Chinese Ambassador;* and *Motion to Require the Chinese Ambassador to Appear as a Witness at the Trial of Clyde Gillis.*

Ben was stunned. "The Chinese ambassador? Liu? You've got to be kidding."

"I'm not, Ben. From Ann Winthrop I've learned facts that you don't know."

"And you really think that Liu had something to do with Winthrop's death?"

"Not something. Everything. The Chinese government was unhappy about Winthrop's Taiwan arms package. They learned that Winthrop employs prostitutes when he travels, and they tried to blackmail him. When he refused to yield to the blackmail, they decided to kill him by sending a woman he thought was a prostitute. A woman dressed as a man and with a fake ID in the name of George Nesbitt. Winthrop thought she was coming for sex. When she was in his house, she killed him."

Ben sat quietly for a long minute, letting her words sink in. "That's quite a story," he finally said.

Jennifer realized that he wasn't prepared to accept her conclusion, based on what she had said. She couldn't blame him. She still had gaps she wanted to fill in herself. "It's consistent with your theory. When somebody close to the President found out about it, they knew that they had a major scandal and a foreign policy nightmare on their hands. They couldn't take that a year before Brewster's reelection. So they initiated the cover-up that you're talking about."

Ben got up and walked around the room, mulling over what she had just told him. "It all fits together," he said thoughtfully. "Somebody in the administration could be covering up Winthrop's murder, arranged by

Liu. Where's the proof, though, that Liu was responsible?"

Instinctively, she hesitated. It was her defense counsel knee-jerk reaction against disclosing evidence to a prosecutor in advance of trial.

Ben knew what was running through her mind. "C'mon, Jenny," he said, "this isn't a normal case. Let go of the defense counsel role. For better or worse, we're in this together. Your client and I both have our lives on the line."

"Sorry, Ben, that was habit. Pavlov's dog at work. You're right, of course."

In a no-nonsense, detailed, factual presentation, she summarized everything that she had learned since Saturday. She showed Ben the pictures Mark Bonner had taken on Monday at the video place and then the ones depicting the pickup and delivery to the Chinese embassy. She played Ann's audiotape of Winthrop's meeting with the Chinese ambassador on November 1. She told Ben how Ann had been accosted in her house and forced to go to the bank vault in order to retrieve and turn over a second copy of the video, by the same man who delivered the first one to the Chinese embassy representative.

When she was finished, Ben said, "Is there another copy of the video?" Reluctantly, Jennifer reached into her briefcase and pulled it out. Having just repeated what had happened yesterday to Ann, she was now scared herself.

"Let's take a look at it," Ben said, leading the way to the living room. He turned on the television and shoved the tape into the VCR. As the screen came to life, the camera was focused on the bedroom of a hotel suite. Ben guessed that the camera had been installed in the hotel room adjacent to the suite and that a special mirror, a one-way glass, had been installed between the two rooms. The camera was shooting through that glass. The picture was clear, not at all grainy. The Chinese had obviously employed a professional camera crew with state-of-the-art equipment.

At first they were looking at an empty bedroom. Then faint voices came from the living room of the suite. Ben recognized Winthrop's voice, off in the distance.

Within a minute, they heard stronger voices. Winthrop entered the bedroom, followed by two women, both blondes, wearing identical black microminiskirts and low-cut black tank tops. Winthrop reached into a bureau drawer and extracted a large roll of British pounds, which he divided between the two women. They counted it carefully and then put the money away.

The three of them were still standing in front of the bed when the women began undressing him. All the while he was laughing and smiling.

"On the chair, big boy," one said to him when he was fully undressed. "First you can watch us play."

They undressed each other, fondling and kissing as they did. Winthrop egged them on with delight.

Finally, the two women pulled Winthrop toward the bed. His penis was fully erect as they pushed him down on his back across the king-size bed. One of the women slipped a condom on him, and then put him in her mouth. The other one squatted over his face, spread out her vagina, and thrust down toward his mouth. "Eat me, big boy, eat me," she cried out. Winthrop began licking her wildly.

Jennifer was filled with loathing and disgust. She reached for the remote control and turned off the set. "You've got the idea," she said. "I played it to the end when Ann first gave it to me. The rest is more of the same. He was scum."

Ben was shaking his head. "That video's dynamite. I see why people are prepared to do anything to get hold of it. I don't think you should be carrying it around with you."

"I won't give it up."

"At least let Art make a copy to lock up in his office."

She nodded. "That I'll do."

Now convinced of Liu's involvement in the Winthrop affair, Ben picked up her motion papers and leafed through them.

"My idea," Jennifer said, "is to confront Liu head-on by making him testify under oath about his involvement in Winthrop's death."

Ben shook his head absently, still flipping through her papers. "It won't work."

"Why not?"

He looked at her directly. "You'll never get a chance to depose him. The White House will blow smoke about diplomatic immunity. While you're fighting that legal battle, they'll let him slip out of the country. And even if you did manage to depose him, he'd admit everything on the tape, but deny he had anything to do with Winthrop's murder. And you know what?"

She gazed at him, waiting for him to continue.

"We don't have a shred of direct evidence linking the Chinese ambassador or his government to the murder."

"But we have the video," Jennifer protested, "and proof of his efforts to get it back."

Ben nodded. "That's true, but it's still a big leap from that evidence to Winthrop's murder. If we put on a case in court against Liu with what we have now, we'd never survive a motion to dismiss."

She wrinkled up her nose, thinking about what he had just said. "So where's that leave us?"

"We've got to get some direct evidence linking the Chinese government and Ambassador Liu to Winthrop's death. Then we can force the administration to let us question him. If they won't, we'll go to the press. The key now is to get that direct evidence."

"Easier said than done."

"You're not kidding. Let's go back over everything one more time. There's got to be a loose thread somewhere we can grab onto and use to unravel the ball."

She started back over her story a second time. In

the middle, he interrupted her. "Peg Barton," he said. "Ann told you on the audiotape, from the night Winthrop and Liu met at Winthrop's house, that the Chinese ambassador said the secretary of state used Peg Barton in London to arrange the evening with the two prostitutes. It's not much, but it's a name. It gives us something to go on."

She still didn't follow. "How can she help us?"

"Your friend, the shrink at NIMH, told you to find out who supplied him with prostitutes. Peg Barton is in London, but at least she moves us in that direction. Besides, she's someone who interacted with both Winthrop and the Chinese. You know what I mean?"

Jennifer didn't. He could read it on her face.

Ben continued, "Peg Barton and her girls had to be in on making the London video."

Suddenly, the telephone rang. Ben glanced at it nervously. What if it was the blonde threatening him again? Demanding to know whether he was taking the confession to Judge Hogan this morning? Telling him that she was watching Amy's preschool?

"You'd better answer it," Jennifer said.

His hands were moist when he picked up the phone. Hearing Campbell's voice, Ben breathed a sigh of relief.

"Can you come over to Clyde Gillis's house ASAP?" Campbell said. "I may have a break for you."

"Jennifer and I are on our way."

"And take your cues from me," Campbell ordered him. "Don't try to seize control. It won't work here."

"Yes, sir."

Excited, Ben hung up and ran up the stairs, discarding his Yale Law sweatshirt and faded jeans on the way. He'd better shave fast and dress like a lawyer. Campbell was always careful, Ben knew. If he had a break, then maybe their position wasn't as hopeless as it had seemed an hour ago.

* * *

Jennifer drove while Ben kept checking through the rear window, looking for the blonde. As far as he could tell, they weren't being followed.

Lucinda Gillis was sitting on the living room sofa when Campbell led Ben and Jennifer into the Gillises' house. Upstairs, two girls were shouting at each other. A television set was blasting downstairs.

Impervious to the noise, Lucinda sat perfectly still, with a composed look on her face. Her arms were crossed in front of her chest. Jennifer sat down on the sofa next to her in a show of solidarity with her client's wife.

"We've come to an understanding of sorts," Campbell said to Ben. "Mrs. Gillis saw you in court yesterday. She knows it's your case. She'll agree to tell you about her husband's confession if you agree to certain things."

"What are those, Mrs. Gillis?" Ben asked politely.

The detective removed a piece of paper from a ledge above the fireplace filled with knickknacks and handed it to Ben. It was in Lucinda Gillis's handwriting. As Ben read aloud, the detective paced.

" 'One. We agree to release Clyde Gillis from jail immediately and not charge him with any crime because we know that he is innocent. Two. We will not charge Lucinda Gillis with any crime if she gives all of the money to the police. Three. We will protect Clyde and Lucinda Gillis and all of their children.' "

What money were they talking about? Ben wondered. That must be the break Campbell had referred to.

There were two signature lines at the bottom. Underneath one, the words *Ben Hartwell for the United States* was spelled out in black letters. *Detective Arthur Campbell for the District of Columbia* was written under the other.

When Ben finished reading, he handed the document to Jennifer.

Campbell said, "I told Mrs. Gillis that we would

sign it if she made one change. We can't release her husband yet because we can protect him better in jail. I'll make sure that he gets treated well. But I told her that you won't prosecute him anymore."

"That's right," Ben replied without hesitation, knowing full well that he could be fired for making a commitment like this on behalf of the United States without Al Hennessey's express approval.

Lucinda nodded her agreement. "Change the paper, Detective Campbell," she said.

Jennifer handed Campbell the paper, and he made the revisions.

As Ben waited, he thought, What a sad commentary on our society. People don't believe the police unless they put it in writing. The two men signed the paper and handed it to Lucinda.

Satisfied, she began talking. "Yesterday afternoon, a woman called me and said she could help me. She asked me to meet her at the Van Ness Metro stop, which I did."

Ben was about to break in, but he bit his tongue. Campbell had said this was his show.

"What did she look like?" Campbell asked.

"She had lovely blond hair and blue eyes. She was pretty, but not as beautiful as Miss Moore," she said, pointing at Jennifer, who blushed. "They look like the same type. Except that she wore her hair long, hanging down, not up like Miss Moore. And she wasn't wearing glasses like Miss Moore."

Campbell reached into his briefcase and extracted the picture the artist had made last night with Ben's description.

"Yeah, that's her," Lucinda said.

Jennifer looked at the picture, then at Ben, knowing that he would have been attracted to her, which must be how he got himself into trouble last night.

"What kind of car was she driving?" Campbell asked.

"It was old and blue. That's all I know. Afterward,

I thought I should have looked at the license plate." She pursed her lips. "You don't think about those things at the time."

Campbell waited patiently, making sure Lucinda was finished with that part. Then he asked, "What happened next?"

"I got into her car. From Connecticut Avenue, she drove into Rock Creek Park. She pulled off into a parking lot. You know, one of those little ones next to a picnic grove? Anyway, there was nobody around. At first I was a little frightened. But she said that she wanted a quiet place to talk."

"What did she say?"

"She told me that she had spoken to Clyde at the jail and promised him two million dollars if he would confess. It would be paid out at a rate of ten thousand dollars for every month of his life. He refused. So she told me that she would kill all of my children one by one."

Ben expected her to start crying at this horrible threat. Not Lucinda Gillis. She had a core of inner strength that she drew upon to continue talking in a flat, unemotional tone.

"She just said it so matter-of-fact, as if she was telling me it would rain tomorrow. She didn't seem like a real person. She showed me a sharp knife to convince me that she was serious. It wasn't necessary. I had no doubt from the cold-blooded way that woman talked."

Instantly, Ben's hand went to his pants, covering the right cheek of his buttocks and the wound. Yeah, she's serious about using that knife, he thought.

"We talked some more. Finally I told her that I would persuade my husband to change his mind about the confession. She said that was good. She asked for my account number at Riggs Bank and promised me that the first deposit of ten thousand dollars would be wired into my account at six o'clock yesterday if Clyde confessed. She gave me a telephone number to call her at five o'clock. I convinced Clyde to confess. Then I called the woman."

Ben looked expectantly at Campbell.

"Mrs. Gillis kept the phone number," he said. "It's a pay phone on the corner of Twelfth and L. Mrs. Gillis also gave me her account number at Riggs Bank." He stopped to pat his pocket. "And a note that lets me get any information about her account."

Ben decided at this point it was all right for him to speak up. He turned to Campbell. "I think we better go down to Riggs Bank and see about that deposit."

They left Jennifer's red SAAB convertible on Quincy Street and set off in Campbell's unmarked car to the main branch of Riggs Bank. The detective didn't take a direct route. He wove around streets and back alleys of southeast Washington until he was certain they weren't being followed.

At the bank, Ben and Jennifer waited in the car, parked on Pennsylvania Avenue, which was off limits to vehicular traffic, while Campbell went inside alone.

In the high-ceilinged marble lobby resembling a shrine as much as a bank, he sat down across the desk from a pale, thin young man with black horn-rimmed glasses resting halfway down his nose. On his desk was a sign with gold letters that said, HARVEY MILLER, VICE PRESIDENT. The banker studied Lucinda Gillis's note carefully.

"Without Ms. Gillis being here," Miller began, "I'm afraid that—"

"If you even dream about giving me any shit like that," Campbell said irately, "I'm going right to Mr. Parker, who always cooperates with the police. You'll be Harvey Miller, former vice president."

The detective's harsh tone, coupled with invoking the name of the president of the bank, had the desired effect. Miller pushed back his glasses and began punching buttons on the computer on his desk. The screen immediately sprang to life.

"Last evening at five fifty-eight P.M., Washington time, a wire transfer of ten thousand dollars was made into the Gillises' account."

"Where'd the money come from?"

"Credit Suisse in Zurich. Number Twenty Bahnhof-strasse."

"From whose account in Zurich?"

"There's no name. Only an account number." Miller didn't wait for the detective to ask. He wrote the Swiss bank's name, the address, and the account number on a small piece of paper, and handed it to him.

With a deadpan expression, Campbell came out of the bank and got into the car. Before he could open his mouth, Ben said, "Well, what happened?"

Campbell looked at Jennifer and smiled. "Was he always so impatient when you used to date him?"

She returned the smile. "He has lots of good qualities. Patience isn't one of them. No way I could change him."

"Yeah, that's what I figured."

Campbell reached into his pocket and handed Ben the piece of paper Miller had supplied. "How good are your contacts at the Department of the Treasury?" Campbell asked. "They might be able to shake some more info free from Credit Suisse, but maybe not. From my experience, those Swiss bankers are tough customers."

"We can't go to Treasury," Ben responded. "If someone high up in the administration's involved, a call to Treasury will set off the alarms bells. I'll be tossed off the case, for openers."

"We need someone in Zurich," Jennifer said.

Ben's mind was racing ahead. "A few years ago I prosecuted a high official at Treasury for corruption. Same as now, I had to make an end run around official connections to Swiss banks. I developed a relationship with Jack Carmack, a CIA operative in Zurich, who hates the Treasury people because of their haughtiness. Carmack's well wired into the Swiss banking industry."

"Would Carmack help you," Jennifer asked skeptically, "in a case like this when you're operating on your own?"

Ben realized it was a long shot, too, and he frowned. "It's worth a try. We'd have to do it in person because the CIA routinely monitors the calls to and from Carmack, and we don't want to tip off people in Washington. What do you think?"

"We've got no choice," Jennifer said.

Reluctantly, Ben nodded in agreement.

"So now we've got a bank in Zurich and a madam in London to work with," Jennifer said.

The detective offered, "Sounds to me like you two are headed to Europe."

At this suggestion Ben instantly looked worried. "What will happen to Amy if I'm gone?"

Campbell responded, "I'll personally spend time at your house and watch her go to and from school. I hate to put it this way, but as long as you're not planning to be with her all day, she'll be as safe whether you're in Europe or downtown."

Ben wasn't satisfied. "No, I can't do that," he said, shaking his head.

"Let me call Ann," Jennifer volunteered. "She'd be glad to stay with Amy while we're gone. She's been dying for grandchildren." Seeing Ben was unconvinced, she added, "To get started, the two of them can spend some time together when Amy gets home from school today—before we have to leave for the airport."

"Ann Winthrop is hardly my idea of a bodyguard," Ben replied.

Jennifer reached into her briefcase and extracted the picture of the man with the broken nose in the video store parking lot. "This gentleman might disagree with you about that."

Voice mail is great, Ben thought. It's the perfect way to leave messages for people when you don't want to talk to them.

From the phone upstairs in the study in his house, he left identical messages for Hennessey, Traynor, and Fulton. "Sorry, I had to go to Chicago for a couple of days on the Young case. This shouldn't pose any problem for the Gillis prosecution because there haven't been any new developments. I have plenty of time to get ready for trial."

He smiled when he hung up from Fulton's voice mail. For forty-eight hours he and Jennifer would simply vanish. Only Campbell and Ann knew their itinerary.

Jennifer walked into the room. "Art Campbell called on the other line. He made a copy of the video, which will be delivered here before we leave for the airport. They finished analyzing Winthrop's pants. It was precoital fluid, no doubt about it."

Ben cringed. He wondered what type of sick game the blonde had played with Winthrop—making him think he was going to fuck her when she blew him away.

Jennifer was looking at him curiously, and he quickly changed the subject. "How are Amy and Ann getting along?"

"Fabulously. Ann's really into dressing up Barbies."

Ben went downstairs to spend some time with Amy before they left for the airport, while Jennifer called her office to check for messages. Kathy said Jim Slater had called but didn't leave a message. Jennifer checked her watch. There was time to return the call.

To her surprise, she heard Miss O'Brien, Slater's secretary, say that she'd pull him out of a meeting. What did he want that was so important? Jennifer wondered.

"I called to see if your workload has changed for the weekend. Is California now doable?" he asked.

She smiled. "Persistent fellow, aren't you?" Her tone was gentle and playful.

"I'm not used to rejection."

"Poor baby. But it's not rejection. Just deferral."

He sounded elated. "Deferral I can handle. Tell you what. The first weekend after the Gillis case is over, I'll take you to London for the weekend. We'll stay at the Connaught. Three shows. Meals at Gordon Ramsey and The Square. How's that sound?"

He sure knew the right things to say to a girl. "Sounds great."

"Good. It's a deal."

"Hope you win your polo match on Saturday."

"I always win."

"Modest fellow, aren't you?"

"Talk to you when I get back."

Ben drove to Dulles Airport in his Volvo. Telling Jennifer to look for any car following them, especially a dark blue one, he tried every trick he could remember from any detective movie. Feeling a little like James Bond, he went up streets one way, and down the other. He made sharp quick turns, pulled to a stop, and waited. He got off the beltway twice—once at Old Georgetown Road and once at River Road— and back on again quickly, always watching the rearview mirror.

All of this time, a mile behind the Volvo, at the wheel of her own car, Gwen watched Ben's antics with amusement. Get into the modern age, you dope, she thought. With electronic homing devices, you don't have to see a car to follow it.

When he finally parked at Dulles, she parked three lanes away and waited until he stepped inside the terminal before exiting her car. From a distance, she saw him and Jennifer in line at the United international counter.

She picked the lock to a dark gray door that said UNITED EMPLOYEES ONLY. None of the flight attendants lounging around between flights paid any attention when she sat down behind a computer. Looking very official, she punched the keys. Before Ben and Jennifer even boarded the plane, she had their entire itinerary. Zurich tonight on United. London tomorrow afternoon on British Air. An open return to Washington.

She exited the room and went to a pay phone downstairs. Using a phony credit card number that AT&T's automated system took, she called Zurich. A gruff-sounding man answered, "Herr Wilhelm."

Then he recognized her voice and cheered up. *"Meine kleine mädchen,"* he said, eager to do the bidding of the blond goddess.

Five minutes later when Gwen hung up the phone, she had a puzzled expression on her face. She knew why Ben and Jennifer were going to Zurich, and she had arranged with the help of Karl Wilhelm to deal with them there. But why London?

There must be facts related to Winthrop in London. But they hadn't told her about those facts. They had concealed them from her. That made her very angry.

Chapter 21

Ben had a strategy for dealing with Jennifer. He waited until the plane had leveled off at thirty-five thousand feet, and they were sipping white wine.

"There's something I've been wanting to tell you," he said in a no-nonsense tone. "Now you're going to listen to me."

She saw the determination on his face and groaned. "We're getting along so well now. You want to ruin it all?"

"I have to tell you the story of what happened."

With her eyes she pleaded with him to stop. People made mistakes. She was willing to move on, but he wouldn't let it rest. "Can't we leave it alone? Just keep on the way we are now?"

"I can't do that. You've got to hear me out."

She could see that she had no choice, and it was too bad. Since this morning, she had enjoyed being with him again. She was starting to feel the old, easy companionship they used to share. He didn't wow her like Slater, but in a way she was more comfortable with that. She was hoping that they could at least be friends.

She made one more futile stab at stopping him. "Really, Ben," she said, trying not to sound dogmatic, "whatever happened, happened. Some things are best left undiscussed."

"Not this one, Jenny. Please let me tell you about California."

He was so serious, she tried to add some levity. "Since I don't have a parachute and it's a full plane, I guess you've got your audience."

"Good, let me start with the bottom line." He whispered, "I didn't do anything with her at all."

Jennifer shook her head in disbelief. "Yeah, right."

"Well, let me explain."

Her voice was ten degrees frostier. "Ben, this was your idea. I'm willing to listen."

"It was a Saturday afternoon when Terry called," he began slowly. He had this memorized.

"I know it was a Saturday afternoon," she interrupted. "I was the one who answered the phone. I happened to be addressing our wedding invitations at the time, as you just might remember."

A little steamed, he replied, "I remember exactly what you were doing."

"When I answered the phone, she asked for you, and I said, in my most polite future-wifely little voice, 'Can I tell him who's calling?' She told me it was none of my fucking business, which was just lovely."

"C'mon, Jenny, she was in bad shape. She was diagnosed a couple days later as being depressive and suicidal. When I picked up the phone, she was threatening to slit her wrists with a kitchen knife."

"So my fiancé, a brilliant trial lawyer without one ounce of psychiatric training, decided to drop everything and fly to Los Angeles."

All of the old anger flared up like it was yesterday. "You knew what had happened to my parents. You knew that Terry and I had been raised as brother and sister. That both of her parents were dead. That there was no one else who could help her. You knew all of that."

"I also knew," she countered, "that you and Terry had dated when you were both seniors at Berkeley. In fact, if I recall, when we discussed our prior relationships early on, you said that before me Terry was the only woman you had ever dated seriously. I think that was your term."

Ben grimaced. Jesus, Jenny had a steel-trap mind. "Yeah, I did say that. I also told you that dating her had been a mistake. She was screwed up even then at Berkeley. Into coke and other drugs, which I didn't touch."

"But the sex with her was great."

Actually, it had been fantastic when they were at Berkeley together, Ben remembered, but the sex was all they had together. He didn't tell Jennifer that.

"I had law school ahead of me. I wasn't interested in a relationship with anyone. Certainly not with her. So I broke it off. She dropped out of school a little while later."

The flight attendant brought a tray with dinner, but Jennifer waved her away. "I'm not hungry," she said.

"It's going to be a long time until we eat again," Ben said.

"Don't tell me what to do," she snapped at him.

His face straining to look polite, he asked the flight attendant to hold both of their meals until later.

Jennifer turned back to the argument. "You told me that you were going out to Los Angeles for two days. Just long enough to get her under the care of a psychiatrist. You'd be back Monday evening."

"That's what I thought at the time. Things got more complicated than that."

"As I later learned."

Here was the nasty side to her again. "What's that supposed to mean?"

"It's your story. Why don't you continue to spin your tall tale? By the way, just for the record, don't leave out the fact that even after what she said on the phone and even knowing that you had dated Terry, I trusted you. I was such a dope. I thought it was a good idea for you to go and help her. I even drove you to the airport."

They were getting to the tough part. Ben drained the rest of the wine in his glass and ran his hand through his hair. "When I got there Saturday night, she was in dreadful shape. She was out on the balcony of her fifteenth-floor apartment in Santa Monica, threatening to jump to Wilshire Boulevard below."

"How touching."

"I called a psychiatrist who had been a fraternity brother of mine at Berkeley, and I leaned on him to come out. He calmed her down and medicated her. He agreed to see her Monday morning. I figured I'd fly home Monday afternoon."

"That's what you told me when you called on Sunday."

"But on Monday he gave her a new medication. He said it would take a day or so for her condition to stabilize. So I decided to stay a little longer. I called and told you that on Monday. Later that day, she took most of a bottle of sleeping pills. I rushed her to St. John's Hospital in Santa Monica, where they pumped her stomach. That's when I decided I'd better move out of the Beverly Hilton and into her apartment to take care of her. I figured I could sleep on the couch."

"Wasn't there anybody else who could take care of her?" she asked suspiciously.

"There was nobody," he protested. "I swear it. Remember, this wasn't the greatest time for me. I was scrambling to complete a brief in the Dobson case that was due to be filed in court in Washington on Friday." That struck a chord of remembrance in her, and she nodded for him to continue. "Tuesday morning, my psychiatrist friend said he would try a different medication. I stayed with Terry Tuesday night and Wednesday night, sleeping on the couch. Then, even though she was pleading with me to stay longer, I told her I couldn't do any more for her. I loved you, and I was going home to you. I tried calling you Thursday morning to say I was coming home, but I couldn't reach you. So I got on the first plane out." He stopped, his voice turning dull. "I returned home to the wonderful surprise you left for me. All the wedding invitations cut in half and placed neatly on the bed. Your engagement ring on top of the pile, that lovely note, and you had moved out of the house. The worst part was you wouldn't even let me explain. You wouldn't even talk to me."

"I can see how shocked you were. You expected a hero's return."

He was surprised at how tough, sarcastic, and sharp Jennifer sounded when she wanted to. He never remembered this side of her from before. Maybe it had developed as a result of the broken engagement and her divorce.

He continued, "Sarah Van Buren came to talk to you when I got back. She told you that I was just taking care of Terry. I never had sex with her. Why didn't you believe her?"

"Oh, c'mon, Ben. She was just telling me what you had told her. She may have believed you, but she had no idea what really happened."

She was right about that. Desperate at that point, he had told Sarah what to say. When Sarah couldn't make any headway, he had decided it was futile.

"I never tried to call you again after that," Ben said. "I figured if you didn't trust me, then there was nothing to our relationship. No point in our getting married. The hell with you. I wasn't going to spend my life with somebody like that. Face it, Jenny, your imagination ran away with you. I know what you thought." He locked eyes with her. "I swear to God I never fucked Terry the whole time I was in L.A. That's it. End of story. By the way, I might add that I've never seen or spoken to Terry since. Now, does that satisfy you?"

"You only left one thing out," Jennifer said coldly.

"What's that?"

"You didn't explain what you were doing asleep in Terry's bed at five o'clock Wednesday afternoon, when I called and she answered the phone."

"What'd you say?" he asked in a weak voice.

"Don't stall for time. You damn well heard me."

"You called on Wednesday afternoon?"

"Yes, darling," she said in a voice dripping with sarcasm. "You gave me the telephone number at both the Beverly Hilton and at Terry's apartment. You hadn't called me since Monday. Wednesday evening, about eight o'clock, Washington time, I decided to call you and see how things were going. First I tried the Beverly Hilton. They said that you checked out two days before. That was a big surprise. So I called Terry's apartment and asked to talk to you."

"What did she say?"

She puffed out her lips in a fake smile. "Let me try to do it in her sexy voice."

"Just tell me," he demanded.

"She said, 'He's sleeping, honey. Do you want me to wake him?' And I responded, like a total moron, 'What do you mean, he's sleeping?' So she said, 'He's right here next to me in bed, his eyes are closed, and he's making little snoring noises. I love that about Ben. After we have sex, he sleeps like a baby. Does he do that with you, too, honey?' Seemed pretty clear what had happened. Wouldn't you say?"

Ben was outraged. "It was an absolute lie. I never had sex with her that week."

"Good try, Ben, but you're not convincing me."

"Jesus, Jenny, I had no idea that you called on Wednesday. I wasn't even in her apartment on Wednesday afternoon." He paused, trying to recall. No, he hadn't been. "I remember distinctly. I was downtown at the U.S. Attorney's office making final changes in my brief in the Dobson case. I can get an affidavit from somebody down there if you need it," he said angrily, seeing her face hadn't changed. "Believe it or not, I was trying to keep up on my work that week. The U.S. Attorney's office in L.A. made an office and secretarial help available to me as a courtesy." He clenched his teeth. "Dammit, Jenny. I didn't do a thing with her. All you had to do was give me a chance to explain. The woman was nuts, for God's sake. That's why I was there in the first place. What happened to trust?"

A flight attendant came over with a bottle of white wine in her hand. "A little more?" she asked Jennifer.

"How about a lot more?"

"Same for me," Ben added.

Mercifully, Ben's stopping to take a sip gave Jennifer a chance to absorb what he had said. His story sounded credible, but so had Terry on the phone that day.

Ben seemed to read her mind. "I'm going to say only one more thing and then I'll shut up. I felt I was wronged, and I'm sorry I didn't push you harder to clear the air. But now I have. So can we forget it and start over?"

Confused, she left his question hanging. She didn't know what to believe or what she thought. Assuming the worst, he had made a mistake and cheated on her with this old Berkeley flame. He was sorry. Should she have forgiven him? She loved him at the time. Still, she thought she had made the right decision. That was no way to start a marriage.

Suppose he was telling her the truth now, which she was beginning to believe. He had still been self-centered and inconsiderate at the time. Not calling after Monday was just one example of that. They were engaged. He didn't care enough to call. She sighed. On the other hand, they had had so many wonderful times together. Was he different now? More thoughtful? She wasn't sure. She doubted it. "Life's not like that, Ben. You can't just pick up from a prior point years ago. A lot's happened to both of us since then."

"Well, we can try."

"We can't," she said emphatically, "because I need somebody who'll treat me as their top priority, regardless of what happens in the rest of his life. And I don't think you're capable of making that kind of commitment."

He frowned, listening to her. There was something more on her mind than what she'd just said. "You're involved with someone else now, aren't you?"

She had no intention of telling him about Slater. "That's not the point."

"But it is. Who is he?" Ben snapped.

"It's none of your business. Discussion closed."

At five minutes past ten that evening, Gwen stood in the shadows behind the statue of Thomas Jefferson watching the figure in the long black coat pace nervously in the dim light from the moon's reflection on the water of the tidal basin. The floodlights on the memorial grounds had been turned off at nine o'clock. GSA was trying to save money.

Before climbing the stairs to the memorial, Gwen had searched the grounds in every direction. She had to be satisfied that no one else was there. They might be trying to kill her. She realized how expendable she had become. She was the only thread linking them to the Winthrop killing. In their shoes, she would have shot her in an instant.

Still, she needed the meeting tonight. She had to know what they knew.

She approached the figure stealthily, moving on the toes of her tennis sneakers. Then she threw a hammerlock around the neck, evoking a scream. "Hey, what—" She tightened her grip and conducted a body search. There were no weapons, so she let go.

"What the hell?"

"Sorry, I had to do that. We're down to the short strokes now. There are no team players. It's everybody for himself."

"Why did you want to see me? I thought we decided that you'd handle the rest yourself. No more meetings."

"Something's happened. Ben Hartwell's gone to Europe. He's taken Jennifer with him."

"Europe?"

"Yeah, Zurich and London. Zurich I can understand. I'm dealing with that. But why London?"

"Ben won't find anything in London. You can count on that."

"What's he looking for in London?"

"You don't need to know."

Gwen reached into her pocket and slipped out the

push-button stiletto. The blade shot out of the end. "I need to know everything."

"Don't worry. London will be a dead end for Ben Hartwell. We're in this together. I have more to lose than you do."

Gwen thought about what she had just heard. "I've taken out an insurance policy," she finally said. "I have a good friend in one of the intelligence agencies. If anything happens to me, he'll receive a letter explaining everything we did."

"Nothing will happen to you."

"Hartwell's becoming more of a problem than I would have thought. I have to be more creative in dealing with him."

"You don't have to worry about London. I told you it'll be a dead end for him."

"If London isn't a dead end for Hartwell, I'll kill you."

She said it matter-of-factly, as if she were announcing that she had to get a cup of coffee. Quickly she turned and disappeared into the shadows.

Chapter 22

The Bahnhofstrasse, running from the train station to Lake Zurich, cuts through the heart of Zurich's most fashionable shopping area. Each side of the wide thoroughfare and its tiny side streets are lined with the most expensive designer shops from France, Italy, and everywhere else in the world. Mixed in with those shops are the main branches of a half dozen of Zurich's largest banks. And under the street, encased in steel and concrete, are vaults that hold gold ingots, row after row, piled high for nearly half a mile.

The taxi Ben and Jennifer took at Zurich airport turned onto the Bahnhofstrasse at the train station and threaded its way slowly along the street in heavy morning-rush-hour traffic. A wet snow was falling with thick, heavy flakes. As the taxi stopped for a red light, Ben yawned and looked around. Off to the left behind the buildings he could see the Fraumünster, a thirteenth-century church, with its slender spire shooting up to the sky and its five stained glass windows, in their current version designed by Marc Chagall.

What he didn't realize was that he and Jennifer had been followed from the minute they cleared Swiss customs by a sophisticated tag team, using cellular phones and several different cars to avoid being detected. Now a gray Mercedes was trailing two cars behind the taxi.

From the airplane, Ben had phoned Jack Carmack to arrange a meeting. He suggested the restaurant in

the Hotel Bar Du Lac at the far end of the Bahnhofstrasse. Low, heavy clouds hung over the lake,
blocking off any view as they scrambled out of the
taxi, under the hotel's canopy.

Ben looked around the lobby and the dark-paneled
hotel restaurant. No sign of Carmack.

"Let's get a table," he said to Jennifer. "Jack must
be running late."

When they were seated and a waiter had deposited
a pot of hot coffee, Jennifer asked, "Suppose your
buddy Carmack doesn't show? What's plan B?"

"Jack'll be here."

"What makes you so sure?"

"On the telephone, he perked up when I said I
wanted to come over and have some fun with him like
the last time. He really hates the people at Treasury.
Says they think they know everything. They're always
freezing him out."

As tired as she was, Ben's enthusiasm was conta-
gious. "What's he doing here anyway?" she asked,
interested.

"He's a CIA operative whose cover is an import-
export firm. What he's looking for is financial crimes
involving U.S. currency. It's one of the CIA's main
missions in the post–Cold War era. Treasury should
want his help, but you know how these interagency
squabbles go."

"I almost forgot how delightful working for the U.S.
government can be. Excuse me."

Jennifer got up to go to the rest room. As he
watched her walk away, he thought, We've been in an
airplane all night, and she still looks so striking. She
had so much natural grace and elegance that even
bankers looked up from their stock listings in the
morning paper. She looks as if she's ready for a fash-
ion show, he thought, while I'm here with a stubble
of a beard, dressed in my rumpled gray suit, looking
like I snatched an hour's sleep on an airplane, which
I did.

Ben sipped some coffee and looked anxiously

toward the door and then around the room. It was about two-thirds full. To the empty table next to them the maître d' led a good-looking, smartly dressed young brunette. She was in her late twenties, being followed by a tall, distinguished-looking man in a banker's blue suit and tie, who must have been at least sixty, Ben guessed. The man was wearing a large hearing aid in his right ear and carrying a copy of *Le Monde*. The woman began rattling on in French about something or other, maybe her shopping plans for the day, while the man half listened and half looked through the paper. Ben smiled. It reminded him of breakfasts he and Nan had had when he traveled with her on a few concert tours.

Where the hell was Carmack? He began to worry. Jennifer had a point. What if Carmack didn't show? He hadn't even begun to formulate a plan B.

Jennifer returned to the table a moment later. Then Ben saw tall, wiry Jack Carmack standing at the restaurant entrance, and he breathed a sigh of relief. Unless Jack had changed his routine, which Ben doubted, at night he was a rakish bachelor playboy. In the mornings he ran five miles every day, regardless of the weather.

Ben was no longer watching the couple at the next table. He didn't see the man reach into his jacket pocket and adjust the buttons on the listening device he had hooked to his ear. By pressing a couple of buttons and aiming a tiny pointer at Ben's table, the man could drown out other noise, including that of his breakfast companion, while amplifying Ben's conversation.

Ben introduced Jennifer, whose hand Jack held for a very long time as he shook it, exchanged a few greetings, and quickly said in a whisper, "I need your help again, and I can't use Treasury."

Carmack looked around nervously. When he didn't see anything suspicious, he answered in a soft, barely audible voice, "You're going after another Treasury official?"

Ben hesitated. He didn't want to lie to Jack. On the other hand, he wanted Carmack to have only minimal information. The names of Joyner, Donovan, or other top CIA officials hadn't surfaced yet in the Winthrop affair, but a foreign government was involved. From Ben's knowledge of how Washington worked, that meant there was a chance some of the roads ran to Langley.

"We don't know yet. But it's not the Company," Ben said.

That was good enough for Carmack. "What do you need?"

"I've got an account number at Credit Suisse, Number Twenty Bahnhofstrasse. It's been used to fund illegal activities in Washington. I need to know whose account it is, as well as the source of any deposits into the account."

Carmack frowned and rubbed his forehead. "Credit Suisse can be tough."

"Suppose I were to go in cold to an officer at the top and wave my prosecutor's ID at him. Do you think I'd be able to get what I need?"

Carmack smiled. "You've got to be kidding. No way. He'd laugh at you."

"That's what I was afraid you'd say. Got any bright ideas of what I can do?"

Carmack broke off an end of a croissant and spread some marmalade on it. He ate it slowly, thinking about Ben's question.

"I've got a pretty decent relationship with Klaus Fenster, who's one of their top people. About as good as any non–Swiss national can have, which isn't saying a lot. But more important, he owes me for some information I gave him a month ago about a money-laundering operation in the Bahamas. It's a valuable chip. I'd be happy to talk to Klaus and see if he'll quietly give you what you want."

Ben looked at Jennifer. "That would be great."

Carmack pulled a tiny cell phone out of his pocket. "The Company doesn't know about this little beauty."

Ben's German wasn't good enough to understand every word, but he got the idea. Jack had just set up a meeting with Klaus in fifteen minutes.

"You're in luck," Carmack said. "He's in today, but I'll have to see him myself first. That's the only way Klaus will do it. That's best for us as well. You wait here for forty-five minutes; then go to the bank and ask for Klaus Fenster. I'll have everything wired. He'll give you the information. If there's a snag, I'll be waiting in front of the bank to stop you before you go inside. So if you don't see me, it's a go."

Carmack got up and hurried out of the restaurant. The man with the hearing aid followed him a few seconds later, leaving behind the smartly dressed brunette.

Ben should have been tired from the long plane ride, but he was feeling a surge of adrenaline. Suddenly very hungry, he ordered a cheese omelet. Jennifer picked at the pastries in the basket on the table. Ben glanced at his watch. It was going to be a long forty-five minutes.

It was five blocks from the Hotel Bar Du Lac to Credit Suisse. The snow was coming down more heavily. The sidewalk was crowded with people with raised large black umbrellas. For the first block Carmack let the snow cake on his hair. Then he brushed it off and slipped a navy Fila ski cap out of his pocket and onto his head.

At the next corner, he stopped for a red light. This was Zurich, where the good burghers waited patiently for the light to change. The snow made him think of Christmas. It had been almost six months since he'd visited his widowed mother in Queens. She continued hanging on, living alone in an apartment and neighborhood that had deteriorated so badly that Jack pleaded with her to move out each time he saw her. But she was too stubborn to leave. He'd go back this year for Christmas for sure.

The light changed to green. Still thinking about his mother, Jack was about to take a step when he felt something sharp enter his left side. In an instant his training told him that it was a knife, and it had struck a nerve. His mind told him that, but his body was powerless to react. He collapsed to his knees. Blood dripped down his side. His mouth was open. Only a low gurgling noise came out.

As he fell, he heard a couple of people scream. That was the last he heard.

With typical Swiss efficiency, it took only twenty minutes for an ambulance to transport Carmack to the hospital and for all of the blood to be cleaned from the street. When Ben and Jennifer passed the same corner, after waiting for forty-five minutes as Jack had directed, everything seemed perfectly normal again. There was no indication that anything out of the ordinary had occurred on the Bahnhofstrasse that morning.

They walked quickly to No. 20, the headquarters of Credit Suisse. Ben paused before entering the large gray stone building to look around. There was no sign of Carmack. It must have gone smoothly with Klaus, Ben thought, feeling happy as they climbed the stone steps. They were on the verge of a major breakthrough.

Inside the bank, his good cheer quickly evaporated. To his surprise, it took Ben fifteen minutes of shouting Jack Carmack's name at three different receptionists and waving around his Assistant U.S. Attorney's ID before he and Jennifer were passed through a metal detector and waved into an office with large gold-embossed letters on the door that said, KLAUS FENS-TER. Obviously, there had been a breakdown in communications. Klaus hadn't told the receptionists to expect them.

The man behind the desk had very little hair on his head, but he had a thick and neatly trimmed brown beard sprinkled with gray, which emphasized his large red round face. When he stood up, Ben saw a portly figure punctiliously dressed, with a gold chain across his vest and immaculately manicured fingernails.

Klaus left the door open and pointed to two wooden chairs in front of his desk. Through the corner of his eye, Ben saw two armed guards move into place at the entrance to Klaus's office. One of them was gripping an automatic weapon.

What the hell is going on here? he wondered.

He began talking slowly in case Klaus's English wasn't too good. "Jack Carmack came to see you this morning about—"

Klaus cut Ben off. In halting English tinged with a heavy German accent, he responded, "Mr. Carmack never came to see me."

"But I was there when he called you about an hour ago and arranged a meeting."

"*Ja,* that is correct. However, he changed his mind. He never came."

Ben was perplexed. What had happened? "There must be a mistake."

"Perhaps, but I don't know what it was."

Exhausted and weary, Ben didn't know what to do next. He glanced at Jennifer.

"We need some information," she said, picking up the ball.

"What information?"

She described for Klaus what they needed.

As she spoke, the banker listened quietly. At the end, he tapped his chubby fingers on the wooden desk next to the computer. All he had to do was access the computer. They could have what they needed in an instant.

Klaus refused to touch a single key.

"I'm very sorry," he said decisively. "We never give out information like that about our accounts."

"I could get a court order," Ben threatened.

Klaus shook his head and smiled. "I sincerely doubt that, Mr. Hartwell. This is Zurich, not Washington, D.C."

Ben leaned back in his seat. He knew it was hopeless. If he continued to threaten Klaus, the armed guards would forcibly evict them.

In the lobby to the bank, he found a pay phone and called the two numbers he had for Jack Carmack, and the one on the card Carmack had given Jennifer. On all three he heard a recording that Jack was unavailable.

When he put the phone down, Jennifer said, "There are only two possibilities. Either your buddy Jack changed his mind after he left us, or somebody got to him before—"

Ben didn't let her finish the sentence. He knew Carmack well enough to be certain that he hadn't changed his mind. The blonde and her friends must have known he and Jennifer were coming to Zurich. Once again, those people had been one step ahead of him and Jennifer. Ben felt the ache in his buttocks where the stab wound was crusting over.

"We'd better get the hell out of Zurich," Ben said.

Chapter 23

"I want Elana to take me to school," Amy said stubbornly. "She always takes me."

The three of them were dressed in coats, standing near the front door of Ben's house. It was Saturday morning, when the preschool scheduled a special reading class for children who were ready for it.

For the fourth time Ann said, "Elana will be taking you to school. I'll just be coming along. It will be the three of us."

Amy sat down on the floor. She started to cry and to kick her feet against the door. "Only Elana takes me to school!" she wailed.

Ann was surprised at the outburst. She and Amy had been getting along so well. She had read Amy a story last night, and Amy had given her a big hug and a kiss before going to sleep. Amy had even asked Ann to play Ben's silly game with her of leaving the room after turning out the lights, then returning a couple of minutes later for one more hug. Poor kid, Ann thought. So many changes, so fast. Ann looked through the window next to the front door. The police cruiser was in place on the street. It would follow Elana and Amy as they walked to school. What further security could she provide? She looked at Elana, who shrugged her shoulders apologetically. Then she decided to relent and let Elana take Amy. She could also pick her up at three o'clock this afternoon by herself. There was no point upsetting the child further.

Ann opened the door and watched them walk down the steps and head up the street. With a lump in her throat, she saw the police cruiser pull in behind them. She followed them with her eyes until they were out of sight. Suddenly the phone rang.

Nervously, she picked it up. It was only Ben calling to say they had arrived in London. When he asked about Amy, she reassured him that everything was all right. It was obvious to her that he didn't want to talk over the phone about what they'd been doing. Ann detected a trace of fear in his voice. It made her even more anxious about Amy.

"That's the last Peg Barton in the London directory," Ben said as he put the phone down dejectedly. "Are you sure that was the name the Chinese ambassador used in the tape?"

They were sitting in the living room of a two-bedroom suite at Claridge's in London. Ben had spent the last half hour in an unsuccessful attempt to locate Peg Barton. Outside it was dark already.

"You heard the tape, too," Jennifer said, irritable because she was tired. "The London madam's name was Peg Barton."

"So what do we do now?"

"I've told you three times that you're going about it the wrong way, but you're so damn stubborn, you won't listen to me. We're not trying to find a dentist. We're trying to locate somebody who runs an illegal call-girl operation."

He wasn't exactly brimming with patience himself. "We can't go to the British police, because we don't want word to leak back to Washington."

"I don't want to go to the police."

"So what do you want to do, genius?"

"Stick with me and you'll find out."

Jennifer led the way to the elevator, with Ben following two steps behind, sulking because she hadn't told him what was up.

On the lobby floor, she headed for the cocktail

lounge and sat down at the end of the bar. Ben moved in next to her, separated by four empty chairs from the nearest patron. With a clang, Jennifer placed her room key on the polished wooden bar so the bartender would know they were staying at the hotel.

"What'll you have?" he asked, coming over.

"Pimm's cup," Jennifer replied.

"The same for me," Ben said.

The bartender brought their drinks. With only a handful of people in the lounge, he wasn't busy, and he lingered near the Americans.

"You over here on holiday?"

"Business," Jennifer replied. "We're with a New York investment banking firm. We flew over today. Meetings on a deal tomorrow. Then back on Sunday."

"Tough to make such a long trip for two days." He had a cockney accent.

"It's a living," Jennifer said, pretending to sigh. "We'd feel better if we could have some fun tonight."

The bartender asked, a shrewd look in his eyes, "What'd you have in mind?"

"A girl for my friend here—and another one for me."

The bartender raised his eyebrows. He didn't much care for the way the Yanks were taking over London, but he sure liked the way they threw around money.

He smiled. He didn't really care, as long as he got his.

Jennifer reached into her purse and carefully extracted a hundred-pound note. She slipped it into the bartender's hand. "A friend of mine back home told me about Peg Barton. You know how I can get hold of her?"

He had underestimated this little lady. She knew her way around at the top end of the pleasure world. He flashed a smile of delight. She had pushed a good button. There would be more money in it for him. "What Peg arranges doesn't come cheap."

Jennifer reached into her purse, extracted another hundred-pound note, and handed it to the bartender. When he didn't respond, she handed him one more and said, "We're New York investment bankers. We can pay the freight."

He was now satisfied. "What's your room number?"

She showed him her room key. "My name's Jennifer."

"Be back in your room in fifteen minutes. Peg Barton will call you. You can make the arrangements for your friend, too, since he seems like the shy type."

Ben cursed under his breath.

Twenty minutes later, the phone rang in the living room of their suite. It was a low, friendly voice, warm and inviting.

"Is this Jennifer? I'm Peg Barton. I heard you wanted some company tonight."

Jennifer glanced over at Ben and gave him a thumbs-up. "Yeah, a girl for me and one for my business associate."

"My girls are expensive."

"How much?"

"Five hundred pounds for the first hour. For each one. A thousand for three hours. Two thousand for the night. That's pounds. I take major credit cards. It'll be billed as Mayfair Enterprises."

Jennifer was ecstatic. This was going the way she had hoped. "That's okay."

"I can have two of them at your hotel in thirty minutes."

"We have to come to your place," Jennifer said firmly. Peg had to believe she wouldn't bend. "We can't take a chance of being seen at the hotel. Business associates of ours are staying here."

There was a long pause.

"The price is double at my flat."

Jesus, that's a lot of money, Jennifer thought. She found it hard to believe people paid that much. "I can handle that. Give me your address."

When Jennifer put the phone down, Ben gave a long, low whistle. "I'm very impressed."

She looked at him quizzically. "Are you being a smart-ass?"

"No, I meant it as a genuine compliment. You played your part well, Miss Moore, famous Broadway actress. Almost as good as New Orleans."

When they had been dating, Jennifer had performed in a scene from *Picnic* one evening at a DOJ lawyers conference in New Orleans. Ben had been bowled over. "Well, thank you, Mr. Hartwell, distinguished prosecutor," she said, and laughed, excited at what she'd done.

Ben was pleased. They were slipping back into their easygoing, joking partnership, just like old times. Maybe that heart-to-heart on the plane was having an effect, after all.

Peg Barton occupied a house on South Audley Street in Mayfair, a few blocks from the American embassy. It was a posh area. Approaching it with Jennifer, squinting in the heavy London mist, Ben counted four Rolls-Royces, three Jaguars, and a Bentley parked on the block. Either the skin trade in London was very good these days, Ben decided, or Peg Barton had inherited a bundle. The latter thought made him smile. Only in England would an heir of the landed gentry relieve the boredom by opening up a call-girl service.

A voluptuous blonde dressed in a short black apron and nothing else opened the door for them. "Miss Barton is expecting you," she said. Then she turned and led the way to a book-lined study where Peg Barton was flipping a log on a blazing fire. She stood up slowly and turned around, taking the measure of the two of them all the while. She had ink-black hair that was closely cropped. She was wearing charcoal wool slacks and a gray cashmere sweater that disclosed a good figure. Ben's gaze leaped from Peg to the Ming dynasty vases on each side of the marble fireplace. His instinct about landed gentry might have been correct.

"Elizabeth's waiting for you upstairs, Jennifer," Peg said. "It's one floor up and in the back. There's a bar and everything up there. Mary's across the hall waiting for your friend here."

"What about the money?"

Peg raised her proper British nose into the air. "Talk to the girls. I don't handle transactions."

"Actually, it's you that I'd like," Ben said.

She smiled softly. "Sorry, I don't work that way."

"No, I mean we just want to talk to you."

Peg drew back in alarm. She grabbed a small black transmitting device resting on a table next to the phone. "The police protect me well. If I punch one button, they'll be here in two minutes."

Ben raised his hand defensively. "We want to talk about Robert Winthrop," he said.

She abruptly put the transmitter back down on the table. Terrified, she asked, "Who are you? Who sent you?"

Ben pulled out his wallet and flashed his DOJ identification. "We're with the U.S. government," he said, "investigating Winthrop's murder."

"I think I'd better call my solicitor."

She started toward the phone, but Ben stopped her in her tracks. "I don't think you want to do that. If your role in this case comes out, you'll be charged with a crime and ruined. We're proposing an easy way out. Just talk to us. Nobody has to ever know what you did."

She stared hard at Ben, trying to determine how much he knew and whether he was bluffing to get her to open up. "Suppose I don't want to talk to you?"

Following their prearranged script, Jennifer took over. "Then an American associate of mine releases an audiotape to the American press. It's jolly interesting, as you say over here. In the tape, the Chinese ambassador in Washington, Mr. Liu, tells Secretary of State Winthrop about a video the Chinese made in his room at Claridge's when Winthrop was with two prostitutes you sent. And by the way, you're mentioned by name on that tape. It's guaranteed to make you an international celebrity."

All of the color drained from Peg's face.

Jennifer said, "I don't know whether you cooperated with the Chinese when they made their little movie, but it will sure look like that in the tabloids when they start to bandy your name around. I don't imagine any of that will be good for your business. It is based on discretion, I take it."

Peg sneered at her. "Do you think I'm stupid? You don't have to draw me a picture."

Jennifer shook her head. "No, quite the opposite. That's why we're giving you a chance to talk to us."

Peg took a deep breath. "What do you want from me?"

"I want to know how you got involved with Winthrop."

Guardedly, she looked from Jennifer to Ben and back again. Stalling for time, she paused to smooth down the material in her pants. She had to give these two credit: They had played it well. She had no choice. If they went public, it would be a disaster for her business. Even worse, the illegal tape would land her in jail after the public gorged on the newspaper articles.

"Winthrop was a referral," she said reluctantly.

"What's that mean?" Jennifer asked.

"A woman in New York by the name of Alexandra Hart called me. She said he was a special client of hers. She told me to take good care of him when he was in London."

Ben took a piece of paper out of his pocket and scribbled down the name.

"Who's Alexandra Hart?" Jennifer asked.

"She operates an escort service in New York."

"You have an address or a phone number?"

She shook her head.

"I don't believe you."

She looked rattled. "I swear it."

"How'd you get the money to her?"

"Some American bloke came by and picked it up.

A big guy. Fat. Dark brown hair. Greasy looking. Pimply face."

Jennifer was in cross-examining mode, and Ben watched, admiring her. "Let's go back a little bit. How did the Chinese get to you?"

The madam was squirming now. "Winthrop used me before on Alexandra's recommendation. The Chinese had been watching him. They picked up one of my girls after she left him at Claridge's about a month ago. She thought they were potential clients. She told them she worked for me."

"So they came to see you, and you played ball with them?"

She looked at Jennifer cagily. "You could say that."

"Did you know they made a tape of Winthrop with your girls?"

Eager to deny her involvement in this critical part, Peg jumped on the question. "I had no idea. They paid me a lot of money to use my girls. That's all I know."

Jennifer looked her dead in the eye, weighing her words as she did with a witness on the stand. She decided that she believed Peg. "What else can you tell us?"

"That's all. I swear. Will you keep me out of the papers?"

"We'll do our best."

Back out on South Audley Street, Ben said to Jennifer, "You did that very well. I think we make a good team."

Jennifer was pleased at the compliment. "I think so, too. There's a good chance George Nesbitt got into Winthrop's house via Alexandra Hart."

"That's exactly what's running through my mind."

Amid the excitement, a yawn involuntarily forced itself out of Jennifer's mouth. "God, I'm bushed," she said.

"How about a nice dinner? We earned it. Then we can get the first plane out in the morning."

* * *

It was late at night when the train pulled into the station at Nanping. As Chen climbed down the steps from the old rickety rail car to the platform carrying his two bags, he thought about Donovan's words: "Two soldiers will meet you at the station. They will address you as Comrade Li. You'll go with them."

A score of other passengers exited the train at Nanping. In a matter of minutes, they scattered, leaving Chen alone on the platform, feeling vulnerable.

What if they didn't come? What if there had been a hitch?

While looking around, he made his way into the small station. It was deserted except for an old woman who was mopping the floor.

Chen walked outside in front of the tumbledown wooden building. The air was damp. It reminded him of Taiwan. Waiting in front was a mud-brown truck with two soldiers from the PLA in the front. Judging from the sound of voices, there were another dozen or so in the back of the truck, which was covered by a heavy brown tarp.

The soldier in the front who wasn't driving, a captain, climbed out and marched over to Chen. "Comrade Li," he said.

When Chen nodded, the captain looked around. There was no one watching. Quickly, he hoisted Chen's suitcase into the back of the truck. Without saying a word, he nodded Chen in that direction. Not waiting for Chen to climb up, he picked up the duffel, then loaded Chen in. Quickly, he scrambled back to the front seat of the already moving truck.

All talk stopped as soon as Chen sat down on one of the wooden side benches in the back of the truck. None of the soldiers glanced at him. They all looked down at their feet.

Donovan had told Chen about this platoon. The so-called Tiananmen Square uprising hadn't been confined to Tiananmen Square or even to Beijing. Protests and riots had been widespread among students and others throughout the country. When the government had decided to use force on June fourth, it had, whenever possible, used units of troops from remote rural areas in the west, outside the cities, not wanting to require soldiers to shoot at their friends and neighbors.

That was the goal, but it wasn't achieved throughout the country. There were some units, like this platoon from Shaoguan, which had been ordered to lead an assault with guns and clubs on the dissidents. In the years since, many soldiers had left the platoon. New ones arrived. However, the smoldering bitterness continued, passed on to new recruits, for the blood of fellow citizens they had spilled. And it had all been unnecessary. The students and their allies could have been dispelled without resorting to force. These feelings were fueled by a growing resentment against the old men who ruled with an iron fist in Beijing.

Donovan had told Chen that Sherman had made contact with one of these soldiers when he was home on leave. He had spoken to his comrades. All were ready to support Operation Matchstick.

Still, as Chen shivered in the back of the truck, he took the soldiers' silence to mean that they were ambivalent about what they had agreed to do.

A few minutes into the ride, one of the soldiers nudged Chen and handed him a brown bag. Inside, there was an army uniform. "Put it on. Now," he directed.

Chen quickly complied, stuffing his own clothes into the brown bag.

As they rode, Chen peeked through a tear in the tarp along the side of the truck. He saw few civilian vehicles on the road, but there were several large military convoys moving toward the Strait of Taiwan. He began to doubt Sherman's prediction. War with Taiwan was imminent. As soon as this was over, he'd get back home and take Mary Ann and the children to the United States until the situation settled down.

When the truck reached the barracks, the soldiers

helped Chen climb out. One carried the suitcase. Another the duffel. Both were placed next to a cot inside the unheated, damp wooden building.

The captain in the front of the truck said, "You'll remain here until we tell you it's time." He walked away without waiting for a response.

Chen felt isolated and alone. If anything happened to him, Donovan and Sherman would never know. Mary Ann and his father would have no idea. He slid the bags under the cot and tried in vain to sleep.

Chapter 24

At two-thirty in the afternoon, a half hour before the Cleveland Park Preschool classes ended, Gwen parked her blue Impala directly across the street from the blue-and-white D.C. Metropolitan police cruiser standing half a block away from the school. Billie Clements was behind the wheel, with his window rolled down, smoking a cigarette, staring off into space, and thinking about what the hell he could do to get Joyce to change her mind about breaking up with him. In the backseat, Charlie Watts was sacked out and snoring loudly. He was counting on Billie to wake him if anything happened.

Billie stopped daydreaming when he saw a sexy blonde get out of the blue Chevy with a map in her hand. She was wearing large white-framed sunglasses. Her raincoat was open in the front, and the first two buttons of her pink blouse were open. Jesus, what jugs, and she wasn't even wearing a bra. So long, Joyce, he thought. If this baby's lost, I'm ready to get lost with her.

"Say, Officer, can I bother you for directions?" she asked politely.

You can bother me for anything, he thought as he tossed the cigarette onto the street.

"What are you looking for?"

She placed the map in the open window and leaned over, pointing with her hand to Georgetown. "I've got to get to the Georgetown Mall shopping center on M Street."

He could have easily given her directions without looking at the map, but looking down was much more fun. God, her tits were beautiful. There was still a half hour till school got out. Maybe he'd wake Charlie to cover the Hartwell kid while he rode down to Georgetown with this broad. After all, city employees should be nice to out-of-town visitors.

He reached over and pointed to the map himself, touching her hand. Goddamn, her skin felt warm. He was so enthralled that he never saw her other hand reach into the raincoat pocket and emerge with a Taser. Before he could react, she fired a shot into his stomach. He could feel himself losing consciousness. He knew what would happen. He would be paralyzed for about two hours. Then he would be okay. In the meantime, he was powerless to do a thing about it. He also had the vague sense that she raised the gun and fired a second shot at Charlie in the backseat, but by then he was fading fast.

She opened the car door and pushed his body across the seat. The keys were in the ignition. She drove to the corner, turned right, then right again into an alley. Beneath a clump of trees, she parked the car, partially hidden by a garage. This was Cleveland Park, an area inhabited mostly by professional families and kids who had lots of activities on Saturday that didn't end until late in the day. Chances were, nobody would notice the police cruiser for at least the next hour, which was all she needed. Even if they did, they would ignore it, figuring the police were on some type of stakeout.

Before exiting the car, she glanced around quickly. The alley was deserted. She stepped out of the police cruiser and walked back to her own car.

With another ten minutes until school was out, she drove a block and parked on Newark, facing downward on the sloping street, directly across the street from the route Elana walked home with Amy. In fact, just as she parked, she saw Elana walking up the hill, coming to collect Ben's precious little Amy.

For two cents she'd kill the girl to teach Ben a lesson, but that wouldn't get her what she wanted. No, she had a much better idea. She would kidnap Amy, take her to Connecticut, and lock her in an old deserted farmhouse near Westport until the world's greatest prosecutor finally decided to stop his meddling and accept the confession that had been dropped in his lap. The beauty was that Gwen wouldn't even have to bother with a note or phone call, which could be traced, because Ben would know exactly why Amy had been taken and what he had to do to get her back. Given his experience as a prosecutor, he might even cooperate quietly, for fear that the FBI would get the child killed, as they often did in kidnapping cases.

Gwen kept her eyes on the mirror outside of her door, which showed the sidewalk across the street. She waited patiently for Elana to walk back down the hill with Amy. They would walk right into her trap.

Art Campbell was at the Washington Savings and Loan, DuPont Circle branch, investigating a robbery that had just taken place, when he decided to call officers Clements and Watts to make certain that everything was OK as they accompanied Amy and Elana home from school. First he dialed the special cellular phone he had given them for this job, but there was no answer. He asked the precinct to patch him through to their regular car phone. Still no answer.

Alarmed, he didn't wait for any further confirmation. Leaving another detective in charge of the robbery investigation, he bolted from the bank.

In a few seconds he was in his unmarked car. The red light went up on the roof. The siren was blaring as Campbell roared across P Street and up Massachusetts Avenue at sixty miles an hour.

* * *

Gwen watched a few other children accompanied by housekeepers pass by. Then she saw them. Elana was on the outside, closer to the curb. They were holding hands and singing a Spanish song. In her other hand, Amy clutched her yellow metal lunch box.

When they were almost directly across from her car, Gwen made her move. She opened the door and ran across the street with a .357 Magnum with a long silencer in her hand.

The instant Elana saw her coming, she knew that this was the blond woman she had overheard Mr. Hartwell talking about. What could she do? Running with Amy in tow was hopeless. Quickly she said to Amy, pointing, "Go up to that house right now, ring the bell, and go inside." Meantime she hoped to delay the blond woman long enough for Amy to get inside.

Sensing Elana's anxiety, Amy immediately obeyed. Once the child released her hand, Elana turned to face the onrushing blonde.

A weapon, I need a weapon, she thought desperately. Without any other choice, she reached down into the grass along the sidewalk and grabbed a handful of dirt and pebbles.

Gwen knew exactly what Elana was doing. To counter it, she ran straight at the housekeeper. When she tossed the dirt and pebbles, Gwen closed her eyes. Scattered shot hit her right in the center of her face. Gwen's eyes stung, but she kept on coming. In the next instant Gwen smashed the gun against Elana's face. She heard bones shatter, and the woman collapsed. Still, she tried desperately to grab Gwen's right leg. With a yank, she pulled free of Elana's grasp. Gwen aimed her toe at Elana's head, precisely where it would knock her out but not kill her. An unnecessary death couldn't possibly do any good. It might make the kidnapping exchange more difficult.

Terrified, Amy watched what was happening. She was standing on the wooden porch of a rambling old Cleveland Park house, clutching her lunch box tightly in her hand. Frantically, she kept pressing the door-bell, but nobody was home.

Stepping over Elana, Gwen ran up the wooden stairs toward Amy.

"Daddy!" the girl shrieked. "Daddy!"

Gwen made no effort to soothe the child. She could tell that Amy was too smart for that. Instead she scooped up Amy's rigid body. As she did, Amy swung her arm with all the strength she could muster, aiming the lunch box at Gwen's face. The metal corner struck Gwen on the bridge of her nose. She felt it break. Then a jolt of searing pain shot through her body.

Dizzy, Gwen put Amy down for an instant. "You fucking little monster!" she shouted. She snatched away the lunch box and hurled it to the ground below.

Then she grabbed Amy again, much harder this time. Blood was now flowing from Gwen's nose. With the gun still in her free hand, she raced back down the steps, wanting to get Amy across the street and into her car before any of the neighbors saw what was happening.

Gwen had made it midway across the street when she heard a man's voice from down the hill shout, "Police! Freeze!"

With her gun arm outstretched, she wheeled around to face the newcomer. Detective Campbell was standing in the street, about twenty yards down from her car. He had his service revolver aimed at Gwen's eyes.

"Drop your gun," he ordered. "Lay it down nice and easy. Nobody has to get hurt."

All the while he was walking slowly and doggedly up the hill, closing the gap between them.

Gwen had no intention of rolling over for some cop. She raised her gun and pressed the end of the barrel against the side of Amy's head. Too petrified to move, the child held perfectly still, a look of terror in her eyes.

"Stop right there," Gwen ordered Campbell. "Throw down your gun."

He kept advancing.

"Do it now," Gwen shouted, "or I'll kill her. Then I'll take my chances with you."

Campbell finally halted. He had no doubt that she meant every word she said. He tossed his gun onto the street and began moving away from her car.

When he had taken three steps, Amy began waving her arms wildly and screaming, "Daddy, I want my daddy!"

The child's thrashing made it hard for Gwen to hold her tightly. She moved her free hand to stabilize her grip on the child.

That was the break Campbell was looking for. Unarmed, he ran for them.

Gwen freed her hand and fired. The bullet tore into the detective's left shoulder. Blood spurted out in a high arc.

"That's just a warning," Gwen said. "The next one will kill you."

He stopped moving. His upper body was on fire with pain. The blood was spreading, staining the front of his shirt and soaking through to his jacket.

Suddenly, behind the blonde, he saw a gray Cadillac come barreling over the crest of the hill, too fast for a residential street. Campbell saw what was going to happen, and he charged them. Amy was screaming and thrashing in Gwen's arms. She got off another shot, but Campbell ducked. The bullet whistled over his head.

As the driver of the car saw the blonde holding the child, he slammed on his brakes. It was too late. The right front of the car slammed into Gwen. Instinctively, she tossed the child aside to protect her head, just as she had been trained to do. For an instant Amy was suspended in midair, screaming at the top of her lungs.

Campbell made a desperate lunge.

He caught the child just before she landed. Cradling her in his huge arms, they hit the ground together. Campbell's two-hundred-pound frame was poised to land on Amy's right leg, but he twisted away. Still, most of his weight came down on the child. He heard the awful crunching sound of her leg breaking, the child screaming. He had her head and face safe, though, buried tight against his blood-soaked jacket.

The blonde was lying on the street, unconscious, bleeding from the face. Campbell called for a police ambulance. With Amy crying in his arms, he stood over the blonde, ready to pounce on her if she moved.

Chapter 25

Ben drained the last of his espresso. "This evening's been great, Jenny," he said. "Really great." He meant it, too. Sitting at a corner table in the small, intimate Marquis restaurant on Mount Street, they'd recaptured some of the spirit of their past relationship. They didn't talk about Clyde Gillis, or Winthrop, or the case. None of those things existed for two hours. They caught up on each other's lives for the past five years. The sarcasm and wisecracks had stopped. They were getting to know each other again. They felt comfortable together. Maybe there was hope for them after all, Ben thought.

He reached across the table and put his right hand on hers. Frowning, she pulled it away and sipped a little of the wine in her glass.

Take it slowly, he cautioned himself. It's been a long time. Don't push her too hard.

After he paid the bill and they left the restaurant, they walked in silence on the deserted Mayfair Street, toward Claridge's. Suddenly, he thought of Amy and began worrying. He glanced at his watch, which was still on Washington time. Amy should be home from school by now. As soon as they got back to their hotel suite, he would call home and talk to her.

"What do you think we should do tomorrow?" Jennifer asked.

He considered their options for a moment. "If

Amy's okay, let's fly directly to New York. We've got to find Alexandra Hart.''

"I sometimes use a PI who's a former New York City cop. Mark Bonner."

"The one who took those pictures about the video and the Chinese embassy?"

She nodded. "He still has great contacts in the NYPD. He'll be able to find Alexandra Hart for us in no time at all."

A heavy mist had settled over London. They reached a corner and turned, three blocks from the American embassy in Grosvener Square. Parked at the curb was a dark green van with the legend A&A PLUMBING COMPANY printed in white letters on the side.

They were walking past the van when suddenly the double doors in back exploded open and two powerfully built men wearing black leather jackets, leather gloves, and ski caps over their faces, with cutouts for their eyes and mouths, jumped out. Ben and Jennifer, their senses deadened from alcohol and lack of sleep, never had time to react. One of the men grabbed each of them roughly from behind and looped an arm around their neck and a hand over their mouth. Quickly, they were hustled into the back of the van.

Two other men, similarly dressed, were waiting there. An instruction was shouted to the driver in front in Greek. The van began moving slowly. They drove for a couple of minutes. During that time, cloth gags were tied over Ben's and Jennifer's mouths. They stood Ben up against one side of the truck and tied his arms and legs tightly to the wooden racks along the side. Meanwhile, they pushed Jennifer down on her stomach, hard, against the dirty wooden floor of the truck. One of them pressed his boot firmly on the center of her back, keeping her flat against the floor of the truck. Her glasses had fallen off and were lying next to her, where a large boot smashed down hard on them.

When the van stopped moving. Ben watched with growing fear as one of the men put on a pair of boxing gloves. An experienced pugilist, he went to work on Ben's body, starting with his chest and working down. Defenseless and unable to cry out, Ben bit his lip as wave after wave of pain shot through his body.

When the thug began working on his stomach, punching hard, Ben threw up his dinner. That didn't stop the hard, stiff blows. Ben twisted his arms to get free, but the ropes were too tight. He started working on Ben's groin, pounding away with blow after blow. Finally, Ben passed out.

One of the thugs barked an order, which was the signal to untie the unconscious Ben. Roughly, a man pulled Jennifer to her feet. He raised the bottom of his mask to uncover his mouth. In English, he said, "You go home tomorrow morning, and take him with you. No snooping around London. You understand?"

She nodded weakly.

"We'll be watching your hotel. We'll be there to make sure you get on an airplane." He paused. "Otherwise, you'll suffer far more than tonight."

Her body convulsed in spasms of fear.

One of the men opened the rear double doors of the van. They pushed Jennifer and Ben out onto a small grassy plot and tossed her shattered glasses after her. Then the van sped away.

Jennifer saw that Ben was still unconscious. She had to get help for him. She wrenched herself to her feet and struggled to the corner. She managed to flag down a cab.

"My friend's sick," she said. "Take us to the nearest hospital."

It was two-thirty in the morning when they got back to Claridge's. The diagnosis on Ben was no permanent injuries or damage. It would take a while, but his body would heal from the pounding he had taken. They had filed the required emergency room police reports, saying that they were tourists who had been attacked and robbed by assailants on the street, whom they never saw well enough to identify.

While they were waiting for a doctor, Ben had taken Jennifer into a corner of the hospital emergency room. "I'm so sorry I got you into this," he said in an anguished voice.

She was frantic with worry about him. My God, they had hit him so hard. She could still hear the blows and see it in her head. "Please don't think about that, Ben. It's not your fault. I had as much to do with it as you did."

She fiddled with the broken, bent glasses in her hand. Suddenly it all became too much for her. She broke down and cried, a soft weeping, with tears rolling down her cheeks. Ben put an arm around her and held her tight. He wiped the tears from her face with his hand.

"I'm all right now," she finally said.

He looked down at her useless glasses. "You never needed those."

"I did, too."

"Not to see, I mean."

"That's true, but I needed them so men like you wouldn't think that because I'm pretty, I must be an airhead."

He summoned up a crooked smile. "You sure didn't fool me."

Confused, she said, "What do you mean?"

"The first time I met you, I had you pegged for an airhead all the way." He smiled, hoping for some levity.

It worked. She returned his smile, saying, "And I had you pegged for a total nerd."

They laughed together. "Boy, were we both wrong," Jennifer said.

"This isn't my idea of a great evening out in London," Ben said, wincing from the aches he felt all over. "We'll have to come back after all this is over and try it again."

Ben's words made her think about Slater. This was

the second invitation she'd gotten to London in the last two days.

Ben groaned loudly. "God, my body's so sore."

"So what do we tell the doctor?"

He had already thought of that. "As little as possible. There's no point getting Scotland Yard involved," he reasoned. "That would only lead to alerting the administration in Washington. Let's face it—there's no possibility that our attackers will ever be found. These people are pros. I'll bet you anything there's no A and A Plumbing. That van probably had magnetic signs on it that have already been changed. Besides, they never touched my face. They even wore boxing gloves to avoid leaving any marks on my body."

"Who do you think sent them?"

"We've got three choices. The Chinese government, our blond friend George Nesbitt, or . . ." He hesitated.

"Or what?"

"Somebody in our wonderful government back home."

A dark shadow crossed her face. "I don't even want to consider that possibility."

"Unfortunately, we have to. The silver lining in this cloud is that they were too late. They were supposed to get to us before we learned anything useful in England. In fact, we already got what we wanted from Peg Barton. Whoever sent them didn't know that, or they would have killed us."

His words made her tremble.

"For once," he added, "we were ahead of them."

A spasm of pain shot through his body, and Ben bent forward. She grabbed his hand and squeezed it, wanting him to know she was there. "A lot of good it did us."

Before they left the hospital, Jennifer checked a London telephone directory. Ben was right, of course. There was no listing for an A&A Plumbing Company.

The lobby of Claridge's was deathly still. The tall bald night clerk showed no emotion when the two Americans asked for the key to their suite. His guess was that they had been out losing their money at one of Mayfair's gambling clubs that catered to wealthy American tourists.

"Oh, and you have a telephone message, Mr. Hartwell," he said, handing Ben a small white envelope along with the key.

Ben's heart leaped, and he could feel his battered chest muscles tighten. Please, God, no, Ben thought. Don't let anything happen to Amy.

Ben ripped open the envelope. The message said, *Call Ann as soon as possible.* There was a Washington, D.C., phone number Ben didn't recognize.

He showed it to Jennifer. "Is this Ann's home number?" he asked frantically.

She shook her head, as anxious as he was.

Ben gingerly walked across the lobby to the elevator with Jennifer right behind.

Inside the suite, he punched out the telephone number before he even took off his coat. His heart was pounding.

A woman answered the phone. "George Washington Hospital."

Ben stammered, his throat dry, "I-I want to speak with Ann Winthrop."

There were several minutes of silence. "It's G.W. Hospital," he said to Jennifer in a panicked whisper. Finally he heard Ann come on the line. "Ben?"

"What's wrong?" Ben asked.

"Everything's all right. Amy has a broken leg, but everything's all right."

"What happened?"

She described what had occurred as she had pieced it together from Amy and from Campbell.

"How bad's the break in Amy's leg?" he asked.

"Not bad. I got one of the top orthopedists in town to set it. He said to tell you that kids' bones heal fast. There won't be any permanent damage. And there are two armed cops outside of her hospital room in case anybody else makes a move against her."

"What about Art?" He held his breath.

"He's in surgery now. I'll know something in about an hour."

"What's the prognosis?"

"Nobody's talking yet. They don't know what may have been hit."

"Oh, Christ. What about Elana?"

"She'll be okay. They're keeping her here overnight for observation."

"And the blonde?"

"Still unconscious. I haven't heard anything beyond that."

"Call me as soon as Art's out of surgery," he said.

"It's the middle of the night for you."

"I don't care how late it is," Ben said emphatically, and hung up.

He was racked with guilt for the harm he had inflicted on Amy and Campbell. What if Amy was hurt worse, and Ann was trying to soften the blow? He should never have left her. He should never have gotten both of them into this mess. His priorities were all screwed up. He was . . .

Jennifer read his mind and tried to reassure him. "They'll both be okay. Ann wouldn't give you anything but a straight story. That's the way she is."

As a result of the painkillers the doctor had given him, Ben was sleeping fitfully when the phone rang an hour later. He grabbed it from its cradle.

"Ben, it's Ann."

"How's Art?"

"They got the bullet. No severe damage. The doctor says he'll be up and around in a week."

"Which for Art means three days. And you're sure it's only a broken leg for Amy?"

"I'm absolutely sure. In fact," Ann said in a lighter voice, "somebody wants to talk to you. She'll sound a little drugged. They gave her medication when they set the leg."

"Put her on."

He was overjoyed to hear Amy's groggy voice.

"Daddy, I'm okay. I was really scared, but Art told me they got the bad lady. Aunt Ann's real nice. She got me a hot-fudge sundae with three cherries. It was yummy."

"I'm so glad, honey."

"When are you coming home, Daddy?"

"I'll be back tomorrow afternoon."

"I love you, Daddy."

"I love you, too, Amy."

When Amy handed the phone back to Ann, Ben asked her, "Any other developments in the case in Washington since we left?"

"Not a thing."

"See you tomorrow, then."

As Ben put the phone down, his forehead was damp with perspiration. He couldn't wait to get back to Washington. Too wired to sleep, he went into the other bedroom of the suite. Jennifer was sleeping on her stomach with her arm thrown across the other side of the king-size bed and hair strewn over her face. He watched her sleeping for several minutes. He had been terrified of what those men in the van would do to her, and relieved that they had decided to deliver their message to him rather than her.

Was there a future for them? he wondered. He certainly hoped so. He knew very well that there was no point even thinking about it until the Winthrop affair was over.

Chapter 26

"Well, we got our shooter," Art Campbell said as Ben walked into his hospital room with Amy in his arms, a cast on her leg.

Art was propped up in bed with a large bandage on his left shoulder.

Ben winked at Paula, Campbell's wife, who was sitting in a wooden chair next to the bed. "The man's hopeless," he said. "He should be resting, and he's doing police work. He'll probably be playing basketball tomorrow."

"That's not the half of it," Paula said. "While they were wheeling him into surgery, he's shouting to one of the policemen, 'Get the blond hair in my center desk drawer and check it against the woman who shot me.'"

"And guess what?" Campbell said.

"Wait a minute," Ben interrupted. "Before we talk about all of that, I want to say thank you." He walked over and squeezed Campbell's hand.

"He's really brave," Amy chimed in, "and I was brave, too."

Ann appeared in the door to the hospital room. She had just driven Elana to Ben's house with Jennifer and left the two of them there. Two guards were posted outside. "And Aunt Ann's really nice."

He handed Amy over to Ann and moved in closer to Campbell. "What happened with the blond hair?" he whispered.

"The hair I found on the carpet at Winthrop's house is a match for the lovely blond tresses on the head of the woman upstairs in intensive care, who tried to kidnap Amy. Also, we brought in Hines and MacDonald, the two guards who were on duty at Winthrop's house that Saturday, to look at her. Hines made a positive ID, despite the disguise. MacDonald says he didn't get a good enough look at Nesbitt to say either way. With all of that, I'd say we have a powerful circumstantial case that she was George Nesbitt and pulled the trigger on Winthrop."

Ben felt a surge of hatred for the woman who had attacked his daughter. "Have you spoken to her?"

"She's in a coma, although the doctors hate that term. They say she's 'nonresponsive.' Suffered a concussion, severely bruised ribs, and lots of cuts and bruises." He smiled. "Oh, and Amy did her bit. Broken nose and face laceration caused by one old metal Barbie lunch box. Couldn't you afford to buy the kid a new one?"

They exchanged smiles. "I will now. I'll tell her the police took it for evidence. So what happens with the blonde?"

"We've got police guards posted outside her room around the clock. If she wakes up"—he paused to take a breath—"and nobody knows when that will be, she just might talk. Then we'd get all of our answers. There have to be people in this town who wouldn't want that to happen."

Ben couldn't wait indefinitely to see if that scenario unfolded. Right now they had nothing. "So we're still left with the question of who hired her."

"And an even more basic question. Who is she?"

"She didn't have ID?"

"Nancy Burroughs from Detroit. Phony, just like George Nesbitt."

"What about prints?"

"Bill Traynor took some fingerprints from her this morning. He sent them over to the FBI lab. We ought to have the results anytime."

*   *   *

When Ben drove up to his house, he was reminded of the movie *Fort Apache, the Bronx*. Three police cruisers were parked in front. Two patrolmen were posted on the front porch with rifles at their side.

Amy was tired. He put her into bed for a nap, nearly tripping over the scooter. He wished she'd keep it in the closet, but now wasn't the time to tell her. He read her a story and stayed until he thought she was asleep. Then he kissed her on the forehead and said, "Sleep tight, honey."

"Don't forget one more hug, Daddy."

He smiled. She was going to be all right. When he returned to her room a minute later for one more hug, she squeezed him tight. "I'm glad you're home, Daddy."

"Me, too, honey."

"And that bad lady won't come again?"

"No more, honey."

On the way downstairs, he looked into Elana's room. She was sleeping as well, with a nasty bruise on one side of her face. Then, as he started down the stairs, he heard an unfamiliar man's voice. Nervously, he came all the way down and looked into the living room. Startled, he saw that he had two visitors—Al Hennessey and Ches Hawthorne.

Hennessey was pacing nervously back and forth across the beige carpet. The AG sat calmly in a high-backed leather chair, rolling an unlit cigar around in his mouth. Ann was explaining what had happened yesterday when Elana picked up Amy from school.

Ben had met the AG only once—a year ago, when he was one of five government lawyers to receive the attorney general's Distinguished Service Award. He doubted Hawthorne would remember him. The AG was one of several Wall Street corporate lawyers whom Brewster had put into key positions. He looked every bit the part—expensively tailored blue pinstripe suit and wing-tip shoes that looked as if they'd been shined ten minutes ago.

Hennessey eyed Ben coming down the stairs with an expression of annoyance, and Ben knew why. Al had been forced to admit to the AG that one of his lawyers had deliberately kept him in the dark. "I thought you were going to Chicago," Hennessey said indignantly to Ben.

"Well, I . . ."

The AG pulled the cigar out of his mouth. "Listen, Ben," he said, taking charge, "I know who you are. I gave you that award last year."

Ben was pleasantly surprised that Hawthorne had remembered.

"I just got back from a Pacific Rim conference in Tokyo, and Al here told me some of what's been happening. I figured we'd better talk." Hawthorne stood up. "Let's go off somewhere quiet. The three of us. You, me, and Al. I've got to know what you've learned about Robert's murder."

Ben shifted his feet nervously, and his head jerked back toward the stairs. "I hear Amy crying," he said suddenly. "Ann, will you come upstairs with me? You seem to be able to calm her down." He looked for all the world like a concerned father. "I'll just be a minute."

He was still in a lot of pain from the beating in London, and slowly he limped back to the staircase. Ann followed him.

When they got to the top of the stairs, he led Ann into his own empty bedroom and closed the door.

"Okay, what gives?" she asked.

"What do I do now?"

"What do you mean?"

"You know the people in the administration better than Jennifer and I do. Do I trust Hawthorne and work with him or not? And take your time answering. All of our lives are at risk: yours and Jennifer's, as well as mine and Amy's." Ann didn't reply at first, and Ben added, "If we're right and what's happening is an administration cover-up of the Chinese government's murder of your husband, then how do we know

Hawthorne's not a part of it? These people are desperate. Violence means nothing to them."

"Ches has been in Tokyo the whole time," Ann pointed out.

"That gives him the perfect cover. Anyone here in town could have coordinated with him by phone. They have secure lines."

Ann walked over to the window and looked out. Softly she said, "I've always liked Ches. I've thought that of the President's top people, Ches was the most decent of the lot. Better than Cunningham or Slater. Certainly better than Robert. He strikes me as one of those lawyers who will bend the law as far as he can, but he won't downright violate it."

"That's a nice thing to say about the attorney general of the United States."

"You ever heard of John Mitchell or Ed Meese?"

"Touché."

"The lesson is that lots of people in this town in high places will do illegal things when their political survival is at stake."

"So where's that leave us with Ches?"

Ann took a deep breath. "In the last analysis, you have to work with Ches because you have no other way to save yourself and Amy. At least with Ches you have a chance."

He nodded. "That's fair enough." He thought about it some more. "But I'm taking out an insurance policy. You and Jenny stay involved in everything. Each night I want you to write up what's happened, deliver the pages to someone in the media you trust, and tell him to publish them if the two of us are killed. With that in place, we can bargain with the AG if he turns on us."

She eyed him skeptically. "With the blonde in the hospital in a coma, you still think there's as much personal risk to us?"

"Ask Jenny sometime what happened to us in London last night." The grim expression on Ben's face terrified Ann. "I don't want to talk about it," he said.

In silence they went back downstairs.

"I'm ready to talk," Ben said. "But I want Jenny and Ann to sit in. They've been part of it up until now. I'm not cutting them out."

"They're not government employees," Hennessey protested.

"It doesn't matter, Al," the AG replied sharply. "We're doing it Ben's way."

For the next hour Ben, with Jennifer and Ann's help, described everything that had happened since Winthrop's death. They played the audio- and video-tapes and showed the AG the pictures Mark Bonner had taken in connection with the video and the Chinese embassy involvement. They explained about Ann's being forced to surrender the second video. The AG listened carefully, without interruption, but frowning from time to time. He continually rolled the unlit cigar around in his mouth and chewed on it until it was a pulpy mess, at which point he got up, walked into the kitchen, and tossed it in the garbage can. A couple of times in the narrative Hennessey made a move to intervene, but the AG signaled him to zip it.

When Ben finished, the AG angrily paced back and forth across the room with a furious expression on his face. "This is fucking awful," he said. "It's even worse than Watergate. I've got to talk to Brewster about it ASAP."

Ben raised his hand. "I'm not so sure that's a good idea, Mr. Hawthorne."

"It's Ches."

"Okay, Ches. We have to keep a tight lid on this for now. If word leaks to the Chinese ambassador, he'll slip out of the country. They'll never agree to send him back. Then we won't have any proof that he hired our blond shooter."

Hawthorne nodded, agreeing with that much. "So what do you propose to do?"

"For now, my recommendation would be that you don't say a word to the President or anyone else at the top of the administration. Let Jennifer and me keep taking it one step at a time, peeling back the onion until we get to the rotten core."

"What's your next step?"

"We go to see Alexandra Hart in New York tomorrow morning."

"Okay, then come to my office in the afternoon when you get back. Mary Beth's piled up a million things that came in while I was in Japan, but nothing's more important than this. Meantime, I'll think about what I do with Brewster."

Jennifer waved her hand in the air. "Hey, what about my client, Clyde Gillis? Anybody remember him?"

The AG replied, "I think we should leave him in jail in a sort of protective custody, but make him comfortable. Hustle him off quietly to Lewisburg. Give him the white-collar-criminal country-club treatment. Single cell. Large cell. Special food. Complete protection until it's over, which should just be a few more days. Meantime, we'll put twenty-four-hour protection on his wife and kids. Can you live with that, Jennifer?"

She was satisfied. "I'll talk to Clyde and his wife. I think that should work."

"Good. I'm still on Tokyo time and tired as hell. Anything else we need to decide now?"

Ben glanced awkwardly at Hennessey, who was going to hate him for what he was about to do, but he couldn't pass up this opportunity. "One more thing. Since day one in this damn mess, I've been saddled with Ed Fulton as a sidekick. I want him totally off the case. He's a pain in the ass, and he's always in the way."

The AG looked puzzled. "Who's Ed Fulton?"

Ben replied quickly, "A young kid. An assistant White House counsel. He works for Jim Slater."

At the sound of Slater's name, Jennifer's head recoiled in surprise. She didn't speak. An angry scowl covered her face.

"Why the hell was he ever on this case?" Hawthorne said.

"You'd better ask Al."

The AG was clearly pissed. He turned to Hennessey. "Well?"

Hennessey sent Ben a dirty look. He'd been ass-kissing Slater so much for that appointment to the open seat of the court of appeals that he'd forgotten that although his nomination came from the White House, it would still need Hawthorne's approval before it went to the Senate Judiciary Committee.

"Slater leaned on me hard while you were in Japan," Hennessey said weakly. "He said because Winthrop was so close to the President, it was important for him to be in the loop on the investigation."

"Oh, for chrissake, you should have called me in Tokyo," Hawthorne said, disgusted at this excuse. "You know what I think about those White House clowns mixing into Department business. First, it's improper. Second, with the Chinese government involved, I don't want White House people within a mile of this case. And third, it's nothing more than Slater trying to expand his turf in domestic affairs." He turned to Ben. "Don't worry. I'll get it straightened out as soon as I leave here. You've seen the last of Ed Fulton on this case."

As Hawthorne walked toward the front door, Ben moved with him. Hennessey was a few paces behind.

"We're going to do the right thing," the AG told Ben, "regardless of whose ox gets gored. Regardless of the political consequences."

Hawthorne had said precisely the words Ben wanted to hear. Still, they didn't make him feel any better. He wasn't sure that he could believe the attorney general. Hawthorne was a very good lawyer. Ben knew only too well that a good lawyer could take any position and make it sound like Moses had brought it down from Mount Sinai.

Once Ben was alone with Jennifer and Ann in the

living room, he said, "It's time to move on Alexandra Hart."

"Actually," Jennifer replied, "when you were at the hospital this afternoon, I already moved on her."

He pulled back in surprise.

"Yeah, without you, I learned how to do some things on my own."

"Very funny. What'd you do?"

"Well, for starters, I talked to Louise Jenson, my associate. She's been going through the personal papers of our distinguished and recently deceased secretary of state. Louise found lots of canceled checks written to Alexandra Hart by Winthrop."

"What are we talking about in dollars?"

"More than a hundred thousand this year, easily."

Ann, who was sipping coffee, put her cup down with a thump. "That bastard. God, he was even worse than I thought. Grace Hargadon was right. He was sick."

Jennifer said, "Louise is making copies of the canceled checks. She'll deliver them to my house tonight. They should help when we visit Alexandra Hart. Chances are, she never declared the income. It'll be nice to have evidence of tax fraud in our pocket when we pop in on her tomorrow. As I remember from my old government-prosecutor days, it loosens a witness's tongue real fast."

"Hey, maybe," Ben said, "we can use the bank-deposit information on those checks to locate Alexandra Hart."

"No need to, Ben." Jennifer smiled, ahead of him again. "Mark Bonner already found her. She lives at 420 East 64th in Manhattan. I have her telephone number, too."

"I'm impressed."

"Wait, there's more. A buddy of Mark's in the vice squad of NYPD told him that Hart runs a high-priced call-girl service. A madam without a bordello, as he described it. NYPD's willing to cooperate with us as long as we don't do anything to upset the New York tourist business. Mark and his buddy have a plan. All they need is a green light from you."

"What's the plan?"

"Tonight New York vice busts two of Alexandra's working girls. They can easily do it by having a couple of their guys pose as johns. Then they lock up the girls in separate pens. The only nearby phone will just happen to be busy all the time or out of service. So they won't to be able to make a call. Then tomorrow morning you, Mark, and I will pay a visit to the diplomatic madam. How's that sound?"

"I love it," Ben replied.

Ann was less pleased. "You two are supposed to be lawyers and officers of the court. What about the constitutional rights of those two girls?"

"C'mon, Ann," Ben replied, "we're doing them a favor. They'll be better off behind bars for the next twenty-four hours than whatever they'd otherwise be doing." He yawned suddenly. The lack of sleep and everything that had happened in the last twenty-four hours was catching up to him. "How about some dinner?" he said. "I'll order pizza."

"Sounds good to me," Ann replied. "I'll stay on here and take care of Amy until this is over and Elana's better, if that's okay with you."

"Are you kidding? I'd love it," Ben said, while turning to Jennifer. "Pizza okay?"

"Sorry, count me out. I've got something I have to do this evening, since we're going to New York in the morning."

Ben wondered what she was being so mysterious about. It was obvious that she didn't want to tell him. You can't push, he told himself. Let it go.

Once Jennifer was outside, alone in her car, she took out her cell phone and punched in the numbers of the White House switchboard. "Jim Slater, please," she told the operator.

Jennifer was passed along to Miss O'Brien, Slater's secretary. When Jennifer said, "I want to talk to Mr. Slater," the curt response was, "I'm sorry, he's in a conference. Can I ask who's calling, please?"

That was enough for Jennifer.

She parked a block from the White House on the street. Approaching the guardhouse, she steadied herself. A cold fury was gripping her. He had used, manipulated, and deceived her. No one had ever treated her like this before.

"I'm here to see Jim Slater," she told the guard.

"Do you have an appointment, ma'am?" he asked.

Jennifer lied. "I don't have a specific appointment. Mr. Slater asked me to come by today. It's an urgent matter."

The guard checked Jennifer's driver's license, then called Slater's secretary. For several minutes he held the phone up to his ear without saying a word, while the secretary must have been interrupting Slater, Jennifer guessed, in his conference. Finally, the guard said, "Miss O'Brien will meet you at the reception area." He pointed to the double doors at the end of the path.

Miss O'Brien was a wizened, gray-haired woman smartly dressed in a tailored suit. "I'll take you over, Miss Moore," she said in a New York accent. Jennifer deduced that Slater had brought Miss O'Brien with him when he had come down from New York. She followed Miss O'Brien along a series of corridors until they ended up in a reception area for a suite across from the Oval Office. The name plaque on the corridor outside said, JAMES SLATER, CHIEF OF STAFF.

Inside the reception area, there were two secretaries' desks facing each other, one on each side of the closed wooden door, guarding access to the inner sanctum of the second most powerful man in America. The other was occupied by Mary Jo Thompson, according to the name tag on the desk, whose short hair, tight blue cashmere sweater, bursting in the front, and brief miniskirt made a great contrast to Miss O'Brien. I wonder who does the office work? Jennifer thought contemptuously.

"He'll be with you shortly," Miss O'Brien said. "Would you like something to drink?"

"No, thanks," Jennifer said, positioning herself in a leather chair that faced the closed door. She glanced at her watch, wondering how long he'd keep her waiting.

Exactly three and a half minutes later, the door opened and out walked a tall, dark-haired woman who not only had beautiful features but a striking sensuality. She was straightening her skirt as if she had just gotten dressed. She had fresh lipstick on her mouth and a smug expression on her face. She wasn't carrying any papers or files in her hands.

Jennifer had never seen the woman before but she gave Jennifer an embarrassed look as she walked past.

Following Miss O'Brien into the office, Jennifer detected the scent of sex in the air. Slater, sitting behind his desk, pretended to be looking at some papers. What struck Jennifer was that the immaculately dressed Slater was just a little messy.

Rising behind his desk, he gave a big smile. "Jennifer, what a nice surprise to see you," he said graciously.

She waited until the secretary had gone. "I obviously didn't pick a good time to come."

"Nonsense," he replied in his usual smooth voice. "Anytime you come is a good time. I was just meeting with one of my aides." Realizing how feeble that sounded, he added, "Going over the various alternatives for tax reform legislation."

Yeah, and I'm shooting up into space on the next NASA mission, she thought.

"Anyhow, did the girls offer you coffee?"

"I didn't want anything."

He came out from behind the desk and pointed to the sofa across the office. The cushions were nearly falling on the floor. That must be where he was screwing her, Jennifer decided. She refused to sit on it, taking a chair on one side, while Slater plopped down on the sofa.

"I don't want to take too much of your time," Jennifer said. "So I'll make this as short as possible."

"All right, I'm listening."

"I came to compliment you." Her voice was dripping with sarcasm.

That put him on the defensive. He didn't know where she was going with this, and he didn't like it. "Compliment me?" he said weakly.

"Yes, I have to hand it to you. You manipulated me with such class and charm that I never had an inkling of what you were after. I see why you're the second most powerful man in the United States."

"What are you talking about?" Slater asked, bemused.

"In plain English, you've been using me from the get-go, and I've been a complete sucker the whole time. Now I know why you were so interested in me."

"Using you how?"

"Don't play stupid. It's insulting. I just found out about Ed Fulton. You had him feeding you information about the Gillis case from Ben, while you were getting it direct from me."

"Whoa," he said, trying to calm her down.

"Don't try to sweet-talk your way out."

"I don't have to." Slater took a deep breath. "Are you ready to stop talking and start listening?"

"Yeah," she said grudgingly.

"Have I ever asked you one question about your defense of Clyde Gillis? Even one?"

She tried to think. She couldn't recall any.

"And have you ever told me anything about the case? Think about it long and hard. Even a tiny morsel?"

"No, but—"

"But nothing," he said, sounding vindicated. "In fact, I've deliberately avoided talking about the case so you wouldn't be able to jump to the conclusion you now did."

He paused for a moment, challenging her with his eyes to dispute what he had said. When she didn't respond, he added, "If I were interested in you for information, I would have tried to extract it. Sorry to disappoint you, but my interest in you is more primitive than that. I've been strongly attracted to you since I first saw you at the funeral chapel in New York. I'd give anything to spend time with you, to get into bed with you, and to show you how a woman can be loved and pampered. Accuse me of those things and I'm guilty."

She sighed. "I knew you'd sweet-talk me."

"Seriously, Jennifer, the proof is that I never asked you about the case."

Partly persuaded by what he had said, she admitted, "Maybe I reacted too strongly."

"You did. Tell you what. I won't call you again until after the Gillis case is over. How's that?"

Furious, thinking about the woman who had just left his office, she didn't respond.

"Then we'll go to London," he added.

She thought about Ben, what had happened to them in London. His offer to go back. She didn't know whom she'd rather go with. So much had happened in the space of a couple days. She needed time to sort it out in her mind.

"Let me walk you out," Slater said, trying to sound caring.

She didn't want him to think he'd won her over. "Thanks, but I can find my own way."

After he and Ann finished the pizza, Ben, dead tired and thoroughly drained, took two more painkillers, went to bed early, and fell into a deep sleep. Yet it seemed as though he'd only started to dream when a tapping on the bedroom door woke him.

Through a crack in the door, Ann whispered, "Ed Fulton's downstairs. He says it's urgent."

"To hell with him," Ben shouted at Ann. "Tell him to come back in the morning."

Ben buried himself under the pillow and blankets, trying to tune out the world, but he knew he couldn't do that. He was feeling a little guilty. He had just gotten Fulton fired from the case. God only knew what the AG had told Slater. Ed's career would be hurt, and the guy wasn't that bad. Granted, he was an arrogant jerk. So were lots of bright young lawyers in Washington. He'd even had Ben out to his house for dinner. Reluctantly, Ben stumbled out of bed and grabbed a robe on the floor. He opened the door just as Ann was reaching the bottom of the stairs.

"Wait a minute, Ann," he called to her. "I'll talk to him."

Fulton was sitting on the sofa in Ben's living room, looking contrite. "Mr. Slater told me I'm off the case."

For a second Ben thought Fulton was going to cry. "Yeah, well, the AG got back from Japan, and I had a review session with him. Of course, I had to tell him you were working with me. He exploded."

All the arrogance was gone. "Did you tell him I was always in the way?"

Ben dodged the question. "It's nothing against you personally. There's a turf battle going on between the AG and your boss. These things happen in government all the time."

From Fulton's expression, Ben knew that he wasn't buying it. Fulton was too smart for that. He could read between the lines of what Ben had just said. It wasn't simply a turf battle. Ben's words to Hawthorne must have been repeated to Slater, and then to Ed. Ben was sorry he hadn't spoken more carefully.

Fulton stared long and hard at Ben. He knew now that Ben had turned on him. The accusation of betrayal showed in his eyes.

Finally, Fulton changed the subject. "I heard about your daughter, and I'm really sorry. I know how I'd feel if anything like that happened to one of my kids."

Ben grew more cautious. "What exactly did you hear?" he asked.

"The AG told Mr. Slater that George Nesbitt was a woman, and she tried to kidnap your daughter. Somehow, I feel responsible."

"Why you?"

"Because I was so certain Clyde Gillis was the killer

that I wouldn't even let you consider other alternatives."

"Oh, don't give yourself a beating over that. I thought we had our killer behind bars as well."

Yet Fulton wouldn't be drawn off track. "What I want to know is why the blond woman killed Winthrop."

Ben shrugged. "At this point, I don't have the vaguest idea. But I sure intend to find out."

Chapter 27

"Wow, three of you," Alexandra Hart said. "I feel mighty important. How about coffee and a piece of danish?"

"We're not here for fun and games," Ben snapped. "You're in trouble, Ms. Hart. Big trouble."

She wasn't fazed. Surly prosecutors didn't intimidate her. Alexandra was about thirty-five, busty, with curly bleached-blond hair. She wore large round gold-framed glasses that made her face look bookish. As soon as she had opened her mouth, her Boston accent had been obvious.

"Well, at least sit down and tell me why you are here."

Ben waited until they were seated. "Trish and Sabrina send their regards from Manhattan South," he said.

She sneered. "That was a stupid trick, not letting them call. You guys must think I'm a babe. I know exactly what goes on at NYPD when it concerns me. Trish was arrested at eleven-ten and Sabrina at eleven twenty-five. The arresting officers were Murphy and Rolfe."

"Then you must also know that they've given the police enough to charge you with two counts of pandering, which the last time I looked is a felony in this state. Since you've sent both of these young women to New Jersey on your business during the last year, that's a federal offense."

"Let's be real clear about this," she said defiantly. "I never mention any illegal act on the phone. My girls are hired out as escorts to go to dinner or the theater. I instruct them expressly never to engage in any illegal act. They sign a paper agreeing that they won't do that. I can even show you the papers Trish and Sabrina signed if you'd like. If they end up doing something illegal, like soliciting for prostitution, there's no way it can lead back to me. So you don't have a thing to charge me with."

"That's not what Trish and Sabrina say."

Alexandra snorted. "Don't underestimate me. My old man didn't do much for me, but he taught me to know when a cop was bluffing. I know those girls. I know what they'd say."

"And in addition, we've got you on income tax evasion."

She shook her head. "Like hell you do. I pay taxes on every dollar I earn."

"Well, there's a certain gentleman who paid you last year in excess of one hundred thousand dollars and—"

"Whoever he was, it was all listed as taxable income. Talk to my accountant. I use Pricewaterhouse. You sure you don't want some coffee?"

As far as Jennifer was concerned, Ben's game plan wasn't scoring any points, so she said, "Yeah, I'd like a cup."

Alexandra started toward the kitchen. "Do you want any croissants?"

"No." Irritated, Ben tapped his fingers firmly on the glass-topped coffee table. "Bitch," he mumbled softly. "We're going to break you, sweetie. Wait and see."

When Alexandra returned with four Wedgwood cups and saucers on a teak tray, Ben said, "This is no joke. You may have bought off the New York police, but I'm prepared to recommend a federal case based on the New Jersey calls you sent Sabrina and Trish out on. I'll pursue it if you force me to."

Alexandra regarded Ben with disbelief. "Please

don't start all that bullshit again. I know what my legal situation is better than you do. I've got a law degree from NYU."

"You're kidding," Jennifer replied.

"Hardly, Miss Moore. I also spent two years working for a large New York law firm. Doing stock-and-bond issues. That life totally sucks. No pun intended. So I decided to go into business for myself. I've been damn successful at it."

"Doesn't it bother you that it's illegal?"

"Going out on a date isn't illegal."

Ben said, "If you've got such a great business, you wouldn't like to be charged with arranging to transport women across state lines for an immoral purpose."

"My lawyers could beat a charge like that faster than you could file it."

Alexandra smugly picked up her cup and sipped some coffee.

"But could they beat a murder conspiracy charge?"

She set her cup down hard, spilling coffee in the saucer. The game was over. "What? Whose murder?"

"Robert Winthrop's."

Fear appeared in her eyes. "You've got to be kidding. I had nothing to do with that gardener."

"Forget the gardener," Ben said. "He didn't kill Winthrop."

"Then who did?"

"A woman you sent to have sex with Winthrop. She brought a gun with her and decided to use it. And we've got you for conspiracy to commit murder because we figure that somebody knew you could get a woman into Winthrop's house. They paid you a lot to get this woman in. That's how we figure it."

Her face went rigid. "What makes you think I knew Robert Winthrop?"

Jennifer jumped in smoothly. "That's what Peg Barton told us in London. You even split her fee for servicing our distinguished secretary of state." She snapped open her briefcase, pulled out a brown envelope, and tossed it to Alexandra. "Copies of canceled checks of payments Winthrop made to you in the last year."

Ben turned up the heat. "I must advise you, Miss Hart, that you are now the target of the criminal investigation into the death of Robert Winthrop. You know what that means. If I were you, I'd hire a good criminal lawyer. You're going to need one."

She raised her hand weakly. "Hold it a second. Time-out. I don't need a lawyer; I'm ready to make a deal. I'll talk to you."

"And what kind of deal did you have in mind?" Ben asked.

"I'll tell you everything I know about Winthrop. In return, I get immunity from any murder conspiracy charge as well as the transporting of women across state lines for an immoral act."

Ben shot back quickly, "I'll give you the interstate transportation. That's it. On murder conspiracy you get nothing. From the facts we now have, you're in deep shit. You've got to clear yourself."

She sipped her coffee and stared off toward the window, weighing her options.

Finally, Alexandra said, "I've got nothing to hide on the Winthrop murder. In fact, I'd like you to catch the SOB who did it," she added bitterly. "He cost me a bundle by taking out one of my best customers. Will you give me the immunity on the other charge in writing?"

Ben replied, "I thought you'd never ask."

He reached into his briefcase, pulled out the document, and handed it to her. She read it quickly and pushed it aside.

Jennifer placed a tape recorder on the coffee table and pushed the record button as Alexandra began to speak.

"On Friday, the day before Winthrop died, a woman called me. She said that her name was Ann

Winthrop, Robert's wife. Naturally, I was worried. It's always messy if a client's wife finds my number and calls."

Jennifer was nonplussed. What was going on? Ann had never told her about this call.

"Well, anyhow, Mrs. Winthrop said that she and her husband had an open marriage. She knew that he used my services. She wanted to give him a surprise for his birthday on Saturday afternoon at two o'clock. At home. A session with one of my best girls."

"This is preposterous," Jennifer said.

Ben shushed her. He wanted to hear where this was going. "What else did this woman who said she was Mrs. Winthrop tell you?"

"That on Saturday I should send the girl down on the Delta Shuttle at nine-thirty, then call Robert and tell him a surprise was coming. I shouldn't tell him who was responsible for the surprise."

Jennifer was looking at Alexandra in total disbelief. The madam had shifted to face Ben before continuing. "Mrs. Winthrop said she or someone else would meet the girl at National Airport with a sign that said Rome Industrial. They would take the girl to Robert. She also told me that she'd have fifty thousand dollars in cash delivered to me in a few hours to cover transportation, the girl and so forth."

"That's a lot of money," Ben said, "for something like this."

She eyed Ben suspiciously. "Meaning that I should have guessed something more was involved?"

The woman was no dummy, Ben thought. How'd she manage to make such a mess out of her life?

"Honey, you'd be surprised when sex is involved how people spend money. I once had a New York Yankee who—"

Ben interrupted her. "Let's stick to this situation. Did you get the money?"

"A courier, a young man, delivered it an hour later in a blank brown envelope."

"What company was the courier from?"

"I have no idea. I didn't pay attention."

"Did you have any reason to believe that Ann Winthrop, or whoever was calling you pretending to be Ann Winthrop, might have been involved with a foreign government?"

She shook her head. "No."

"So you took the money?"

"Yes. Which I will, of course, report as taxable income at the end of the year."

"No doubt. And?"

"Saturday morning, I told Betsy to take the nine-thirty Delta Shuttle to Washington. She's gorgeous. A new girl from Iowa. She was excited about the idea of being with the secretary of state." Alexandra's mouth turned down. "It was the worst thing I ever did in my life."

"What do you mean?"

"Well, obviously, it led to Robert's death. Like I said, he was one of my best customers. Dummy," she muttered, angry at herself. "I was stupid. I should have seen through it. The money blinded me."

Ben brought her back to the story. "What happened to Betsy when she got to Washington?"

"I didn't find out about any of this until she got back. But a blond woman met her at the airport. Said she was Ann Winthrop's secretary. When they got into the blonde's car, the blonde handed Betsy ten thousand dollars, and said the plans had changed. Robert was tied up on some urgent state department business during the afternoon. The blonde said she was taking Betsy to the Washington Hilton Hotel. She handed her the key to room 742 and told Betsy to be there that evening from six on. Robert would come by as soon as he could."

Jennifer shook her head in dismay. Ann Winthrop didn't have a blond secretary.

"What'd Betsy do?"

"She'd never been in Washington before. So she

did the monuments in the afternoon, went to the top
of the Washington Monument, touched old Abe Lincoln, and looked at Thomas Jefferson.

"Then she went back to the Hilton at about five-
thirty. She turned on the TV and heard about Robert's
death. In two seconds, she packed up and came back
to New York."

"Where's Betsy right now?" he asked.

"At home, I think. Over on East Seventy-second."

"Get her over here now."

Alexandra was hesitant. "Can I ask why? I'd really
like to spare her."

"Well, you can't. I want her to make an ID from
some pictures."

Betsy arrived fifteen minutes later. One look at her,
and Ben knew that Alexandra wasn't exaggerating. The
woman was gorgeous. About twenty-four years old, she
was large-busted with sandy brown hair and a smooth,
clean complexion. Straight from the farm, she had an
innocence about her. New York hadn't yet hardened her.

He could see the fear in her eyes as her gaze darted
from one of them to the other. "Are you cops?" she
stammered.

"We're helping them," Ben responded in an author-
itative tone. "As long as you cooperate with us, nothing will happen to you. I promise."

From Betsy's expression, she wasn't persuaded. Alexandra took her into a back bedroom. When they
returned a few minutes later, Betsy's look had
changed. She had been intimidated into following her
whoremaster's command.

After she corroborated Alexandra's story, Ben
handed her a picture of the blonde, taken that morning at George Washington hospital. Betsy's fingers
were wet and clammy. "Is that the woman who met
you at the airport?" Ben asked.

She stared at it for a long moment. The bandage
on the nose and facial bruises were making the ID
difficult. Finally, she squinted, then nodded.

"You're sure of it?"

"I'm sure. I'll never forget what she looked like. She gave me the creeps."

"What do you mean?"

"She had a dead look in her eyes. She was a killer, that one. I could tell."

Ben told her to write her address and telephone number on a small piece of paper. With a trembling hand, she gave it to him.

"Please, you won't tell my parents what I'm doing in New York, will you? They think I'm working for an advertising agency."

"You guys don't believe for a minute Ann Winthrop made that call, do you?" Jennifer said as soon as they were in Mark's car on the way to LaGuardia. She was in the front seat. She turned around and looked at Ben in the back.

He put his hand on her arm to calm her. "I agree. There's no reason to believe Ann did it. Anyone could have paid a woman, or asked a secretary or a woman friend to make the call, pretend she was Ann Winthrop, and follow the script. Our George Nesbitt could have even made the call. Personally, I think Ambassador Liu arranged it. We learned how deft he was at setting up encounters of this type from Peg Barton in London. Still . . ." he hesitated. He hated asking Jennifer because she'd chew his head off, but he had to. "You'd better touch base with Ann to close the loop."

Jennifer sighed. "All right, I'll call her." Jennifer pulled the cell phone out of her purse.

After she explained to Ann what had happened, Ann laughed. "That's the most preposterous thing I've ever heard. Me arranging a prostitute for Robert?"

"That's what I told Ben. Did you ever talk to Alexandra Hart?"

"I never even heard of the woman until we found Robert's checks to her. And by the way, Robert's birthday is April fifteenth, tax day. A wife would know that. She'd never use a phony birthday as an excuse for a surprise gift to her husband, because it's so patently false."

"Okay, I get it," Jennifer said.

When she told Ben what Ann had said, he was convinced she hadn't made the call. Somebody had arranged for another woman to make that call to Alexandra Hart. It was Liu, Ben was now certain.

Chapter 28

Ben and Jennifer went immediately to the Department of Justice from National Airport.

"It's time for us to go see Ambassador Liu," Ben announced as they walked through the door into the AG's office.

Hawthorne was in the midst of dictating to his secretary. He rose from his chair with a start. "Let's take a break, Mary Beth."

When she had departed, he shut the door. Ben and Jennifer gave the AG a rundown while he rolled an unlit cigar around in his mouth.

"You're right," he said when they were finished. "Your next stop is the Chinese ambassador."

Ben tried to look hopeful. The moment of truth had come as to whether they could count on Hawthorne. "We'll need your help getting to interview Liu."

"I've already started the process. I've arranged for us to meet this evening with the President to discuss the issue. He's expecting us at nine o'clock in the Oval Office."

Ben was pleasantly surprised. "Should we bring anything?"

"All your stuff. We're only going to get one chance to do this. The tapes, the pictures, and Jennifer's motion papers relating to the deposition of the Chinese ambassador."

Jennifer patted her briefcase. "They're all right here. I never leave home without them."

"There's one more loose end," Ben said.

The AG tossed his cigar into the wastebasket. "What's that?"

"The FBI report on the blonde's fingerprints."

"You underestimate me, Ben. When we hadn't heard anything by eight this morning, I went directly to Murtaugh. There had to be some reason it was taking so long."

"And?" Ben held his breath.

"It turns out that George Nesbitt doesn't have fingerprints. At least not ones we can use to make a match."

Ben was nonplussed. "That's crazy. Everybody has fingerprints."

Hawthorne smiled. "That's what I said, but we're both wrong. They can be surgically removed, which is what happened here."

"Holy shit. So we're dealing with a real pro."

"Precisely. And once she wakes up we may be able to make a deal with her and find out who hired her. The Chinese ambassador or someone else."

Ben thought of the woman's assault on Amy, and his face burned with anger. "No way I'm going to agree to let this psycho walk."

"Let's cross that bridge when we get to it."

Hawthorne stood up, signaling that as far as he was concerned, the meeting was over. Ben remained in his chair, deep in thought.

"What's bothering you?" the AG asked.

"I'm trying to puzzle this all out. I can see the Chinese ambassador getting someone to call Alexandra Hart and making all the arrangements for the hit on Winthrop. That's doable, all right, but an awful lot's happened since then. Threats and bribes on the Gillis family. An attack on me and my daughter. And a helluva lot of other things intended to cover up Winthrop's murder. The Chinese ambassador couldn't have done those himself."

Hawthorne sat back down, regarding Ben closely. "What are you saying?"

"I think he needed help from an American. Do you have any idea who was close with Liu?"

"The only one I know of is Marshall Cunningham, but Marshall wouldn't—" Hawthorne stopped in mid-sentence. "Jesus, this is turning into a fucking nightmare."

"Should we invite Cunningham to the Oval Office this evening?" Jennifer asked.

"Great idea," Hawthorne said. "Let's see how he deals with this."

Ben thought the President would explode with anger, or at least have a heart attack behind his desk in the Oval Office, when he and Jennifer finished the summary of their investigation, including Mark Bonner's photos showing the pickup of the video taken from Ann Winthrop by someone from the Chinese embassy. He shot to his feet. His face was beet red, and his breath was coming in short spurts. He ripped a page off the pad on his desk, rolled it up into a ball, and flung it into the wastebasket. Ben couldn't remember ever seeing anyone that angry.

"Those bastards," he said, "spying on Robert like that and killing him. God damn them. We can't let them get away with it. I'll send Liu home. I'll cut off all diplomatic relations with the Chinese government. I'll—"

Hawthorne interrupted him. "At this point, Philip, we don't know for sure that the Chinese government was responsible for Robert's death."

"But just blackmailing him that way. That's enough to let Ben here do the interview he wants. We'll see where it leads."

Ben was watching Cunningham, as he had during much of the presentation. The secretary of defense had a hostile scowl on his face.

Jennifer knew that she should be watching Cunningham as well, but she kept glancing at Slater out of the corner of her eye. When they arrived, he hadn't acknowledged that he knew her, for which she was relieved. Throughout the entire presentation he had been silent, showing no visible reaction.

The President turned to Cunningham. "What do you think, Marshall?"

He tried to sound helpful. "Let's face it, the whole thing's a mess. The more poking around we do, the more likely we'll end up reading about that part of Robert's life in the newspapers. Equally important is our current relationship with Beijing, which is so sensitive right now, with their troops on the move toward Taiwan and our forces streaming toward China. I'm afraid the kind of interview Ben wants to do with Ambassador Liu could have serious foreign-policy repercussions. To be blunt, it could be the spark that lands us in a major war in Asia. For this reason, I think it would be a terrible mistake even to request this interview."

"But if Liu was somehow involved in Robert's death . . ." Hawthorne said.

"That's the whole point, Ches," replied Cunningham vehemently. "Ben's got no credible basis to believe Liu was involved."

"I do have the two tapes Ann supplied."

Cunningham snarled, "This is the first I've heard of this Chinese effort to blackmail Robert. What's clear is that it's a red herring as far as Robert's death is concerned."

There was a brief silence. All of the others turned toward the President, waiting for Brewster to speak. Meantime, he picked up Ann's videotape and turned it over repeatedly, trying to sort out in his mind what to do.

The President glanced at Ben. "How do you respond to what Marshall just said? You're the experienced prosecutor."

"I think it's a mistake to wait. In any murder case the trail gets cold with time."

Hawthorne jumped in to support Ben. "That's precisely right."

"But doesn't Marshall have a point? There is no

direct link between Robert's death and what was said on Ann's tape."

Hawthorne nodded to Ben, who answered, "The circumstantial evidence is strong. If this were any other case, I wouldn't hesitate to interview a witness in Liu's position."

"But this isn't any other case. Is it?"

"That's correct, Mr. President," Ben said respectfully.

"Shouldn't we follow Marshall's advice and wait until you have some direct evidence?"

Dammit, Ben thought. Cunningham was winning. He would get away with it unless Ben stopped being intimidated by the Oval Office and became more assertive. Ben took a deep breath and decided to give it his best shot. "I've been doing criminal cases for a long time, Mr. President. I've learned to be suspicious about coincidental events. It's my experience that when two closely related events occur at about the same time in a serious criminal matter, it's not a coincidence. It's like hitting the same number twice on a roulette wheel. Yes, it could happen. But personally, my guess would be that there was a rigged wheel."

Brewster smiled. "Actually, I'd put my money on a rigged wheel, too." The President looked over at Slater. "What do you think, Jim? You've been awfully quiet."

Slater tugged on his blue suspenders. All eyes in the room were turned to him. Looking pensive, he said, "I'm in a funny position. I was the one who was pressing hard for a quick arrest and conviction of the gardener because I honestly thought he was guilty. I gave Ben a pretty rough time over that."

He glanced over at Ben, who muttered, "That's an understatement."

"But," Slater continued in a flat, even voice, "I'm a big enough person to admit if I make a mistake. Listening to everything Ben and Jennifer have said, I think it's probably more likely that Liu was responsible."

Ben saw Cunningham squirming in his seat.

"So I'd let Ben do the interview," Slater said. "As for how the Chinese will react?" He shrugged. "We'll never have their respect if we literally let them get away with murder."

Brewster looked at Hawthorne. The AG leaned forward in his chair and cleared his throat. "I agree with Jim," he said. "My gut as a trial lawyer tells me Ben should do the interview with Liu. I'm not sure what we'll get. There's a good enough chance we may get something."

Cunningham looked angry. "Oh, that's a great way to make national policy, Ches, based on your gut and his guess. I still think—"

President Brewster cut him off. "I'll set up the interview through Dalton at State. If that doesn't work, I'll call Beijing myself."

"The Chinese might not agree to it," Cunningham said.

"Then Miss Moore will file her motion papers, and we'll take the diplomatic immunity issue to a judge. Robert was my best friend. One way or the other I'm going to get their cooperation."

Cunningham was beaten, but he wasn't finished yet. "This is sensitive politically and diplomatically. At the interview, we'd better have somebody present from DOD. There's a lawyer on my staff who—"

"If that's your concern," Hawthorne said, "then I'll get Bruce Girard to send somebody from his legal office at State. Can you live with that, Ben?"

"Yes, sir."

"And I think," Cunningham added, "that your interview should be informal and off the record. No transcripts. No tape recorders. You can take notes. Nobody attends besides you and this representative of State. Nothing obtained during the interview can be disclosed to anyone other than the people in this room without express approval from the President."

"I can live with that, too," Ben said.

As the meeting was breaking up, Slater came over

to Ben. "Listen, I meant what I said. I am sorry that I pushed you so hard on the gardener."

Ben was still pissed at Slater for inserting Fulton into the case, but he decided to be gracious. "We've all been under a lot of pressure."

"It wasn't that. I'm used to pressure. The reports I was getting from Ed were so strong and so definitive. He was absolutely convinced the gardener did it."

That was the opening Ben had been looking for. He was getting an idea. "He wanted to impress you with an early arrest." In a low voice he said, "Do you think Ed could have planted the phony evidence in the gardener's truck?"

Slater's eyes lit up with alarm. "Jesus, I hadn't thought of that." He stopped to consider what Ben said. "I guess the money's easy. But where would Ed get the gun to plant in the truck?"

Ben shrugged. "One of the FBI people could have found it at Winthrop's house. Ed tells him not to say anything. Presto, he's got a way to look like a hero in the eyes of his boss."

Slater looked appalled by this idea. "What are you going to do? Follow up by talking to Ed? Or do you want me to?"

Ben shook his head. "Leave it alone for now. Ed's not going anywhere. Liu has to be our focus. We have to find out who was responsible for the murder. There'll be time enough later to deal with an overzealous government lawyer."

Slater nodded his acquiescence. "On that subject, if you want my opinion, I think you're right on target going after Liu." The chief of staff looked around nervously to make sure no one could overhear them. Cunningham was at the far end of the room talking to Brewster. "I'll give you some advice, though. Liu's going to be tough to nail. He has a powerful friend"—Slater paused to cock his head at Cunningham—"right here in this room, who's not going to let that happen."

While pretending to gather up her papers and tapes,

Jennifer had been watching Ben and Slater engaged in conversation. They were quite a contrast, those two. Even late in the evening Slater was perfectly dressed and clean shaven, with his hair slicked down. Ben's hair was uncombed, his suit and shirt were rumpled, and the dark shadow on his face indicated that morning had been a long time ago. Ben was emotional, moving his hands and questioning with his face. Slater looked smooth, calm, and cool. So what does all of this tell you? Jennifer asked herself.

"I'm not afraid of being interviewed," Liu said to Cunningham. They were in Cunningham's house sipping armagnac. The tall antique grandfather clock in the corner of the wood-paneled den had just struck midnight.

"Ben Hartwell's smart," Cunningham said. "Don't underestimate him."

"I don't have anything to hide."

"He knows about the two videotapes taken from Ann. He has photographs to establish that someone at your embassy was responsible. Those aren't matters to be proud of."

Liu shrugged his shoulders. "It's all part of the normal conduct of foreign affairs."

"Assassinations don't fit into that category."

"I quite agree." He leveled his gaze at Cunningham. "We didn't assassinate anyone."

Before Cunningham had a chance to respond, the ambassador yawned. He'd had enough of Cunningham for one night. He had a wonderful young staffer waiting in his bed. He wanted to go home to her. He drained the rest of the armagnac and rose to leave.

Cunningham said to him, "There is one other thing."

"What's that?"

"I think it would be best if you clarified to Hartwell that I had no idea about your effort to blackmail Winthrop until the meeting at the White House this evening."

Liu smiled weakly. "You said it would be best. Best for whom?"

Cunningham bit his lip, suppressing his anger. "Think long and hard tonight about what you just said."

"Meaning what?"

"If you plan to shoot at a king, then you'd better kill him."

"But I don't see a crown on your head, Marshall Cunningham."

"It's time to move, Comrade Li," the captain from the front of the truck said as he poked Chen, who was dozing in his cot.

Chen bolted upright and rubbed his eyes. It took him a few moments to orient himself. "I'm ready."

The captain took Chen's suitcase and duffel bag and exited the barracks with Chen two steps behind. Outside, Chen, dressed in an army uniform, climbed into the back of the truck, which seemed to be the same one in which he had arrived. There were only five other soldiers in the back. This time, a second truck with six soldiers followed behind. The two trucks headed out on a deserted road under a cloudy sky.

Chen was surprised that no one wanted to review the plan with him. These men were either too nervous, or knew what they had to do. No one said a word. Chen reassured himself that the beauty of Donovan's plan was its simplicity. There was no need to discuss it. When they reached the missile battery site, both trucks would enter the site, being passed through by a guard at the gate who had been well paid. No record would be made of their entrance. The two trucks would pull up close to the missile battery and then stop. While the soldiers scrambled out of Chen's truck into the other one, he would set the bomb, then join them in the second truck. He would wait until they left the site to detonate it.

At the entrance to the missile base, the two trucks came to a halt. Looking out, Chen saw thirty tall cylindrical C55–6 missiles on fixed launch pads pointed at Taipei across the narrow strait. Thirty matchsticks with a range well beyond Taiwan, each with a potent warhead that could kill Mary Ann and his children.

Chen heard the guard and driver laugh; then they were moving again. Security was light inside the deserted base. Chen guessed that was because it was almost three in the morning. Also, the regime couldn't conceive of anyone attacking the site.

Chen took another look at the missiles. The explosive he would be leaving behind in this truck was powerful enough to destroy the missiles and the launching pads. It would blow the whole site sky-high.

The trucks went slowly along a narrow, winding road that led down toward the water. After ten minutes, both trucks stopped. Without saying a word to Chen, the five soldiers scrambled out of the truck, leaving him alone in the back.

He opened the brown suitcase and looked inside. Everything was in place.

It was dark inside the back of the truck, and Chen needed light to assemble the bomb. Donovan had prepared for this contingency, though. Inside the suitcase was a flashlight, which Chen turned on. He propped it against the duffel bag so it would shine on the suitcase.

His fingers were cold and stiff. Before pulling the pieces of the bomb out of the suitcase, he rubbed his hands together. With great care, he removed each piece and laid it on the floor of the truck. Then he began the methodical assembly, without needing to consult the instructions. He had committed them to memory.

Four connections down and four more to go, Chen thought. He felt as if he were back at MIT doing an experiment in electrical engineering.

Everything was going like clockwork. Three more minutes at most, he told himself. Then it's done. It's over. I'll never do anything like this again.

His concentration was so great that he didn't notice

through cracks in the tarp the bright helium lamps that came on suddenly, lighting the whole area as if it were noon. But he heard the blasting sirens, and a sickening feeling grew in the pit of his stomach.

From the outside, someone ripped the tarp off the truck. Soldiers climbed inside. Rough hands grabbed Chen and tossed him out, where other muscular arms caught him and tied his wrists and ankles with rope. They packed him in the back of a dark green van, where four soldiers sat with their rifles aimed at him.

Shoot me, Chen pleaded with his eyes. Shoot me.

He knew that would be far too kind a fate. Something much worse awaited him. As he thought about it, he felt a trickle of warm fluid go down his leg inside his pants.

Chapter 29

Michelle Weinberg was the lawyer from the legal adviser's office at State who was picked to accompany Ben. When the black State Department limo pulled up in front of his house, she climbed out and introduced herself to him at the curb. She was tall, with lots of leg. For a woman to get a job in that office, she must have lots of smarts as well, he guessed. She wore brown-framed glasses and a very proper charcoal-gray suit.

As they climbed into the car, Ben eyed her suspiciously, wondering if the State Department had its own agenda in this morass. The limo started moving.

"How long have you been with State?" he asked, probing.

"Oh, about eight years. Ever since a D.C. circuit clerkship."

"And did someone tell you what your role is today?"

"Not exactly."

"Well, it's to be a potted plant. Can you handle that?"

Without responding, Michelle reached into the briefcase resting on her lap. While she searched for something, Ben looked at her legs, which were mostly exposed, as her skirt had ridden up high on her thighs. Finally, she found a piece of paper and handed it to him. Then she promptly pulled down her skirt. He was embarrassed that he had been so obvious.

The paper contained a bio of the Chinese ambassador she had prepared.

Ben started to read it. "Hey, this is great," he said. "And here I thought you only wanted a potted plant."

"Touché."

"You'll note that he spent four years in England at Cambridge."

"Studying physics, no less. He must be one smart dude."

"He's a champion bridge player, too. A very pragmatic man. And he's an expert judge of people. So don't sell him short. Also, be careful when you try to guess what he's thinking from his facial expressions. He's enigmatic and difficult to read."

"Gotcha."

"One other thing. Don't interrupt him when he's speaking. In China, it's polite to let each person complete his thoughts. You think about what he said. Then you respond. Here, we're continually interrupting everybody."

"You know these people?"

"I'm not sure what you mean by 'know these people,' " she said sharply. "I studied Chinese at Yale. I spent two years in China. My language skills are adequate. But none of that is enough for me to believe that I truly understand one of the most complex societies in the world."

The limo reached Connecticut Avenue and turned right, heading south.

Chastened by her advice, Ben said more humbly, "What else should I do to make a good impression?"

"Accept his offer of coffee or tea even if you don't want it. And generally try to be a mensch, if you know what that means, instead of a mad dog prosecutor, which I suspect you are."

There was that term again that Senator Young had used. It rankled Ben, but he decided to grin and bear it. "I get the picture."

Ben was gaining respect for the woman, and he

added, "Do you know what this interview is all
about?" he asked her.

"The attorney general briefed me himself."

"What do you think?"

"What do I think about what?"

"Am I wasting my time?"

"You mean, did Ambassador Liu arrange for the
murder of the secretary of state?"

Ben nodded.

"On his own, he would never have done that. It's
not his style. But it's reasonable to assume that Ambassador Liu wasn't on a frolic of his own. Some other
Chinese officials had to be involved."

"Why can we assume that?"

"He needed help from the Chinese embassy in London to arrange the video at Claridge's."

That was a reasonable assumption. "So where's that
leave us?" he asked.

"Some of the leadership in Beijing play a rough
game. Still, I would be very surprised if they gave an
order to assassinate our secretary of state. They might
have thought about it. My guess is that they decided
the risks outweighed the benefits. So they tried this
elaborate blackmail scheme. But that's just a guess
on my part. You can form your own conclusion from
the interview."

"If he's so hard to read, how am I going to reach
any conclusion?"

She smiled. "Attorney General Hawthorne said you
were a crack trial lawyer. You must have cross-
examined difficult witnesses in your brilliant career at
the U.S. Attorney's office. Now that it's showtime,
don't get stage fright on me, Clarence Darrow."

She was reminding him of someone else he knew—
before she decided she liked him again. "Do you always put people down like this?"

"Only when they tell me to sit in the corner and
keep my mouth shut."

"I never . . ."

She glared at him. "Save that potted-plant line for some of your dull-witted male colleagues. Maybe they'll take it better."

"Hey, you don't have to get so upset."

She responded by crossing her arms in front of her chest and staring out of the side window.

Feeling like a jerk, Ben looked down at the floor of the car. He couldn't remember anyone ever putting him down as fast and effectively. But he could hardly blame her.

The Chinese embassy occupies what was formerly the Windsor Hotel on Connecticut Avenue just above downtown Washington. When the great breakthrough in diplomatic relations came during Nixon's presidency, there was a lot of speculation about how large a presence Beijing would have in Washington. That ended with the announcement that they had bought an eight-story building that could comfortably house a staff in the hundreds. In that era of the Sino Soviet rivalry, two facts were readily observed: The Chinese embassy not only dwarfed its Sixteenth Street Soviet counterpart in size, but it occupied much higher ground.

Ben remembered that bit of Washington trivia as the limo pulled up in front of the embassy. Two members of the American Executive Protective Service eyed Ben and Michelle carefully and asked for IDs. The next security check was just inside, where two plainclothes members of the embassy staff checked IDs again and passed them through a metal detector. When the elevator doors opened on the eighth floor, a secretary met them and led the way down a long corridor to the ambassador's spacious corner office.

Ambassador Liu was sitting behind a heavily polished teak desk entirely devoid of papers. He stood up, came forward, and greeted Michelle warmly in Chinese. She introduced Ben to the Chinese ambassador and to the only other occupant of the room, whom she identified to Ben as the chief legal officer of the embassy. Ben didn't catch the man's name, but Michelle was obviously on good terms with him.

Coffee and tea were graciously offered on a lacquered tray in the most beautiful floral cups Ben had ever seen. He was ready to decline; then he remembered what Michelle had said in the car. He took a cup of coffee, thanking the ambassador for his hospitality. He waited for Ambassador Liu to settle down behind his desk. Ben began speaking slowly. "Mr. Ambassador, I sincerely appreciate your willingness to meet with us voluntarily."

"Let's be clear," Liu replied in careful, precise English tinged with a British accent, "my government has instructed me to do everything possible to cooperate in the unfortunate death of Mr. Winthrop. I intend to do that."

To put the ambassador on the defensive right off the bat, Ben unsnapped his briefcase, pulled out the audio machine, and played Ann's tape from Liu's visit to Winthrop's house. As the sprockets turned and the recording filled the room, Ben picked up a yellow legal pad and pencil. He studied Liu's face carefully. There was no reaction. Absolutely none at all.

When the tape ended, Liu looked at Ben. "That's an accurate recording of my conversation with Mr. Winthrop. But now I have something for you."

He pointed to his legal aide, who handed Ben a manila envelope. "It's the video recording from Claridge's Hotel mentioned in your tape. Mr. Winthrop told me that he destroyed the one I gave him. In the spirit of cooperation, I wanted you to have it. Of course, we haven't given it to anyone else."

To Ben, the implication was clear. Winthrop might be dead, but he had still been the President's close friend. Liu no doubt had other copies of the video. Even now its release would be embarrassing to the occupant of 1600 Pennsylvania Avenue.

"How do you know Winthrop destroyed the other tape?" Ben asked.

"We spoke by telephone the day after we met at his house. I called him at his office."

"What did he say?"

"He told me that he had thrown the video into the Potomac River."

"But you didn't believe him."

"Why do you say that?"

"Because you sent a thug around to Winthrop's house to steal back the tape." Ben locked him in a stare. "And you sent him back a second time to get any copies Mrs. Winthrop had made."

"That's preposterous."

The blatant lie infuriated Ben. It took all of his self-control to keep himself in check. "Is it?" he replied coldly.

"It is."

Ben reached into his briefcase and pulled out Mark Bonner's photographs, showing the video being delivered to the Chinese embassy. Remembering what Michelle had said about Liu being a champion bridge player, Ben said, "You might call this the ace of trump."

Liu gave Ben a wry smile, then glanced at the photos quickly without comment and handed them to his legal aide. Ben had been hoping that the photographs would fluster Liu, but he wasn't the least bit surprised. Someone must have tipped him off.

Ben could feel himself tightening with anger. This was the last time anybody was getting confidential information from him. Every time he disclosed information, he got screwed.

"You may not know this, Mr. Liu," he said in a voice heavy with sarcasm, "but in this country we take human rights seriously. Breaking and entering is a crime."

"So is the hiring of prostitutes. I imagine Mr. Winthrop must not have been aware of that fact."

Ben ignored this. "How did you get to Peg Barton?"

"Through contacts we have in London. She services

the diplomatic community. She is known to most embassies there. Her girls talk. Once we became aware of Mr. Winthrop's outside interests, she was a likely candidate."

"How did you become aware of what you just called Mr. Winthrop's outside interests?"

Liu cracked a tiny smile. "Really, Mr. Hartwell, that fact was well known to every embassy in Washington. His sexual needs frequently overcame his discretion."

"How long have you known Alexandra Hart?"

Liu's forehead wrinkled. "I'm sorry. I don't recognize the name."

"Don't play games with me."

Michelle moved to the edge of her chair.

"It's not a game, Mr. Hartwell. I've never heard of that woman."

"Then why did you arrange to have me attacked in London?"

"I had no idea you were attacked."

Ben stood up suddenly, took off his jacket, and pulled up his shirt. His body was filled with black-and-blue marks. Michelle started to get up as well, then thought better of it, and stayed seated. She was clearly taken aback by the condition of Ben's chest and stomach.

"I had nothing to do with that. I assure you."

"You hired the Greeks who did this, didn't you?"

"This time you're mistaken, Mr. Hartwell," Liu said coolly.

Ben sat down, tucked his shirt back in, and pointed to the photographs Mark had taken. "But you hired that man."

"Yes, I hired him."

"And you hired the Greeks who beat me in London."

"I had nothing to do with that. Anyone could have hired them."

Michelle said, "Let's return to Mr. Winthrop."

Ben shot her an irate look, but picked up on the hint. "You said that you had a telephone conversation with Mr. Winthrop the day after you met at his house. That's when he told you that he threw your video into the Potomac River?"

Liu nodded.

"What else did he say?"

"He told me that he wouldn't resign. Also, he wouldn't change his policy on the arms package for Taiwan. He told me that our effort at blackmail was ridiculous because we wouldn't dare release that videotape. It would come back to haunt us, he said, and in any event he would survive the bad press and be in a position to punish my country. He was playing what you Americans call hardball."

"Did you ever see or talk to him after that phone conversation?"

"Never."

"What did you do after that telephone conversation with Mr. Winthrop?"

"I called Marshall Cunningham. I went to see him at his office at the Pentagon that afternoon."

"So that would still be the day after your meeting at Winthrop's house?"

"That's correct."

"Why did you go to see Cunningham?"

"To describe everything that had happened with Mr. Winthrop in the last twenty-four hours and to urge Mr. Cunningham to intervene and to compel Mr. Winthrop either to resign or to change the American government's policy on the Taiwan arms transaction."

"Who else was at that meeting?"

"Only the two of us."

"Why did you select Cunningham to obtain support for your blackmail attempt?"

Liu scowled and shook his head furiously. "I resent your characterization of my efforts at persuasion as blackmail."

Ben glanced at Michelle, who was shaking her head at him. He revised the question. "Very well, why did you select Cunningham to help with your effort at persuasion?"

Liu was happy to put all of this on the table. If Cunningham was trying to set Liu up to take the fall, he wouldn't sit back and let it happen.

"I knew that Mr. Cunningham had a deeper understanding of the relationship between China and Taiwan, of political and military realities in Asia, and—"

"And what?" Ben asked, ignoring Michelle's advice and interrupting Liu in midsentence.

"Perhaps it's not appropriate."

"I thought there was to be full cooperation."

The ambassador looked at his legal aide, who nodded, and he continued. "I also knew that Mr. Cunningham and Mr. Winthrop disagreed on many issues, including Taiwan. I was hoping that Mr. Cunningham could use this evidence of Mr. Winthrop's personal indiscretions as the basis to force Mr. Winthrop from office."

Ben paused for a minute to leaf through his yellow pad. He soon found what he was looking for. After he had left the White House last evening, he had gone through his notes and had carefully written down everything that was discussed while it was still fresh in his mind. Cunningham had said that he had not heard about the Chinese effort to blackmail Winthrop prior to the discussion last evening in the Oval Office. One of them was lying. Ben pressed on.

"What exactly did Mr. Cunningham say at your meeting?"

"He listened carefully to my report of the discussion the evening before with Mr. Winthrop, and my telephone conversation with Winthrop earlier in the day."

"And then?"

"I played the London video for him on the VCR in his office. I asked him if he wanted a copy."

"Did he?"

"He said that he collected wine, not porn movies."

"What else did he say?"

"He asked if I would agree to withhold releasing the video to the press and to take no action for a period of one month. He said that he hoped to be able to persuade Mr. Winthrop to resign in that month. I agreed to his request."

"Then what happened?"

"Nothing. Mr. Winthrop died within the month. I took no further action on this matter."

"But you did steal back your tape from Mrs. Winthrop and a copy she made."

"I recovered my property."

"I must ask you, sir, were you involved in any way in the death of Robert Winthrop?"

Ben expected Liu to react in indignation. Instead, there was only a tiny smile, with the edges of his mouth turning up ever so slightly, and the simple response, "No, Mr. Hartwell. Neither I nor any other official of my government had anything to do with the death of Secretary of State Winthrop."

"Why should I believe you?" Ben asked, boring in. "With all the other things you've done here, why would you stop at murder?"

"Because my government doesn't assassinate foreign leaders," he said in a clipped British accent. "We don't think that's proper behavior in the civilized world. Your government, on the other hand, has different moral standards. Witness what you tried to do with Saddam Hussein, Fidel Castro, and Qaddafi."

Ben bristled, listening to this lecture coming from a diplomat whose government was responsible for the massacre at Tiananmen Square. No doubt, Ben thought, plenty of high Chinese officials had mistresses or used call girls. And what was more, secretly filming someone's sexual activities in a hotel room was hardly a high moral act. "At least we don't arrest and torture people who raise their voices against the government."

Michelle reached over to touch Ben's hand, cautioning him to stick with the subject of this interview. He yanked away.

Liu didn't need help, in any case. "You strike me as an intelligent man, Mr. Hartwell. You no doubt appreciate the irony here."

"What do you mean?"

"Your secretary of state purported to be supporting Taiwan for moral reasons, the honoring of American commitments. He felt good making that very moral, high-minded judgment. Yet, at the same time, that same secretary of state was behaving in his own life in a most immoral way, as the videotape that I handed to you demonstrates." His tone was not emotional but pedagogical. "To me, that's ironic. No, more precisely, it's hypocritical. Your Mr. Winthrop lost his moral compass. Don't you think so, Mr. Hartwell?"

"What I think is that you, with your high-minded morality, hired a woman to kill Mr. Winthrop in order to gain a reversal of the United States' decision to sell certain arms to Taiwan. That's what I think."

Liu clenched his fists. "Who made up such a ridiculous story?" he said in a quavering voice.

"I think it's very clear from all the facts."

Liu tapped his fingers abruptly on his desk. His brief show of emotion was over. "Though we had nothing to do with it," he said calmly, "personally, I'm not sorry someone killed Robert Winthrop. In fact, I'm pleased. The world needs statesmen who are principled and stick to those principles, regardless of whether I agree with them. The world doesn't need hypocrites who wear their morality like an overcoat—on those days and in those places where it suits them."

Ben shrugged in boredom. He had gotten what he could from the interview. Tired of being lectured by Liu, he put away his legal pad.

But the ambassador wasn't finished. He decided to go on the offensive. "I'll offer you a suggestion," Liu said, "in your search for Mr. Winthrop's killer."

Ben looked up. "What's that?"

"It's likely to be someone similar to Secretary of State Winthrop. Someone who also lost his own moral compass."

"I appreciate the advice. More to the point, are you planning to remain in the country for the next week, or do I have to obtain a court order?"

"I wouldn't consider leaving, Mr. Hartwell. I want

to be right here when you find your killer—in order
to accept your apology."

From the back of the limousine, Ben called the attorney general to report on his interview with Liu.
Before he had a chance to focus Hawthorne's attention on the contradiction between what Liu and Cunningham had said about when Cunningham first
learned about Liu's blackmail of Winthrop, the AG
picked up on it.

"I don't like that at all."

Ben was relieved that he had an ally. "What do you
think we should do?"

"Without any warning, I'm sending two top FBI
agents over to Cunningham's office to get any documents relating to his contacts with Liu, meeting logs
and so forth."

"Good idea."

"Then I'm demanding that he come to my office for
a four o'clock meeting this afternoon. Bring Jennifer
with you. We'll see what he says about this contradiction."

"That's great. Jennifer and I will be there at three
to look at the documents."

To say that Marshall Cunningham was incensed
when he walked into Hawthorne's office was one of
the great understatements of all time. The man's face
was bright red. He was scowling and his eyes were
firing dirty looks, which, if they were laser beams,
would be sawing through everything in sight.

Ben wasn't intimidated. "We know you don't like
doing this. We had no choice."

Cunningham shot a look at Hawthorne. "You had
no right removing files from my office when I wasn't
there."

The AG wasn't intimidated either. "I gave that
order. The files belong to the United States government. Talk to the President if you don't like it."

That ended the discussion. Cunningham knew that

Brewster would approve of anything that might help
to find Winthrop's killer. The four of them settled
down around a conference table in the AG's office.

Still, Cunningham remained on the attack. "So what
did you find from this great search of my files?"

Ben took his time answering. He refused to let Cunningham dictate the order of the discussion. "Let me
tell you why we're bothering you."

"Yeah?" Cunningham snarled.

"We interviewed Liu this morning. There's a contradiction between what Liu said and what you told us
at the meeting in the Oval Office yesterday evening.
You said that last night was the first time you had
heard of the Chinese effort to blackmail Winthrop."

Cunningham didn't respond. He knew where this
was going. Liu was trying to point a finger at him to
distract Ben.

"But Ambassador Liu told us this morning he came
to your office at the Pentagon and talked to you about
it the day after he was at Winthrop's house."

Cunningham looked wary. "What difference does
that make?"

"Well, it affects Liu's credibility in general. If he
was lying to me about this, then he might have been
lying about other things. I'd have to reevaluate my
conclusion that the Chinese weren't involved."

Cunningham saw through Ben's ploy. It was a clever
effort to get him to drop his guard, which he refused
to do. Ben was looking at him innocently. Jennifer
was on the edge of her chair, anxious to hear what
Cunningham said.

"You must have misunderstood what I told you last
evening," Cunningham finally replied. "I never said
that I didn't know about the Chinese blackmail attempt at the time. What I said, or at least what I
meant to say, is that I never knew Ann made a tape
of Winthrop's meeting with Liu until you told us about
it yesterday."

Ben hesitated. He had a precise recollection of what
Cunningham had said last evening, which was consis-

tent with his notes from the meeting. The man was lying now. There was no doubt about it. On the other hand, nothing would be gained by a frontal attack. He conceded, "I guess it's possible that I did misunderstand."

"I'm sure of it. What was the date that the ambassador claims he came to see me?" Cunningham asked.

"I think it was November second. The day after his meeting with Winthrop."

"Well, is that right?" Cunningham said sarcastically. "You guys have my records."

Ben looked at Jennifer, who opened up a black diary. "On November second," she said, "you had a three-thirty meeting with Ambassador Liu."

He nodded. "I keep notes from most of my meetings and phone calls. I'm sure you found the notes from that meeting." His tone and mood had changed to arrogance. These people weren't about to nail him for anything. "So what do they show?"

Jennifer handed him a white sheet of lined paper with handwriting on it. "I think it would be better if you read it."

He took the page from her and glanced down. "My notes show that the Chinese ambassador told me he had an embarrassing video of Robert. It says here, 'He wants Robert to resign or change policy toward Taiwan. If not, he'll go public with the video. He'll agree to delay for thirty days release of the video.' "

"What else?" she asked.

"Underneath there's a note I made later in the day. Robert and I attended a briefing with President Brewster on the Middle East. I took Robert aside after we left the meeting with the President and asked him about what Ambassador Liu had said. My note reads, 'W is leaning toward resigning. I am hopeful.' "

"What did you mean, you were hopeful?"

"I meant that Robert was contrite and ashamed. He made it clear that he would probably resign within the thirty days. I always liked Robert. We were good friends. I thought, under the circumstances, that would be the best choice for him personally and for the administration. The President's chances for reelection would be destroyed by the release of that video." He handed the document to Hawthorne. "You can read it for yourself, Ches."

Ben picked up the questioning. "Did you discuss the Chinese video with anyone else?"

"I told Jim Slater about it shortly after this meeting."

"What did he say?"

"He just listened and nodded, the way he does."

"What happened then?"

"Nothing that I was involved in. I decided that I'd wait three weeks before I turned up the pressure on Robert, or get Brewster to talk to him. I didn't think I'd have to do that. As I said, I was convinced from what he told me that he would resign. Then he was killed, and that was the end of that." Cunningham paused. "Are you satisfied now?"

Ben was convinced that Cunningham was lying, but he knew that he'd never be able to shake the former general. "I just have one other question. Does the name Alexandra Hart mean anything to you?"

Cunningham looked perplexed. "Never heard the name. Why?"

"Winthrop ever mention it to you?"

"Never. Was she a girlfriend of his, or one of the girls the Chinese filmed him with in London?"

"I'm not sure who she was. I'm just trying to find out who hired the blond shooter."

"That's what we're all trying to do."

"I don't know what to think about Cunningham," Ben said.

It was nine in the evening. They were seated around the dining room table in Ben's house with boxes of pizza in the center. Ben and Jennifer were on one side, Traynor and Campbell on the other, Ann at the end of the table. Amy was upstairs sleeping.

"What about the contemporaneous notes of his meeting with Ambassador Liu?" Traynor asked.

"For all we know, he could have prepared that piece of paper after our meeting last evening at the White House and backdated it."

Jennifer turned to Ann. "Cunningham said that after Liu gave him the tape, Robert was leaning toward resigning."

Ann choked on a piece of pizza. "That's a total crock." She took a sip of beer and cleared her throat. "In fact, I asked him whether he was going to resign. I wanted to know if we'd be moving back to New York."

"What did he say?"

"He replied in typical Robert Winthrop style. 'Fuck 'em. They're bluffing. I'm going to tough it out.' Something like that. The point is, he didn't seem worried at all by the Chinese threat."

Trying to recall Cunningham's precise words, Ben asked, "Would you say that Robert was contrite and ashamed?"

She laughed. "Robert? Are you kidding? You knew him, Jennifer. Try arrogant and bold if you want a couple of adjectives. But he was always like that. He cleaned up at poker because he'd ride a pair of deuces so hard that everyone else would fold."

"Do you know whether he ever talked to Marshall Cunningham about the Chinese government blackmail?"

Ann closed her eyes, trying to remember. "You know, that same evening, the second of November, when I asked Robert whether he'd be resigning and we'd be moving back to New York, he said, 'You sound like Marshall. That's what he told me to do today. I told him "Hell, no." I'll tell you the same thing.' Then he launched into his diatribe, 'fuck 'em' and so forth."

Ben looked around the table. "That doesn't really help us, though. Even assuming that Cunningham did lie to us, big whoop. Liu and Cunningham have managed to play off against each other so well that we're now at a total dead end. Alexandra Hart hasn't gotten us anywhere. There is absolutely nothing else we can do to find Winthrop's killer."

He waited, hoping someone would challenge him with an idea.

It was Jennifer who spoke up. "We still have one other chance."

"What's that?"

"Once our blond shooter comes out of a coma, she may be willing to talk if we can cut a deal with her."

"And when will that happen?" Ben asked glumly.

She returned his discouraged look. "I've got some information you're not going to like."

"You can't make it any worse."

"While you were interviewing Liu this morning, I talked to Dr. Marks, who's the attending for the shooter at G.W."

"What'd he say?"

"She. It's Dr. Deborah Marks. Could be tomorrow. Could be a week from now. Could be never."

Chen had no idea how long the beatings continued, how many men took turns pummeling him with their fists and clubs, or how many times he had passed out. His body was so battered and bruised that he prayed for death. But they were good at their work. They wouldn't let him die. Not until he told them who sent him on this mission.

He didn't betray Donovan even after the beatings. They hooked up electrodes to his genitals and sent ever-increasing surges of electricity through his body, but he still didn't talk.

He was barely conscious, hanging upside down with his feet tied by a rope to a metal bar, when the sadistic colonel who had been directing Chen's interrogation walked into the prison cell with a swagger. "Cut him down," he said.

They put Chen in a chair and tied him to it so he wouldn't fall over. Blood was oozing down his face.

"We know all about you, Chen," he said, smiling with a mouth missing several teeth. "Your father in Taipei is the owner of Diamond Computers. Your wife is Mary Ann. Your children are Ted, Walter, and Donna. We know where they live."

The colonel's words jolted what was left of Chen's senses to attention.

"You have a choice," the colonel said. "Do you understand what I'm saying?"

Chen nodded.

"You have a choice. Either you tell me who arranged this despicable crime of yours, there will be an explosion tomorrow night at your house when they're asleep. An explosion large enough to kill all of them."

That broke Chen. "No . . . No . . . No . . ." he stammered.

"Then talk," the colonel said.

Chen told him the entire story, beginning with his recruitment by Chip Donovan in Boston. He told him about Donovan's proposal for Operation Matchstick and then its execution.

When he was finished, the colonel picked up the phone and reported to a superior. As if Chen weren't listening, they discussed the alternatives for his fate—a show trial followed by the death sentence, or killing him now.

In the end, someone in Beijing decided that a show trial would embarrass the United States and Taiwan, but it would also expose to the Chinese people and to the world how lax security had been at the missile site, which was humiliating for the regime.

The colonel put down the phone. "Take him outside and kill him."

Chapter 30

"You must come to my office immediately," Liu said to Cunningham on the phone. It was eight-fifteen in the morning, and the secretary of defense was scheduled to begin a review of American military movements in the Pacific with the Joint Chiefs in fifteen minutes. That would have to wait. The urgency in Liu's voice persuaded Cunningham that he had to drop everything and get to the Chinese embassy ASAP.

Mired in heavy rush-hour traffic Cunningham sat in the back of a black Lincoln Town Car on the tedious ride from the Pentagon into the city, trying to guess what new development had occurred. Was this more nonsense about Winthrop's murder? Or had the Chinese decided to ignore the agreed-upon December seventh deadline and attack Taiwan? Had Taipei, frightened by the reports of Chinese troop movements, decided to launch a preemptive strike? Each scenario he envisioned terrified him more than the previous one.

His anxieties were increased when he was ushered by a secretary into the ambassador's office. Instead of the Liu he had come to know, cool and unflappable, the man looked distraught. Liu's eyes were bloodshot, evidence that he had been up all night. His hair was tousled, his tie loose, and his shirt open at the collar.

"An extreme provocation," Liu said as he rose from his desk to confront Cunningham.

"What happened? I don't understand."

"You've tricked me. Strung me along. You might as well have been signing my death warrant."

Cunningham was horrified. "What are you talking about?"

"Please don't insult me by pretending you don't know."

"Don't know what? So help me, God, I have no idea what you're talking about."

"The CIA plot to blow up one of our missile batteries."

"The CIA plot to do *what*?" Cunningham raised his voice in astonishment.

"You heard me."

"I swear I don't know anything about that. You must be mistaken. The CIA couldn't do something like that without my knowledge. Not now, not with the tension between our governments."

Liu motioned to Cunningham to sit down on the sofa, while he took a chair across a small teak table. "Don't tell me that nobody in your government can control Chip Donovan."

At the sound of the name, Cunningham cringed. When the Chinese had forced down and stripped the American reconnaissance plane, Donovan had argued and cajoled in White House strategy sessions for a prompt and forceful response. In the end, at the request of the President, Margaret Joyner had stopped bringing him with her to meetings. What in the hell had Donovan done on his own?

"We've always been straight with each other," Cunningham said. "I won't lie to you now. I'm not sure anybody in my government does control Chip Donovan. You have to believe me when I say I knew nothing about any action of this type. And if I didn't know, the President didn't know either. So you'd better tell me what you've heard. We can deal with it together."

Liu hesitated.

His face set in determination, Cunningham pressed, "If it's that bad, you don't have anything to lose by talking it through with me."

"You don't understand. I'm supposed to file an official protest with your President. Then I've been recalled until further notice. I don't want there to be any misunderstanding about how seriously my government views this action."

Cunningham sucked in his breath. Jesus, recalling Liu was one step short of a declaration of war. "I appreciate how grave the situation is. Now tell me what happened."

In short, staccato sentences in his British accent, Liu described everything Chen had done since leaving the Shangri-La Hotel in Shanghai. He walked over to his desk and returned with a faxed copy of Chen's signed confession, which he showed to Cunningham.

Shaking his head in disbelief, Cunningham read the document twice. "Was he tortured to sign this?"

"He was questioned at length," Liu replied.

Cunningham raised his eyebrows. "Can I be blunt?"

Liu nodded.

"In view of how the confession was obtained, is it worth anything? Perhaps the whole episode is a fabrication by hard-liners in your country to find one more excuse for launching an attack on Taiwan."

Liu frowned. "That was blunt."

"We don't have time for beating around the bush. Are you prepared to respond to my last point?"

Liu had no problem with that at all. From everything he had heard this morning, the confession, though coerced, was accurate. "You can rely on the confession."

"You're certain of that?"

"Quite. Now I need your help. If I'm to have any chance of surviving the next several days in Beijing, it's imperative that I get in to see your President to lodge the protest with him before I fly home."

Cunningham grimaced. In two hours Brewster was leaving for Paris to attend an economic summit with European leaders. Cunningham would have to find a window for Liu, but only after he got some facts from Joyner.

Liu gave Cunningham a private office to call the White House. Using his cell phone, Cunningham said to Brewster's secretary, "Listen, Doris, I need thirty minutes with him before he leaves. Fifteen alone and fifteen with the Chinese ambassador."

"You're kidding."

"I wish I were. Tell him it can't wait." At a moment like this, Cunningham was glad his relationship with Brewster went back so far.

"Hold on. I'll go ask." She returned to the phone a minute later. "Come in an hour. Senator Burns will be upset that he lost his slot. I'll get a tongue-lashing, but I can take it."

After telling Liu about the meeting, Cunningham added, "It's your call, but I don't think you should raise the Taiwan arms package with the President. I'm working on the issue. I need more time."

Liu didn't reply.

Once he was back in his car, Cunningham called Margaret Joyner at her office at the CIA. "All hell has broken loose," he said. Then he reported what Liu had told him.

"If it's true, I'll kill that damn Donovan with my own bare hands," Joyner shouted into the phone.

Cunningham was relieved. Unless Joyner was the world's greatest actress, which he doubted, this had been an unauthorized rogue operation, if in fact it had occurred.

"Keep your cell phone on," Joyner said. "I know Donovan's in his office today. I'm going to pay him a surprise visit and see what he has to say."

A half hour later, as Cunningham's car was passing through the gate to the White House, Joyner called him back. "He did it," she said, sounding upset. "The whole thing, just as you described it."

"Oh, shit."

"That pretty well sums it up."

"Was he defensive?"

"He's proud of it. Says we behaved like a bunch

of pussies when they took our plane. Says all they understand is brute force."

"Jesus, what'd you say?"

"Blew sky-high. Chewed him out. Told him that I'm going to take disciplinary action against him. He told me I was a gutless weasel. We'll see about that."

Cunningham reminded himself that high-profile, unauthorized spy actions that failed were an embarrassment for all governments from time to time. That didn't lessen his fury and outrage. Cowboys like Donovan had to be reined in. With everything on high alert with China over the Taiwan arms deal, this was no time for provocation, which was undoubtedly why Donovan had launched it now: to provoke a Chinese military response that would lead to war.

"You want me to come into town and join you at your meeting with the President and Liu?" Joyner asked.

Cunningham looked at his watch. He would have liked Joyner there, but she'd never make it in from Langley in time. "We'll put you on the speakerphone if need be. Meantime, have somebody keep an eye on Donovan. We don't want him walking out with any of the Agency's confidential documents."

"This is the worst month of my life." President Brewster moaned as Cunningham finished his briefing in the Oval Office. Off to one side, Slater shook his head, showing his disbelief at Cunningham's report.

The President turned back to Cunningham. "What do I tell Liu?"

"That you deeply regret this unauthorized action. You apologize to his government. You tell him that Donovan will be sacked from his job and dismissed from the Agency."

"Will Margaret go along with that?"

"I think so. Let's get her on the speakerphone."

Waiting for Doris to place the call, Slater said, "You really think it's wise to sack Donovan like this?"

"We have to do it," Cunningham replied. "What's bothering you?"

"He knows where a lot of bodies are buried, so to speak. You put someone like that out of the tent and he could come back to haunt us."

They both looked at the President. "Donovan goes unless Margaret disagrees," Brewster said without hesitation.

The President didn't even finish asking Joyner about the proposed disciplinary action on Donovan before she blurted out, "He'll be out of this building for good by the end of the day."

The decision to fire Donovan, along with an official, albeit private apology, meant a great deal to Liu, Cunningham could tell when they met with the Chinese ambassador a few minutes later. It was something he could tell the leaders in Beijing he had extracted from Washington. Cunningham knew that Liu was itching to press his case with the President for a reversal of Winthrop's decision on the Taiwan arms package, but, following Cunningham's counsel, he kept silent on the issue.

"We did as well as we could," Cunningham said to the President and Slater when Liu left.

"You think they'll respond with an attack on Taiwan?" Brewster asked.

"As usual with the Chinese, it's hard to know how they'll react." Cunningham added, "Our ships are in the area. We're ready to respond if that's what you decide to do."

Doris stuck her head in the door. "You said to remind you when it's time to leave for Paris."

Brewster sighed. "This trip couldn't come at a worse time. You think I should cancel?"

"Absolutely not," Slater said. "It sends the wrong signal to the Chinese and the rest of the world. We'll be in close contact with you from here on a secure line. If they attack, you can get back in a matter of hours."

Cunningham nodded in acquiescence.

"You know," Brewster said, "the more I think about what this guy Donovan did, the angrier I get. Firing him is not enough." The President was seething. "I want to throw the book at this . . . what did you call him?"

"Cowboy," Cunningham said.

"Yeah, cowboy."

"You really think that's wise?" Slater asked.

"You're damn right." Brewster hit the intercom. "Doris, get me Margaret Joyner again on the squawk box."

Once the CIA director was on the line, Brewster said, "I want you to call Ches Hawthorne. Tell him to have Sarah Van Buren or one of her people at DOJ find some laws that Donovan broke and charge him. That bastard's going to pay with a criminal conviction for what he did. You got that?"

"Done."

Slater was stunned. "You're willing to put the country through a public trial? Donovan could reveal plenty of our dirty little secrets."

"It'll never go that far. He'll plead."

"And if he doesn't?"

Brewster turned back toward the phone. "Also, Margaret, tell Ches I want to know how he's coming on the Winthrop investigation. Tell him to call me on Air Force One. I can't believe they haven't caught the people behind the Winthrop murder. The man was my best friend and a devoted public servant. This is a top priority for me. Tell him I said to use all the resources of this government."

Joyner summoned Chip Donovan, dressed in his usual black suit and black turtleneck shirt, to her office, where Sarah Van Buren was waiting. As soon as he heard the words "head of the criminal division" in the introduction, he knew what was coming. In stony silence he listened to Joyner. "You're being removed from your job for cause as of right now. You'll have ten minutes to clean out your office and to leave the building. You'll be watched the entire time. And that's not all. We're throwing the book at you." She turned to Van Buren. "Sarah, tell him what charges you're filing."

Before Van Buren could respond, Donovan said, "Why don't you people stop and think for a damn minute? China's hell-bent on their rise and our decline. Nations like that have to be stopped early with a show of force. What I did was right. Cunningham and Brewster are like Chamberlain was in the thirties. How far did appeasement get England?"

Joyner bristled. "You're not running the country."

"But what I planned was brilliant. Knocking out that missile battery would have been a powerful blow for Beijing. They'd think twice the next time before they behave like pirates and grab one of our planes out of the sky."

"Are you finished ranting?" Joyner said.

"No point trying to talk to people with blinders on who refuse to look at the facts."

Donovan didn't care about the dismissal from the agency. He was tired of working for a bunch of wimps. As for the ten minutes to clear out, that was a joke. He had hidden in a safe at home false passports and cash if he ever had to beat a hasty exit from the United States. He did not like the idea of being charged criminally, however.

He was scowling when Van Buren began talking about the laws he had violated and the charges that would be filed. She was in the middle of a sentence when he fired back, "You can charge me if you want to, but you'll lose your chance to find out who killed Robert Winthrop."

Startled, Van Buren said, "Run that by me again."

Donovan snarled. "You heard me. His Royal Highness, Brewster, wants to know who killed his great buddy who couldn't keep his pecker in his pants. Why don't you ask him if he wants to know badly enough that he's willing to let me walk?"

Joyner took off her glasses and fiddled with them, wondering what Donovan was talking about. "Tell us more."

He paused, letting the tension build. Then, like someone who was tossing a live grenade on the table in Joyner's office, he said, "I know who killed Robert Winthrop. You want to know? Then you have to play ball with me."

Mystified, Van Buren looked at Joyner, who was cringing inside, but trying not to show it. My God, Joyner was thinking. I hope to hell Winthrop's murder wasn't another clandestine CIA operation, like the attack on the Chinese missile base.

Van Buren asked, "What do you want?"

Donovan gave her an icy stare. She'd better realize that his terms were nonnegotiable. "I'll step down from my job at the Agency. You'll have to paper it over to make it look like a voluntary retirement, so I get my pension. Also, I want total immunity from any criminal charges in connection with the attack on the Chinese missile base and the Winthrop murder." He paused. "And finally, I can't be forced to testify in any proceeding about either event. That's it. Take it or leave it."

He looked like a poker player who had just bet the limit and laid down a straight flush. Contempt was mixed with arrogance in Donovan's steel gray eyes.

"You've got to be kidding," Van Buren said. "You don't have anything like the leverage you need to drive a deal like that."

Donovan pounded the table. "Oh, really? Try this for openers. I can tell you now that someone who works in the White House was very much involved in Winthrop's murder. You can take that back to His Royal Highness."

The women exchanged horrified looks. "You've got to give me more than that for what you're asking."

"Sorry, that's all you'll get from me until you sign on the dotted line."

"It's not enough."

Donovan pushed a hand through his thick gray hair.

"I hope Brewster never finds out that you two passed up a chance to learn who killed his bosom buddy."

Though she found Donovan despicable, Joyner, who less than an hour ago had heard the President refer to finding Winthrop's killer as a "top priority," took a softer line. "We'll let you wait in a conference room outside while we talk this over."

"Make sure you lock me in. You wouldn't want me stealing any documents."

"Don't worry," she snapped. "We'll have an armed guard at the door."

Once he was gone, Van Buren said to Joyner, "You think he knows anything about Winthrop's killer? Or is this just a game?"

"It's hard to know. I don't want to make that decision."

They called Ches Hawthorne at DOJ, who was flabbergasted. "This one gets made at the top. You two hold on while I get the President on another phone. He should be on Air Force One by now."

Minutes later, Hawthorne was back. "Brewster said, 'Hell, yes, take the deal, and keep me informed. Finding out who killed Winthrop means more to me than putting this cowboy in jail.' His words. My thought is, you get Donovan out of the CIA building. Set it up for a four-o'clock meeting with him somewhere in town. That'll give us time to draw up the papers. I'll get somebody drafting ASAP. When you tell him we'll give him what he wants, emphasize that if anything he tells us isn't true, the deal's off. That term goes into the immunity document."

"Will do," Van Buren replied.

"Oh, and one other thing. When you set the meeting with Donovan, I want Ben and Jennifer there. They've been working the Winthrop case. They'll be in the best position to decide whether that scumbag Donovan is telling the truth."

Gwen had regained consciousness over a period of several hours. She could move her toes. Her eyes fluttered. The room, which had been fuzzy and clouded, grew sharper, like a camera lens being focused. Along with her sight, her sense of smell and hearing returned. The odor, unmistakably a hospital, told her where she was even before she heard the announcements over the PA system that said, "Dr. Nielsen to surgery, stat. Dr. Goldberg to O.R., Dr. . . ."

As she looked around, her recollection of what had happened returned. She touched her face and nose, felt the large bandage, and thought about that little monster with her yellow metal lunch pail. "I'll kill her," she growled. She remembered the detective and the car. She could feel her entire rib cage aching. She had cuts and bruises over much of her body. She reached down, touching the IV tubes and monitors hooked up to her arms, then leaned up a little from her prone position in bed. How long have I been unconscious? she wondered.

In the doorway she saw a guard in a blue police uniform sitting on a wooden chair. He had his back to Gwen, chatting with a nurse, who was holding blood samples in a metal tray.

For the next hour, Gwen kept her eyes closed, pretending to be unresponsive as nurses went in and out of her room. She was waiting for the right time to make her move.

Suddenly, there was a commotion in the corridor. She heard a nurse shout, "Code blue in room eight." Half a dozen medical personnel raced past Gwen's door.

They won't be looking at the monitors, Gwen thought. I've got to move fast, before they know I'm awake. One by one, she disconnected the tubes and apparatus. With great effort, biting down on her lip to block out the excruciating pain, Gwen lowered her feet out of the bed.

Spotting a couple of towels in a chest, she snatched one. Then, after twisting the towel around like a rope between her hands, she made her way across the floor on her toes, sneaking up on the guard.

No one was in the corridor. In a single swift motion, she looped the towel over his head and around the front of his neck. Mustering all of her strength, she pulled him back into the room, chair and all, and kicked the door shut. He struggled, thrashing his arms, going for his gun, which was buttoned in the holster at his waist, as she tightened the noose. With his air cut off, his face turned red and then blue as she continued pulling. She waited for him to stop moving, then held on for another minute, making sure he was dead. As she let go of the towel, his body fell off the chair and onto the floor.

Move fast, she told herself. A nurse could pop into the room any minute. She opened the door to the closet. Sure enough, her clothes and coat were hanging inside. Her personal things were in a brown shopping bag, including her cell phone. All that was missing was her gun. Fighting the pain, she stripped off her hospital gown and got dressed. She removed the guard's loaded gun and stuffed it into the pocket of her black leather jacket.

Peeking from the edge of the door, she made sure the corridor outside her room was still deserted. Then she slipped out. She decided not to risk the elevator. Walking almost normally, she headed toward the exit stairway at the end of the corridor.

Once inside, slowly walking downstairs, she felt better. But where could she go? In a matter of minutes there would be a huge manhunt under way to find her. Not only the neighborhood, but trains, planes, and highways. With the huge bandage on her face, she'd be easy to spot.

Think, she told herself. You've been on the run before. If you make it back to Connecticut, you're safe. Paul will take care of you. Chip will never let them know where to find you. Then you can heal, come back, and even the score with Ben and that little monster of a kid. But first you have to get out of Washington.

She cracked the staircase door on the first floor and

took a quick look. A sign said GEORGE WASHINGTON UNIVERSITY HOSPITAL. She knew the hospital was in a crowded urban area, ironically only a few blocks from the late Robert Winthrop's office in the State Department. It was also filled with medical buildings, since doctors wanted to be close to the hospital. She could slip into one of those. She might even be able to take an elevator without anyone paying attention to her. Patients with bandages showed up in doctors' offices all the time. A plan was beginning to take shape in her mind.

She walked into a nondescript glass-and-stone eight-story building on Pennsylvania Avenue and scanned the board listing the tenants. In 808 there was a general surgeon, Dr. Malcolm Herbert. A surgeon was perfect. He'd have nerves of steel.

She rode the elevator to eight. Halfway down the corridor was the women's rest room. As she expected, it was locked. While she rummaged through her purse for a paper clip or some other object to pick the lock, the door opened from the inside. A very pregnant woman emerged. Trying to shield her face with one hand, Gwen used the other to hold the door for the woman and then entered when she was gone. She checked her watch. Three forty-five. She had a couple of hours to kill.

She went to one of the toilet stalls, locked the door from the inside, and sat down gingerly, to minimize the pain. Anyone who came in would see her feet and nothing more. She was safe for now. Safe until it was time for her to make her next move.

Chapter 31

It took Donovan five minutes to clean out his office at the CIA. With great pleasure, he was getting the hell out of a building occupied by a bunch of wimps for the last time. At his insistence, the interview was set for four in the afternoon at his house on N Street in Georgetown, about a block from where John F. Kennedy had lived when he'd been a senator. Jennifer and Ben arrived first, but waited in front of the house until Joyner and Van Buren came.

With a glass of single-malt scotch, straight up, in his hand, the last of America's Cold War superspies opened the door with *The Marriage of Figaro* filling the town house.

"Hang up your coats and go into the living room," Donovan said, pointing to the closet. "I'll turn off the music. Anybody want a drink?"

When they all declined, he disappeared. A minute later the music stopped. On his way to the living room, Donovan passed by the entrance hall, out of view of the others now in the living room. In a single swift motion he slipped into a pocket of Van Buren's coat a small black object that resembled a button.

Donovan was still carrying his drink when he joined the others. "Show me the immunity agreement," he said.

Handing him the document, Van Buren said, "The terms of this agreement are highly unusual."

Donovan smiled. "If you want something good, you have to pay for it."

Charming fellow, Jennifer thought.

Once Donovan signed the agreement, Ben turned on his tape recorder. With a pen in hand, poised to take notes, he nodded to Joyner to begin the questioning.

"I want to remind you, Chip, that under the agreement, if you make any false statements you lose your immunity."

Donovan finished his drink and put down the glass. "Understood."

"Now tell us what you know about Winthrop's murder."

Donovan began in a soft voice. "About a week before his death, Winthrop found out from a Taiwan leader about the operation I was planning to run in China, Operation Matchstick, to blow up a Chinese missile battery aimed at the island."

"Do you know how he learned that information?" Joyner asked.

"My guess is that Chen was shooting off his mouth. I haven't been able to determine that. Anyhow, Winthrop called me down to the State Department and began shouting at me as if I were a little kid. What was I doing setting up a hostile act that might provoke war? That kind of thing. He threatened to go to the President or to you, Margaret, unless I agreed to call it off."

"What'd you say?" Joyner asked.

"I told him he was being a hypocrite. He was advocating his arms package for Taiwan while jumping on my 'little adventure,' as he called it. He told me there was a big difference between permitting Taiwan to defend itself and attacking China. So I acted properly chastened and told him that I'd call off Operation Matchstick."

"What'd you do then?" Joyner asked.

"I wasn't sure what to do." Donovan took a deep

breath. Well, here goes the fat into the fire. He spoke slowly, letting the words drop out of his mouth like jewels. "I went to see Jim Slater. I told him that Winthrop had found out about Operation Matchstick and Chen. That Winthrop was threatening me."

Jennifer's head snapped back. From the corner of his eye, Ben noticed her extreme reaction. "Who, did you say?" Jennifer asked.

"Jim Slater, the President's chief of staff," Donovan replied.

"Had Slater been part of your Operation Matchstick?" Joyner asked.

"Negative."

"Then why'd you go to see him?"

Donovan's eyes sparkled. "Slater was close to the President, without a lot of historical baggage with Brewster like Winthrop. I figured that he could give me a good fix on how Brewster might react if Winthrop told him about my little adventure. Also, he has a reputation of knowing how to solve problems."

"What did Slater tell you?"

"That Brewster would never approve Operation Matchstick. He said that if Winthrop and Cunningham were against something in the foreign policy area, it would never happen. I knew that Winthrop was opposed. Cunningham had to be a no for sure. Hell, he's practically in bed with the damn Chinese."

"That's out of line," Joyner said.

Donovan glared at her. "Well, regardless, Slater said that he had his own problems with Winthrop on lots of issues. Slater told me that he had learned from Cunningham about the Chinese blackmail of Winthrop for his whoring around and the London video, and so forth. . . ." He paused and shifted in the chair, taking his time, wanting to select his words carefully.

" 'Winthrop's a liability to the administration,' Slater told me. He said that *we* had to find a way to get Winthrop to resign because it didn't look like the Chinese blackmail was going to work. 'Perhaps a little helpful persuasion for Winthrop to step down coming from another source might help.' Those were his words."

"Then what?" Ben asked in his crisp prosecutor's tone, taking over the questioning now that Donovan had moved into the Winthrop case.

"Slater asked me if I had any ideas."

"Did you?"

"As a matter of fact, I told him that I didn't have any. Then he said that he had a kid on his staff who was smart and could 'think out of the box.' Those were Slater's words. Slater's notion was to put this kid on the project. He was a former marine."

The pen fell out of Ben's hand. Holy moly, he thought, a former marine. It had to be.

"Well, anyhow," Donovan continued, "this kid on Slater's staff came to see me."

"Who was he?" Ben asked, knowing the answer.

"Ed Fulton."

Not having known about Fulton's marine background, Jennifer hadn't made the deduction. "Ed Fulton?" she blurted out. "Your cocounsel, Ben."

He shot her a look to keep quiet.

"So what happened then?"

"Fulton came to see me. The kid was ready to do anything. Fulton asked if I could recommend a good-looking woman. Someone who had been trained by the CIA, but was no longer with the Agency. Someone who could be trusted."

"How did you respond?"

"I gave him the name of a woman who had worked for me at the Agency in an elite anti-terrorism unit. She's retired from the Agency." He shot Joyner a surly look. "I was forced to dismantle the operation."

Joyner nodded to Ben, signaling that she had no intention of taking the bait.

"What was the woman's name?" Ben asked.

"Gwen."

"Gwen what?"

"Just Gwen. It was an operational name. No one in

the unit had last names. They had half a dozen false names and IDs that they used from time to time."

"She must have had a name at birth."

Donovan suppressed a smile. This straitlaced lawyer had no idea how the shadowy world of undercover agents operated. "Janet Murphy. She was born in Boston. I recruited her as a teenager from a juvenile prison. Her mother was dead. She had no idea who her father was. No knowledge of any family members."

"What's Gwen's address?"

Donovan pursed his lips together. "Try G.W. Hospital. The ICU. She got there trying to kidnap your daughter."

Ben tightened the grip on his pen. Everything was now falling into place.

"What about before that? When you gave Fulton her name?"

Donovan looked squarely at Ben and shrugged. He knew that the chances were slim that Gwen would ever escape and make her way back to Connecticut, but he'd be damned if he'd let them know where they could find her if she did. "I have no idea. All I had for her was a cell phone number, which I gave to Fulton." He gave it to Ben.

"Washington, D.C., area code," Ben said, thinking aloud.

"That means nothing for a cell phone number. I have no idea whether Gwen lives here in town or somewhere else. All I know is that once she left the Agency, she had extensive plastic surgery, including fingerprints. She started a new life in the private sector. Put the new identity together herself so nobody in the Agency could find and eliminate her if they became nervous about disclosure of one of her missions. That's all I can tell you about her."

Ben felt Donovan was concealing something. "Then why did she give you her cell phone number?"

"She called one day and said she might want to freelance from time to time to relieve the boredom of her new life. That's when she gave me her cell phone number. Told me I should feel free to pass it along to someone if I thought a project might appeal to her."

Ben raised his hand and pointed a finger at Donovan. "I want to remind you," he said sternly, "that if we find out that you lied to us, you lose your immunity."

Donovan cracked a smile. Did this lawyer really think he could intimidate him? "I haven't forgotten that, but I appreciate the reminder."

Looking at Ben's face as he leafed through his notes, Jennifer knew he felt Donovan was hiding something about Gwen, a view that she shared. But how was he ever going to break this guy?

"Let's go back to Fulton," Ben said.

Donovan nodded.

"So you gave him the name of the blond psychopath who's in G.W. Hospital."

Donovan scowled. "Gwen's no psychopath."

"All right. Pass that."

"Yeah, as I told you, I gave him Gwen's cell phone number. He said he would call her. That's all I know."

Ben locked eyes with Donovan. "So you and Slater set up Winthrop's murder this way?"

An outraged expression appeared on Donovan's face. "We just thought Fulton would try to find a way to intimidate Winthrop. We had no idea Fulton planned to kill the guy."

"Yeah, right, and I'm the tooth fairy," Ben said.

Donovan stood up in protest. Red in the face, he said, "I resent that."

"You can cut the act and sit down. What else was said at your meeting with Fulton?"

Donovan paced around the room a couple of times, then sat back down. "Not a thing. You've got it."

"That's it?" Jennifer said incredulously. "You expect us to believe that Jim . . . I mean, Slater was responsible for your getting Gwen involved, and then . . ." Her mind was a jumble. She lost the thread of her question.

"That's all she wrote."

"Didn't you check back with Slater?" Ben said.

"Nope. That was it. I never talked to Slater about it again."

Ben bored in on him. "So you're asking us to believe that you turned over the name of a trained killer in response to a request by someone you called a kid without talking to Slater or Mrs. Joyner."

"As you may have noticed, Mrs. Joyner and I rarely see eye to eye. We don't talk much unless we have to. You may not believe it, Ben," he said, glancing at Joyner, "but then again you didn't have your nuts put in a cracker on six different occasions in the last decade by congressional committees who have been tearing apart the agency for projects we initiated for the good of the country. As a result, with two more years left to go before retirement, whenever someone in the White House asks me to do something, I do it. If those things head south on us, which they usually do, I can point the finger, first or second, at Sixteen-hundred Pennsylvania Avenue and say, 'Talk to those boys.' In this case, Ed Fulton."

"So you want us to believe that Ed Fulton masterminded Winthrop's murder?" Ben asked.

"Yep, that's the story. I set up the operations I believe in, like Operation Matchstick. As for the rest, I don't give a shit. My wife died last year. I'm planning to sell this house and move to the mountains in North Carolina, home of the greatest fishing and golf in the world. Give me that and an annuity of single-malt scotch, and I'll be one happy country boy."

Jennifer glanced at Ben, waiting for him to formulate the next question, hoping that he could break Donovan on this pack of lies.

Donovan interjected, "Before you ask about documents, let me tell you that I've spent my whole career dealing with lawyers. I know what I need to protect myself. In the vault in my office at Langley, there's a written statement I made the day Fulton came to talk to me. It verifies my story. It was witnessed by my secretary and notarized. I didn't take it when I cleaned out my office today."

"Did Ed Fulton ever come back to you for additional help after your initial referral of Gwen?" Ben asked.

Donovan shook his head. "Negative," he said flatly. "We talked once. That was it."

"Did you ever talk with Gwen yourself about any of this?"

"Negative. I had no intention of getting in the middle of it."

"Who else was Ed Fulton working with?"

"As far as I could tell, he was on his own."

"Wasn't he being directed by Jim Slater?" Ben asked.

"I've got no reason to believe Slater was pulling the kid's strings, but I didn't try to find out. As I said, the less I knew the better."

"Did Slater ever talk to you about this matter at any other time before or after Winthrop's murder?"

"Negative. I've described the one conversation I had with him."

"I want to remind you again that if you're lying in this interview, the immunity deal is off. I'll charge you with conspiracy to commit murder, because that's sure as hell what you set Gwen up to commit."

"Believe me, I understand that. I'm choosing my words carefully."

Ben wasn't convinced. "I can't see Ed Fulton pulling all this together himself."

"Oh, I don't know. The kid may be lacking in people skills, but as I look at it in hindsight, he has plenty of brains. All he needed was a shooter. And unhappily I supplied Gwen."

"Unhappily?" Ben asked skeptically.

"Yeah, not only didn't I want to kill Winthrop, but Gwen was beaten up pretty badly as a result, which is a shame." He smiled, reveling in the disgusted faces all around him. "A number of years ago, I spent six months in Paris with Gwen on Agency business. We ended up living together. It was the best six months of my life. The only time in my life I've been in love. I was ready to toss my marriage away. The trouble was, she told me that she wouldn't marry anybody who had less than ten million in the bank. So that ended that."

"Don't leave town," Ben said. "We may want to talk to you again."

Once they were gone and Donovan was alone in the house, he ran upstairs and grabbed a red phone concealed in a desk drawer. From memory, he punched in a Washington number. As soon as he heard a voice on the other end, Donovan said, "May Day."

Donovan then turned on the receiver for the listening device he had slipped into Van Buren's coat. The four of them were conferring on the sidewalk in front of his house.

"Should we believe him?" Joyner asked.

"Not for a minute," Jennifer replied. "Donovan was lying through his teeth. Does he really expect us to fall for his country-boy routine and that cock-and-bull story?"

"I don't know what to believe," Joyner said. "One thing, though, Sarah, you'd better get a couple of FBI people over here to keep tabs on Donovan. Don't let him leave the country under any circumstances."

"Smart idea," Van Buren replied. "I'll have people here within a few minutes."

Upstairs in his house, Donovan laughed. By the time his FBI watchers arrived, he'd be on his way to Dulles Airport. He opened a wall safe behind a picture, from which he extracted wads of cash and four fake passports with matching IDs. Deciding to travel light, he pulled from the closet a duffel bag he had packed as soon as he got home from Langley today. He set the automatic light timer in the house to turn lights on and off at different hours each morning and evening. To anyone out on the street, it would look as though he were still home. It would be days before anyone discovered he was gone. By then, they'd never find him.

Jennifer and Ben walked in silence to Ben's car, which was parked two blocks away. He was deep in thought, trying to absorb what Donovan had said. Ed Fulton was responsible for Winthrop's death? he wondered. I can't believe that he conned me so thoroughly. I feel sorry for Theo and the kids. Then there was Jennifer's bizarre reaction to what Donovan had said. Why was she so shaken by the mention of Jim Slater?

He looked askance at Jennifer. "What part of Donovan's story did you believe?"

"Not much of it."

He decided to follow his instincts, attacking in a voice tinged with bitterness. "You mean, you don't want to believe that Jim Slater is guilty of conspiracy to commit murder? Is that it?"

"What's that supposed to mean?"

"How well do you know Jim, as you referred to him in the meeting?"

When she didn't respond, Ben's pangs of jealousy increased. "Does Slater have the hots for you?"

Her face flushed with anger. "What I do with my personal life is my own business."

"Wrong. If you're seeing Slater, then you'd better disqualify yourself from working on this, because we now know that he's involved up to his eyeballs. You'll compromise our case."

She retorted, "All we have to implicate Jim so far is a lot of lies from Donovan." She paused to take a deep breath. "And I haven't compromised a thing."

"Bullshit!" he shouted. "Keep telling yourself that."

"Just stay out of my life. And keep the little green monster under control."

Ben was seething. Dammit, she was seeing Slater, and dammit, he was jealous. "Your boyfriend's also a shit," he said. "Last night after the White House meeting, he tried to dump the whole blame on Fulton for trying to railroad Gillis."

Jennifer didn't like that, but she didn't know if she could believe Ben. "Can we talk about the case now?"

"How can we, in view of your involvement with Slater?"

"Don't start in on that again. Slater's not the issue."

"Then what is the issue?"

"Somebody who just made up the world's tallest tale, which you're buying hook, line, and sinker because you want to believe Jim is involved. The idea that Jim would want to murder Winthrop because he was a liability to the administration, which is what Donovan told us, is absurd. That's no motive for murder. Why don't we confront Jim and give him a chance to defend himself?"

They reached the car and climbed in. Before starting the engine, Ben thought about her suggestion. It was tempting to rush down and confront Slater, but also foolish. "We can't do that. We've got to work our way up the chain of command. We start with Fulton. We're going to talk to that son of a bitch right now." He glared at her. "I assume that no one will tip off Slater in the meantime."

She shot him a furious look. "That was nasty and uncalled for."

Ben took a deep breath and pulled back. In a softer tone, he said, "I'm sorry, Jenny. That was horrible. I apologize. It's just that a lot of emotional baggage got thrown into an already difficult case."

Wanting to back away from the confrontation as well, she put her hand on Ben's arm. "You've got the Fulton complication, too. Wanting to see him now may be an emotional response on your part because he duped you."

Ben nodded. "You think it's a mistake?"

Behind the glasses, her blue-green eyes sparkled with intensity. "Let's play it out. If we confront Fulton right now, he'll deny everything. Then where are we? We can't make Donovan testify. We could make a plea bargain with Gwen and get her to testify against Fulton. The trouble is, there's no telling how long it will be until she can answer questions. Without corroborating evidence, we've got nothing. Also, we don't have the vaguest idea of Fulton's motive."

"That's easy," Ben replied. "He was following Slater's orders. Trying to please his boss. That's the kind of a guy he is. I want to hit him with this cold before Slater hears from Donovan and tips off Fulton."

"I think it's a mistake."

Ben wouldn't listen to her. He was aware that his stubbornness was being fueled by jealousy, but he wasn't about to give in to her on anything right now. The clock in the car showed it was a few minutes to six. While he expected Fulton to be in his office, Ben decided to call first to make certain. To his surprise, he heard Fulton's secretary say, "His wife called. One of the kids is sick. He went home early."

Ben hung up the phone. "Okay, we'll go out to his house," he said to Jennifer.

When Ben turned left on Wisconsin Avenue, his cell phone rang. It was Art Campbell. "I've got bad news."

"What happened?"

"She escaped from the hospital."

Ben gasped. "This is a joke, right? You're kidding."

"I wish it were."

Ben's hands started shaking so badly he pulled off to the side of the road and turned off the car. "I don't fucking believe it. How could they let that happen?"

"Don't shoot the messenger."

"Oh, c'mon, Art. It's your police force. This is pathetic."

"She must have regained consciousness when the guard was looking the other way."

"I hope you fire that clown."

"He paid for it with his life."

"Shit. What happens now?"

"The D.C. police and the FBI have a huge manhunt under way. We've got all the area airports covered. Train and bus stations. Roadblocks on the highways. We're putting her picture out everywhere. We'll find her."

"I doubt it," Ben said grimly.

Jennifer had been tugging on Ben's arm, and he finally turned to her. "What happened?" she asked anxiously.

"Hold it a minute," he told Campbell. Then he turned to Jennifer. "Gwen escaped from G.W."

"Oh, my God. I'll call Ann on my cell phone and tell her to keep Amy in the house. Also away from the television," she said, thinking aloud, "so she can't hear about Gwen's escape. Make sure Campbell gets some cops out to your home."

Ben got back on the phone with Campbell. "I don't have to tell you I'm worried about Amy."

"As soon as I heard the blonde was on the loose, I reinstated the police protection at your house around the clock."

"Don't you think she'll be more intent on escaping than on getting back at Amy or me?"

"We're dealing with a psycho. Let's not take any chances."

"I guess you're right," Ben said, dejected.

"Listen, I know you wanted to make a deal with her to find out who hired her."

"We just found out who it was. You're never going to believe it."

"Who?"

"Ed Fulton."

"That asshole."

"Jennifer and I are going out to his house now to confront him."

"Just the two of you?"

"Yeah."

"Oh, no, you're not. The guy's a former marine. If

he hired a killer, there's no telling what he'll do if he feels cornered. Bill Traynor and I are going with you. They don't need us for the manhunt."

"C'mon, Art, you have a gunshot wound."

"Reports of my demise were premature. I've got a bandage on my shoulder. Big deal."

"You sure?"

"I wouldn't miss it."

Art was right. They might need to make an arrest. "Good. Meet us in the parking lot of the Safeway on Connecticut near Livingston, say, in thirty minutes. I'll brief you then. We'll go over in one car."

At five forty-five, Gwen made her move. She walked out of the rest room and down the corridor to room 808. Opening the door a crack, she looked around. As she expected, at this hour the waiting room was deserted. Behind the counter was a heavyset woman wearing a white nurse's uniform. Over the pocket was a name tag that said Agnes. Gwen hoped the doctor was in the office. If not, she'd try another door on the floor. They were all doctors.

"Can I help you?" the receptionist asked.

"I'm here to see Dr. Herbert."

"What's your name?"

"Irene Ross."

Agnes looked at the screen on the computer that held the doctor's schedule. Without looking up, she said, "I'm sorry, Miss Ross. There must be some mistake."

"Well, I spoke to Dr. Herbert myself this morning. Could you go back and ask him?"

The second Agnes left her desk, Gwen went through the door that led to the examining rooms. She caught up with the slow-moving receptionist a few yards from Dr. Herbert's closed door.

"Hey, you shouldn't be here," Agnes said.

Gwen pulled the gun out of her jacket pocket and held it by the barrel. The nurse was too stunned to react as Gwen smashed the butt end of the gun over her head, knocking her out. Gwen rolled the receptionist into an examining room, closed the door, and squeezed her hands around the woman's thick neck. She maintained the pressure until she felt the life leaving the receptionist's body.

Then, she stood up and straightened her brown leather jacket. With the gun in her hand, she walked down to Dr. Herbert's office. Before opening the door, she looked at one of the telephone panels on the wall, making sure that he wasn't on the phone and could tell someone about the intruder. Good. None of the lines were lit.

Opening the door, she pointed the gun at a bald-headed man in his sixties with a round jovial face, who was sitting behind his desk.

"Hey, what is this? Agnes, come in here right away," he shouted to the receptionist.

"I'm afraid Agnes is dead," Gwen said in a stone-cold voice.

The doctor blanched. "Dead?"

"That's what I said."

"What do you want? Drugs? Prescriptions? Anything you want."

She grimaced from the pain. "Actually, I do want some Percocet, but that's not why I'm here."

He reached for the phone and picked it up. Before he could dial, she yanked the cord out of the wall.

Sitting down in front of his desk, she pointed the gun at him. "Now, let's get down to business."

She gestured toward the framed picture on a corner of his desk, showing Dr. Herbert and his wife, four children, and six grandchildren. "If you want to see them ever again, you've got to do something for me, which is quite easy. If not, you'll end up like Agnes."

"W-what is it?" he stammered.

"I assume you've got a car parked in the garage under the building."

"Absolutely," he said. He reached into his pocket,

extracted a Lexus key ring, and tossed it to her. "It's a black Lexus sedan on level L-two in space twenty-eight. It's all yours."

She gave him a sinister smile. "It's not that easy. We're going together. You're driving. I'll be on the backseat covered by a blanket, which you're going to supply. When we're in the car, I'll tell you where to go. Just remember, I'll have the gun in my hand at all times. We may come across a police roadblock. If I hear anything from you that sounds the least bit suspicious, I'll blow your head off. Then I'll blast my way out of the car. Is that clear?"

He nodded rigidly.

"Now get a blanket and the Percocet. Let's get moving."

A sly look came into his eyes. "I could give you something a bit stronger for pain."

She scowled. "What do you take me for? You think I'm going to let you knock me out?"

"I didn't mean that. I—"

"Just get the stuff and let's go. Don't make me re-think my decision to let you live."

Chapter 32

Rather than have four people descend on Fulton, the decision was that Ben and Traynor would go inside while Jennifer and Campbell waited in the car.

Ben's fingers were moist with perspiration when he rang the bell.

Theo opened the door, wearing a white apron that said SUPER MOM in red letters on top and SUPER WIFE in blue letters on the bottom. "Ben, what a nice surprise," she said, smiling warmly.

"I called Ed's office and heard he came home because one of the kids is sick. I'm sorry."

"Kirstin was throwing up and has a high temperature. It's that time of year."

Ben introduced Bill Traynor.

"I'll get Eddie," Theo said.

Startled to see them, Fulton led them into his first-floor study and kicked the door shut. He glowered at Ben. "I'm still pissed at you for getting me tossed off the Winthrop case. You made me look incompetent before Mr. Slater and the attorney general. It might kill my career. So if you're here to apologize, you can stuff it."

"That's not why we came."

Fulton's frown lifted. "A new development in the case?"

"Yeah, we found out who hired Winthrop's shooter."

"Hey, that's great. Who?"

His interest seemed genuine. Everybody in this case was an actor, Ben thought. "What do you know about a man named Chip Donovan, head of special ops at the CIA?"

Fulton shrugged. "I may have heard the name. Never met the man."

"C'mon, Ed," Ben said, going easy. "There's no reason for you to take the rap for Jim Slater."

His eyes bulging, Fulton looked at Traynor. "What the hell's he talking about?"

The FBI agent nodded to Ben, who said, "Donovan fingered you as the one who hired the blond shooter."

"Me?" Fulton sounded astonished. "He fingered *me*? Is he crazy? What kind of bullshit is this?"

"He gave us all the details," Ben said. "How Slater sent you to see Donovan. How Donovan gave you the blonde's telephone number."

"It's all a crock," Fulton shouted. "A total crock."

Ben looked at him sympathetically. "You don't have to take the rap for Slater. I can cut a good deal for you."

"You don't get it, do you? There's no deal to cut. Donovan's screwing you over, and you can't see it."

"I know Jim Slater's responsible. Just confirm it," Ben pleaded with Fulton. "I'll make sure Slater takes the rap. You shouldn't have to walk the plank for his crime. Come on. Talk to me."

Fulton leaned in close to his face. "Are you stupid or deaf, or both?"

"If you go down alone, you're looking at murder one."

"What evidence do you have other than what some spook told you?"

"Nothing yet. We wanted to give you a chance to cooperate."

"You think Hawthorne will let you take that to a grand jury?" Fulton asked in disbelief.

"I'm betting he will. Winthrop was the President's best friend."

"The jury would see in a minute that I'd been

framed. The next convenient scapegoat when your case against the gardener didn't stick."

Ben held his hands wide. With a voice full of sympathy, he said, "Listen, Ed, I can cut a deal with you. The case doesn't have to go to any jury. Just tell me why you did it and who else was involved with you."

"You really don't get it, do you?" he said, raising his voice. "Someone's trying to frame me, and you two numbnuts fucking don't get it."

Ben was starting to lose his temper as well. "Instead of shouting at us, why don't you tell us who's trying to frame you?"

"The Chinese government, you idiots. They were clever enough to arrange the video setup in London. They pulled this off the same way. They hired Gwen. They worked with Alexandra Hart. With the kind of money they have to play with, they easily could have pulled this off."

Ben shook his head. "I questioned the Chinese ambassador myself. They didn't do it."

"He conned you, Ben. He was eating you for lunch, and you couldn't even tell what was happening."

"I'm trying to help you," Ben said testily.

"Get the hell out of here. Both of you."

Back in the car, Ben and Traynor reported to the others.

"You were right," Ben said, looking at Jennifer. "Confronting Ed this soon did us no good at all. He won't bend until we can show that we have a strong case against him."

"If he wants evidence," Campbell said firmly, "we'll give him evidence."

Everyone in the car looked at the detective.

"Let's go back to your house, Ben. I assume you've got a fax machine." Ben nodded. "We'll get some phone records. I'll bet anything Ed Fulton made calls from one of his phones to Gwen. We can nail him that way."

"You can't be serious," Ben said.

"Trust me. The guy's no pro. He was in over his head. I know how people like this operate the first time they commit a serious crime."

Campbell turned to Traynor. "When we hit the Safeway, you take your car downtown to the U.S. Courthouse. I'll call you if I get a hit. Then you can get a warrant for this asshole's arrest."

Ann and Amy were playing a board game when Ben arrived with Jennifer and Campbell. After Ben hugged his daughter, Jennifer scooped her up in her arms and said, "C'mon, big girl. We're going upstairs to read a story."

"I pick out the book," Amy said, delighted with this new baby-sitter. "I pick it out."

While Campbell went to work with the phone company, Ben brewed a fresh pot of coffee. Ann found him in the kitchen. "The AG called. He wants to know what's happening."

"Uh-huh." Ben had no intention of returning the call until Fulton had implicated Slater and they were both behind bars. He didn't want to risk having his investigation go south one more time.

Twenty minutes later, Ben tucked Amy into bed and returned for "one more hug." As he came down the stairs, he heard the fax machine running. He saw Jennifer studying what looked like telephone records. "Son of a gun," she murmured.

Ben ran the rest of the way downstairs, joined by Campbell.

"Well?" Ben asked impatiently.

"Phone company records show that two calls were made from Ed Fulton's house to Gwen's cell phone and . . . Wait a minute. . . ." She scanned another document. "There was also one call from his cell phone."

"Why didn't he make the calls from his extension in the Executive Office Building?" Ben exclaimed. "He could have argued that there was an unauthorized use of his phone. Now we've got him dead in the water."

Campbell responded, "Fulton was playing in a game he didn't understand. He was probably worried someone would overhear him. I'll call Bill Traynor and have him get the arrest warrant."

After Campbell made the call, Ben said, "Call back the phone company. Maybe they can use Gwen's cell phone number to get her address. If she's going home, let's have a reception party waiting for her."

"Great idea," Campbell said, sounding hopeful.

Minutes later, those hopes were dashed. The address for bills for the cell phone was in the name of 'G. Gwen' at a P.O. box in midtown Manhattan."

"So we've got no way of finding her," Ben said.

It was slow going in the Lexus. Traffic was a nightmare. At the entrances to the interstates and major exits from Washington, the police had erected roadblocks. Under a cloud-laden sky, with only a sliver of a moon, it was pitch-dark outside. The police were shoving flashlights into car windows, looking for a blonde heavily bandaged on her face.

In the garage of Dr. Herbert's building, before they left, Gwen had checked a road map in the trunk and given him a route that kept them off the beltway and other main thoroughfares. The Lexus stayed on local city streets and county roads as they made their way north and west from Washington. While the doctor had hunted the map, she saw that the Lexus had a special feature she could use. Once the center armrest in the back was removed, a lid could be lifted, permitting objects like skis to be passed from the back seat to the trunk. This meant that Gwen didn't have to ride in the backseat under a blanket. She rode in the trunk, keeping the lid open. That way she could watch Dr. Herbert— and shoot him if he did anything suspicious. Meantime, she kept the trunk unhinged, but tied to the frame with a loosely knitted piece of rope, for a hasty exit.

For the first hour and a half the back road route worked. They didn't encounter a single roadblock. Once they were deep into Montgomery County, Gwen decided it would be safe to enter Route 270 at Montrose Road.

She guessed wrong. "Roadblock ahead," Dr. Herbert soon said, sounding calm. He was now in his role as a surgeon. His own life was at stake. He wanted this operation to succeed.

"You let me know when a cop approaches your car, and I'll lower the lid," Gwen said.

"Got it," he replied in his curt operating room voice.

A minute later, he said, "Now."

She lowered the lid all but a crack, not trusting the doctor. Through that crack she saw a light shine through the window. She heard a policeman say, "Anybody else in the car?"

Gwen held her breath.

"No, sir. Just me," Dr. Herbert replied in an even voice.

The policeman shined the light in the back and didn't see a thing. "Okay. Proceed."

"Thank you, Officer."

She gave a sigh of relief.

"West of Frederick," she told Dr. Herbert, "take the road for Charles Town, West Virginia, just after the Hagerstown turnoff."

As they crossed the Potomac River, she was beginning to feel safe. She doubted if they'd encounter any other roadblocks.

She was right. It was clear sailing to a remote area in West Virginia, where the CIA maintained a safe house high on a bluff overlooking the Shenandoah River. It had been used to stash and interrogate defecting Russians in the Cold War days. With those days over, the house was rarely used. Gwen knew about it because she and Chip had spent a long sex-filled weekend there about a year ago.

As they got nearer, she ordered Dr. Herbert to stop the car so she could climb into the front to give him directions for the several turns over the narrow, winding dirt roads.

"When do you release me?" he asked nervously.

She pointed with her gun at the house on the top of the hill. "That's where we're going. I'll call friends to pick me up. Once they come, you can split."

"Okay," he said wanting to believe her, but not convinced.

"If you tell anyone, I'll come and kill you and your whole family," she said.

"You don't have to worry. I won't."

He eased the Lexus to a stop next to the house, a large wooden A-frame with a deck that overlooked the river.

As he held his breath, she said, "Get out of the car."

All he wanted was to get free of her as soon as possible. "I'd rather just wait in the car."

"Get out! Or I'll kill you!"

As she opened the car door, she kept her gun trained on him. When he was clear of the car, she pointed with the gun toward the house. Then, without saying a word, she fired a shot into the back of his head, sending his brains and tissue splattering onto the unmowed grass.

After taking more Percocet to alleviate the pain, she buried him in a shallow grave using a shovel in the house. With a bucket she cleaned the grass of his blood and tissue. It wasn't perfect, but then, who would come to look?

Inside the house, she went to a second-floor closet where Chip had shown her a secure phone that couldn't be traced, and which scrambled the receiving number. Before calling Paul in Westport, she considered her options. Paul would do whatever she wanted without asking questions. Driving Dr. Herbert's car to a local airport was too dangerous. Not only would she be seen, but police would no doubt be looking for the doctor's car once the building cleaning crews found his receptionist's dead body.

When he answered, Paul sounded worried. "I know I'm not supposed to ask where you go, but you've never been gone this long. Are you all right?"

"Actually, I've been in an accident. Nothing I can talk about. A car hit me."

"My God! Are you hurt?"

"Not serious. I need to get home, though."

"I'll come for you. Tell me where you are."

"Don't come yourself. Call Hal, the pilot you use. Tell him to get a seaplane. I want him to pick me up on the Shenandoah River in West Virginia tomorrow morning at eight and take me home."

"Give me your precise location. He'll be there."

Once she hung up the phone, she felt better. Everything was coming together. She'd get medical treatment at a private clinic in the Westport area where questions wouldn't be asked. By the time she was recovered and strong enough, the police manhunt would be over. Then she'd come back to Washington for Ben Hartwell and his little monster.

Chapter 33

"We're making a big mistake if all of us barge in and arrest Fulton," Ben said to Jennifer and Campbell. They were standing in the deserted Safeway parking lot, waiting for Traynor to join them with the arrest warrant.

"What do you want to do?" Campbell asked.

Ben took a deep breath and said, "I want one more shot at him by myself."

"Forget it," Campbell said. He didn't need to consult with Traynor to make this decision. "Bill goes with you. No way I'm letting you go in alone. We're at the point now where the perp could lose his grip on reality and start doing crazy things. Fulton could attack you. He could hold you hostage. For all we know, he's got a cache of arms in the house."

"I'm willing to take that chance," Ben said boldly.

"Sorry, Ben," Campbell replied. "It's not your decision. There's more than your life at stake. Fulton's got a wife and two kids in that house as well. I've seen enough of him to know that he's somebody who's so tightly strung he could easily pop at a time like this. The last thing I want is a hostage situation, with a woman and two children inside while a White House assistant, armed with rifles and grenades, has a stand-off with the cops. If that happens, I'll be cleaning the sidewalk in front of the District Building for a very long time. No, we'll can take him downtown. You can go at him there."

"You're absolutely right," Jennifer said.

"Okay, okay." Ben turned to her. "But I do want to know something. Since you reject my Slater puppeteer theory, why do you think Fulton did it?"

Ben's question hung in the air. Jennifer didn't have an answer. She was beginning to doubt her conviction that Slater couldn't be this venal, that she would never have been attracted to such a man. She refused to believe it. What possible reason could Slater have for killing Winthrop? Disagreements over governmental policy couldn't be a motive for murder.

Ben pressed ahead with an idea that had been forming. "With Ed's driving ambition, he wanted to keep moving ahead in Washington. If the President didn't get reelected, he'd be out of the government—for at least four years. If he helped Slater solve this problem and get rid of Winthrop, whose indiscretions would wipe out the President's chance for reelection, he'd get a bigger job in the White House or somewhere else in the government."

"What a waste," Campbell said, ready to buy the idea. "Even though he is a pompous prick."

When Traynor pulled up, they all loaded into the large unmarked FBI sedan. There was room for a third passenger in the backseat—Ed Fulton, when they arrested him.

In front of Fulton's house, Ben and Traynor got out and walked toward the door. The FBI agent was in front, holding his hand inside his jacket, close to the shoulder holster, ready to go for his gun.

Standing next to the car, Campbell took a cigarette out of his pocket and lit it.

"Still haven't quit?" Jennifer said.

"Only at moments like this. You know," he said, gesturing toward the ritzy house, "I hate to see people pissing away their lives. Doesn't matter to me whether it's a black kid stealing sneakers or a fancy-ass Harvard lawyer living in Chevy Chase."

Jennifer was shivering from the chill in the air as

she watched Traynor ring the doorbell, with Ben two steps behind. The woman who opened the door seemed vaguely familiar to Jennifer. From the distance, with her view clouded by the dirty glass storm door, Jennifer couldn't see the woman well enough in the few seconds before the door shut to remember where she had seen her before.

Inside, Theo was alarmed by this second visit in one night. Sensing from his face that this wasn't just another meeting to discuss the Winthrop case, Theo said to Ben, "What's wrong?"

"We have to talk to Ed."

"He's working in the study. I'll go tell him you're here."

"Thanks."

As Theo walked across the living room to the closed door of the study, Traynor moved up, placing his body between the door and Ben. In a single slick motion he unbuttoned his jacket and pulled the pistol out of the holster.

Ben began to say, "Is that necessary?" Then his better judgment prevailed, and he swallowed the words.

Traynor was pointing the gun at the study door when Theo opened it.

As soon as she looked inside, she gave a blood-curdling scream, the most piercing, anguished, heart-wrenching scream Ben had ever heard in his life. Loud enough that Jennifer and Campbell heard it on the sidewalk and raced toward the house.

With the gun in his hand, Traynor ran toward the study. Ben was right behind.

There was no need for the gun. Fulton was sitting in his desk chair with his head slumped over the desktop and his hands next to his head. To the right was a glass with a little water and an opened brown plastic pharmacy container of pills without a label. On the left was a half-eaten bowl of dark chocolate mousse.

Traynor felt Fulton's pulse.

"I'm awfully sorry, Mrs. Fulton," he said to Theo, who was standing ashen-faced in the doorway. "Your husband's dead."

This time she didn't scream. She began crying hysterically. "What did you do to him? Get out of my house, you murderers."

Running through Ben's mind was the thought that Theo was right. They had killed Fulton. If they had gotten to the house sooner, he would still be alive. It was obvious what had happened. Once Fulton remembered that he had used his own phones to call Gwen, he realized that they'd be back with the evidence. He must have gone upstairs, kissed the children, and kissed Theo good-bye. Then he walked into the study, and . . .

"Get her out of here," Traynor said to Ben, "and find Art for me."

The latter order was unnecessary. Jennifer and Campbell were pounding on the front door. As Ben opened it, Theo disappeared upstairs to be with Kevin and Kirstin who had been awakened, terrified by their mother's screams.

Traynor said to Campbell, "Let's do it the right way this time. You get your medical examiner and forensic people here. We'll give you backup if you need it."

Campbell picked up the phone and called police headquarters.

Meanwhile, Ben began looking around the study, searching for some confirmation that Slater had orchestrated Winthrop's death.

"Don't touch a thing," Traynor said.

Ben didn't have to. What he found lying faceup on the floor next to the desk chair was a computer-generated note that said, *I'm sorry for what I've done. Theo, Kirstin, and Kevin, never forget. I love you always.*

As Ben read the note, he became despondent. How could he have been so stupid to let Fulton kill himself and take his secrets to the grave? They'd never find

Gwen. They had nothing. Slater was safe. They would never get him now.

Back in the living room, Ben told Jennifer what he was thinking.

She nodded in agreement. "You're right. The Winthrop case is over."

Her face tearstained, Theo came downstairs after putting Kirstin and Kevin back in bed, without telling them what had happened. She planned to deal with that later, when she was alone with her children.

Jennifer got a good look at Theo for the first time. Bells instantly went off in her head. Oh, my God, she thought, barely restraining herself, that's the same woman who came out of Jim Slater's office the evening of my surprise visit. Jennifer had known from the rumpled clothes and the scent of sex that they hadn't been writing a speech. What an idiot she'd been to fall for Slater. All the time he'd been fucking the wife of a subordinate. She'd never have anything to do with that bastard again.

Through her rage and jealousy other thoughts began to emerge. What was Theo's relationship with Slater? Ben had been pushing the theory that Slater was involved in Winthrop's death. Maybe he had a point. But Theo was mixed up with Slater. Was she involved in the Winthrop affair too?

Jennifer went into the study and looked around. "Art," she whispered, pulling Campbell aside, "make sure the medical people take the chocolate mousse as well as the bottle of pills, and have them dust the room for prints, including the computer keyboard."

"What are you looking for?" Then he got it. "You don't think Theo . . . ?"

"Let's talk later. Not here. I know something that you don't."

"Would you like another drink, Mr. Rogers?" the flight attendant asked as United Flight 924 made its way over the Atlantic from Washington Dulles to London Heathrow.

"No, thanks. I think I'll just finish this scotch," Chip Donovan replied.

He leaned back in his seat in first class and thought about what he would do when he reached London. The first thing would be to discard the James Rogers passport. It was probably unnecessary, but he couldn't afford to take any chances. Besides, the James Rogers identity was expendable.

Once he hit London, then what?

He'd take it one step at a time. Check into a small, out-of-the-way B and B in Belgravia, then wait for the coded message that Ophelia, his secretary at the agency, had promised to leave on his answering machine at home.

It was possible that everything might blow over, and he could go home again, retiring in serenity to North Carolina. The more he thought about it, though, that seemed wishful thinking.

Figuring he would need to be alert when they landed, Donovan tried to sleep, but his mind refused to stop running. He wasn't only concerned about his own situation. Something else was gnawing at him, as it had been ever since Joyner had called him on the carpet about China and Operation Matchstick. Who the hell had compromised Chen? That was what had set in motion all of this trouble. He was determined to find that out if it was the last thing he ever did.

Chapter 34

Jennifer and Ben filed slowly into the attorney general's office. Hawthorne looked grim. On his desk was the morning *Washington Post* with a front-page picture of Ed Fulton and a headline that read, PRESIDENTIAL AIDE TAKES HIS LIFE. CAUSE UNKNOWN.

The White House spin doctors had worked late into the night. Just in time to make the *Post*'s deadline, a nameless "White House source" had leaked the information that Ed Fulton had been overworked and depressed. In addition, the young man had unspecified personal problems.

Ben said, "We should have known this would happen."

"That's enough," Hawthorne replied. "You did what you thought made sense at the time. Hindsight's always twenty-twenty."

"The issue is, what do we do now?"

"I don't think there's anything left to do," the AG said. "The Winthrop case is closed."

Ben didn't respond. Last night Jennifer had told him about Theo's connection with Slater. "I saw her coming out of Slater's office. She's involved sexually with him. There's an element here we're missing." Ben wasn't so sure about Slater's involvement with Theo—it sounded like female jealousy to him—but he was convinced that Slater has been Ed Fulton's puppeteer. He desperately wanted to continue with his investigation.

At the same time, he feared that if he shared these thoughts with Hawthorne, the AG would tell him to stop further work on the case. The last thing the administration needed now after bad press from the Winthrop murder and Fulton suicide was a sex scandal involving the President's chief of staff and the wife of the aide who killed himself. So Jennifer, Ben, Traynor, and Campbell had agreed last night when they took stock over a nightcap at Ben's house to operate on the q.t. until they had more solid evidence.

"Where are we now?" Art Campbell asked.

The four of them were sitting around Ben's kitchen table sipping coffee with glazed doughnuts.

"If that were the clue for a seven-letter word in a crossword puzzle," Ben replied, "the word would be 'nowhere.' "

Traynor and Jennifer laughed.

Ann poked her head in the door. "Ben, can I talk to you for a minute?"

He got up and followed Ann to the living room. "We've got a problem with Amy. She doesn't know that Gwen escaped, but she can see from her bedroom window in the back that the police have returned. She's scared to death. I offered to take her out, to get some air, let her sit on the swings. As soon as I suggested it, she ran into her bedroom and started screaming."

"Let me talk to her," Ben said.

With Ann behind him, he went into Amy's room. "It's going to be okay, honey," he said. "You can go outside with Ann."

Amy's eyes filled up with tears. "I don't want to go. That bad lady could come back and get me."

"She's not going to come back."

His words did little to allay Amy's fears. "Do I have to go, Daddy?"

"Honey, you can't stay in the house forever."

A few seconds passed while she thought it over.

Ben knew she loved her swing set. "Okay, I'll go," she said reluctantly.

"I'll come out in a few minutes."

Once Ben saw Amy sitting on the swing and Ann pushing her gently, he returned to the kitchen. "Poor kid," he said. "She's absolutely terrified."

"We've got two men here around the clock," Campbell said. "One in the front and one in the back."

"I know that." They exchanged grave looks, and Ben realized he couldn't sit there and bemoan his fate. He had to make things happen so it would all go away. "Now, where were we?"

"We were talking about Gwen," Campbell said, "and how we might find her."

Jennifer spoke up. "Donovan knows where. I'll bet he knows where she lives. We can shake him down by telling him the immunity's off because he lied. Let's at least go back and make another run at him."

Ben looked at Campbell. "What do you think, Art?"

"We've got nothing to lose. Only this time try talking to Donovan in the courthouse. You may get a little intimidation factor that way."

Ben picked up the phone and called Joyner at the CIA. When he told her what they wanted, she was in agreement.

"One of the FBI agents at the house just called me. Donovan has been inside the whole time. The lights have been going on in the morning and off in the evening."

"Good," Ben said. "Have one of them tell him we want him down at the courthouse in an hour. And make sure they stick with him the whole time."

"Will do."

Ben gave her his telephone number. "Call me back when it's all set."

He thought he'd be called back right away, but for the next fifteen minutes, all four people in his kitchen stared at the phone nervously, waiting for it to ring.

"I don't like this," Ben said, now coming around to Jennifer's view that Donovan had deceived them.

When the phone rang, Ben grabbed it.

Jennifer knew exactly what had happened as she listened to Ben, with a sullen expression on his face, saying, "Yes. I see. . . . No, it couldn't have been predicted. . . . You shouldn't blame yourself. . . . We're all at fault . . . all four of us were there at the time."

Ben slammed the phone down. "We're too late again. Donovan flew the coop. It had to be right after we left, before the FBI arrived."

Jennifer looked away, angry at herself for not being more forceful yesterday about her distrust of Donovan.

Ben continued in a mournful voice, "Margaret asked the FBI agents to break in and do a quick search. They couldn't find his passport or any cash. Margaret's guess is that he left the country because he knew that we'd find out he was lying yesterday and charge him in Winthrop's murder." In his frustration he banged the phone, making it rattle. "She's fit to be tied. She's screaming that the immunity deal's off because he ran, and she'll toss him in jail for the rest of his life for skipping out. Personally, I think that's the least of her worries. He knows lots of secrets. She's scared he may be taking them to a foreign government. For now, she's confining the news of his flight to CIA personnel. She's leaving the FBI people stationed at his house in case he shows."

"Which will never happen," Traynor said bitterly. "Now we're finished for sure."

"We still have Theo," Jennifer said.

"That's right. We still got Theo," Ben said doubtfully. "Which only proves Slater is a crumb. You should have figured that out long ago."

Campbell, who knew the history between Ben and Jennifer, said, "Knock it off, Ben. The Slater-Theo connection is the only horse we've got in the race right now."

Just then Campbell's cell phone rang. As he listened, his eyes lit up. This time Jennifer knew they had something.

"It was the medical examiner," Campbell said when he finished the call.

"And?" Jennifer asked, holding her breath.

"Fulton died from a lethal dose of amitriptyline." When the others looked at him, puzzled, he explained. "It's a strong antidepressant, available by prescription. In a large enough dose, it shuts down the heart. It was in the opened pharmacy container without the label on his desk. Fulton's prints were on the container. The water glass had his prints and saliva."

"Which is consistent with the idea that he popped a bunch of pills," Traynor said.

"Precisely," Campbell responded. "But here's the twist. The drug also showed up in the chocolate mousse."

Jennifer pounced on that. "Which means that Theo poisoned him by grinding up the pills and putting them in the mousse. She staged the scene to make it look like a suicide."

"Then why didn't she remove the chocolate mousse, discard it down the disposal, and run the dish through the dishwasher?" Ben said.

Jennifer thought about that for a minute. "Suppose she didn't have time. We arrived without notice, and the doorbell rang." She looked at Traynor for support. "You touched the body first. Was it still warm?"

He nodded.

"What about fingerprints?" Ben asked.

"Only Ed's on the pill bottle and water glass."

"She could have used gloves," Jennifer said.

"Nothing on the computer keyboard on which he typed the note?"

"Wiped clean. The rest of the room had a lot of other prints, as you might expect in a room in a house like that."

Ben turned to Jennifer. "Isn't your imagination running wild? This was a suicide—"

"Then why did Ed take the label off the bottle. What's the point of that?"

Jennifer had that look in her eye, and he conceded, "I can't answer that one."

"I can," she said. "Because Theo bought the stuff. She didn't want her name on the bottle."

Campbell perked up. "Now we're talking. Pharmacies keep records of prescriptions. Let's divide up the local jurisdictions and start making calls."

Three and a half hours later, Jennifer had a hit. A pharmacist near Middleburg, in Virginia's horse country, remembered selling amitriptlyine in generic form to someone named Fulton a week or so ago. "Let me go back to my records and check," he said to Jennifer on the phone.

Horse country had to be familiar territory for Slater, Jennifer thought. She raised her hand high and gave a victory sign. The others stopped their calls and watched her.

"It was exactly a week ago today," the pharmacist said. "Patient was an Edward Fulton. Prescription phoned in by a D.C. doctor, Dorothy Knapp, ID number 70452."

Jennifer felt like a balloon that had just been pricked. If Ed Fulton had bought the poison himself, it had been a suicide.

"You want to know who picked up the order?" the pharmacist asked.

"What do you mean, who picked it up?"

"I keep records of that, too. It was picked up by his wife, a Mrs. T. Fulton. She signed for it."

"Please keep those records," Jennifer said. "Someone from the FBI will be out to pick them up."

Putting down the phone, she shouted, "Yes! Yes!"

Campbell called Dr. Knapp's office. The doctor's ID number was right, but she had never treated Ed or Theo Fulton. Theo had gotten hold of it or Slater had given it to her to phone in the prescription.

"I think it's time we paid the grieving widow Fulton a visit," Campbell said.

"Let's do one other thing first," Jennifer replied.

Campbell looked at her. "You've got the hot hand here. Fire away."

"Alexandra Hart, the madam in New York, told us

that Mrs. Winthrop ordered up the prostitute for her husband by phone."

"Uh-huh."

"So that means a woman made the call. If—"

Campbell cut her off. "I see where you're going. We'll put a tap on Theo's phone line and get a voice recording. Then we'll hop on a plane and take it to Alexandra in New York."

"It was a long time ago," Traynor said. "You expect Alexandra Hart to remember?"

"Can't hurt to try."

"We'll lose time," Ben said.

"One day doesn't matter," Campbell replied. "Without Alexandra Hart, we have a descent case based on the pharmacist and the chocolate mousse. If Alexandra Hart helps us out, we've got a lock. Right, Mr. Prosecutor?"

Ben nodded enthusiastically. He was now on board. Theo was going down. Slater was going with her.

Donovan used a red public telephone box in Piccadilly far from the B and B in Belgravia where he had spent last night to call his home answering machine in Washington. He didn't care if the agency got his location from the call. He had his carry-on with him. If he had to run, it was a few yards to the Green Park Underground station and a short ride to Victoria Station. There, he'd take the Chunnel train to Paris.

The phone booth was lined with pictures for escorts. *Hot and Busty, Blonde Devil* and *All U Want* were some of the messages. Donovan didn't pay any attention to them. His hand was firm, his blood cool when he placed the call. He hadn't been in the field for years, but an agent never forgot what he needed to survive.

Once his recording on his home answering machine started, he bypassed it. Then he heard Ophelia's voice, "Mr. Donovan, this is Ophelia. . . ."

God bless her, sounding like a secretary concerned for her former boss and not a sensuous woman trying to help a former lover escape, though she knew if he succeeded, she'd never see him again.

"Mrs. Joyner has been looking all over for you. I gather it's something urgent. I said that I would try to find you. I even went to your house in Georgetown in case you weren't answering the phone, but no one was there. Except two men in front of the house, which worried me. When I started up the stairs to ring the doorbell, they said, 'Don't bother. He's not home.' Anyhow, I'm leaving this message for you in case you call in. Please call Mrs. Joyner."

He kissed the phone, whispered, "Thank you, Ophelia," and hung up.

Donovan now had a clear picture of the situation in Washington. Joyner knew he was gone. She must have concluded that he had been lying when he told them his story yesterday. That meant the immunity deal he had made wasn't worth the paper it was typed on. Going home meant being charged as a conspirator in Winthrop's murder. There was no way he would let that happen. Not now. Not ever.

That didn't worry Donovan. He wouldn't spend the rest of his life running and hiding. He had a safe place to go where he'd be welcome. The United States government, even with its long tentacles, would never reach him.

Chapter 35

"Both kids left for school," the guard in front of Theo's house said to Campbell on a cell phone.

"Showtime," the detective said to Traynor, Jennifer, and Ben, who were in his car.

In Ben's briefcase, he had the tape they had obtained from Alexandra Hart yesterday in New York. On it was the recording that she had made of her conversation with the so-called Mrs. Winthrop arranging Winthrop's Saturday afternoon treat. Defiantly, Alexandra had told them that she recorded all of her phone calls for protection, to have a hook to gain the help of important men if the cops tried to bust her. The voice on the tape was unmistakeably Theo's.

They went up the walk and rang the doorbell. Dressed in a white terry-cloth bathrobe, slippers with bunny rabbits on the toes, and her hair up in curlers, Theo answered the door.

"More follow-up on Ed's death?" she asked.

She sounds sincere, Jennifer thought. And the other night she was convincing. I doubt if I acted that well when I was in the theater.

"Afraid not," Campbell told Theo.

"What then?"

It was Miranda time. "Theodora Fulton, we have a warrant here for your arrest for the murder of your husband. You have the right to remain silent—"

"I know what my rights are," she said flatly.

"Then you know if you ever want to see your kids again, you'd better cooperate with us," Ben said.

"I'm not talking without a lawyer."

Campbell pointed to a phone on the table. "Better call him now and tell him you'll meet him down at the U.S. Courthouse cell block, because that's where we're going."

For the first time she looked rattled. "Why don't we talk here?"

"Because I don't want to do that," Ben said. "I'm running the show now, not you."

In one short call Theo arranged to have Fred Talbot from Bishop & Talbot meet her at the courthouse. Ben and Jennifer were impressed: Talbot was one of the best criminal lawyers in town. Either on her own or with Slater's help she had made contingency plans if everything went south on her. "We may be a while," Ben told Theo. "What about the kids?"

"A woman comes in," she said, worried. "She'll stay until I get back."

The same woman, Jennifer thought, who comes when you go off to sleep with Slater.

Gwen laid her head back on the pillow and closed her eyes. It was good to be home in Westport. Paul had been marvelous, not asking any questions, and getting her to the nearby Stone Manor Private Clinic, which had an excellent plastic surgeon whose specialty was facial and body makeovers for aging dowagers.

He reset her nose and cleaned up her face.

"You're going to look as beautiful as ever," Dr. Fairview said. "All of the faces I do are works of art . . . worthy of being in a sculpture garden."

Gwen was less interested in being a work of art than knowing how long it would take to heal.

"Use lots of ice," the doctor said. "The bandages will come off in five days."

That meant Tuesday morning, Gwen thought as she

lay in bed letting her ribs heal. She made plans in her mind for that day. From Dr. Fairview's office, she would go to the beauty parlor and have her long blond hair cut short, then dyed flaming red. After adding a large pair of black designer sunglasses to cover the bruises on her face and putting on a stunning Armani suit, she'd go to Washington to get revenge. No one would ever guess that she was the same woman who had escaped from G.W. Hospital.

It took an hour of legal jockeying in an interrogation room at the U.S. Courthouse to strike a deal. If Theo told the truth and implicated someone else as calling the shots, she'd get a lesser plea, but she had to do two years in jail. The jail time was the toughest part of the deal for Theo to take. Only after Talbot told her repeatedly that she'd be crazy to turn it down, did she swallow hard and sign the agreement.

Now Ben had center stage. Picking up his pen, he turned on the tape recorder. Theo was sitting across from him with Talbot next to her. Jennifer, Traynor, and Campbell were at the far end of the table.

"Please state your name and address."

"Theodora Fulton, Ninety-five-twenty Western Avenue, Washington, D.C."

"I'm here to ask you questions about the Winthrop affair. Do you understand that?"

"Yes, I do."

"On November tenth, did you call a woman in New York by the name of Alexandra Hart and ask her to send a prostitute to Robert Winthrop's house the day he was murdered?"

"I did."

"You want to tell me how you happened to do that?"

She took a deep breath. "I'm not good on dates. A couple of months before that, Eddie, my husband, invited Jim Slater, his boss, over for dinner. I had never met the man before. After the main course, I went into the kitchen to make zabaglione for dessert. . . ."

Jesus, that's what she made for me, Ben thought. Not only is she the mother of the year, but now she's Martha Stewart.

"Kirstin had a nightmare, she started screaming. Eddie went upstairs to quiet her down. Jimmy came into the kitchen and watched me beating for a couple of minutes. I do it by hand, the old-fashioned way. He came over and rubbed my shoulder. 'That's tough work,' " he said.

"What did you say?"

" 'You're right. My shoulder's killing me. That feels so good.' "

"And then?"

She hesitated.

"And then?"

"You've got to realize that I'm not a loose woman. Sometimes you marry someone and they change. They become less likable than the person you married." She was looking at Ben for understanding because he had known her husband. "You know what I mean?"

Ben nodded.

"In contrast to Eddie," she continued, "here was Jim Slater, so suave and debonair, and he showed genuine caring. I know it's a small thing, but in all the years I've made zabaglione, Eddie never asked me if my shoulders got sore."

"And then?" Ben repeated.

"Jimmy moved in close to me from behind. He pressed his body against me and cupped my breasts in his hand. 'That feels so good,' he said."

At the end of the table, Jennifer was cringing.

"And then?" Ben asked.

"I stopped beating and turned around. He kissed me. His mouth felt good. His hands started unbuttoning my blouse with an urgency that Eddie hadn't shown in years. I knew this was crazy. That Eddie would be back any moment. So I pulled away and buttoned up. He pleaded with me to see him. So we began dating."

"Dating?"

"We'd get together at his house every couple of days for dinner or lunch and . . ."

"Sex?"

"That too," she said happily. "He swept me off my feet with his charm and charisma. Jimmy can be that way."

Ben shot a glance at Jennifer, who looked away.

"So you had an affair with him?"

"You make it sound so squalid. We love each other, and we have plans. His marriage was nothing. A formality. In a year he expected Brewster to pick him to be chairman of the Federal Reserve Board. Then he planned to divorce his wife. I'd divorce Eddie, and we'd get married. After a couple of years as chairman of the Fed, he was planning to run for the presidency. I'd be the First Lady. That was the plan."

Jesus Christ, Ben thought, do I really need to know how Slater gets women in the sack? Trying to curb his impatience, he asked, "So how's this relate to Winthrop?"

Her brow darkened. "He found out about us and ruined everything."

"Who?"

"Winthrop," she said, as if it were a vile curse. "Jimmy told me that once Winthrop knew about the Chinese video, he blamed Jimmy for putting the Chinese up to it. He had become paranoid about Jimmy. He hated Jimmy because Jimmy was so much better and was gaining the President's respect. But it wasn't true."

"What wasn't true?"

Her tone remained venomous. "Jimmy had nothing to do with the video. The Chinese did that themselves. But Winthrop decided to get even by finding some dirt on Jimmy, knowing his wife was out of town and so forth. So he used private detectives. He had a picture of me going into Jimmy's house one night. He also had one of Jimmy kissing me good-night at his front door. Winthrop planned to tell the President about Jimmy and me at Camp David on Sunday—the day after he was killed. He figured that way Jimmy's career in Washington would be over."

Puzzled, Ben looked over his notes. Something wasn't making sense. "But what about the compromising video the Chinese had on Winthrop? If Slater told Brewster about that, wouldn't Winthrop go down in flames as well?"

"According to Jimmy, Winthrop was convinced the Chinese would never go public with the video. That they were only bluffing. He was prepared to stare them down. 'To tough it out,' he told Jimmy. As for Brewster, Winthrop felt that when it came right down to it, Brewster would stick by him because of their friendship. You know how it is when somebody excuses a friend regardless of what he does." She stopped and fiddled with her wedding ring.

Ben was surprised to see she was still wearing it. "So how'd you get hooked up with Gwen?"

"Jimmy told me to call Chip Donovan from the CIA. I went to meet him at his house in Georgetown one night when Eddie was working. He gave me her name. I called her and had a couple of meetings with her at the Jefferson Memorial."

So Donovan had cleverly shaded the truth to them, substituting one Fulton for the other. Jennifer had it right: He had been lying all along.

"And Alexandra Hart?"

"Jimmy knew her from his investment banking days in New York. He used her to set up escorts for clients. He gave me her phone number, and I called her pretending to be Mrs. Winthrop, just as Jimmy told me to do."

"So he had you doing all the dirty work?"

She grimaced. "Jimmy said that he was too public a figure to have meetings with these women. He told me I was doing it all for our future."

Ben could only shake his head. She read his thoughts and looked away at Jennifer, who refused to meet her gaze.

"What about the gun and money? Did you plant those in the gardener's truck?"

She shook her head. "Once Eddie told Jimmy that the gardener had emerged as a suspect, Jimmy had someone put the gun and money in his truck."

"Who?"

"I don't know. He didn't tell me."

Ben glanced through his notes.

"Okay, now let's turn to your husband's death. When did that idea come about?"

"On Sunday evening when you and Jennifer returned from London. Jimmy said the situation was dicey. We had to do some contingency planning in case things went south on us. We had to fix it so Eddie took the fall."

"And the amitriptyline?"

"Jimmy told me what to buy and where. He gave me a doctor's name and ID number. He said he knew the pharmacist, who would never check."

"And you went along with all of this?"

She looked troubled. Clearly Slater had had to convince her. "Not at first. I argued with him that I didn't want to kill Eddie. He said that he didn't want to either. We should just have the stuff in the house as a last resort. Only if it was absolutely necessary, Jimmy said."

"And then?"

"Jimmy called."

"When?"

She sighed and rubbed her eyes. Ben saw she was on the verge of tears. "Christ, I don't know. A couple days ago, I guess. The day Eddie died. I can't remember exactly."

"And?"

"Jimmy said that he'd heard from Donovan, who had to give them Eddie's name. Now we'd have to be vigilant. Eddie would deny his involvement. As long as he did that, it could never get traced back to us. So I was supposed to keep my eye on Eddie. Then Jimmy asked me what phone I'd used to call Alexandra Hart and Gwen. I told him that I'd used the phone at my house and Eddie's cell phone. Jimmy didn't yell, but I could tell he was unhappy about that. He said that would come back and hurt us, which I guess was right. So I reluctantly agreed to give Eddie the large dose of amitriptyline and make it look like suicide. Jimmy said he was so sorry, but we didn't have a choice."

"Did he tell you to do it?"

She thought about the question. Ben was giving her a way to lessen her guilt. She hesitated, then rejected it. "We arrived at the decision together, I guess. Neither of us wanted to do it, but we didn't have a choice. I called Eddie to come home early. I had to really yell at him. Then you guys came the first time. I listened behind the door and called Jimmy to report. He told me that I had to do it. I agreed." She stopped, wiping away tears. "So I did it."

"You put the amitriptyline in the chocolate mousse you gave Ed?"

She nodded. "Uh huh. I also wiped the water glass on his mouth and his fingers against the glass and the bottle of pills. I was wearing gloves. My plan was to take away the chocolate mousse and run the dish through the dishwasher. Unfortunately, I didn't have time. I had just finished typing the note when you rang the bell."

"Have you seen Slater since your husband's death?"

Looking despondent, she turned her head down toward the table and fiddled with her wedding ring. "He hasn't called me since Eddie's death."

You were as big a fool as I was, Jennifer thought.

"Have you called him?"

"No, we haven't spoken."

"Let's take a break," Ben announced.

While a guard escorted Theo and her lawyer to the cafeteria in the courthouse, Ben remained behind with Jennifer, Campbell, and Traynor. The FBI agent stood up and wrote the name *Slater* in chalk on the blackboard. "What do we have on him?" he asked.

"Write 'not enough,' " Ben said.

"She's given you powerful testimony," Jennifer interjected.

"But it'll come down to a question of whom the jury believes. I don't like cases like that. Particularly with someone smooth and convincing like Slater on the other side. We need more."

While Ben looked over his notes, Jennifer's mind was racing on all cylinders trying to find a way to build an ironclad case against Slater. Suddenly, she had it. "Have her arrange a meeting with Slater and wear a wire."

Ben shook his head in disbelief. "After Slater finds out she's been arrested, he'll never talk to her."

"What if we don't book her, and we don't hold her?"

Ben gave her an outraged look. "How can we release a murderer just like that? Besides, if Slater calls, she'll warn him. She's still got the hots for him."

Jennifer was two steps ahead of Ben, though. "We station a couple of female undercover cops in Theo's house posing as nannies—on revolving shifts. We tell Theo to act normal. The nannies stick with her at all times and listen in on all calls. If she does anything to tip Slater off, she loses her immunity and faces murder one. That's the arrangement."

Ben nodded. "I like it, I guess.

"So what's the script for her conversation with Slater?"

"Let me take a crack at a draft," Jennifer said sourly.

"He won't be easy to nail. He's smart and savvy. Somebody like that won't say, 'Oh, I'm so sorry that I told you to kill your husband.' "

"C'mon, Ben," she said in disgust. "I know that. But don't forget she did a good job of acting the night her husband died. She sure as hell fooled you."

Ben pulled back. "Ouch, that stung."

The old tension between them was coming back. "Well, it's true."

"And what if he starts messing around with her first? He'll see the wire and—"

"Give me credit for some smarts. At this point, you know I want to nail him as much as you do."

That was a certainty, and he was relieved. Deep in thought, Ben cut across the room to the blackboard, where he picked up a piece of chalk and flipped it from hand to hand a couple of times.

Jennifer knew that something was bothering him. "What don't you like about my idea?"

Without responding, Ben turned toward the blackboard, wrote down *Gwen,* and put a circle around it. "Even if your plan works, it's not enough. At least not for me. Sure, I want to nail Slater, but it still leaves Gwen out there somewhere. That means I'll have to spend every minute of my life worrying about when she'll come to get revenge on Amy. I know she'll come. Make no mistake about it."

As Ben looked around the room for agreement, it was deathly still. Silence from the others meant assent, he thought grimly.

"So let's bring Gwen to the party too," Jennifer said. "Theo can call Gwen on her cell phone and tell her things are turning bad here. They've got to do some damage control."

Traynor scratched his forehead. "She's a real pro, that one. She may smell a trap."

Excited by Jennifer's suggestion, Ben brushed aside Traynor's concern. "Suppose she doesn't take the bait? We haven't lost a thing."

"Oh, she'll come, all right," Campbell said in a dark tone that alarmed the others. "She'll come because she'll want to kill Theo—the only witness against her for Winthrop's murder."

Ben was charged. "We can protect Theo. It's a question of the right setup." He turned to Traynor. "Why don't you go find them in the cafeteria and bring them up?"

Traynor didn't move. "Not so fast, Ben. We've got to think this through. We're asking a lot from Theo to put her life on the line. You gave her as much as you could by agreeing to a two-year sentence. She's met her end of the bargain."

"I'll lean on her hard. Tell her it's part of the deal."

"And Talbott will tell you to fuck off unless we've got something else to motivate his client—like eliminating jail time."

Ben ran his hands through his hair. "To hell with that. She's already got the best deal we can offer."

"Then you'd better come up with something else."

Ben looked dejected. Traynor was right. "What do you think, Jenny?" he asked.

"I've got an idea."

Ben smiled. "That's what I figured. I could smell the wood burning."

"She always has an idea," Campbell quipped. "Which is what's been saving your ass in this case."

"Put Theo in a cell overnight," Jennifer said. "In solitary. Let me talk to her in the morning."

Ben was puzzled. "What'll you do then?"

"You wouldn't understand. It's a girl thing."

"Mr. Peng, please," Donovan said to the operator who answered the phone at the Taiwan Trade Mission in Paris.

"And who should I tell him is calling?"

"Gus Brock from New York," Donovan said in French, using the code name that he and Peng had used for communications over the last several years they had worked together.

A few moments later, Peng came to the phone.

"My company is interested in building a plant in Taiwan," Donovan said. "I was told that you could help me."

Peng knew that Donovan wanted to meet him to discuss an urgent matter. "Perhaps we can meet over lunch today and discuss this new plant," Peng said. "I'll make a reservation at Pre Catalan for one o'clock. We can meet in front of the restaurant. Is that agreeable?"

"Excellent. I think it best if we discuss this matter ourselves before advising others."

"I understand."

Two hours later, Donovan entered the large grassy park known as the Bois de Boulogne. Approaching Pre Catalan on foot at twelve thirty with a copy of the morning *Herald Tribune* in his hand, Donovan scanned the park in every direction. Satisfied that no one was there, he sat down on a bench about fifty yards from the entrance to the restaurant.

The wind was whipping through the park, blowing the leaves. Donovan turned up the collar on his coat against the cold. Calling Peng was a gamble on his part. He was betting that Joyner hadn't put the word out among intelligence services of friendly governments that Donovan had jumped out of the boat, as they said at Langley, and shouldn't be rescued. Or if she had, that Peng was willing to entertain a better offer.

At precisely one o'clock, Donovan saw a black BMW pulling into the restaurant's parking lot. Peng climbed out and walked slowly toward the front of the restaurant. As he looked around, he saw Donovan on a park bench holding up a newspaper. Peng turned and walked that way.

"Would you like to talk over lunch?" Peng asked. "The tables are well spaced."

Donovan was relieved. Peng would never have suggested talking in a public place if he had known that Donovan was on the run from Joyner and the CIA. So the news wasn't out on the street yet.

"I would prefer to walk," Donovan replied.

He took the path that led away from the restaurant back toward the city. If this was a setup, he wanted the option to avoid being trapped in the deserted park.

"What happened with Operation Matchstick?" Peng asked.

"Chen was compromised. They were all arrested at the missile base before the bomb was set. They tortured Chen. He coughed up my name."

"How do you know that?"

"Liu, their ambassador in Washington, told Cunningham."

Peng didn't like that news. "Who compromised Chen?"

"I wish I knew." Donovan hesitated, shoving his hands into his pockets. "I thought it might have come from your end. Somebody sympathetic to Beijing."

Peng shook his head. "It's possible, but I don't think so. Is that why you wanted to see me?"

"It's more complicated than that."

Peng took a package of cigarettes out of his pocket and pointed to a bench. "Let's sit."

Satisfied no one was around, Donovan followed Peng to the bench. The moment of truth had come. He wasn't certain that he could trust Peng. The trouble was, he didn't have a better idea. "I'm persona non grata in Washington," he said quietly. "If Joyner finds me, she'll put me under arrest."

Peng took a deep puff on the cigarette, blowing out the smoke in circles while absorbing what Donovan had said. "Because she didn't authorize Operation Matchstick?"

"That's part of it." Donovan stopped there. Taiwan had viewed Winthrop as a friend. Donovan didn't dare say that he'd played a role in the secretary of state's death.

Peng sat silent. A patient man, he was waiting to hear why Donovan had called this meeting.

"I want to make an arrangement with your government," Donovan said.

"What kind of arrangement?"

"I want to come and live in Taiwan. It'll have to be done in secret, because if Joyner finds out and Washington seeks extradition, I suspect your government will turn me over, regardless of what your laws provide."

Peng nodded, then took another drag on his cigarette. "You're asking us to risk a lot. Washington will be furious if they ever find out. Without their backing,

Beijing would gobble us up in a minute." He let the cigarette smoke flow out in a thick stream. "So what do we stand to gain?"

Donovan had known all along they'd get to this question. "I'll tell you everything I know about Beijing's intelligence operations. I'll give you suggestions for operations you can launch against them. I'll tell you where your own points of vulnerability are."

When Peng didn't respond, Donovan added, "Don't forget that at Langley we've spent years playing war games that involve China and Taiwan. I know a lot about them."

Peng put out his cigarette. "I can't make this decision myself."

"I appreciate that. How long will you need to consult with Taipei?"

"A few days. Until, say, next Tuesday."

"Good. I'll call you Tuesday morning and suggest a meeting place. Will you assure me that no one on your side will leak this to Washington?"

"I can't assure that." Peng paused to ponder how he could deal with Donovan's concern. "When you call, if I mention the word 'Paris' in my response, then you'll know someone did talk to Washington."

"That's fair enough. I trust you."

Peng rose to leave.

"There is one other thing," Donovan said, now believing that Peng was hooked by what Donovan could tell him about China. "A sweetener that I need from you to seal the agreement."

Peng was wary. "What's that?"

"I want you to find out how Beijing learned about Operation Matchstick. Who compromised Chen?"

"You can't possibly expect me to get that information."

"C'mon. I know that you have moles deep inside the Chinese intelligence agencies. Make contact with one of them."

"I don't know . . ." he said, hesitating. "How important is the information to you?"

Donovan's face tightened in hatred. If it weren't for that traitor, he'd be back in Washington drinking single malt scotch in his house instead of being on the run. "Without it, we don't have a deal."

Chapter 36

"I'm worried about my kids," Theo said to Jennifer.

They were alone in the prison cell. Jennifer opened up a brown paper bag, handed Theo a cup of coffee and a muffin, then pulled out a second cup for herself. She settled down on an old battered chair facing the bunk where Theo was sitting. Jennifer's guess was that Theo hadn't slept a minute all night. Her eyes were red and bloodshot from crying. Her hair was falling over her face and touching the shoulders of her orange prison outfit.

"I stopped by your house on the way down," Jennifer said, without explaining that she had wanted to see if Slater had called. "Kevin and Kirstin are both doing well. They miss you. Your sitter can stay on indefinitely."

Theo took a deep breath. "Thank God for that." She paused to sip some coffee. "Did anybody call me?" she asked hopefully.

"You haven't heard from Jim, if that's what you're wondering."

Theo looked away, beaten down. "I can't believe that I got myself in such a mess. I'm in jail, and Eddie's dead."

What a great opening, Jennifer thought. She had been wondering how she was going to get started. "The fact is that you didn't get yourself into it. Jim conned you and used you, the same as he did me. We were both fools."

Theo stared at Jennifer, wondering if she'd heard right. "He was sleeping with you, too?"

"We didn't get that far. But I have to say if all of this hadn't broken, he'd probably have had me in bed before long."

As Jennifer hoped, Theo responded with bitterness. "He must have fed you that line of his about how special you were and how he could do so much more if he had you with him. Improve the country and all that."

"Yeah, he laid it on thick." Jennifer touched her tongue to her lips. "And all he wanted was me in the sack."

At the thought Theo's face turned crimson with rage. "That man is scum."

"He's smart. He's smart enough to push our buttons."

"In my case," Theo said angrily, "he didn't have to work very hard. Hell, just the idea of his power made me wet. Christ, if I had to do it over again, I'd feed that chocolate mousse to him rather than Eddie."

Jennifer kept fueling the fire. "You know what really ticks me off? Jim will remain free as a bird while you leave your kids and stay in jail."

Theo was horrified. "What do you mean? I gave Ben the facts to hang Jimmy."

Jennifer shrugged. "It won't do the trick. It's your word against Jim's. Ben's got no chance of establishing guilt beyond a reasonable doubt. I don't even think he'll bring the case."

"There has to be a way to get that bastard. To put him away for a long time."

Jennifer said, deadpan, "You really want to nail Jim don't you?"

"More than anything in my life! He made me kill Eddie."

Jennifer stared out through the cell bars as if she were thinking. Finally she said, "There is a way, but it'll be dangerous for you."

"I don't care. What's your idea?"

"Suppose," Jennifer said slowly, "just suppose you don't let Jim know you've spoken with us. Call him for a meeting. We'll put a wire on you, and we'll give you a script that will let him spill out enough incriminating information to hang him. What do you think?"

Theo shot to her feet, a determined look in her eyes. "I'd do it in a minute. Why not? Where's the danger?"

This was the crucial moment. "Ben won't set it up unless you invite Gwen as well as Jim. That way he can wrap up the whole thing."

All of the color drained from Theo's face. "Gwen," she said softly. "That woman's a psycho. She scares the hell out of me." Her eyes opened wide. "Besides, she'll want to kill me to eliminate a witness against her. Won't she?"

"They'll set it up in a way that protects you."

Jennifer could see that Theo was torn. Two years in jail was a long time, but at least she'd see her kids that way. Not if she were dead. Jennifer switched gears, letting Theo realize the dangers. "Look," she said, "you're right. Gwen may try to kill you. And no matter what Ben says, the cops may not be able to stop her. So don't do it if you're not comfortable. They can't force you to do it."

Jennifer got up, snapping her coffee lid tightly closed. "Think about it for twenty-four hours. I'll come back tomorrow."

As she started toward the cell door, Theo called, "Don't go. If I agree to do it, will they let me out of here?"

"Until the meeting. I'm sure of that."

"And afterward?"

Jennifer didn't respond to the pleading look in her eyes. "If the meeting goes well, you can make another run at Ben to reduce or eliminate the two years in jail. I can't promise he'll agree, but I'll help you persuade him. You can count on that much."

Theo seized upon the new terms. "I sleep in my own house until the meeting?"

"With female plainclothes cops there posing as nannies."

"Okay, let's do it. Get me to a phone, and I'll make the calls setting it up."

Jennifer was ecstatic. "It's better if you call from your house. They may have caller ID."

When Gwen's cell phone rang, it was resting on the table next to her bed, where she had been stretched out counting the hours until Tuesday.

"Things have gotten dicey in Washington," Theo said, knowing that Gwen would recognize her voice.

"They always do," Gwen replied in a flat, unemotional tone that concealed her surprise. All of her senses went on alert. Gwen had read about Ed Fulton's death in the newspaper. Had the cops nabbed her? Were they trying to lure Gwen back to Washington?

"I think we should talk," Theo said.

Gwen decided to let Theo play her cards. Here was a chance to kill Theo and eliminate the only witness who could tie her to the Winthrop murder. "What do you have in mind?"

"Tomorrow evening at nine," Theo said, following the script Jennifer had given her. "There's a bar in the lower level of the Hay Adams. It should be deserted then."

"Tomorrow doesn't work for me." Gwen didn't want to tell her about the bandages and surgery. "It has to be Tuesday night."

Theo was delighted by the delay, which meant she'd be out of jail longer. "Tuesday's okay with me. The Hay Adams at nine in the evening."

"Not the Hay Adams. It has to be the Lincoln Memorial, at midnight. In the chamber. Next to the Lincoln statue."

"I'll be there," Theo said, and hung up.

Ben was furious when he heard what Theo had agreed to. "The Lincoln Memorial?" he blurted out. "It's the single worst place in Washington to try to defend someone." He looked at Campbell and Traynor. "You guys know I'm right. Don't you?"

Theo was chagrined. "Gwen insisted on the Lincoln Memorial. What could I say?"

Jennifer jumped to Theo's defense. "You did the right thing." She shot a look at Ben, irritated with him for shooting his mouth off when they were still with Theo. "Don't pay attention to him. He gets emotional. We'll make it work." She pointed at the phone. "Now call Jim Slater. Let's get the other guest for this party."

Reminded of her anger at Slater, Theo sounded hard and cold when she told Slater's secretary that she should "interrupt the great man" in his conference to tell him that she was on the line.

Slater cleared two aides out of his office in record time. There was a wariness in his voice as he said, "Theo, how nice to hear from you."

"We have to talk, Jimmy. I hesitated calling you so soon after Eddie's death, but I've missed you so much. I want to see you."

"There's nothing I'd like more than that. How about coming by my place tonight. Say around nine?"

"Complications have developed. We can't risk being seen together." Her voice was shot through with anxiety. "I'm scared, Jimmy."

"Don't worry, honey. Where do you want to meet?"

"The Lincoln Memorial. It'll be deserted. We can talk freely."

"What?" he said, astounded. "Why the Lincoln Memorial?"

"That's the the first place Eddie and I went when we moved to Washington. . . ." She let her voice trail off, making him think she was losing it. "Please, Jimmy. Do it my way."

When he answered, his voice was much more cautious; he obviously wanted to keep her calm. "I'll be there. Whatever's bothering you, we'll deal with together. You can count on me."

"At midnight, Tuesday night. That's the best time."

"What?" Then his voice lowered instantly to a purr. "Fine, honey. Midnight, Tuesday night."

When Theo put the phone down, she said, "I know it's eleven in the morning, but if you guys don't mind, I'm opening a bottle of wine."

In Ben's kitchen, Traynor finished a turkey sandwich and said, "It's not perfect, but here's the plan for Tuesday night."

Ben, Jennifer, and Campbell were watching him carefully.

"Point one is that at midnight all the park rangers and people are gone. The memorial and grounds should be deserted. Point two. There's only one way up or down from the memorial—via the seventy or so steps in front. Point three. We can't put a SWAT team anywhere around the memorial. There are no office buildings within range. Gwen's certain to case the place ahead of time. If we put armed agents in the bushes or the trees, she'll see them and run. Same result if we try to move them in once the meeting starts. The whole area will be dark, but she'll have the commanding view from up on top."

"So how do we protect Theo?" Jennifer asked.

"There are two green wooden booths at the end of the reflecting pool on the memorial side that have information about POWs and MIAs. They're manned twenty-four hours a day. The people who run those booths will cooperate with the park service, which lets them use the grounds. So an hour before the meeting we put one FBI sharpshooter in each of those booths, pretending to be manning them."

Jennifer was tapping her fingers on the kitchen table. "But the meeting will be in the chamber where Abe is. With all those marble columns in front, how will these sharpshooters be able to hit Gwen?"

"I told you the plan's not perfect. They could get her when she goes up the stairs, but Ben doesn't want that because he needs Theo to talk with Slater and Gwen so he can get a tape of the incriminating information. Right?''

Ben nodded. "Precisely. Theo will be wearing a wire."

"Wrong," Traynor said. "We'll give her a microphone to attach to the base of the statue, just in case one of them decides to check her for a wire."

"That's a good idea," Jennifer said. "But I assume that you'll still put a Kevlar vest on her."

Traynor nodded. "I wouldn't do it any other way. It'll be cold. It shouldn't show under a heavy coat."

"That's okay with me," Ben added.

Jennifer was still worried about Theo. "I don't see how you're going to get Theo out and capture Gwen after we get what we need on the tape."

Traynor took a deep breath. "The four of us will be in a van on the other side of Memorial Bridge listening to their conversation while it's being recorded. Another van with an FBI SWAT team will be behind us. Once we hear and record the incriminating evidence, our van drives to the front of the memorial with the other van behind. The instant we're in front all the lights go on around the memorial, and the two sharpshooters sneak out of the green booths and up the stairs. A chopper with more armed agents heads across the river as well. I jump out with a bullhorn and tell the three of them to come down with their hands in the air. If Gwen makes any move to resist, the sharpshooters take her down. That's it."

Ben was nodding his approval. "I like it. It'll work."

Jennifer eyed the silent Campbell. "What do you think, Art?"

He glanced nervously at Traynor. "It's Bill's show."

"You can tell them," Traynor said.

Campbell crossed his arms over his chest. "Personally, I hate it. I think we'll end up with a hostage situation with Gwen grabbing Theo or Slater, or both. I think a lot of lives will be lost before it's over, and

I think a stone killer like Gwen may be able to slip away in the confusion."

Jennifer looked glumly at Ben. "Theo's got two young kids. It's crazy putting her at risk like this."

Ben wasn't budging an inch. "I've got a young kid, too. The world's full of young kids, and they're all at risk as long as that psychopath is on the loose. Besides, I want Slater, and this is the only way I can get them both. With the Kevlar vest, Theo will be okay."

Jennifer and Campbell weren't convinced.

"And if it doesn't work," Traynor said, "Ben and I will both be selling drinks to tourists along the reflecting pool for the rest of our lives."

Nobody laughed.

"This is Gus Brock," Donovan said when Peng picked up the phone.

"I'm ready to meet with you again to discuss that new plant. Would lunch at Pre Catalan be acceptable to you?"

"Le Divellec on the Left Bank would be more convenient. It's a nice day. Why don't we meet on the Left Bank, at the Pont des Invalides, in thirty minutes and walk from there?"

As Donovan hung up the phone, he replayed in his mind Peng's words. Paris hadn't been mentioned. There was no tension in the man's voice that Donovan could discern. He'd have to take a chance.

He had given himself another measure of protection. He had made the call from a cell phone in a brasserie one block from Invalides Bridge. From this spot, he could watch the meeting place for the next half hour. He wasn't wearing a coat over his black suit and black turtleneck shirt, but he didn't need it. The adrenaline was keeping his blood warm. This was the endgame.

Donovan was relieved when nothing happened in those thirty minutes. Once Peng arrived, Donovan nodded to him, then began walking along the Seine past artists' stalls with paintings for sale. Peng fell in beside him. This time the Taiwanese had no illusion they would be eating lunch.

"I have good news for you," Peng said.

Donovan held his breath. "Yes?"

"You'll be welcome in Taiwan, and your presence will be kept a secret. A comfortable house is being prepared in the mountains."

"It doesn't have to be lavish."

"We view you as an honored guest."

Feeling pleased, Donovan said, "I'm a man of simple tastes."

Peng laughed. "I know what you like. You'll have an excellent chef. A woman to provide comfort and other recreation. A constant supply of Macallan."

"What else is there?"

"Indeed." Peng took out a cigarette and lit it while Donovan watched a barge pass by. "When will you arrive? I want to be there to meet you."

"I'll come over on Friday. A flight from Tokyo. The passenger's name will be John Green. I won't select a plane until the last minute. Check all manifests of incoming planes from Tokyo."

"Will do."

"They must regard you as a hero in Taiwan for landing me."

Peng nodded. "Nobody believed it fell into my lap."

"That's the way I wanted it. Now that you owe me, tell me who compromised Chen."

Peng blew a fat, lazy circle of smoke in the air. "It wasn't at our end. The leak to the Chinese came from Washington."

Donovan was mystified. "But I ran the operation myself because there are so many Beijing sympathizers in the American government. I even kept it from Joyner." He began searching his mind. "Winthrop found out about Operation Matchstick from somebody in Taiwan," he said, thinking aloud. "When I told him that I'd call it off, he seemed to accept that." Donovan ran his hand through his thick gray hair. "I only did that so I could buy time. So I could talk to Slater about what I should do—" Then it hit him. "Oh, shit, Slater. It can't be." Wide eyed, he looked at Peng. "Slater?"

Peng nodded. "Slater leaked your plans for Operation Matchstick to Ambassador Liu in Washington."

"Why in the hell would he do that? He hated Winthrop."

"According to my source, Slater wanted to curry favor with the Chinese. He saw himself being President one day. He wanted to have a major IOU in Beijing. He sees Beijing as a world power. Taiwan he views as a 'pimple on the elephant's ass.' Those were words that Slater used."

Donovan looked mortified. "I had no idea that he was sympathetic to Beijing. He deals with domestic policy and economic affairs. Not foreign policy."

"He may not have any ideological views on the subject of Taiwan, but I gather that he's pragmatic and opportunistic."

"That's the understatement of all time."

"So when you handed him the chance to put Beijing in his debt, he jumped on it." Peng shook his head in disgust. "I hate seeing him get away with it."

Donovan thought about Ophelia's message. If Joyner was ready to arrest him, chances were that by now they had found out that Slater's foxy girlfriend, Theo, and not her dumb-ass husband, had come to Donovan for Gwen's name. That meant they were all going down. Winthrop and Fulton were already out for the count. Slater and Theo would be making license plates in prison. Donovan would be the only survivor. He'd be fucking his brains out and drinking single-malt scotch in tropical splendor. Maybe, as his late mother used to say, everything happened for the best. There were always winners and losers.

Chapter 37

Gwen parked the rental car along Constitution Avenue, a few minutes' walk—or a two-minute run if she had to beat a hasty retreat—from the Lincoln Memorial. It was almost ten, and heavy clouds and fog had moved into the Washington area, as they often did in November, snuffing out the light from a half-moon. Rain was expected, but not until daybreak Wednesday morning. Gwen thought the conditions of poor visibility were perfect. She was wearing dark-lens infrared night-vision glasses that let her see objects as if it were daylight. Dressed in a dark brown leather jacket, denim jeans, and black running shoes, she wouldn't stand out. In her hand she clutched a black canvas bag containing an Uzi as well as other weapons. As she walked, the .380 Waltham PPK automatic with a sionics suppressor in her jacket pocket bumped against her bruised rib cage, which was healing slowly. She didn't mind the pain. It reminded her of Ben and Amy . . . her second stop tonight, his house on Newark Street. She hoped Ben didn't show at the memorial. Killing him here meant that she wouldn't have the pleasure of having him see his precious Amy suffer and die before his eyes.

She angled off along a path that led toward the reflecting pool in front of the memorial. Then she cut to the right, following along the pool. She unzipped her jacket pocket so she could go for the gun on an instant's notice. The area was deserted. The park rangers and tourists were gone. The lights had been turned off inside and around the memorial.

Her eyes were constantly in motion as she checked the area, perusing the trees on both sides of the pool. If this was a setup and the FBI had a SWAT team in place, here was where they'd be, although she knew how they operated. It was unlikely they'd be here two hours before the meet. One hour was SOP, which was why she had come so early. Still, she couldn't take a chance.

Approaching the end of the pool closest to the memorial, she spotted what appeared to be soldiers on the other side of the pool behind the trees. What the hell? There were at least six men in army uniforms. She darted onto the grass, behind a large oak, and pulled out a pair of night binoculars.

A smile of relief came over her face when she realized what it was. The Korean War Memorial consisted of statues depicting soldiers in army uniforms. She had forgotten it was buried in a clump of trees, where very few tourists ever saw it.

Satisfied no one was around, she crossed the road and began the long climb up the stairs to the memorial. First there were ten steps. Then a flat area. Ten more and another flat area. After that she began a steep climb up thirty stairs. She walked along a short flat area and began her final ascent of twenty more steep marble steps.

As she climbed, she glanced over her shoulder at the two green POW/MIA booths. Nothing looked out of the ordinary there. Eager to seem like a tourist and not wanting to draw attention to herself if the people manning those booths were awake, she decided to forgo more careful scrutiny of them until she reached the top of the steps. She moved over to the right, examining the bushes on the ground below for any movement, but they were still. She angled across the steps to the left and looked there. Again nothing.

Maybe, just maybe Theo had set this up alone, Gwen thought, but she wasn't willing to bet her life

on it. At the top of the stairs, she slipped behind one
of the thick marble columns. Dropping her bag at her
feet, she took the binoculars out of her pocket and
surveyed the entire scene below. Nothing looked unusual. There were no armed men in the trees. The two
men, one in each of the POW/MIA booths, looked
precisely like the grizzled Vietnam vets she expected
to see there. The Washington Monument straight
ahead was barely visible in the heavy fog. There was
no shadow for it to cast over the reflecting pool.

She nodded a greeting to Honest Abe sitting on his
marble throne, then reached into her bag and pulled
out a small round white object resembling a shirt button. On one side, the button had a sticky adhesive.
She jumped up and stuck it on the top of the monument base under Lincoln's feet. It was a microphone
that would let her hear anything said in the chamber
via a set of earphones in her bag. The color of the
buttonlike object was a perfect match for the aged
marble of the statue. If Theo or anyone else saw it,
they would think it was simply a rough spot in the
marble.

Feeling in control, Gwen moved toward the wall
that had Lincoln's second inaugural speech cut in
stone—across from the Gettysburg Address. In front,
on her right was the door to the closed gift shop. She
ignored that one and headed toward the rear of the
chamber and a door leading to a maintenance room.
It was locked, as Gwen had expected. In a few seconds, she picked the lock and entered the pitch-dark
room.

Rather than turn on the light, which might be seen
under the door, she took a small flashlight from her
bag and looked around. There was a chair next to a
desk that she could sit at with her earphones on. The
desk would hold her weapons. There was another door
at the far end of the maintenance room. Very few
people knew about that door. It opened to an internal
staircase running to the exhibit room downstairs. If

need be, it provided another means of escape for Gwen.

She checked her watch. An hour and fifteen minutes until midnight. She had some cold chicken in her bag, which she ate and washed down with coffee from a thermos. She needed her energy. It might be a long night. She was now ready for anything. If Theo came alone, Gwen would come out and talk to her. If not, and it was a trap, she knew precisely what she'd do—and heaven help them.

Ben and Traynor established the command post for the operation in a ground-floor conference room at the FBI building, a five-minute drive from the memorial. When the round white clock on the wall read ten-fifty, Traynor said to the two FBI sharpshooters who would be pretending to be manning the POW/MIA booths, "Time to get in place. Don't use the road in front of the memorial. Enter from the side, cutting through the trees from Constitution."

"Will do," they snapped back, and headed toward a van waiting on Pennsylvania Avenue.

Fifteen minutes later, a van with Ben, Jennifer, Traynor, and Campbell set off for their waiting spot on the Virginia side of the Memorial Bridge. All four of them were dressed in dark green military camouflage uniforms with greasepaint on their faces. They were wearing Kevlar vests. Without telling anyone, Jennifer had decided to bring her gun in her jacket pocket, just in case. A second van followed with armed FBI agents. Behind it was a car with one female FBI agent driving and another in the back with Theo.

At eleven-thirty the car dropped Theo behind the memorial where Gwen couldn't see them. On her own now, Theo circled the memorial on foot, toward the stairs in front.

The driver called Traynor to report, "subject is on her way up to the memorial. We're heading toward your waiting location. Over."

"Roger," Traynor replied.

"Hey, wait a minute," Ben said in the back of the van. "Who's watching Theo now?"

"Nobody," Traynor said. "She'll be on her own for a couple of minutes until she attaches the microphone for our recording device, and the others come."

"Suppose she runs on us?" Ben said nervously.

Jennifer responded, "Get real, Ben. She won't run on those kids. Our problem will be to make sure she stays close enough to the microphone and gets the other speakers there as well. It's a large chamber. If they drift away from the microphone, we'll never get what we need on the tape."

In a voice crackling with tension, Traynor said, "I told her sixteen different times that's key—to stay close to the microphone. I think I got through to her."

Jennifer was sorry she'd said it. They were all feeling the pressure. "Sorry, Bill. I know you did. I just hope she doesn't forget."

As she climbed the steps to the memorial, Theo's knees were knocking. I must have been insane to agree to do this, she thought. She'll kill me. I'll never see my kids again.

In the maintenance room, Gwen heard footsteps through her earphones as Theo's heels clicked along the marble floor of the chamber. Gwen peeked through the door and saw the target. A great wave of relief washed over Gwen's body as she saw that Theo was alone. Her relief dissipated as she watched Theo head straight for the base of the statue, extract a small object from her purse, and stick it to the monument base. Well, well. You disgusting cunt, Gwen thought. You're working with the Feds. Big mistake, Theo. You picked the wrong team.

Gwen's first instinct was to shoot Theo and then head down the internal staircase and blast her way out if they had troops in place. She grabbed her gun and aimed at Theo. Then she pulled back. She was developing a better scenario. Right now they didn't know she was here. That put all the advantage on her side.

She checked her watch. It was five minutes to twelve. She closed the door to the maintenance room and resumed listening.

At precisely midnight, Theo saw Jim Slater get out of a car and begin climbing the steps. She moved close to the microphone and said, "Jimmy is on his way up. No sign of Gwen."

In the back of the van, Traynor gave a thumbs-up sign. At least they had landed one fish so far.

"Hello, Jimmy," Theo said when Slater reached the top of the stairs. She moved forward to great him.

"Helluva place you picked to meet," Slater said, regarding her up and down. "It's freezing out here."

Theo was trying to remember the script Jennifer had written for her and gone over a dozen times. "I wanted a place where nobody could see us. After all, this soon after Eddie's death I couldn't take a chance."

"Well, if that's what you had in mind, you certainly picked the right spot." There was a tinge of sarcasm in his voice.

Nervously, Theo looked down the stairs and around the area along the road, wondering if Gwen was coming.

Slater picked up on it. "What are you looking for?" he asked, turning around and glancing down the stairs himself.

Theo was furious at herself for being so obvious. Slater was smart. She'd better be careful or he'd be tipped off. Her best bet now was to assume that Gwen wasn't coming and follow what Jennifer had said was script two, for Theo and Slater alone. "I just want to make sure you weren't followed," she said in a deep, throaty, sensual voice.

That sounded more like the woman he knew. "You don't have a thing to worry about. We're in the clear."

She remembered that she'd better be close to the microphone, or they wouldn't hear a thing in the van.

"I'm also cold," she said. "Let's move back away from the wind."

She backpedaled toward the statue, with Slater following her. "Poor baby," he said, "let's see if I can warm you up a little."

He leaned forward and kissed her, with his tongue darting into her mouth. When she didn't respond, he began unbuttoning her coat. She was afraid he'd find the Kevlar vest, which would blow the whole thing. With a sly smile she slipped away from him. At the base of the statue, he caught up to her. From behind, he pressed his erection against her. He slipped a hand under her skirt, around to the front, and into her panties. "No, Jimmy," she said, forcing her legs together.

He looked confused and disappointed. Afraid of losing him, she stopped and rubbed her hand against his crotch, massaging the bulge in his pants. "You want me, Jimmy," she said. "You want me. Don't you?"

"Do I ever, honey. Yeah, stroke my prick like that. It feels so good."

In the back of the van they listened to the amplified voices in disbelief. Ben turned to Jennifer and said, "That was quite a script you wrote for Theo."

Jennifer blushed. "At least we know the mike's working."

With Theo's hand still on his crotch, Slater said, "I could drop my pants and take you from behind, the way you like it. It'll warm both of us up."

Theo abruptly pulled her hand away. Then, to cover, she said, "I can't do this now," pretending to be crying. "I'm too scared. I've got to talk to you. Maybe later we can make love."

"What's wrong, honey?" he said, stroking her cheek.

"What's wrong is that you never think about anybody else. Only yourself."

Slater was startled by her mood change. "What do you mean?"

"When I called you, I said that we had to talk. So far, you never even asked me why." She broke into tears that weren't entirely pretend.

"Hey. C'mon, Theo, what happened?" He awkwardly patted her hair, trying to comfort her.

"You don't even care."

"Of course I do. I just asked."

She wiped her nose and sniffed back more tears.

"Your protégé deserves an Oscar," Ben said in the van.

Jennifer was too engrossed in Theo's conversation with Slater to respond.

"The cops won't quit about Eddie's death," Theo said.

Slater stiffened in alarm. "What do you mean?"

"They keep coming back to the house. They're checking every prescription we have for names of pharmacies. They've dusted the den for prints twice. They're checking phone bills and phone records. They know it wasn't a suicide. It's only a matter of time until they find the pharmacy where I bought the shit. Then what?"

"They'll never find it," Slater said, trying to sound confident. "You'll be okay."

"I thought of a better solution."

Slater was wary. "What's that, honey?"

"You've got all that power in the White House. The President controls the FBI and the police. You could get them turned off."

Slater fidgeted. He didn't like where this conversation was headed. "How are your kids?" he asked, trying to change the subject. "How are Kevin and Kirstin doing?"

Theo snarled. "How the hell do you think they're doing? They miss their father. They cry all day. I don't know what to do."

"Take them away over Thanksgiving."

"We're going to my parents'." She started to cry again. "I should never have killed him."

Slater stood apart, not knowing how to handle this. "Neither of us wanted to do it. We did what we had to do," he soothed.

She shouted, "We could have let him live!"

"C'mon, Theo," Slater said, "you've got to calm down. Remember where we were." He tried to sound regretful. "I didn't want to make that call to you. I would have given anything to let him live. We had no choice. I had to protect you and our dream. Look at the big picture. In five years, you'll be in the White House. First lady. You'll be far away from all of this."

She kept on sobbing.

"Sometimes little people like Ed have to die," Slater said. "So people like us can achieve our dreams. Can help the country. That's what you have to remember."

She began crying louder, sounding hysterical. "You don't hear my kids at night. You don't know how awful it is."

Slater was losing his patience. "C'mon, Theo, get hold of yourself."

"Don't be so fucking cruel."

He'd had enough of her whining. "This isn't why I came here tonight. To take shit like this."

"You don't know what it's like to have children. You and your wife never—"

"Cut the sob story," he said, raising his voice. "Don't get carried away. If you hadn't made the calls from your house, I wouldn't have had to tell you to kill him. What the hell were you thinking of? Or I guess you weren't thinking, huh?"

She punched her fists against his chest. "How did you think I was going to make the calls? I have two little kids. I can't just leave them by themselves. I should have told you to call Alexandra and Gwen yourself. Killing Winthrop was your idea. I never even met that man."

"Don't be a goddamn moron. I explained it to you six times. If Winthrop told the President about us, we could have kissed it all good-bye. Our dream together."

"Big fucking deal," she cried. "Right now our dream's been flushed down the toilet."

"Oh, forget it," Slater said, exasperated. "I'm leaving. This isn't why I came to see you. Call me if you come to your senses."

He was about to walk away when she caught the lapel of his coat. "Don't go. I'm sorry, Jimmy." She was almost whimpering. "I shouldn't have said those things."

At last he smiled and kissed her. "Don't worry. I'll always take care of you."

In a quiet voice, against his cheeks, she said, "Then you've got to talk to your friend, the President, and get the cops off my back so they won't prosecute me. You can do it."

He jerked back away from her. "It's not possible," he said in a hard voice. "And don't ever fucking ask me again."

"You dirty bastard," Theo replied, equally sharp. "Either you get me immunity, or I'm going to testify against you and that monster Gwen. I'm going to bring the two of you down to save myself. I can do it. You watch me. You'll both fry."

Slater laughed at her. "For sure you'll be able to bring down Gwen, because the two of you plotted Winthrop's murder, but you can't touch me. I've covered all of my tracks. You'll never even be able to establish we had an affair. You keep your mouth shut, or you and that psychopath witch will fry."

Slater's taunt made Gwen explode. With gun and rope in hand she burst out of the maintenance room and advanced toward Theo and Slater. They were too stunned to speak. While Theo watched in horror, Gwen went directly to the microphone Theo had planted on the statue base. She ripped it off and hurled it onto the grass below.

Then she turned to Slater. "I'm Gwen. Here, let me show you what a psychopath witch can do."

She kicked him viciously in the balls. He made a choking grunt of pain, then toppled to the ground.

Pointing the gun at Theo, Gwen tossed her the rope. "Tie his ankles together and tie his wrists with his arms above his head," she barked.

In the van they weren't hearing any more sounds from the recorder.

Jennifer was alarmed. "What's going on?"

"Theo must have moved away from the microphone," Traynor said.

"Let's get over there," Ben snapped. "It doesn't matter if Gwen didn't show. We've gotten all we need to nail Slater. Let's close up shop."

Traynor shouted, "Move it," to the driver of their van. Then he told the driver of the second van to remain in place. There was no need for an army at the memorial with just Slater and Theo. Likewise, he told the chopper to remain back for now.

In the memorial chamber, as a shaking Theo bound Slater's ankles and wrists, Gwen sneered at him. "You're not pinning this on me. You were responsible for the whole thing."

"What do you want?" he pleaded. He was still doubled up in pain, lying on his back, his arms and legs tightly bound. "I'll give you anything."

"What a gutless wonder you are," she said, disgusted. "You know what I want? Your manhood. That's what I want."

Gwen turned to Theo. "Pull down his pants. His shorts, too."

"Oh, Jesus, no," Slater cried.

"Do it, you cunt."

With trembling fingers, Theo complied. Slater's shriveled penis looked pathetic exposed in the cold air.

Gwen took a stiletto from her jacket pocket and pressed a button, springing open the blade. She handed it to Theo.

"Cut off his dick," she ordered. "Then toss it down in the bushes. After that, his balls."

Theo didn't move. Her hands were quivering.

"Do it now, cunt, if you want to stay alive. If not, I'll kill you and do it myself."

As Theo bent down, tears coursed down Slater's face. "Oh, God, please. Not that. I'll give you anything."

On the road below, the van roared to a stop. That was the signal for all of the lights to go on in and around the memorial. Traynor jumped out of the van with a bullhorn in his hand. "Jim Slater and Theo Fulton," he called. "Walk down the stairs slowly, with your hands in the air."

When nothing happened the sharpshooters scrambled out of the green booths and took up positions behind the van. Traynor and Campbell cautiously started up the steps, guns raised, weaving from side to side, with Ben and Jennifer behind.

Up in the memorial chamber, Gwen grabbed the stiletto from Theo. She aimed it for Slater's balls, but as she noticed Theo running away, her eye jumped and she missed, driving it into his abdomen instead. He screamed in agony. Gwen snapped off a shot at Theo, taking cover on the other side of the statue, and Theo went down. Gwen didn't have time to see if she'd killed her.

Gwen heard a rifle shot from one of the sharpshooters below and ducked behind a marble column at the top of the stairs. From that vantage point she saw Traynor and Campbell, with Ben and Jennifer behind. She didn't want to expose herself to the sharpshooters, so she couldn't get a clear shot on the four figures moving up the stairs.

She decided to wait until they reached the top. As Campbell and Traynor appeared, she fired out a burst, which echoed loudly in the chamber. One of her shots nailed Campbell in the leg. Another got Traynor in the shoulder. Both men went down. That left Ben and Jennifer. She waited, but they didn't appear. Where the hell were they? Gwen wheeled around, looking for them.

As Jennifer saw Gwen turn, she hurried to the back

wall of the chamber before Gwen spotted her. Alerted
by the gunfire, she had run across the steps to the
other side. But where could she hide? There had to
be a small space between the back of the statue and
the wall of the chamber. Had to be. There was no
other place for her to go.

There was a space. And it was narrow.

Standing upright, sandwiched in that space, Jennifer
clutched her pistol tightly, her heart pounding. What
am I going to do now? she thought. I'm no match for
her with that machine gun of hers.

To the right, she heard Theo moaning in pain. Jennifer wanted to go help her, but she didn't dare move.
She stood still and held her breath. All she had now
was the element of surprise.

Suddenly she wondered: What happened to Ben?
Had Gwen shot him? Was he hiding?

More shots from the sharpshooters rang out, rico-
cheting from the column Gwen was behind. Peeking
out, Jennifer watched as Gwen reached into her jacket
pocket, took out a grenade, and pulled the pin. She
threw it down at the van behind which the sharpshooters were taking cover. In another moment the van
exploded, sending a large ball of fire into the sky.

In horror, Jennifer watched as Gwen spotted Ben
cowering in a corner of the chamber next to the door
of the gift shop, breathing heavily from the climb up
the stairs.

"Get over here fast," Gwen barked at him.

When Ben stood frozen to the spot, she fired a
warning shot over his head. He had no choice but to
obey. Slowly, he walked over to her, stalling for time.

She backhanded him hard in the face. Gliding behind him, she looped her arm around his neck. She
raised the gun in her other hand until the barrel was
pressed hard against his cheek. She had no intention
of dying in the electric chair. Keeping Ben in front of
her, she started down the stairs.

It's up to me, Jennifer realized. If I stay here, Ben
will be killed.

She couldn't let that happen.

Gwen was walking slowly down the center of the first group of twenty marble stairs, making certain that any other law enforcement people on the scene saw Ben and the gun held to his face.

Jennifer moved to the top of the stairs on the tips of her toes. By the time she could look downward, Gwen had reached the first small landing. She's too far away, Jennifer worried. I'll only have one shot. If I miss, we're both dead. Despite the cold, her hand holding the gun was sweating and clammy.

Jennifer waited until Gwen was about to descend the next group of thirty steps.

She dropped to one knee, took aim, and fired. The center of Gwen's back exploded with blood. Her arms flew out to the sides. Freed from her grasp, Ben fell to the side, catching himself before he tumbled down the stairs.

Not Gwen. Still clutching the gun in her hand, she rolled down, hitting the steps one after another like a rag doll. At the bottom she summoned all of her energy to raise her gun one more time. Her face was contorted in a grimace of hatred. She had Jennifer dead in her sights when she was struck by a hail of bullets. The sharpshooters in the second van had arrived. The gun dropped from her hand and she went limp.

Jennifer ran down the stairs, Ben two steps behind her. They stood next to Gwen's body as it gave one final shudder. Even in the throes of death, her face was a mask of cunning evil.

Epilogue

Ben and Amy arrived early at Dulles Airport for their flight to Aspen. As he carried Amy, her leg in a cast knocked against his chest. In his other hand he held his guitar case.

At the gate, he looked around anxiously, but Jennifer wasn't there. It was still early, he told himself. Then he recognized what a fool he was being. Of course she wouldn't be here. Three days ago he had asked a messenger to deliver a vase with twelve red roses and a gift-wrapped box to her house. Inside had been a gorgeous white teddy from La Perla. In the tissue paper was an envelope containing a one-way airplane ticket to Aspen and a handwritten note that read, *I hope you can come to Aspen with Amy and me. I lost you once. I don't want to make the same mistake again. Love, Ben.*

He had received a voice confirmation from the messenger that the package had been delivered to a woman who had signed for it, Jennifer Moore, but Ben had never received an acknowledgment from her. He had called her four times in the last three days, leaving messages on her answering machine. She didn't even have the courtesy to return his calls. How could he possibly think she would be on the plane? Still, she had saved his life. He was grateful to her for that.

Reaching the front of the line, he was relieved to

set Amy down on the counter. "Hey, you're getting heavy, kiddo."

The ticket agent, whose name tag said Dixie, looked at their tickets, and then said to Amy, "Wow, a vacation in Aspen. That sounds like fun."

"We're not on vacation," Amy replied. "My daddy and me are moving to Aspen."

"That's a great place," Dixie said.

"Time to start over," Ben added. "I'm getting out of this nasty town."

Dixie laughed. "All those politicians get to you?"

"Something like that."

She handed him two boarding passes. "We've got a small load today. I gave you an extra seat to stretch out her leg. If the passenger shows for that seat, I'll move her somewhere else."

In the boarding area, waiting for Dixie to call the plane, Ben suddenly saw a messenger in a gray uniform rush up with a box in his hands. "Is there an Amy Hartwell here?" the messenger called out.

"Hey, that's me," Amy shouted.

He handed her the box and quickly departed.

"Wait," Ben called to the messenger, but he was too late. The messenger was gone.

"Can I open it now, Daddy?"

"Sure. It's yours."

She eagerly tore off the wrapping. Inside there was a new Barbie doll with a whole array of clothes. Amy shrieked with joy. There was also a note. Anxiously, Ben read it to her: " 'I hope you have fun playing with your Barbie on the plane.' "

Ben was dejected as he carried Amy on board. Their seats were at the back of the plane: 25A, B, and C on the wide-body. As he got Amy settled next to the window, he tried not to think of who should be in the empty seat. At least she should have had the decency to return the ticket to him, he thought. So he could get a refund.

"I thought you said Jenny was coming, too," Amy commented.

He tried not to snap at her. It wasn't her fault. "I said she might come, honey. She must have gotten busy."

"Like you're always busy?"

"No more, Amy. I'm going to be a different kind of a lawyer now."

"What kind?"

"A real lawyer. Helping people with their problems."

He remained hopeful until the door closed. Then he gave up. Amy quickly became busy putting clothes on the new Barbie. He was glad she couldn't see the tears in his eyes. Fool, he thought, you blew it. You let her get away again.

They were the last ones to exit the plane. Ben struggled with Amy in one arm and his guitar case over the other shoulder, while his daughter held aloft her new Barbie doll. He was deep in thought, his mind fully occupied thinking about the details of starting a new life, like rental cars and temporary apartments, when Amy suddenly screamed, "Jenny . . . Jenny."

Stunned, Ben raised his head and saw her standing by the gate, dressed in ski clothes with sunglasses on her head. There was a gift-wrapped box on a chair next to her.

Jennifer walked over to them, took Amy out of his arms, and placed her on a chair next to the package. "That is for you."

Turning to Ben, she threw her arms around him, and kissed him passionately. "We're not going to waste any more time," she said pulling back. She gave him a wink. "Underneath, I'm wearing that gorgeous white teddy you sent me."

Ben hugged her tight.

"Listen," Jennifer said, sounding excited, "I've got a lead on a great house for us to look at."

He smiled. "Not until I see that teddy."

They both glanced at Amy, who had opened the gift. Inside was a Ken doll. Amy was pressing her two dolls together and crying, "I love you. I love you. I love you."

People passing by stopped to watch. They burst into applause.

Ben looked embarrassed. "I think it's time to get out of this airport."

Acknowledgments

Enormous thanks to my wife, Barbara. Together, we've added this new dimension to our lives. Barbara read and we discussed each draft. She contributed perceptive insights on the characters that helped shape the novel. Our children, David, Rebecca, Deborah, and Daniella, and in-law children, Stacey and Larry, all offered enthusiastic support. On medical issues, Deborah, as a physician, supplied the information I badly needed without my having to do research.

Henry Morrison, my superb agent, was critical to the development of this project from its conception. His knowledge and insights about all of the elements of a novel kept me on track. The long hours he spent reading drafts and the revisions he proposed were invaluable.

Finally, I owe an enormous debt of gratitude to Doug Grad, my marvelous editor at NAL. Doug has an incredible ability to take a manuscript, decide what it needs, and offer outstanding suggestions for the revisions. He constantly helped me push the envelope.